AKIN TO DEATH

CARROLL LACHNIT

BERKLEY PRIME CRIME, NEW YORK

AKIN TO DEATH

A Berkley Prime Crime Book / published by arrangement with the author

PRINTING HISTORY
Berkley Prime Crime edition / September 1998

The Penguin Putnam Inc. World Wide Web site address is http://www.penguinputnam.com

ISBN: 0-425-16409-8

Berkley Prime Crime Books are published by The Berkley Publishing Group, a member of Penguin Putnam Inc., 200 Madison Avenue, New York, NY 10016
The name BERKLEY PRIME CRIME and the BERKLEY PRIME CRIME design are trademarks belonging to Berkley Publishing Corporation.

PRINTED IN THE UNITED STATES OF AMERICA

10 9 8 7 6 5 4 3 2 1

Acknowledgments

A number of people made time in busy professional lives to give me technical assistance. Sincere thanks to attorney Harold La Flamme and Judge Robert Polis for their expertise on paternity suits and troubled adoptions. To Southwestern University School of Law Professor Robert Pugsley, for fielding ethical questions. To Sharon Kaplan Roszia, for her invaluable insights into the heart and psychology of adoption. To Dr. David Barinholtz, Dr. Joan Whelchel, Dr. Jeff Morris, and Dr. Barton Wachs for medical expertise. To Paul Sedgwick, Robert Cravey, and Larry Ragle for their toxicological and forensic acumen. To Timm Browne, for help on aspects of police investigations. To Cliff Munson, Lynn Jacobson, and Dale Holdmann for information on natural-gas explosions.

As always, I am grateful for the support of Hillary Cige, Susan Ginsburg, and the Mavericks writing group. My deepest thanks goes to Alec, the best husband any woman could have. And a hell of a lawyer.

I received invaluable help from all these sources, but any errors in the story are mine alone.

AKIN TO DEATH

Prologue

On the last day she could legally call herself Matthew's mother, Laura Benson took him to the park. They always went on Thursdays, and Laura didn't think the hearing should interfere with that.

At nine months, Matthew's mission in life was to walk. Holding the edge of the bench, he managed three weaving, bobbing steps and then faced a woman in her sixties, who sat with a ball of thread and a crochet hook in her lap. She smiled and spoke to him, but he stared, wide-eyed, lost his balance and sat down hard on the grass. He started to cry, a piercing wail of frustrated locomotion.

Laura went to him, picked him up and held him, feeling the fast, fearful beat of his heart. The woman leaned down and stroked Matthew's fuzzy head.

"I'm so sorry," she said.

"No problem," Laura replied. "He's nine months, and now he's decided to be picky about adults."

"Only trusts his mother and daddy?" The woman's eyes were a murky brown, but kind.

Laura nodded. He trusts his mothers, she thought, both of us. And he treats us the same. A hot surge of resentment flared through her, fast as a flash fire. And then it was gone.

The woman gooed and gaaed at Matthew. He smiled at her, now that he was wrapped in Laura's arms. Laura didn't mind the attention Matthew got. It flattered her when people told her how beautiful he was.

She had her Polaroid with her, for some shots with the

judge that afternoon. But those pictures would include the Drummonds. She wouldn't have one alone with Matthew. She asked the woman if she'd take a picture.

"Love to, dear. He looks very much like you."

As the images rose out of the milky-green film, the woman launched into a story about her own son, working backward through his life until she was telling Laura how she'd conceived him. It was a hot July afternoon. She and her husband had finished the gardening and drank cold beer that left them tipsy. They went inside, to the cool bedroom. She knew that was the very moment she had become pregnant.

Laura lied to shut her up, telling her how romantic the story was. Then she concentrated on buttoning Matthew's sweater. Laura wasn't going to reciprocate with her own story, which was where the conversation seemed to be leading.

Her story was different. Exciting—erotic even, if you factored in the fear, but it wasn't romantic, not the way this woman would have thought of it.

The dim room. The hastily bought Bombay gin she gulped. The shiver she felt as he penetrated her. Laura remembered it all, but not because it was a shimmery valentine. She remembered because it had turned out right.

Her periods were as regular as Kurt's tantrums: each month, she could count on both for several days of blood and ache. But there was no bleeding on the expected day, or the next. There was nothing to tell her she was pregnant, other than what was missing. There was no magical *ping* in her womb, no sign of some fertility godmother touching her egg with a spermy wand and creating life, wonderful life. That was some stupid notion out of the romance novels Evelyn read. That bitch, her so-called mother, Evelyn. Thank God she wasn't around for all this.

She noticed changes from the start: she felt good. Even the morning sickness was mild, and didn't last long. She thickened in the waist, her breasts swelled. She felt herself softening, the sleek lines of her body rounding, like dough rising.

She was scared during the pregnancy. How could she not be, given the situation? But her body counseled her: *You're fine. The baby will be fine.* Even when she felt panicky and couldn't talk to anyone, she learned to pay attention, to find solace in her belly and its new, undeniable gravity. Later, she felt him, like a restless kid tangled in blankets, kicking and turning. She laughed, and felt him giggle with her.

She was careful. She quit all the bad things she loved. She ate right, took the folic acid, and started drinking the milk delivered to her, although she loathed the taste of it. This baby will be healthy, she thought as she drained the glass. And loved. He will have a home and the kind of parents she never had. He will have people who care about him, who will knit him into the family fabric. It wasn't going to be like it had been for her, in short. She wasn't going to continue the sick pattern that started long before she arrived. She made a lot of mistakes in her life. Her decision about Matthew wasn't one of them.

No one would ever hide his background from him. No one would tell him that his mother hadn't loved him. No one could say she wanted him out of her womb and out of her life. Obviously, that wasn't how it was. He was loved. And she was still in his life. Along with the Drummonds, of course.

Sometimes, she panicked, second-guessed herself. Was she doing the right thing for her son? For herself? It happened again later that morning, after the visit to the park. As she was getting ready for the hearing she looked at Matthew's pictures, which lay on the floor next to her futon. The hot wave, the rage and bitterness, overtook her. She could see his father in him, the suggestion of the mouth that had been on hers, trembling. That started the thoughts, and she fought them back, calming herself with the memory of the promise she had from the Drummonds.

She remembered the moment when Stephen and Rebecca kissed her forehead in the delivery room. When all three of them cuddled Matthew, all nine and a half pounds of him. When his screaming woe at a rough splashdown in the world of cold air and bright light mingled with their laughter, and Laura's tears.

You don't covet something you already have, she told herself as she put one of the pictures on her pillow. He's the child of my heart and my body always. Nothing will change that.

1

Hannah Barlow stood back to survey the transformation. Paper streamers in yellow and blue, an array of red and white balloons, and a rattle-shaped layer cake had turned the law office of Terry & Barlow into a passable imitation of a nursery school.

She wondered what the cleaning crew would make of the party debris, accompanied as it would be by an empty bottle of Dom Pérignon and a soiled diaper or two. It would look like they were celebrating the arrival of a very junior associate.

Hannah checked her watch. Bobby Terry, her law partner, would be back from court soon. Even factoring in time for pictures with the judge, finalizing an adoption didn't take long. It was a formality. The real work had been done months ago.

She hadn't yet met Matthew Drummond, the guest of honor. She'd been briefly introduced to his parents, Stephen and Rebecca Drummond. She had talked to the mother, Laura Benson, but hadn't met her. It was going to be an interesting party.

When Bobby first told her about the case, Hannah thought of Laura Benson as Matthew's "real" mother, but Bobby told her the term was disfavored. Was Rebecca Drummond less "real" for not having conceived Matthew? No. *Biological mother* was technically correct, but it had the taint of the petri dish about it. And *natural mother* implied that Rebecca was somehow unnatural.

Birth mother was the preferred title. Although the term sounded Birkenstock-ish to Hannah, she was willing to concede that it fit best. Laura Benson had conceived Matthew, carried him, and given birth. She would go on being the woman who had done that, even now that the adoption was finalized and the Drummonds were legally Matthew's parents.

Hannah got the champagne out of the refrigerator in Bobby's office, the biggest of the five rooms that Terry & Barlow occupied on the third floor of the Orange Empire Building on Grove Street, in the center of old Las Almas. The downtown core of Las Almas had been overlooked so far, and was a virtual museum of the county's distinctive past. Its streets had an adobe of the last century, bungalows of the teens, and this office building, a white Art Deco palace from the thirties. Downtown Las Almas was where the county stored its memories and its soul while it plunged into its toll-roaded nightmare of a future. Hannah was beginning to think that she didn't want to see the dawning millennium in Orange County. If the television preachers were right, this was a perfect site for Armageddon. And she wasn't sure how lawyers would fare in it.

But if she had to be in Orange County, Las Almas was the best choice. She was glad that Bobby had been able to take over a law practice here. He bought it from Dan Barkin, a pockmarked, hard-charging attorney in his fifties who had decided twenty-five years of law was enough for him. With the sale of the practice and his forty-percent cut from the settlement of a big med-mal case, he was ready to live out his dream: a round-the-world trip on the *Cutthroat,* his beloved sailboat. He'd left behind several matters with Hannah and Bobby, including the Drummonds' adoption case.

Vera, the secretary Hannah brought with her from her last job, was clearing newspapers and magazines from the reception room's center table and arranging the six crystal champagne flutes Hannah had brought from the forest of stemware accumulated over the lifetime of her landlady,

Mrs. Snow. It was a special occasion, and it called for something more elegant than Big Bird cups.

"Nice job, Vera," she said.

Hannah went back to her office and shoved piles of paper aside. Her daybook was gone again. She had hoped that bailing out of a big law firm might mean less paper to clutter her life. She was wrong, but somehow having her own stake in the business made her less cranky about dealing with it.

Hannah had started her legal career at Cone & Downey, but lasted less than a year before taking a leave of absence. She used the time to consider whether she should climb permanently out of the gilded, high-rise snake pit it turned out to be. She loathed the people there: Steve Judge, Norma Chavez, John Cone—the whole fanged, venomous lot.

When Bobby, her former law-school study partner, asked her to join him in the practice he'd bought from Barkin, she didn't think for more than a moment before saying yes. From her computer at home, she E-mailed Vera, asking if she was interested in a new job. Vera sent back a screen-filling, flashing yellow happy face that screamed "YES!!!!"

So Hannah arrived with Vera—crack computer user and world-class eccentric. Hannah's dowry also included a Stickley table and chairs for the conference room and a stack of potential clients' phone numbers. Most of the callers had tracked her down after reading about the Maria Luz Duran case. Hannah just wanted to forget about the Duran case. It had cost her a lifetime of illusions. It had cost her Michael, her brother.

She focused on work and building their practice when she made the return calls. Otherwise, talking about Michael would have been nearly impossible. People inevitably offered her condolences before they got down to business. It was strange to be comforted when she was the one responsible for the loss. If not for her, Michael would be alive today. Her love failed him. Worse—it killed him.

The chirp of Hannah's computer broke into her brooding— E-mail from Vera, whose transition from a three-hundred-lawyer firm to a three-person office hadn't made her any more comfortable with face-to-face contact.

Judging by the ungodly squalling in the hallway, the infant entourage has arrived. Anyone who calls for the next two hours will think they got Kinder Care, not a law office.

Then she heard the crying and saw the people clustered in the outer hallway. The frosted-glass door scumbled their outlines into shifting blocks of color—white dress, orange dress, a white-and-yellow bundle, gray suits. Then a quartet of voices, two men and two women, belted out snatches of baby songs: "Hello My Baby." "Yes Sir, That's My Baby." "Baby, I Need Your Lovin'." It seemed to work. The crying, somewhere between the sound of mewling cat and braying mule, stopped. She heard Bobby's voice.

"Okay, let's get a picture."

The figures shifted: white dress next to gray suit, orange dress to the left. He was posing the four of them—Rebecca, Stephen, Matthew, and Laura—around the name on the door.

The flash blossomed on the glass. Then the door swung open and the group, laughing, spilled into the room. Nine-month-old Matthew, turned out in ducky-print white overalls, squirmed in the arms of a tall woman in an eggshell-white wool suit. He giggled as the man in the gray suit tickled him.

The Drummonds looked younger than Hannah expected, but in dress, haircut, and bearing, they were the quintessential Orange County professional couple—architect and surgeon—that she had pictured. Rebecca was nearly five-foot-ten, and as she spun the delighted baby her skirt whirled to show long, thin legs. Her dark hair was cut in a sculptural bob. Her jewelry, fine silver geometric links that could have come from the lines of her blueprints, shook and shimmered as she nuzzled Matthew's stomach. Drummond, the surgeon, was a shade taller than his wife, and shared her thin, strong build. His black hair was coarse, thinning, and threaded with silver, but he otherwise looked to be in his mid-thirties—ten years younger than he really was.

Bobby introduced Hannah, and as the parents sat down, Rebecca smiled rapturously at her son. As she turned in profile Hannah noted the fine features, lightly tanned skin, and a peppering of freckles across her nose. Her dark blue eyes were happy, but the longer she gazed at her baby—her baby, for real, for keeps, Hannah thought, bonding finally blessed by the court—the closer she came to the threshold of a sob. She fought to stop it.

Bobby had hinted at a string of tragedies that brought the Drummonds to this moment, but in the press of work, he hadn't elaborated. In short, he'd only said, "Thank God for Laura Benson and her one-night stand."

Rebecca passed the baby to Laura, who legally ceased to be his mother at two-fifteen. The blood ties to Matthew were obvious. Like his mother, Matthew had fine sandy-blond hair. His snubbed nose, even in its doughy softness, suggested hers. There was one clear difference, though. Laura's eyes were brown, with a sad, downward slant that hadn't been passed on to Matthew. There might be other divergences—in cheekbones, body shape, skin tone—but they were hidden for the moment in infancy's pink cocoon.

Hannah had glanced at the file while Bobby was at court, and knew that Laura was twenty-four. As Laura twisted to hand Matthew to Stephen, Hannah saw her nipped waist, flat stomach, and narrow hips, all outlined in a short Day-Glo orange knit dress. It didn't look like she'd ever been pregnant.

But the signs of a hard life showed elsewhere in Laura Benson. As she took a glass of champagne Hannah saw that her hands were ruins—wrecked cuticles, stubby, torn nails, and tough, reddened skin. Lines already were branded deeply at the corners of her mouth. She was nervous, jumpy. Her laughter didn't so much bubble as spurt, as though under pressure. Her eyes were wary, and had a slight puffiness. Like the Drummonds, Hannah guessed, she had spent part of the day crying. Joy or sorrow? Maybe, for Laura Benson, a mixture of the two.

"Time for a toast!" Bobby said.

As they raised their glasses Hannah caught Laura looking at Rebecca. Or rather, at her clothes. Hannah had seen Rebecca's white suit at Barney's in South Coast Plaza. It was the work of a minimalist designer, understated to the point of severity, and would have strained Hannah's credit card, even in a good month.

Laura was staring at it, an expression first of desire and then of resignation. She would never have a suit like that. Hannah wondered what she was doing to support herself. By law, the Drummonds' payments for her living expenses would have ended soon after Matthew was born.

Bobby cleared his throat and held his glass high. "To Matthew, and his family."

Very diplomatic, Hannah thought.

"To Matthew, the fabulous Droolbaby," Laura said. Her voice was breathy, weightless. She tilted her glass to Stephen and Rebecca. "And to his wonderful parents."

Rebecca leaned in for Stephen's kiss. Laura glanced down at her feet.

"To Matthew, and his wonderful birth mother," Rebecca said, turning to Laura. She looked up, and the two women smiled at each other. The shine in their eyes reflected a feeling too rich and layered to name.

Stephen Drummond tapped his ring against the rim of the glass. "Come on, ladies, enough with the bonding. Let's drink to the real man of the hour: Matthew!"

Hannah wondered how Laura could stand to be there. She understood Laura's decision to give up a child. In fact, she applauded it. After all she'd seen as a beat cop and a detective in the sexual assault unit, she only wished more people would put their procreative egos on ice and realize they weren't capable of being parents.

But she didn't understand hanging around once the surrender had been made. How could Laura blithely toast the couple that supplanted her? Hannah couldn't quite imagine herself as a mother. But if she did have a child, and had to give it up for some reason, she would cut clean, cut forever. And if she were an adoptive parent, she would want it that way, too. At some level, she would be afraid that the child would love the other mother more.

Apparently, the Drummonds had overcome that fear. That morning, before Bobby left for the finalization hearing, he showed her the document Barkin drafted for them. In it,

Laura and the Drummonds agreed to a close relationship: regular visits, pictures, and as much contact as both sides found acceptable. The agreement described a life in which Matthew would still be linked with his "family of origin." But to Hannah, it sounded like Laura was being grafted onto the Drummond family tree as much as Matthew was.

"Whose idea was this?" Hannah said.

"Barkin said it evolved. At first, the Drummonds just wanted an exchange of letters, sending pictures of the baby—stuff like that. But Rebecca and Stephen liked Laura so much that they gradually agreed to much more."

Hannah looked at the signatures at the bottom of the agreement—the architect's crisp near printing, the doctor's angular scrawl, and the young mother's rounded script.

"What's Laura's recourse if the Drummonds renege?" she asked Bobby. "Could she get Matthew back?"

"No, not for limiting contact. The only way she could undo the adoption is if she could prove fraud somehow. It's too late for her to get him back just by changing her mind. The law allowed her a few months right after he was born, and she didn't even consider it."

"What could the Drummonds do if Laura decides, ten years from now, that she wants nothing further to do with her son? Can they allege emotional abandonment and seek monetary damages?"

Bobby shook his head. "The agreement is unenforceable. It's really just a statement of their good intentions. They all know that."

So paper wasn't going to hold the relationship together. Only trust and respect would. In some ways, that was more impressive. Hannah wished them luck. She knew she wouldn't be able to live up to something like that. You could share a lot of things in life: books, clothes, maybe even a house, if you worked at it. Share your child? No.

Bobby nudged Hannah and gave her the camera. Hannah got a shot of Stephen and Rebecca carving up a chunk of cake for Matthew. Then another, as he crumbled it in his fist, screeching with delight as the frosting oozed through his fingers. In a third frame, he deposited a dollop of the sugary yellow mess on Rebecca's nose.

"Becca can have him run the company plastering crew in a few years," Stephen said.

"If he's genetically predisposed to play with squishy messes, let's have him follow in your footsteps instead," Rebecca said. "Surgeons make more money than contractors."

"A third-generation Drummond surgeon?" Stephen laughed. "My mother would be incredibly proud."

"She is proud. Wherever in the hereafter she is," Rebecca said dryly.

Stephen let the comment go. Hannah repositioned the viewfinder and saw that Laura's smile had dimmed. Her son—a doctor. Would she be invited to graduation? Would Matthew, at that point, want to share his life with two mothers? As Bobby explained it, children in open adoptions didn't seem to have a problem with the concept of a birth family and an adoptive family. The adoptive parents called the shots. The birth mom was like an aunt. The adoptive mom got the title of Mom. Laura would just be Laura. But Matthew would be a son to them both.

It was too complex a relationship for Hannah to think about for long. She was a square behind on life's board, struggling with the concept of permanent pairing.

For months, Guillermo Agustin, her onetime law-school professor and lover of more than a year, had been hinting at marriage. He hadn't proposed. He gently explored what Hannah might think of the idea. Ever the law professor, he couched it in hypotheticals.

Even hypothetically, she found she couldn't answer him. Once, before Michael died, she could have considered marriage. But Michael's death had roiled bad memories. Her fledgling attempts at prayer and meditation, the only solace she could claim after he died, hadn't dissipated them.

When Hannah was growing up, there were three emotional states in the Barlow house: building up to a fight, having one, and getting over one. Instances of lasting peace could be counted on one hand. Her father, a brooding, taciturn sergeant with the Las Almas PD, drank heavily, right up to the day her mother died. Her mother had been a drinker, too, but only in spurts. When her body's own fizzy-mood factory malfunctioned and sent her sliding into a black pit of depression, she drank iced-tea glasses of Tyrolia to apply the brakes, to stop the momentum, to keep the manic high alive. But it seldom worked. Drinking heated up her sadness, boiled it to rage. Then she and Hannah's father fought. Usually, it was screaming and broken dishes. Only once was it more than that, and Jimmy Barlow stayed out of jail because he knew the cops who responded. No one suspected that Hannah made the call. Jimmy thought she understood: cop families kept their business private.

She saw the toll her parents' marriage took on her brother and her sister. Michael retreated to God. Theresa found solace in dolls, and then boys. Hannah took refuge in being the adult, the strong one who held the family tiller steady.

This was what she went through every time Guillermo talked about marriage, as he had been doing for the last six months. Rational thought turned into a panicked run through the underbrush of her parents' disastrous life together. He deserved better, she thought.

The stress of not talking about commitment had worn out Hannah and Guillermo. He called her less in the last month. He claimed to be busy at school, where the semester was nearly over. Then he phoned to say he was going to Durango for a few weeks. His mother had suffered a mild heart attack, and was recovering from triple-bypass surgery. The import business she ran with a collective of Central American weavers and artisans would fall apart without some hands-on attention. Guillermo's father was too overwhelmed by his wife's sudden illness to be of any use, so Guillermo volunteered to handle it.

Hannah was sorry that Amelia Agustin was ill. Guillermo's absence was going to be a relief. She couldn't stand seeing the hunger for *la familia* in his eyes.

They were waiting at John Wayne Airport for his flight to Denver when he put down his magazine and took her hands.

"Where do you see this relationship going?" He was trying to look at her, but she avoided his eyes.

"Guillermo, not now."

"Yes, now. Do you want to 'date' forever? Shall we just screw and watch movies and eat out a couple times a week until we're bored? Will we break up and do it all again for another couple years with other people? That's not what I want. What about you?"

"I don't know what I want," Hannah said. She looked up to see a spark of anger flare in his face. His flight was boarding. He released her hands, stood up, and kissed her, a harsh, cold brush across her mouth. "I suggest you think about it." And then he was gone.

That had been on Monday, three days before, and Hannah's lips still felt frostbitten. She had been thinking about it. Maybe the desire to be a wife and mother was an emotional virus. She might be able to catch it if she immersed herself in the world of couples, parents, and children.

Rebecca turned to her, smiling.

"Do you want to hold Matthew for a minute?"

Hannah wondered if she was sending out vibrations. She nodded and slipped her hands around Matthew's solid midsection. He was as warm and yeasty smelling as a loaf of French bread. She held him up and looked into his delft-blue eyes. He stared back at her as though he knew this was some weird adult test of maternal readiness, not a real demonstration of devotion to him, the true center of the universe. His pink underlip faltered and he began to wail, his face as crimson and plump as the balloons over the door.

Rebecca reached for him. Hannah saw Laura's arms open, too, a quick, involuntary movement. She snatched them back and glanced at her feet.

Stephen hadn't noticed. Rebecca had. She kissed Matthew's head, quelled his tears, and passed him to Laura. The baby was midway between the mothers when Hannah heard running footsteps in the hall.

A form hovered outside the door for a moment and then a stringy-haired man staggered in. He wore ripped jeans and a flannel shirt. Blond stubble covered his cheeks. He glanced at the cake and the empty champagne bottle and then turned to Laura, who had Matthew in her arms. She was on her feet as soon as she saw him.

"It's true," the man muttered. Then he gathered a breath and bellowed at her. "You goddamn bitch, it's true!"

He lunged at Laura and the boy. She shrieked and ran for Bobby's office. Matthew began screaming.

Bobby and Stephen tackled the man from the side and back, shoving his face against the wall. Vera, frozen, cowered by her desk. Hannah grabbed the phone and punched 911. She looked over her shoulder and saw Bobby's ample back, Stephen's anxious face, and the man pinched between them.

His eyes were wide with rage and the cords in his neck were stretched tight. He winced as Bobby pinned his shoulder. Laura peered out from Bobby's office, her arms wrapped around her wailing son. Rebecca, dark with anger, hovered next to her.

"Get out," Rebecca yelled.

"Fucking baby snatcher!"

Silence then, except for the sound of Matthew's staccato, gulping cries.

"Laura." The man's voice cracked on her name. "How could you do this to me?"

She didn't answer, and that reignited him. He almost shuddered free of Stephen and Bobby.

"You're my wife," he cried. "And he's my son, goddammit. You can't just give him away."

2

After the police were gone, Hannah gave the Drummonds whatever reassurances she could muster and calmed Vera enough so she could drive home. Then she went to Bobby's office. He sat on the couch with a half-dozen aspirins in one hand and a bottle of extra-strength Maalox in the other. He tossed the pills in his mouth, spun the cap, and poured half the bottle down his throat. Hannah had never seen him resort to medicinal treatments. Bobby's idea of pain relief was a plate of orecchiette in cream sauce, topped with shaved black truffles. Food was also how he celebrated and mourned and fought back boredom. Some people wore their hearts on their sleeves. Bobby wrapped his in his gut.

"Where are the Drummonds?"

"I sent them home," Hannah said. "Rebecca finally got Matthew to settle down. I've never seen a baby shake like that."

"It's a fucking nightmare," Bobby groaned. "For a minute I thought we were going to have the SWAT Team in the hall."

"Was he telling the truth? Is he Laura's husband?"

"Looks that way." He handed Hannah an envelope. Inside was a copy of a Washington-state marriage certificate, showing that Kurt Sundstrom and Laura Benson had been joined in marriage on July 7, three years earlier. A five-by-seven picture showed the bride and groom at Pike Place Market, lip-locked, surrounded by grungy, plaid-wearing friends. In the background, a fishmonger was tossing a salmon.

"Is fish tossing what they do in Seattle instead of throwing a bouquet?"

Bobby smiled wanly and didn't answer.

"They didn't seem very loving out there," Hannah said. "Are they still married?"

"I don't know. If they're divorced, why didn't Laura say so?"

She hadn't said a word. She watched silently as Bobby shoved her husband into the hall and into the arms of the police, who impressed on him the advisability of leaving the building quietly. Kurt gave Bobby the evidence of his claim to Matthew before he slammed his way out of the building.

"The Drummonds are going to fire us," Bobby said. "Then they'll sue us for malpractice. Us, and Billy Budd Barkin. If he hadn't been so goddamn busy outfitting the Kon-Tiki, this mess wouldn't have happened." Bobby excused himself and lumbered to the bathroom that adjoined his office. The slamming door didn't dampen the sound of the sudden uprush of cake, champagne, aspirin, and antacid.

Hannah felt queasy, too. *Us* and *malpractice* were two words she hoped never to hear in the same sentence. She hadn't worked on the adoption, except to bring the glasses, photograph the truncated party, and pay for the champagne. But Bobby was her partner, and so it was as much her problem as his.

He came out, wiping beads of sweat away from the curling hairs on his forehead. "Where's Laura?"

"She's in my office. Are you okay?"

Bobby ran a hand through his hair, grabbing it at the crown as though he'd like to rip his head off. "I'll be fine. Talk to her, would you? All I want to do right now is strangle her."

"Bobby. I know it's a bad time, but how—"

Bobby dropped into his chair and motioned for her to stop.

"It is a terrible time, Hannah. The last thing I want to do right now is enumerate for you the ways I fucked this up."

"You didn't do anything. Barkin—"

"Whatever Barkin did or didn't do, it's our problem now. Go talk to that little bitch and see what you can find out, okay?"

Laura stood at the window in Hannah's office, staring out over Grove Street. The afternoon light filtered through the jacarandas, casting a lacy shadow on her face. She hummed softly to herself and pivoted one toe in the carpet, a ballerina tuning up.

At the sound of the closing door, she turned, and Hannah saw a smile drain away. Hannah sat down at her desk.

"Are you doing okay?" she said.

Laura nodded too quickly.

"You know how serious this is," Hannah said.

Her face flushed pink. "I know. But I also know what Kurt is doing. He's trying to get back at me. And it's not going to work. Is . . . are Stephen and Rebecca still upset?"

After she said it, she caught her lip in her small, chalk-white teeth. If this kittenish gesture was meant to signal repentance, Hannah was unconvinced.

"Yes," Hannah said. "Very."

"And Bobby?"

"He sent me to talk to you. Does that answer your question?"

She shrugged, nodded.

"Are you still married to Kurt Sundstrom?"

"Yes."

"And is Matthew his son?"

"No. I don't even know how he found out I had Matthew."

"You slept with other people, and one of them was Matthew's father?"

"Not other people. Another person. I'm not a slut."

But you're a liar, Hannah thought. "You didn't tell Barkin or the Drummonds that you were married, did you?"

She shook her head.

"Why was that?"

Laura shrugged again and stared down at her feet. The gestures, so childishly helpless, infuriated Hannah.

"You didn't think it was important, Laura? You forgot? What?"

"I'd like to go home now," she said.

Hannah wanted to strangle her, but knew that anger wasn't going to work.

"Laura, you might be confident that everything will work out, but I'm not convinced of that. If Kurt is still married to you, he is Matthew's father in the eyes of the law. Fortunately, that's not the end of the story. We can present evidence that he isn't the father. But by not being honest with the Drummonds, Barkin, or Bobby and me, you've made this much more complicated that it had to be. I think we're going to hear from Kurt again. I don't think he's just going to disappear, do you?"

She began to shrug again and, as if she'd thought better of it, shook her head.

"If he presses for his parental rights, the Drummonds will have an expensive legal fight on their hands. And Matthew's future will be in jeopardy. I don't think you want that."

"I don't." Laura paused. "I think I'd like to talk to Bobby about this—later. Don't take it personally, but he's the one I've dealt with, besides Dan . . . Mr. Barkin. Bobby is the one I trust, now that Mr. Barkin's gone. And I'd like to do it tomorrow, not now. This has been very upsetting."

She brushed her hair over her shoulder and folded her arms. She had been a fragile music-box doll a few minutes ago. She was a stone bitch now.

Hannah felt the shimmer of rage racing through her nerve endings. She also folded her arms, the better not to smack Laura's smug face.

"Fine," Hannah said. "Can I call a cab for you?"

"No, thank you." She swept past Hannah, leaving a stream of lemony perfume in her wake.

Hannah went to the window and watched as Laura emerged from the lobby. She walked a half block to the city parking lot, tying a wispy silk scarf around her head as she walked. Then she slid into the driver's seat of a black Fiat.

The tires squealed as she peeled out and cornered hard, cutting off an old orange Dodge truck. The blond strands of her hair danced, gold-bright and young in the breeze. Everything about her—the car, the smile, the careless lies—made Hannah's heart sink.

Bobby had moved to the sofa. A bottle of Glenfiddich sat on the floor, and a tumbler awash in Scotch was resting on his stomach. At least he's using a glass, Hannah thought.

She pulled a yellow pad out of Bobby's desk drawer, sat down next to him, and slid off her shoes. Bobby opened his eyes and took a sip of his drink.

"Tell me Kurt had a vasectomy the night before the wedding," Bobby said. "Or tell me he was early-onset Alzheimer's and forgot about his divorce."

"Okay. It's just like that." She doodled on the pad so she wouldn't have to look at Bobby.

"Liar. They're still married, aren't they?"

"She says so," Hannah said. "But she says he's not Matthew's father. Whoever it is, didn't you have to get him to relinquish his rights?"

"We don't know who Matthew's father is."

"I knew she was a slut."

"No. It's all in the file," Bobby said.

Hannah picked it up and leafed back to the first pages.

"It was a one-nighter?"

Bobby nodded. "She told Barkin she met the guy at a bar in San Francisco. The financial district, months after she broke up with her boyfriend. That's who Kurt was—an ex-boyfriend. She neglected to mention he was a current husband."

Hannah was writing it all down. "So this guy in the bar, who's he?"

Bobby's brow crinkled in annoyance.

"Are you deposing me, counselor? I wasn't there."

Hannah shook her head. "Sorry. It helps me think. Want me to stop?"

He shrugged. "No. Barkin is somewhere off the leeward side of Palau, and has arranged it so that no one can reach him, so we're on our own. We don't really know who the guy was. Laura told Barkin she was hitting the bars around the Embarcadero and financial district that night, and the exact locus of their initial meeting escaped her recall. He was a businessman, she thought. Medium height, blue suit, blondish hair. She didn't get his name. It seemed like he had a lot of money and he talked as though he'd been to college. They went to some motel—details here are even more vague—did it, then *adios* before the break of day."

"What else about him? Eye color? Beard? Double chin?"

"Blue eyes, she thought. She was a little fuzzy on the other facial features. When she met him, it was Halloween, and he was wearing a tiger mask. So that's what she called him. Tiger."

"I hope he took the damn costume off when they did it," she said.

Bobby shook his head. "To tell you the truth, I didn't ask Barkin to elaborate. I was afraid I'd hear this guy's outfit had a tail, and that led to images that were just too kinky for me."

Hannah smiled. She was glad his sense of humor had rebounded.

"Barkin did what was required: he put a notice in the *Record* down here, asking for any putative fathers to step forward. He even put it in the *San Francisco Chronicle*."

"Hoping to catch Tiger?"

"Him and Kurt, too, just in case the ex-boyfriend wasn't really so ex. Laura said he lived in the Bay Area."

"Did he?"

"No. Kurt said he and Laura lived in Seattle. For four years."

"In other words, she made sure that if Kurt got wind that she was pregnant, and he was looking for her and the baby, he'd miss the legal notice."

"Jesus," Bobby said. "I can't believe how she misled everyone. Barkin said he'd checked her out."

"For a criminal history?"

"That, and to be sure she really was pregnant, and really intended to give up the baby. There are some real horror stories—women who agree to an adoption, get their rent and their bills paid for five or six months, and then suddenly change their minds."

"Never intending to give up the baby. That sounds pretty awful."

"It is. And Barkin said Laura checked out. She was clean. God knows if that's true or not."

"What else did he find out about her?"

"I really don't know. Whatever it was, it satisfied the Drummonds. Barkin said Laura and Rebecca had bonded. They shopped, they went to lunch. Rebecca became very protective of Laura. Almost motherly. Barkin said Laura had a tough life."

"Tough how?"

"What you'd expect. Alcoholic father, emotionally with-holding mother, hardscrabble existence in some Long Beach neighborhood—the place reeked of fish, she told Barkin. The particulars were too painful for her to talk about, but she hinted at deprivation and cruelty. She hit the road when she was seventeen. That kind of history puts up red flags for drug use, so Barkin asked Laura's permission to talk to her doctor. She didn't balk at all. The doctor said there was no sign that Laura was taking anything. She'd told him the hardest drug she'd done was marijuana, in high school. What everybody did."

"Everybody but you."

"Thanks for taking this moment to remind me how much of a geek I was." But he was smiling when he said it. He took a slug from the glass before going on. "Laura, erstwhile pot smoker, passed a drug screen and was as healthy as a horse. So far, so good. No drugs, she was really pregnant, and she had no criminal record."

"Did Barkin check for marriages?"

"In California. Apparently he didn't bother checking in Washington, even though Laura said she'd lived there for a few weeks. Try a few years. Jesus, what else is she lying about?" He got up, wobbled to his desk, and unsteadily sat down. Hannah decided she would drive him home.

"I think it's time to let her know we won't be her lawyers

anymore," he said. "She can get her own attorney and lie to him exclusively. Representing her and the Drummonds has bothered me from the start."

Hannah agreed with him on that score. State law allowed one lawyer to represent the adoptive parents and the birth mother, if she agreed to the arrangement. It seemed a crazy conflict of interest to Hannah. If the birth mother changed her mind about an adoption, she was likely to be stranded. The lawyers most often aligned themselves with the bill-paying adoptive parents. As they were about to do.

Hannah went to the reception room and came back with a champagne glass. She rinsed it in the bathroom, poured herself two inches from the bottle of whisky, and sat down.

"If Laura's so down on her luck, what's she doing with that car?"

Bobby, who had been staring out the window, turned with a frown. "The Gremlin?"

"Laura has a brand-new black Fiat."

"Oh, Jesus." Bobby and Hannah stared at each other for a moment. She spoke their mutual fear first.

"Did the Drummonds buy it for her?"

"Christ, I hope not. It wasn't in the support records I submitted to the court. For six months the Drummonds paid her rent, put maternity clothes on her back, and bought her groceries. They paid the hospital bill. That was it, clean and legal, as far as I know."

"You never saw this car before?"

He shook his head. "Only the Gremlin. She was complaining about it last week."

"I thought buying cars was pretty much out of the realm of the permissible," Hannah said.

"It is. Judges see four wheels, they see baby buying."

"The car worries me," Hannah said. "It's one of the reasons I think it would be a bad idea to drop Laura right now."

"I don't follow."

"If we cut her loose, she'll be flapping in the breeze alone, without an attorney or money to get one, while her husband starts a full-court press to get his alleged son back.

If she's pissed off at the Drummonds for abandoning her, what's the quickest way to get back at them?"

Bobby held the glass to his forehead, as though he had a fever that needed cooling.

"She could line up with Kurt and identify him as the real father, whether that's true or not," he said. "She can allege the Drummonds bought her off with a car and God knows what else to get the baby. She would say she was desperate, destitute. She wasn't thinking right. Maybe they coerced her in some other ugly way. With all that, she could try to get this adoption undone."

"Right. I'm a little surprised she let it go on this long."

"I'm sick." Bobby laid his cheek on the arm of the sofa, closed his eyes for a moment, and then opened them. "Wait. Are you saying Laura did this on purpose?"

Hannah swigged the last of the Scotch. It burned all the way down her throat. "Bobby, if we're smart, we'll assume that's exactly what she did."

3

The Drummonds didn't talk on the way home. Stephen drove, despite the headache that pounded behind his eyes. It was like waking up from a bad dream, the same shaking, sweaty unreality of it. He wished it had been a nightmare.

Goddamn Laura. He knew from the start that she was unstable. But instability was the keystone of an adoption: secure, settled, happy, psychologically adjusted women didn't give up their babies. Maybe Mary Catherine was right about blood and breeding. It was a concession he would never have made to her when she was alive.

His mother's finely tuned sense of pedigree extended well beyond the beagles and horses she raised at the ever-shrinking Drummond Ranch. (The rising commercial value of Orange County property meant that the sere hills and grasslands would sooner or later be plowed under for houses and golf courses.) Mary Catherine's snobbery would have been almost forgivable if she had been born into it. But she only had married into the family's money. They called her the Duchess of Las Almas, and although the title was a mocking one, she never heard it that way.

There was no doubt of her love for Andrew Drummond. Stephen was eight when he died, and she turned all that keen devotion to him, the elder son. Stephen remembered her hands on his arms, clenching so tight that he winced, telling him that he was his father's son. And through him, Andrew lived.

It was about a year later when Stephen first heard her

pronouncements on adoption. A Sunday afternoon. His new best friend had visited, and gone home. He'd barely been in Stephen's class for a week, but Mary Catherine already knew his history.

She was serving coffee and gossip to a neighbor, a social climber that Mary Catherine deigned to educate to the ways of the Las Almas elite. Stephen didn't think his mother could see him as he sat cross-legged on the sofa in his father's study with the door three-quarters closed. In case he was discovered, he took down his father's copy of *Gray's Anatomy,* and began memorizing the bones of the hand.

Mary Catherine was telling the woman that she knew the parents of Stephen's new friend. "The adoptive parents, I mean. Not the real ones."

Stephen's ears pricked up. Adoption was a topic kids only whispered about. There had been times, recently, when he wished he was adopted. Mary Catherine's devotion felt like a pillow stuffed up to his face. Stephen had contemplated running away, but knew it would only end in his mother's wailing tears and clenching embrace.

"It was a generous impulse, of course."

The woman agreed, crooning like a mourning dove.

"They're well-to-do people, and they're generous, charitable. But you can carry that too far. I mean, what do they really know about the boy's parents? Poverty-stricken, I'm sure. Immoral, we can take that for granted, given the mother's state. Diseased, probably. Short bones and subpar intellect. It'll come back to bite the people who took that boy in. Wait and see. Blood will out."

Stephen's face burned as he listened to her. Although he wanted to be loyal to his friend, to prove Mary Catherine wrong, he could never see him quite the same way again. He caught himself sizing up his frame, wondering about the mother's sins. Without really meaning to, Stephen found himself too busy to cultivate the relationship. The boy found other kids, and nothing was said. But in a game of dodgeball, he hammered Stephen in the stomach, and then smiled.

Stephen didn't want to let his mother's prejudices take

root. In high school, while he had to live in her house, he blocked her lectures on family, on blood, on keeping his father's spirit alive. He thought distance would help, so he went north for college, medical school, and his residency. But in the second year of his first marriage, when his career-minded wife tried to renegotiate their agreement to have children, he could feel Mary Catherine's lessons unfold in him, like leaves and flowers and thorns. Especially thorns. He filed for divorce before the month was out. Mary Catherine was right. A career, a marriage, wealth, and achievements would not last forever. He would die, his wife would die, and they would slip under the wake of time. But with a child to love him, he would live forever. As Andrew lived in his memory.

Then he met Rebecca, a treasure. Someone who saw family just as he did: the center of a life. When they learned they couldn't have children of their own, the only way to fulfill his mother's only desire—his desire now—meant violating her blood rule. He could hear Mary Catherine in his head, and everything he read seemed to confirm it. Genes dictated so much: temper, health, emotional stability.

The risk they'd taken, the uncertainty of it—it still made him queasy. But he was learning to live with it. Matthew made it all worthwhile.

Stephen made the last turn at the top of the hill and parked in the driveway. Rebecca looked exhausted, although he saw with relief that the silent tears had finally stopped. She didn't seem to notice that the spilled champagne had stained her suit. He'd buy her another one. He squeezed her hand as she was getting out of the car, and she managed a smile. But she still didn't want to talk.

He glanced back at Matthew. He had dozed off in his baby seat. In sleep, he had an obstinate face, like a dour little bureaucrat. He made Stephen smile, even in the midst of the worst day of his life so far. The thought of losing Matthew panicked him. In a way, that reaction was a relief. It demonstrated that there was a bond. He had wondered how his feelings toward Matthew would take shape, given everything the adoption entailed. Now he knew. Mary

Catherine would not have agreed with what he'd done. He could imagine her horror and scorn. But he had what he wanted: Rebecca, and his son. Family. Fatherhood. And that was all that mattered.

4

"This is the last load."

Mike, the proprietor of Mike's Movin' On, handed Hannah a bill for the cleanup and nibbled on a toothpick while she got her checkbook. It was a late Saturday afternoon, two weeks after Kurt burst into the office and rifled the Drummonds' lives. Hannah had spent the morning in the office, catching up on the cases that languished while she and Bobby immersed themselves in the study of troubled adoptions. She came home in time to see the last of Mrs. Snow's dubious collectibles loaded on Mike's truck for the drive to the dump.

Mike's fuzzy sideburns were flecked with dust and he smelled of mildewed paper. "You know, we found newspapers in the attic from 1960," he said. "Why did the old lady keep all that crap?"

"Insulation," Hannah said. From the here and now. If Emma Snow threw away the past, she would have to think about living in the present, or facing the future. Hannah's landlady didn't want to do either of those things.

For fifteen years, since the summer Hannah graduated from college, she lived in a second-floor apartment that Mrs. Snow carved out of her huge Victorian house in Las Almas. The apartment suited Hannah when she was a beat cop who spent most of her time in a patrol car. It was just right for a newly promoted detective who virtually lived in the squad room, proving her dedication. And its low rent was particularly welcome when law school chewed up her savings.

Hannah's Stickley furniture, the first pieces an inheritance from her grandmother and the rest collected at flea markets and swap meets, fit in nicely. When she had a decent income, she convinced Mrs. Snow to let her replace the kitchen cabinets, install a new kitchen floor, and repair some of the draftier panes of leaded glass. It was the perfect home, even if it wasn't technically hers.

She could afford to move. But she didn't. She worried about Emma Snow, whose good health and resilience had brought her to a sorry state: she had outlived everyone she loved. Mrs. Snow's husband, Walter, had been dead for forty-odd years, though she occasionally talked about him as if he'd just gone down to the market for a quart of milk. If there were children, Mrs. Snow never discussed them.

As Mrs. Snow shrank and paled and bent like a twig of steamed birch, Hannah ran errands for her. In her second year of law school, she used her research skills and command of legalese to straighten out a Social Security snafu. For the last three years, Hannah's biggest challenge had been cajoling Mrs. Snow into parting with some of the ephemera she found so precious. She couldn't give up paper. She saved string. She created basketballs out of rubber bands.

And then she had began to accumulate fouler refuse. Hannah would never forget what she found one day in fourteen milk cartons, neatly stacked in the bathtub. Mrs. Snow, Hannah thought sadly, was trying to hang on to herself, any way she could. Hannah proposed a trade: the cartons for two weeks' worth of newspapers. Hannah dumped out the cartons. The old lady clucked joyfully and stacked the papers atop a yellowing account of Nixon's resignation.

She read up on conservatorships and gently questioned Mrs. Snow about any stray nieces or nephews she might have forgotten to mention.

"I've got no one but you," Mrs. Snow said. She put her hand to Hannah's face. It felt like a fall of dusting powder.

Staying on in Mrs. Snow's house wasn't all altruism,

though. Hannah knew that if she was indispensable to Mrs. Snow, she couldn't possibly move in with Guillermo. The fragile widow was her mighty bulwark against commitment.

Then, one afternoon six months earlier, Hannah had gone downstairs to bring Mrs. Snow a rent check. All the lights were on in the living room, which struck her as odd. Using the key Mrs. Snow had given her for emergencies, she let herself in.

She found Mrs. Snow in her bedroom, wearing a silky pink nightgown and lying on her side. Her hand dangled in the space between her bed and Walter's. As Hannah knelt next to her she smelled the tea-rose scent of Joy perfume rising from hollow of her throat. She kissed Mrs. Snow's icy forehead and called her doctor. He said Hannah could take her pick of causes: heart failure, kidney failure, a touch of malnutrition. Hannah felt her eyes fill, thinking of the old lady's tea-and-toast diet and quiet resistance to anything else. The doctor shrugged. She'd lived ten years longer than he'd expected.

No relatives surfaced in the weeks after her death. Hannah tried to find papers in the house that would offer a clue to where they might be, but what she found instead was a will. It was not, as she would have expected, scrawled on the back of Chinese restaurant take-out menu. It was neatly printed in the old lady's handwriting, on clean yellow legal paper. She had signed it and clipped to it a business card for a lawyer in Santa Ana. The lawyer remembered Mrs. Snow—she'd told him he charged too much for his services. She'd do it herself. He tired to warn her about the trickiness of wills, but she didn't listen.

He looked over the holographic document for Hannah—he'd graduated from Douglas, as Hannah had—and said it appeared to be in order.

Emma Snow left Hannah her house. And everything else she owned.

Hannah didn't believe it. Yes, he said, the will was quite explicit and plain. Everything went to Hannah. Yes, there were estate taxes. But upon some checking, he decided Mrs. Snow had enough assets to ensure that the house wouldn't have to be sold to pay them. That surprised Hannah, who thought Social Security and her own rent checks were the only things that stood between Mrs. Snow and poverty.

Cleaning out the house had occupied several of her weekends, but she couldn't seem to make much progress in the midst of so much—stuff. Mike, the professional, took a shovel to the place, sifting out and saving only papers and other items that seemed important or valuable.

Hannah finished writing the check and gave it to him. In return, he handed her a stack of papers tied up with decaying brown cotton ribbon. Resting on top, rubber-banded together, were a half-dozen passbooks.

"My mom did the same thing," he said. "Opened a bunch of accounts—five bucks here and there. I think the banks were giving out Corning Ware or something. She got her dishes and never made another deposit after that."

Hannah nodded. "That's probably just what Mrs. Snow did."

When he was gone, she flipped open the books. Emma Snow had savings accounts all over Orange County, but unlike Mike's mother, she paid them a visit every year to keep them active. Hannah added up the balances. Nearly $265,000, plus unposted interest.

Hannah walked to the edge of the lawn and looked back at the house and yard. They needed work, of course. Maybe that's what the cash was for. She imagined what it would be like, coming home on a summer evening.

The rosebushes burst with flame blossoms. Rustling, leafy liquidambars and ficus trees shaded the yard. The house, a white, gingerbreaded island, lay in the center of a shimmering green lawn, damp from watering. She saw herself opening the door, turning from the entryway into the living room. Her fumed-oak settle and Morris chair, the only family legacy that wasn't tinged with violent loss, were there now. At her desk, head bent over a book, glasses slipping on his nose, sat Guillermo. A few blades of the wet grass clung to his bare feet, bridging the border of tanned and paler brown skin. He looked up and smiled.

Hannah blinked the daydream away, went inside, and

came back to the porch with a notecard and her address book. She though for a moment only—any longer and she would lose her nerve. Then she wrote:

The house is cleared now. I'm sweeping out the last rooms, and throwing away all the junk that has piled up and blocked my way. I've found that this place is much too big for one person. When you come back, would you consider living here with me?

She sealed the envelope, double-checked the zip code for Durango, and dropped it into the mailbox on the corner. The second-guessing hit immediately, melting the cartilage in her knees. But it was done now. Short of filing a Postal Form 1509, "Sender's Application for Recall of Mail,"— and she'd done that once, after firing off an angry letter to her sister—she was stuck.

When she got back to the porch, Bobby was waiting for her. He must have seen her wobbly gait and her money-dazed expression.

"What's wrong?"

"Mrs. Snow didn't just leave me the house. She left money—a lot of it. I'm rich."

He grimaced, leaving an impression of a man having his teeth drilled without Novocain.

"Just don't tell me you're going to quit. Not with what's coming at us."

"I thought everything was under control."

"The hearing's set. Laura, Matthew, and Kurt are having blood drawn for DNA testing. But Kurt's clamoring for visitation."

"Oh, great."

"I filed an opposition. I just hope the court will see that he's trouble."

"He is for the Drummonds."

"He is for himself, too. He's got history." He tossed her a packet of paper-clipped pages. "Once I knew he lived in Seattle, it was a cinch to find it. It would have been for Barkin, too. If he'd tried."

She flipped through the first pile of papers. Kurt had been arrested for possession of a small amount of cocaine. He pled, and did six months. She skimmed the next page, a police report:

Officers responding found the suspect and victim in the bathroom. Suspect was kneeling on victim in the bathtub, battering her around the face and chest with his fists. Victim, who identified the suspect as her husband, sustained cuts to the cheek and eyelid. . . .

"The victim was Laura?"

Bobby nodded. "She wouldn't press charges, but the DA was a stand-up gal and filed on Kurt's ass anyway."

"Good for her." She read the next pages. "Sixty days in jail. And busted again after that, on an outstanding warrant. Thirty days that time. This should all be helpful."

"I certainly hope so. I'm sick that this has happened to the Drummonds. After what they've been through already."

Hannah put the report down. "I've heard that infertility is devastating."

"That's not even the half of it. Invite me in for coffee and I'll tell you the story."

5

Bobby knew most of it secondhand from Dan Barkin, whose connections to Stephen went back several years. They'd gone to high school together and played tennis on Stephen's weekends home from college.

"Stephen's and Dan Barkin's families are old Orange County," Bobby said.

"These days, that means they got here in 1980," Hannah said.

"You'll be impressed. Stephen's mother is Mary Catherine Drummond."

"The Duchess? I didn't make the connection," Hannah said.

"Stephen prefers to keep a low profile."

She was still alive, Bobby said, when Stephen met Rebecca through mutual friends. The couple married six months later, when Stephen was thirty-nine. Rebecca was thirty-four. That was six years ago.

"Is Rebecca pedigreed, too?" Hannah asked.

"No. She's blue-collar, not blue-blood. The family's Irish-American, loaded with earned money. Her dad built up his construction business from nothing. But once they got established, they never denied Rebecca anything. Architecture school at Columbia? Fine. Postgrad at Berkeley? Sure. Mega-wedding at the Ritz-Carlton? No problem. Rebecca's family is pretty solidly non-Ritz, though. I saw the wedding pictures. Stephen's half of the room was Armani. Her half was Sears."

"Snob. Who would you rather spend eternity with?"

"I'd like Armani women and Craftsman tools," he said.

Hannah laughed. "I'd like to see you drive that bargain with God."

"Me, too. He never lets you get the best of both worlds. Anyway, I think Mary Catherine regarded Rebecca as a bit déclassé. But she's gone now, and so is his dad. Meanwhile Rebecca's family had its own qualms. Stephen's family is Presbyterian. The Malones are serious Catholics. And Stephen's divorced. They didn't like that."

"What happened to the first wife?"

"Something about kids. She didn't want them, he did. It wasn't negotiable, I guess. Stephen got out."

"I thought it was Rebecca who was kid-crazy."

"She comes from a big family. Ten kids. Her mom's very proud of that."

"God, it would exhausting. Even the pope's be-fruitful medal wouldn't make it worthwhile."

"Cynic."

"Is that what Rebecca's mother expected of her? A litter?"

"A couple of kids would have been acceptable. Rebecca had no expectations—except that she would be a mother."

"Because that's what her mother taught her: women are either moms in waiting or moms in fact."

"Stephen wanted children, too, more than most guys I've ever met. He lost his dad young. Family was important."

"So they're soul mates," Hannah said.

"They get married, she works a little for her dad's construction and renovation business, but mostly she concentrates on their house. Five bedrooms, kid-ready."

"And the kids didn't come."

"Nope."

"It's the career-woman syndrome," Hannah said. "We're supposedly at peak fertility in our twenties. If we wait until our late thirties, things start to go sour."

"I think it's Stephen's problem, actually. Barkin tried to ask once, but Stephen got pretty defensive—sent out some very strong none-of-your-damn-business vibes. Stephen just said they couldn't have kids."

Hannah shook her head. It was just what you could expect from life. People who didn't want kids—like herself, for instance—busily used contraceptives and feared the day the rubber broke or one too many pills was forgotten. But the people who were dying for children couldn't have them. Hannah sometimes wondered if God enjoyed having a sick sense of humor.

"So off they went to the fertility clinic?"

"Stephen was prepared to do just that. Rebecca made the mistake of telling her family there was a problem, and that they were thinking about it. They freaked."

"This is a Catholicism thing, I assume."

"'Artificial means' is a papal no-no, apparently. Rebecca's mother said prayer would work, if you would let it. So Rebecca prayed. Her mother had novenas said. Bought her a medal and statue of Saint Gerard."

"Patron saint of . . ."

"Childbirth and mothers. And when, as the Drummonds saw it, God didn't come through, she and Stephen tried in-vitro. Then there was GIFT, which the Church doesn't mind, apparently. And ZIFT."

"Whoa, Too many acronyms. You're talking to a woman who's best versed on the contra part of conception."

"Sorry. GIFT is Gamete Intrafallopian Transfer. ZIFT is Zygote Intrafallopian Transfer. Don't ask me how this stuff works. I just know the penis isn't anywhere near the vagina when conception takes place."

"But it didn't work for them?"

"No. And surrogacy was out. They'd heard the horror stories about surrogates changing their minds and trying to get their babies back. They were going to try the fertility route one more time. Then the egg mess broke."

Hannah nodded. It was indeed a mess. A trio of famous fertility doctores at UC Irvine were alleged to have taken some couples' fertilized eggs without permission and implanted them in other infertile patients. Every day, reports of more cases surfaced, until it seemed that half of Orange County's children had been purloined, defrosted, planted, and grown to term without their biological parents' knowledge. Alleged embryo-napping. The idea made Hannah's head ache.

"That's why Rebecca finally called it quits," Bobby said. "She thought the pope and her mother might be right about what happens when you try to play God."

"Why didn't they just adopt in the first place? The foster homes are full of kids who need families."

Bobby shook his head. "Well, I think Rebecca could have talked herself into it. But let's just say Stephen wasn't really interested in adopting the children the county has to offer."

"You're talking about mixed-race kids, older kids, crack babies. Damaged goods."

"It sounds heartless, but do you blame them? People don't even like to buy used cars. Why would they want a thrown-away child? And the Drummonds wanted a baby. A baby who looked like them. Stephen's mother was alive then. . . ."

"God forbid the Dutchess would have a Latino grandson," Hannah said in mock horror.

"Did you ever meet Mary Catherine?"

"No. Why?"

"Apparently that was exactly her attitude. Pedigrees. Genealogy. Bloodlines."

"So they went for a white baby, of course. But wasn't Stephen still little apprehensive about this unknown father, since his family's so into heritage and all?"

"His mother was the Nazi, not Stephen, Hannah."

"I suppose you're right." Stephen wasn't the warmest person Hannah had ever met, but he seemed to love his wife and baby. And he was rational enough to see that families were about love, not blood. He'd managed to get over his mother's odd eugenical outlook, and that said something about his character.

"He knows adoptions are about imperfections," Bobby said. "It's the pregnancy somebody didn't expect. Or the boyfriend who was someone else's husband. Or the father's a petty thief in jail. Or he's a pimply, scared seventeen-year-old who can't deal with algebra, let alone fatherhood. If birth fathers were Princes Charming, women wouldn't need to give up their kids, would they?"

Hannah nodded. "I suppose most people are more worried about the mother and her habits, anyway."

"Right. She's the one growing the little guy for nine months."

Hannah sighed. "Still, the whole idea of demanding a perfect little baby who looks like you bothers me. It's narcissistic."

"I don't see you adopting any disadvantaged children."

"That's because I have no illusions about building the perfect family. I'll never be Donna Reed."

"I doubt that's what Guillermo wants you to be. He'd settle for you as an imperfect mother to Agustin kids."

Hannah felt her hackles rise. Sometimes she was sorry she confided in Bobby. She and Bobby had become best friends in law school. Apparently he thought that gave him the right to toss advice her way, when warranted. There had been a lot of such lobs, lately.

She smoothed her hair and gave him a thin back-off smile. "I hate it when you hijack a conversation and land it in my life. We're supposed to be talking about work."

"Sure. As if this isn't mostly gossip."

"Yes, but it's not about me."

Bobby raised his eyebrows. He knew he'd hit a target.

"Moving right along, then. So Rebecca and Stephen decided on an independent adoption. No agency. They would find a birth mother through a lawyer or friends, or the newspaper—"

"Ads? I thought you couldn't do that."

"It's illegal to advertise in California, but it's okay to do in other states' newspapers. Some national magazines run ads, too."

Hannah nodded as Bobby went on : The mom-to-be and the couple meet. The couple is allowed to pay her pregnancy-related expenses. When the baby is born, it goes home with the adoptive couple. The state does a home study, and six to nine months later the adoption is finalized.

"And here is where Laura comes in?"

"No. This is where it turns ugly. Rebecca and Stephen signed on with an adoption attorney recommended by one of Stephen's rich, knows-everybody uncles. This guy had been written up in the papers. He's got a waiting room full of happy-family pictures. He was so unctuous that the Drummonds called him the Slug, but he could deliver. His fees were high, but the Drummonds aren't poor, so that wasn't a problem."

"But there was a problem?"

"There was. I think they lost a baby."

"Lost it?"

"The adoption went south somehow. The Drummonds wouldn't say much to Barkin about it. But Rebecca told Barkin she was a basket case, no sleep, heart palpitations. She was really messed up. Clinically distraught. The marriage almost ended."

"Did they separate?"

He nodded. "For three months or so. Then they got back together and decided to try again. But it would be different this time. They hired Barkin, someone they really, really trusted, to handle the legal stuff. Barkin had done a half-dozen independent adoptions without any trouble. That was right around the time I began to talk to him about buying the practice. I was in the office when they called him. They'd found Laura. They were ecstatic."

"Too bad it was so short-lived. I hope we can untangle this for them," Hannah said.

"Well, at least I've got the matter of Laura's Fiat under control."

"Good. Where did it come from?"

"Laura's father gave it to her."

"I thought he was a penniless drunk."

Bobby shrugged. "That was the impression Laura gave Barkin. But now, no big surprise, the story has changed, although Laura claims she never said her family was poor. We can verify that pretty easily."

"Good."

"And now the Drummonds have a challenge for which I

think you'd be perfect. They want us to do a little checking on Laura."

"So much for mutual respect and trust. Not that I blame them."

"Laura's not making things any easier. She hasn't returned the Drummonds' phone calls. She stood up Rebecca for a lunch date. No explanation."

"Those are bad signs."

"I think so, too. They want to know what else she might have kept from them. And they want us to find Tiger."

"The masked inseminator?"

"If we find him, get a blood test, an acknowledgment of paternity, and a relinquishment, that's the end of Kurt."

"Kurt is history as soon as the DNA shows he's not Matthew's father—if that's the way it turns out. I wouldn't lay money on Tiger being the dad, though, just on Laura's say-so."

"The Drummonds are hoping that she told the truth about him. But they want us to sew up that daddy loophole, once and for all."

Hannah looked at Bobby's big, slightly doughy face for a moment. She tired not to smile at his earnest expression, but she couldn't help it.

"*We* and *us* really means me, right? You want me to put on a tight black dress and a pair of fuck-me shoes and teeter around the San Francisco financial district's nicer bars. I'm Tiger bait."

Bobby shrugged "I figured you'd have better luck than me. I look lousy in Lycra."

"Let's get a nice, shapely San Francisco PI to do it."

"No. The Drummonds don't want that. Delegating to people who didn't care got them into this mess in the first place. That's what Stephen said."

"He means Barkin."

"Right."

"And since he's gone and we're here, our penance is to personally clean up this mess."

"I think we owe them that, after Barkin's sloppiness. Besides, you're the best PI-without-portfolio I know."

"You're a major bullshitter, you know that?"

"Thank you. And since you're rich now, you can take me out to dinner. Gravad lax at Gustav Anders would be nice." He passed her a folded square of paper. "Before you go up to San Francisco, we should probably check out Laura's story about the car. Here's an old address of Laura's thanks to the morgue at the *Press-Telegram*. If we're lucky, Mr. Benson still lives there."

"Is this clipping going to tell me she committed a heinous crime she didn't bother to tell the Drummonds about?"

"Nope. She was Miss Naples."

Hannah unfolded the page. There was Laura, in a bathing suit and beauty-queen sash. A canal, gondola, and stylish villas were visible beside her.

"Our Naples? Or the Italian one?"

"Ours. The one in Long Beach."

"You know, I've never been there. It looks nice."

"It's no slum. I figured they posed her near home. You can make out the house and the street name in the picture. Her comment about her neighborhood reeking of fish would be funny if she hadn't used it to get the Drummonds' sympathy."

Hannah put the page in her daybook. "You're turning into a pretty good detective yourself."

"Only because Dan Barkin was a bad lawyer," Bobby said. "My only consolation is that if his sailing is this sloppy, he's shark chow by now."

6

Hannah surveyed the Cape Cod saltbox cottage and the neighborhood of Naples surrounding it. She decided that if Laura's father still lived here, he had the means to buy her a brace of Fiats.

Naples was more Venetian than Neapolitan, with its with canals, boat slips, and gondalas-for-rent. But in any country or city, it would stand out as a precinct of wealth. Hannah guessed that million-dollar houses were typical here. The setting didn't jibe with the impression of a deprived, miserable childhood Laura Benson described. But the address was right.

A low brick wall encircled the yard, merely hinting that privacy was desired. (The armed-response sign made the message more forthright.) A poster for a congressional candidate shouted a message from the perfect patch of lawn. SUSAN BECKETT: VALUES FAMILY, FAMILY VALUES. The name on the mailbox said Gerald Lawrence. Maybe the Bensons had moved.

Hannah let herself through the knee-high gate and knocked. She heard footsteps inside, and then a man in his sixties opened the door. He was bent by what Hannah guessed to be arthritis, and strained his neck to look up at her. His hair had once been blond, but now it was a yellowing gray. His eyes were small, pale, and shrewd.

"Mr. Lawrence?"

He surveyed her, looking for tracts or brooms or whatever it was she was peddling on a Sunday morning. "What is it?"

"My name is Hannah Barlow, and I wonder if you could tell me about some people who I think used to live here. The Bensons? They had a daughter named Laura."

Lawrence's face darkened.

"What's happened to my Laura?"

His Laura? "Are you Laura's father?"

He nodded. His eyes hardened and he managed to pull himself up straighter. It seemed to Hannah that this wasn't the first time some stranger had brought him bad news about Laura. Now he was steeled for the worst.

"You're with the police?"

"No. I'm a lawyer. And Laura is fine."

"Not dead, or hurt"

"No."

"In trouble, then?"

"Well, not with the police. But there's a situation. . . ."

He nodded. Of course there was a situation, she'd been in those before. He looked past Hannah to the lawn and its campaign sign, then the canal beyond. He narrowed the door's opening and fiddled with the lock, as though anxious to shut himself away from the news she had.

"Mr. Lawrence, I'm sorry if I upset you. May I come in for a few minutes and talk with you?"

The old man shook his head. Before she could ask another question, he shut the door in her face. She knocked and knocked again. But there was no sound inside the house. It was as though he'd never been there.

Hannah stood on the walkway, thinking of what tack to take next. Suddenly Lawrence barreled out of the house. He had put on a moss-colored windbreaker and Top-siders. With his head jutting out from shoulder level, and his narrow, hard-metal eyes, he looked like a tortoise, but moved much faster. Hannah followed him.

"Mr. Lawrence, if you'd please just give me a moment."

He ignored her as he made for a gate that led down to the canal.

"Laura has a son," she said. "Did you know?"

He blinked once, the reptilian face revealing nothing. Then, for an instant before he turned away and continued down the ramp, Hannah saw a smirk, an expression of bitter triumph. Lawrence stepped onto a sailboat, a single-master forty-footer, trimmed out in teak and brass. He started the auxiliary motor and cast off. He didn't look back.

The question of whether or not he bought Laura a Fiat seemed trivial, suddenly. Hannah wanted to know why he thought Laura Benson was dead. And why did the news of a grandson fill him with such an ugly glee? They struck Hannah as a sign full of portent, and she spent the next days waiting for its fulfillment.

It came a few days later, in the form of the court order for visitation. Kurt won that round. So on Wednesday, Hannah pulled into the driveway of the Drummonds' house, sat in her car, and told herself she was pausing to admire Rebecca's creation. But she was putting off the moment when she would take Matthew to see his alleged father.

Rebecca had selected a site in a hilly district called Las Almas Acres. The house, a multilevel assemblage of slate, mauve, and tan boxes reminded Hannah of an Anasazi cliff house that had been detached from its canyon wall. The home was on the crest of a hill, surrounded by an artful planting of penstemon, salvia, and verbena that trailed away into the slope's native chaparral. In Rebecca's design, half the house's surfaces were windows and glass doors, giving views in every direction. The house was spare and restrained, suggesting that its owners had no need to flaunt their wealth. Even the marine-blue Porsche parked in the driveway was understated.

Hannah got out of her car and approached the house. Behind the bars of a metal gate, the backyard curved out and down the spine of the hillside. One leveled area had a shaded deck, overgrown with trumpet vine. Steps led from there down to another flattened area and a stack of what looked like lodgepoles. At the bottom of the garden stood a small glass-and-concrete pavilion in the Bauhaus style. The canvas shades were up, and Hannah could see a desk, chair, computer, and tackboard covered with blueprints. It must be Rebecca's office.

Near the front door, she heard a trickle of water. There was a long, troughlike fishpond that wrapped around the atrium. Hannah stopped to look at the koi, bright as gold coins and just as expensive. She'd heard that fish-watching could be a calming meditation. She gazed at the gilded fins and fanned tails and checked her pulse. Still racing. She'd need a couple hours with the koi to feel better.

The doorbell rang melodiously. Then Stephen was there in a pale green scrub shirt and jeans, holding Matthew and scowling.

"I can't believe this judge is letting Kurt be alone with a baby that probably isn't even his," he said. "She doesn't have the sense to decide a dog show, let alone decide a little boy's future. And appointing a lawyer for Matthew? He's a baby, for Christ's sake."

Matthew stared at Hannah, his blue eyes wide. His thumb was planted in his mouth, and the faster Stephen talked, the harder his son sucked.

"It's standard operating procedure in a contested adoption," Hannah said. "Bobby and I have talked to the lawyer Judge Baxter appointed for Matthew. We're on the same wavelength. He doesn't think much of Kurt, or his claims."

"Kurt," Drummond said with disgust. "He's a lying druggie low-life scum, even if he did manage to get this Pabst guy, some pro bono lawyer from a bleeding-heart legal clinic, to make a good impression in court."

Hannah nodded. The stringy, disheveled Kurt who battled Bobby and Drummond wasn't the one who appeared in court before the Honorable Elizabeth "Bitsy" Baxter. He was in an olive-green suit. He'd been shorn and scrubbed. Big deal, Hannah thought. She'd known murder suspects who cleaned up even better than Kurt. It merely was a way to create an aura of respectability in court, an effort aided by Pabst and a third guy, whose role Hannah didn't quite grasp at first. Until he stated his affiliation: Higher Ground Recovery House. Having Kurt's rehab counselor show up in court was a smart move.

Kurt also had refashioned his manners. He exuded paternal concern. He kept his temper in check and apologized for crashing the adoption party, but he was so darn upset. Darn? Hannah wanted to throw up. He sprinkled his answers with the right amount of *yes ma'ams*. That did it for Bitsy. She said Kurt reminded her of her own son. Hannah knew then that they were sunk.

"I don't like this either," she told Stephen. "But until we prove otherwise, the law recognizes Kurt as the baby's legal father. And thanks to the drug counselor, Baxter thinks those problems are in the past." She looked at Matthew, who was babbling softly to the koi. He lunged for them, and Stephen had to shift him to the other hip to save the fish from infantile contact. Matthew frowned.

Drummond sighed, picked up the diaper bag, and handed it to Hannah. Good, she thought. He's not going to try to stop the visit. He's just venting.

"That was a load of bullshit," he said. "Did Kurt twelve-step his way out of wife beating, too?"

"That's what Laura said."

"Why did the judge even bother asking Laura? She's obviously afraid of Kurt. That's why she left him, supposedly. But now I can't tell whose side she's on. Can you?"

Hannah couldn't. After several unreturned phone calls, Bobby got through to Laura on the morning of the visitation hearing. She promised to fight so that Matthew would be the Drummonds. But then she'd gone merciful toward Kurt in her testimony before Baxter. He might have changed, she said. Their problems were a long while ago. Afterward she seemed perplexed at the Drummonds' anger. Hadn't they wanted her to be honest? She had been.

Hannah decided that anticipating Laura was like predicting an earthquake. No one knew when the next temblor would hit, or where the shaking would be worst. "Have you talked to Laura since the hearing?"

He shook his head. "Rebecca did, for a few minutes. She claims to understand why Laura is doing this. Something about being a people pleaser. I, for one, am not pleased. I want this crap with Kurt to be over. I want him out of our lives, as quickly and cleanly as possible."

"You make it sound like surgery."

"You're damned right," he said gleefully. "When in doubt, cut it out."

"And what about Laura? Do you remove her, too?"

Stephen's face grew serious as he considered her question. The relationship that enmeshed Stephen, Rebecca, and Laura was made as much from tension as from trust. Laura gave the Drummonds their deepest desire—a child. But he came with a string attached—Laura herself. Their longing for a baby was so strong that Hannah couldn't imagine them saying no when she asked for an open adoption. But even as they agreed to keep her in their child's life, they knew they were making a promise they could break without legal repercussions. And Laura knew it, too.

Stephen finally shook his head and kissed his son on the cheek. "Laura gave us Matthew. We love her for that. We made an agreement with her, and we're going to make it work."

Hannah nodded. "Okay."

"Don't leave Matthew alone with Kurt."

"I promise."

Drummond walked with her and cinched the infant seat into the backseat of Hannah's Integra. He slipped Matthew in and kissed him again. The baby whimpered slightly and narrowed his eyes at Hannah.

"The only smart thing Baxter's done is let you monitor the visits," Drummond said.

Hannah hadn't expected Kurt to go along with it. But he just smiled magnanimously and said Hannah would suit him just fine. If Kurt thought he could manipulate her, he was going to find out differently today.

"We're grateful, Hannah, despite all the bitching we do," Stephen said. "When are you going to San Francisco?"

"Tomorrow. And we'll talk about how else to check out Laura after that. Where's Rebecca?"

"I asked her to stay upstairs. I don't think she can handle this right now."

"We'll be back by noon. It will be fine. A few weeks from now Kurt will be out of your lives forever."

She watched Stephen walk back to the glassy, angular

house. He paused in the entryway and scattered some fish food on the surface of the pond.

In no time Matthew would be able to grab the koi. Then it would be time for Montessori preschool, the first in a succession of good choices. The Drummonds would fill his vacations with skiing in Colorado and dinosaur-appreciation trips to museums. He'd meet other affluent children. There would be soccer games, dances, and dates. He would pick a profession that would do his parents proud. Of course, he might hit eighteen, rebel, take massive doses of Ecstasy, and move to a tepee in the Mojave Desert. But it would be his choice: embrace or reject a life of privilege.

If Laura had decided to keep him, it would have been different. At best, she would have pulled herself together and managed a scrappy, honest pink-collar life for her baby. At worst, Matthew would have been consigned to watching *Brady Bunch* reruns in a cheap motel room while she cowered under the fists of her latest coke-snorting beau.

"Hey, Matthew," she said, turning to smile at him.

Now he looked brightly at her. His fuzzy hair glimmered in the sun. The blue eyes loomed huge in his face. Every moment, experience flooded through those eyes, and she imagined Matthew trying to make shape and sense of them. Did he have any sense of what was going on? Hannah thought he must, on some neural, instinctive level. His mother's anxiety, his father's anger. The cradle was a rocky place to be in the Drummonds' house these days.

Matthew smiled toothlessly. "Dada?"

"And Mama, too. You hit the jackpot."

He squealed and patty-caked his hands.

Kurt had taken a room at the Saddleback Inn, a moderately respectable motel in Santa Ana, not far from the courthouse. Hannah expected him to revert to his grunge wardrobe, but he came to the door in khakis and a fresh, melon-colored golf shirt. He smelled of cologne.

"Nice outfit," she said. "Did you think there might be a surprise inspection?"

Kurt shrugged. "It's for Matthew."

"I'm sure he appreciates the effort." Matthew was writhing in her arms. He kicked her in the side and Hannah wished that Guillermo were there. One look at her clumsiness with a baby would check his family fantasies.

"I just hope he doesn't spit up on that shirt," she said to Kurt. "Looks like a Nordstrom buy. Did the personal shopper help out?"

Kurt held his arms open. "Let me have my boy."

"He's not great with strangers," Hannah said. "Let's give him a few minutes."

But Matthew gurgled and reached for Kurt, scat-singing dadas like a little Ella Fitzgerald.

Kurt smirked. "He knows me."

"He called me dada all the way here," Hannah said. "It's random vocalization."

Kurt glared and then motioned her inside. She wondered how Kurt was paying for the room, the lawyer, and the clothes. His affluence didn't extend to transportation: there was a junky, rust-colored Maverick parked near the door to his room. Stickers for Seattle grunge bands were plastered on the car's windows.

The day after the scene in the office, Laura told Bobby that Kurt fancied himself a musician. But his band, Suture, had only a couple paying gigs before it fell apart. He occasionally supported himself with menial jobs — barrista in one of Seattle's ubiquitous coffee bars, doorman at clubs like the Off-Ramp. More often, though, he dealt cocaine, she said.

Hannah sat down in a fading but still visually assaultive yellow-and-green floral chair and watched Kurt. He threw himself on the floor, grabbed a corner of the bedspread, and started a game of peekaboo. Soon he had Matthew in peals of laughter.

After a few minutes he asked Hannah if she'd brought Matthew's bottle. Kurt deftly popped the nipple cover and tipped the bottle into Matthew's mouth. He sucked happily and danced his fingers across Kurt's face.

Kurt looked up to see Hannah watching him. "Nice technique," she said.

"First job I ever had was baby-sitting at the Calvary Baptist Church on Sundays. Me and a nurseryful of newborns. Who's my Droolbaby?"

The nickname clanged in Hannah's ear. Jesus Christ, she thought.

"When Laura and me were together," Kurt was saying, "we talked about having kids. We'd get our shit together. We'd get clean. We'd have a boy. And now we do."

"I didn't know Laura had a drug problem." She hoped she sounded casual. Her stomach was writhing.

"Oh, sure. Coke to get up, pills to take the edge off—Laura wasn't particular. I was much worse off, though. When Laura decided to stop, she did, just like that."

"That was before she was pregnant?"

He shrugged. "I guess."

"She never told you she was pregnant, did she? How did you find out?"

Kurt's face reddened. "We're not in court now, are we? You can't ask me this stuff."

"I'm thinking about Matthew. If Laura used cocaine while she was pregnant, that's something I think we'd all want to know, for his sake, right?"

"Yeah. Okay. Laura did coke, but she's not stupid."

"But she liked feeling good."

"Who doesn't? She would have stopped as soon as she knew about him." Kurt held Matthew up and looked closely at him. "Besides, he looks fine. He's kinda white, though. Does he go outside much?"

Hannah shrugged. "I think so. Laura takes him to the park a couple times a week."

"There's a park right across the street. And there's a zoo, too."

"Okay. Let's go."

"I'd like some time alone with him."

Hannah was ready for this. "I can't do it, Kurt. I'm the court-approved monitor, and I intend to monitor."

"What do you think I'm going to do?"

"You're angry at Laura for leaving you. Sometimes people play out their anger through innocent third parties.

You could be one of those people. I'm not letting you two out of my sight."

"Fine," he said. "Though it's the stupidest thing in the world for that shit Drummond and his wife to pay someone like you a hundred bucks an hour to baby-sit Matthew when he's with his own father."

Hannah smiled at him. "For baby-sitting, I drop my rates to thirty an hour. And I don't even raid the refrigerator."

For the next two and a half hours Hannah trailed several steps behind Kurt as he showed Matthew the Santa Ana Zoo. Matthew stared at an angora rabbit, which twitched its nose and nibbled vegetable pellets from Kurt's hand. He frowned at the macaques in their cages. He sat easily in Kurt's arms and dipped his head to his shoulder when he got tired.

Hannah checked her watch as Kurt bought Matthew a hat that looked like a lion's mane.

"Time's up," she said.

Kurt cuddled the boy and handed him back to her. In the parking lot, as Hannah pulled away, Kurt waved and called to them.

"See you next week, Baby of Drool!"

During the drive back to Las Almas, she realized that she had spent the morning watching a man who acted exactly the way she'd expect a father to act. How would she tell the Drummonds that?

Rebecca was upstairs at the window, frowning intently as her legs pumped, scaling invisible heights on a stair climber. She glanced down, saw Matthew in Hannah's arms, and the fierce face melted into an expression of joy, mingled with relief. Maybe a trace of envy, too. Rebecca could see that Matthew hadn't spent the morning crying.

She met them at the door. Sweat stained the chest and underarms of her T-shirt. She gathered Matthew in her arms like a bunch of sweet-smelling flowers, kissed his cheek, and motioned for Hannah to come into the slate-floored foyer.

For the first time Hannah realized that this was hardly a

house built for children. Stone floors, glass everywhere. The staircase rose steeply, and the balusters were widely spaced. The fall could break a child's skull.

"The kid-proofers are coming next week." Rebecca had been watching her, reading her mind. "Plexiglas along the stairs, padding for the edges of the fireplace, plugs in all the outlets. We might carpet the entryway."

Hannah nodded. "Sounds like a good idea."

"But you can't imagine why I designed it like this in the first place?"

Hannah was wondering that. Some parents fit their children into the spaces and niches of their lives, while others built their worlds around them. The house told her that the Drummonds fell in the former category, even if Rebecca behaved like a mother from the latter.

"Well, I had heard you wanted to build a house for a family," Hannah said.

She sighed. "I did. This isn't it. This is my act of despair."

"I don't quite understand."

"We were never going to have children, so I thought I might as well build a house for adults only. Plenty of rich clients are like that. I built a showcase to impress them."

"But all the bedrooms . . ."

"I tried to take them out, but I just couldn't. None of the designs would work without them. Some part of me wouldn't give up." She fingered what looked like a medal that hung from a silver chain around her neck. "Stephen took the day off. He's waiting for us in what was supposed to be study. But it kept coming out as a family room, no matter what I did."

The cool formality of the house disappeared here. The sofa and chairs were was covered in washed-out blue denim and the fabric looked to Hannah as though it could withstand any punishment Matthew could concoct. Everything was right for a child—without retrofitting.

"Well?" Stephen was sitting on the edge of the sofa with a glass of wine in his hand. "How did it go?"

"Fine." Hannah sat down and decided she would have to tell them. "Mostly."

The lines in Rebecca's forehead deepened. "What happened?"

Get it over with, Hannah thought. "Kurt says Laura did cocaine. A lot of it."

Rebecca and Stephen looked at each other. Then Rebecca watched Matthew as he pulled himself up by grabbing the coffee table's edge. He wavered there for a moment, and then sat down with a thump.

"He said she was clean during her pregnancy," Hannah said. "But if he's telling the truth, then she was lying when she told her doctor that she'd dabbled in marijuana in high school, but hadn't done any other drugs since. What did she tell you?"

"She told us she'd never used drugs at all," Rebecca said. "And we believed her. She didn't—"

"Rebecca didn't think she looked like that kind of person." Stephen's voice carried an edge of sarcasm. "I tried to tell her that drug users don't come in types, but she didn't believe me."

Hannah nodded. In her time she had seen a few fat heroin addicts and some very chic, composed speed freaks.

"More lies," Stephen said. "It's par for the course."

"What else happened?" Rebecca said.

"He called Matthew Droolbaby."

Stephen put down his glass and stared at Hannah for a moment, perplexed. Then he got it. "That's what Laura calls him."

"How would he know that?" Rebecca said.

"Laura could have told him," Hannah said.

"But that means they're talking." Rebecca knit her fingers until the knuckles were white.

"Becca, get Hannah some iced tea."

"Stephen . . ."

"Honey." He squeezed the endearment through a tight smile. "Get our guest some tea."

She rose uncomfortably and went to the kitchen.

"She's going to go back to him, isn't she?" Stephen was whispering, holding the paper-thin bowl of the wineglass in his hand.

"I'm concerned about the way they're talking. That she's treating him like he's the father."

"Goddammit," he said. He clenched the glass so hard that it shattered. Wine and blood trickled over his fingers.

Rebecca rushed in at the shout and tried to stanch the bleeding with a dish towel, but he pushed her away.

"A Band-Aid, please."

She returned with one, and picked up slivers of glass from the table.

"I don't think she loves him anymore. I don't know how he'd get her back, unless it's a drug thing." The words were a rush, a chant of denial. "He really hurt her, that last time."

Stephen shook his head. "Rebecca, I'm sick of you making excuses for her. Whose side are you on?"

Rebecca barely glanced at him, but her voice was icy. "I'm on Matthew's side. How about you?"

"Look," Hannah said, wishing she had a striped shirt and a whistle. "I understand the pressure you're both under, but this isn't getting you anywhere."

Stephen grabbed the phone and punched a number. "You're right. But confronting that little bitch will."

Hannah shook her head. "Stephen, do you want her to be more afraid of you than of Kurt?"

"Maybe I do." He put down the receiver. "It infuriates me. After everything we've done for her."

"So she owes you a baby, is that it? Think how that would sound to Judge Baxter."

Stephen fell back on the sofa. "We never know what the hell she's going to do next."

"I don't blame you for being worried and angry," Hannah said. "You might be right about trying to talk to her. But I think it might be more productive to have Rebecca do it."

"I'm too pissed off, is that it?"

"Yes, frankly, you are. Rebecca, it wouldn't be a bad idea to remind her how bonded you are to Matthew. And how much you care about her, too."

Rebecca nodded. "That's easy. I do."

"Jesus, she's got you so bamboozled," Stephen said.

"She's coming around. She called here yesterday and left a message saying she wanted to talk to me."

"She called?" Stephen's voice was sharp. "You didn't tell me."

"I . . . thought it would upset you. She's been afraid of how we felt about her, after her lies about Kurt. But I care about her. I don't want her to go back to him. If she's even thinking about it, it's because he's manipulating her into it."

"See if you can convince her to stay away from him," Hannah said.

Rebecca nodded. "I'll try."

"Good luck," Stephen said. He stalked out of the room, kicking a toy on the way.

7

Even if Bobby thought it was the shortest route to Tiger, Hannah simply refused to squeeze herself into a low-cut little black cocktail dress for her trip to the bars of San Francisco's financial district. After checking into the Savoy on Geary, she slid out of her jeans and T-shirt, took a shower, and shook out the suit she'd brought.

It was black watered silk with a cropped jacket, braided-frog closure, and a skirt that rode above the knee. She put on black nylons and black pumps. Red lipstick? Sure. In lieu of cleavage. She considered wearing her hair down. Being a redhead had its advantages on occasions like this. A stream of coppery, curly hair was as good as a beacon in a dimly lit bar.

By six-thirty, she had sipped mineral water in the bars of four Embarcadero Center restaurants. At each, she chatted with the bartender and approached the customers identified as regulars. She worked the conversation around to Halloween, eighteen months before. She described the man, as best she could, including the tiger mask, the assignation with a blonde, and the nickname she'd given him. She didn't tell them that a child had been the result.

The jokes were inevitable.

"Quite a piece of tail, huh?"

"Did she think he was grrrrrreat?"

At Equinox, a slightly scruffy man in a blue pinstripe suit, referred to her by the bartender, listened to her story thoughtfully.

"Do you know him?" she asked.

He shook his head slowly, as though trying to find a memory in a darkened past. Then, without warning, he stood up and declaimed, with his martini glass held high:

> "Tiger! Tiger! Cunning, wise,
> Lapping at those tender thighs,
> The son of Blake's bright-burning cat
> Could not resist a taste of that."

The patrons clapped softly. The bartender chortled into his coffee and wouldn't meet Hannah's frosty eyes.

After four more stops at restaurants and clubs, she came to the Gold Coast, on California Street. She doubted she'd find poetry among the masses of young men crowding the room. Peanut shells crunched under her feet as she wended a path to the bar. She had earned a real drink. She hung her purse from a brass hook at her knees and asked for dirty Ketel One martini.

A man to her left slid a basket of peanuts within her reach. He was about Hannah's age, with a babyish face and a nice smile. They talked about the mayor, the vote on the new stadium, and the high cost of living in the city. Then he asked what brought her to San Francisco. Hannah would have liked to forget that, for a minute, but that was what she was there for.

"I'm looking for someone who was celebrating in a bar around here, in a tiger mask, Halloween before last. He's a blond guy. Thirties. Blue eyes, blue suit."

"What's he done?"

"Nothing illegal. I'm trying to locate him for a client."

The man looked at her suspiciously. "Lawsuit?"

"No. Someone he celebrated with is looking for him."

"Lost love?"

"Something like that."

"Somebody wants money?"

"No."

"In that case, I think I know somebody who might fit that description. He's into dressing up on Halloween and hitting the bars. He's a corporate type, works for B of A. And I think I saw him here a while ago. He might be over at Tadich's. Will you wait a couple minutes? I'll go see if he's done with dinner."

"Sure. Thanks."

The man he brought back was blue-eyed, blond, broad-shouldered. He wore a gray business suit. In a basso voice, he introduced himself as William, firmly shook Hannah's hand, and sat down. She bought him an Anchor Steam.

"So someone's looking for me? Barry said no lawsuits. I hope you're telling the truth."

"There's no lawsuit. I just want to ask a question or two. Were you a tiger Halloween before last?"

He unshelled a peanut with one hand and popped it in his mouth.

"Maybe. That was the end of my wild period and I'm still a little hazy about what I did then. Now it's one moderately crazy night a year, then back on the path of righteousness." He took a drink of his beer. "What did I do?"

"Charmed a blonde."

"It's narcissistic, but I do like the golden-haired ones. Did we go to bed?"

"Yes."

"Hmm. It might be coming back to me. What's the problem?"

"She thinks she made you a father."

William nearly choked on his drink. "Well, Hannah, I am definitely not your man. I'm a blond that prefers gentlemen."

She felt her face turn red. "Sorry. I guess I jumped to a conclusion."

"Oh, I get mistaken for a heterosexual all the time," William said. "Some of my straight friends, who seem to think they're living in the virus-free past, still have anony-mous celebratory liaisons—particularly on holidays. I'll pass on your card."

He offered to buy Hannah a drink. But she declined, pleading an early flight home. Her humiliation was com-plete. She'd fallen prey to bad jokes, dirty poems, and her own prejudices. It was time to call it a night.

8

A voice-mail message from Rebecca was waiting for her at the office. Once again, Laura wasn't returning calls, Rebecca said, her voice strained with worry. She didn't answer no matter what time Rebecca called. She had even gone to the apartment and seen Laura's car parked there. But when she knocked, Laura didn't come to the door. Stephen was about to boil over. Was there something, anything, that Hannah or Bobby could do?

"Want to flip for it?" Hannah said to Bobby when he made the mistake of wandering in as she was playing back the call. "Laura likes you. I don't think she's crazy about me."

"I've got a status conference at eleven," he said. "It'll go at least two hours. By this afternoon, the Drummonds will be basket cases. You call her."

But Hannah decided to go in person. Bobby gave her the address, and she recognized the neighborhood immediately: it was semirural when she was a beat cop fifteen years before. Orange groves stretched back to the foothills, suffusing the spring air with the rich, bee-addling perfume. Fruit stands appeared in summer. Smudge pots smoked the winter nights when the temperature dropped low enough to threaten the crop.

The groves had a darker side, too. Hannah had gone there to investigate body dumps more than once. The isolation and the dark, neat, dense rows of trees made the groves a perfect choice.

Now Las Almas had gobbled up the agricultural land that created its wealth. Few relics of the orange's golden age remained. The streets leading to the foothills were newly mapped and freshly paved. Where trees dangled orange fruit, there was now a new mall. In a week, a warehouse-sized bookstore would open, along with a franchised coffeehouse, a franchised pasta restaurant, and a franchised Western-boot store. Hannah knew that if someone dropped her onto one of these promenades and asked her to name the city in which it stood, she wouldn't be able to do it. From San Diego to Willits, they were as identical as cloned sheep.

She glanced across the street a felt a rush of relief. Something had been spared the latest retail landgrab: a citrus packing house. And according to the address Bobby had given her, it was where Laura lived.

The warehouse, where oranges and lemons were packed, had been built next to the rail line to make for easy shipment of crated fruit. But the weeds that thickly covered the ties were evidence of how long it had been since any boxcar stopped here. The fresh paint was a sure sign of gentrification and commerce reassignment. It was that way all over the county. When Las Almas Savings and Loan's president was sent up to Lompoc to serve his sentence for fraud, the fine old Moorish-influenced bank building became a chic women's clothes store. When the Moose Lodge membership dwindled down to the level of endangered fraternal species, it became a furniture emporium, selling crushed-velvet sofas, tasseled in gold.

The packing house had been made over into shops, too. All the spaces were vacant except for one: the Orange Section, a health-food market. Signs in the window offered specials on raw bran, bitter melon, and "Tofu Pups." Hannah's stomach turned a backflip.

The placement of the packing house's upstairs windows suggested the second floor was used for offices, or apartments. Hannah couldn't see any stairs. There, at the far end of the parking lot, Laura's black Fiat baked in the sun.

An Indian brass bell tinkled as Hannah opened the Orange Section's door. Behind the counter, a middle-aged guy with a mane of black hair, a lush black beard, and black-rimmed glasses was sipping a glass of something algae green. A copy of *The Celestine Prophecy* was propped up on the cash register. Hannah had an unnerving suspicion that the music sweeping the room was Yanni or, worse yet, John Tesh.

"Hi!" The man pulled out a checkered handkerchief and ran it under his nose. "Can I help you? Special on grains today. Triticale, bulgar, quinoa."

"I'm looking for Laura Benson. I had this as her address."

His friendly demeanor disappeared. He wiped his nose again, stuffed his handkerchief in his pocket, and scowled at her.

"What do you want with Laura?"

"Well, not that it's any of your business, but I'm her attorney."

His face reddened slightly, and he tried a tentative smile. "Oh, for the adoption. What a mess with Kurt, and everything, huh?"

"I really can't discuss this with you, Mister . . . ?"

"Gibbons. Cleve Gibbons. Sorry. It's just that I've been worried about her. Is he, or somebody, you know, bothering her?"

"Have you seen someone bothering her?"

He didn't seem to hear her. "Because she's a real special person, you know? Vulnerable, I think."

Hannah couldn't think of anyone less vulnerable than Laura Benson. But she decided to keep her observations to herself.

"And she should take better care of herself." Gibbons seemed distraught at the thought of what a bad job Laura was making of it. "When she was pregnant, I used to make up some fresh juices for her—wheat grass, carrot, all the good stuff. She wouldn't drink them at first. Not unless I begged her."

Hannah nodded, closing off the dietary monologue.

"Who is this person who's been bothering her? Kurt?" It sounded to Hannah as though it might be Gibbons himself. She could imagine downing a glass of wheat-grass juice, if that would get rid of him.

"I don't know if it was Kurt. I didn't see anything. I just heard."

He had gone up to the deck of her apartment, he said, to water the container garden he had given her. Fresh herbs and fresh vegetables would be good for her, and she grudgingly accepted the gift. But after a week or so the cherry-tomato vine was withering and the basil drooped. She wasn't what he'd call a diligent gardener. So he went up there, once a day, to water. Or pinch back the plants, whatever.

Ogle, swoon, Hannah thought. Whatever. "When was that?"

"Last week. Laura invited me in. She was going to make me some tea. The phone was ringing and ringing, and she wouldn't answer it. It seemed to be making her real mad that the person wouldn't give up. And then the answering machine came on, and she picked up the phone and went back to where her bedroom is. Actually, there's no room, exactly, just a divider. . . ."

He stopped, tangled in the description of her apartment, his face red. He'd imagined that bedroom many times, Hannah thought.

"I was leaving, but I could hear what she was saying." He dithered with some bags of blueberry granola. "She was yelling. Really mad."

"About what?"

"I don't know. But she said: 'Why would *I* do this to you? Think about it. Think what you did to me. And then you try to pay me off? You can't buy people.'"

"Who was she talking to?"

"I don't know. I left. It felt very creepy to be there, hearing her blow up like that. I think she knows I heard something. She has kind of avoided me since. Is she okay?"

"If you tell me the way to her apartment, I'll go find out."

He seemed relieved. "Go out the door, turn left, take the path around back, and keep going until you come to some metal stairs. Follow them up and you're there. I'm pretty sure she's home. Could you wait a second?"

"Sure."

He scuttled into a back room and returned with a covered pottery casserole dish. "I know she's not eating right lately. I see what's in the trash. Anyway, this has basmati rice, lentils, and veggies in a nice sauce—yogurt and turmeric. Very healthy."

"I'll take it to her. No promises, though."

"Tell her to give it a half hour at three-fifty." He entrusted the dish to Hannah, watching it as anxiously as a kid handing his first valentine to the postman. "And tell her, no microwaving! It's a killer, the microwave oven. I wish she'd listen."

Hannah followed the paving stones that led through a stand of scraggly palm trees. Over her head, their browning fronds clicked in the breeze. To her right, a concrete channel fell steeply, ending in a trickle of slime-choked green water.

Terra-cotta pots in wide saucers lined the upstairs landing. The oregano was holding its own. The tiny tomato plant needed horticultural CPR. The basil? RIP.

A corner window gave the apartment a view of the path, trees, and the pitiful dribble of a creek. It was open, and a breeze stirred the sheer curtains. Hannah could hear music— a keening Irish rock singer—playing at low volume inside. She knocked, and in an instant Laura swung the door open. She had a glass of vivid-orange carrot juice in her hand.

"Jesus, Cleve, could you just leave me the—oh." Hannah caught a whiff of something stronger than carrots on her breath. Was it gin?

She presented the casserole. "Cleve sent me up with this. He says it's healthy. Reheat at three-fifty and don't use the microwave. It will—"

"Kill me. I know." Laura allowed a tight smile. "He has some wacky ideas. What brings you here?"

"Rebecca and Stephen are worried. You haven't returned their calls."

She shrugged and looked down at the glass. "Well, I've been busy."

Hannah nodded. "I paid a visit to your father."

She flicked Hannah a defiant look. "My father? As far as I'm concerned, my father is dead."

"Funny you'd say that. He was afraid that's what happened to you."

"Wishful thinking." She looked far away for a moment. His worry had touched her in some way, but she was determined that Hannah not see that. She covered it with annoyance. "Look, who gave you the right to go poking around in my life, anyway?"

"If you didn't lie like other people blink, I wouldn't have to bother."

Laura pulled in a breath for her next salvo. But she didn't fire. Instead, she sighed, letting her shoulders slump. "Everyone is bearing down on me, all right? I just wanted to have some time alone. And Gerald? Well, for all the contact we've had, I might as well be dead. I guess he's waiting for someone to confirm it."

"Did he think you were dead when he bought you the Fiat?"

She shook her head. "It's really complicated, and I don't want to get into it. If you only came here to hassle me about him, you can—"

Hannah shook her head. "I'll drop it. May I come in?"

Laura hesitated for a moment, glancing back at the skylit room. Hannah saw a jumble of half-filled cardboard moving boxes stacked next to the door. A bottle of Bombay gin sat on the coffee table. "Sure. Why not?"

Hannah stepped inside. The space was huge, three times the size of Hannah's little apartment at Mrs. Snow's house. The living-room area was at the right. To the left stood a fabric-covered screen. It partitioned the sleeping area and bath, Hannah assumed, from the rest of the loft.

Laura whisked the gin off the table and started clearing

the kitchen counter. A plastic bag, half-filled with dirty-white clumps, disappeared into a drawer. Hannah did a quick scan of the living area, looking for other things Laura might not have had time to hide. There was nothing now on the coffee table except for a stack of Polaroids. Matthew grinned in the one on top.

The room scan was a cop reflex, a habit that still kicked in without Hannah willing it. She expected to see a pipe for the crack. That's what the little chunks in the bag looked like to her. Kurt said she'd quit coke. He never mentioned that she had a taste for crack, an even more addictive version of the drug.

Matthew showed none of the stiff-bodied, colicky hypersensitivity that hinted at a drug baby's neurological damage. Still, Hannah thought, Laura could have started using again, after Matthew was born. Hannah finished examining the loft. She couldn't see a pipe, or any other telltale druggie detritus.

Laura took the casserole from her, returned from the kitchen, and sat on the sofa. The angles of it and the expensive fabric suggested Rebecca had supplied it—a hand-me-down from the couple's house. Hannah sat on the matching chair and nodded to the boxes.

"Moving?"

"It's a pain," Laura said. "I'm out of here at the end of the month. I found a place in Tustin, not far away from where Rebecca and Stephen live, so I'll be able to see Matthew, if . . ."

She stopped and looked away for a moment. "Anyway, this apartment was only supposed to be mine while I was pregnant and getting back on my feet. If it goes on too much longer, somebody—Kurt—will scream baby selling."

"Probably. You've found a job?"

She nodded, looking down at her ragged nails. "Waiting tables at a nice place in Newport Beach, right on the water. Big-money people eat down there. The tips are good."

"Won't you miss Cleve's carrot juice?"

Laura smiled wryly. "I actually like it so much that there's a half gallon in the fridge now. Cleve's okay." It pleased Hannah that he'd managed to thaw her heart. "I guess I'm lucky to have someone who cares about me." Laura's happy look faded. "Is . . . are the Drummonds still mad?"

That was an understatement, Hannah thought. As if hearing her, Laura sighed. "They must be. They've been so good to me. Stephen's really angry, right?"

"Yes. And Rebecca's afraid. They don't know what's going to happen."

For the first time Laura looked remorseful. "And so Stephen is blaming you for this, because Barkin's not around. He can be like that—blaming."

"You would make the Drummonds feel a lot better if you'd give them a call."

Laura shrugged. "I know. Would you like something? Some of the juice, maybe?"

"Got anything less . . . orange?"

Laura laughed. "Tea?" She went into the kitchen and took two cups out of one of the brushed-steel cabinets that looked like they'd come from a doctor's office. She poured bottled water into a kettle and put it on the stove, a big industrial-steel box with six burners.

"You can do some serious cooking on that," Hannah said.

"I guess. I haven't. It came with the apartment, and it's a pain in the ass." She turned the knob under the left front burner, and nothing happened. "The damn pilot doesn't work."

She struck a match and turned the knob again. A blue-orange flame came to life. She put two cups on the counter and sat down on one of the tall stools. Hannah joined her.

Laura fiddled with her hair for a moment. "So you saw him?"

Hannah knew who she meant. Her father. "He's worried about you."

She shrugged. "He worries too much."

"I thought I was at the wrong house at first. How did you get to be Benson, when he's Lawrence?"

Laura looked up sharply, sensing an accusation. "I wasn't married to a Benson, if that's what you're getting at. I always hated the way Laura Lawrence sounded. La-la. I think Gerald did it to me on purpose. He wanted some Goody Two-shoes, debating-society, class-president type. As though running for office would ever interest me. A coming-out party was bad enough. But politics really make me sick."

Hannah listened to the anger in the young woman's voice. "So you picked Benson out of the phone book?"

"I knew a guy named Benson, and he was nice."

"And what does your father think of that?"

"Who gives a shit what Gerald Lawrence thinks?" The kettle howled in the kitchen and Laura got up to fix the tea. "Look," Laura said. "About Rebecca? I haven't called her because of—everything. Not telling her and Stephen about Kurt, I mean. It was a mistake, I know that. I never meant to hurt her. Really."

It sounded sincere enough. But there was something about her face that soured the sentiment. Hannah decided to flush out the lies. Laura was less able to calculate when she was mad.

"And what about the drugs?" Hannah said. "Not just pot, but the whole pharmacy you and Kurt used when you were together. Were those lies a mistake you're sorry about, too?"

Laura's face reddened. "Whatever he told you, he's lying. I told the Drummonds how it was. I smoked pot in high school, and I did use coke, but I quit. That's the truth."

"What about crack?"

Laura's eyes wavered, but she managed not to look toward the drawer where she'd stashed the Baggie. "That's Kurt's problem."

"Still?"

She shrugged. "No. I don't know."

"Was he using crack when he hit you?"

She didn't answer for a long time. "It's a part of my life I just want to forget."

"You made believe it never happened at all."

"I need some more tea. You?"

Hannah didn't but she wanted Laura to keep talking. "Sure."

Laura filled the kettle, relit the stove, and stood in front of it as the water came to a boil.

"When I found out I was pregnant, Kurt and I were over. Completely. I knew he wasn't the father, and I meant to get a divorce, but everything was so . . . fucked up. I was freaking out about being pregnant. I didn't want to have an abortion, but I came close. I was afraid I wouldn't be able to work. Waitressing in really nice places, where you can make some real money, is tough when you're pregnant. They want thin girls in tight clothes. I was broke, and I was hiding out from Kurt, and I just wanted to do right by my baby." Her chin quivered, but she stayed in control. "I was afraid that if I told the Drummonds the truth, that I was still married, they'd back out. And I liked them so much. I knew they'd be good to Matthew. I couldn't stand thinking about what they'd do if they found out I lied to them."

"Tell me about leaving Kurt. Wasn't he through with drugs then? You told the court he stopped beating you. If he was working on getting better, why did you leave?"

"I knew it wouldn't last. It was his life—the band, the clubs. He wouldn't give that up, even though drugs were everywhere, and he had no self-control. No talent, either. He always was better at playing around, pretending he was a musician, than he was at playing.

"It was bad for me, just being near him. I'd stopped doing drugs. I'd stopped partying. I was working a couple jobs. He was lying around, doing nothing. My money would just disappear, and he'd be high. And he wouldn't leave me alone."

"You mean he was possessive?"

She nodded. "At first, when he was clean, and so sorry about hitting me, I thought it was sweet. He said he couldn't live without me. That he wanted me to be his, always. Then it began to bother me. I didn't have anything that was mine. My money was his money. I was his, when he wanted a piece of ass. I was afraid of what he'd do if I tried to leave. I was afraid he'd kill me."

"Was he trying to kill you that night, when he beat you?"

She stared at the burner's flame. "He went crazy."

Hannah mulled that for a moment. "But you went back to him. Weren't you worried about what would happen to the baby if he went crazy again?"

"I didn't think—" She stopped and coolly looked at Hannah. "I told you. I wasn't pregnant then."

Oh, yes you were, Hannah thought. You're lying, as sure as I'm sitting here.

She was about to ask Laura why she'd agreed to let Kurt see the child if she was so afraid of him. But the phone rang. Laura started at the sound of it.

"Go ahead," Hannah said.

Three rings. Four. Laura's shrugging, glancing, and girlish evasion were gone. "Please tell Steve and Rebecca I'm sorry for all the trouble. I'll be there, in court, and if it's necessary, I'll tell the judge everything about Kurt."

Five rings.

"That's good," Hannah said. "Although I wouldn't think it would be necessary."

Laura tried not to look at the phone. She shook her head to show she didn't understand what Hannah was talking about. Six rings.

"If Kurt isn't Matthew's father, there's not much chance the judge will worry about his past, right?"

Seven rings. Eight.

"I just meant . . . if there was any question, I'd tell the judge that I'm afraid of what he might do with Matthew."

Nine rings. And no more. Now Laura glowered at the phone as if it had betrayed her.

"If that's so," Hannah said, "why did you tell the judge visitation was fine with you?"

Laura colored. Hannah had caught her.

The phone began ringing again. Laura opened the door for Hannah. "Please. I'd like you to leave now." Hannah got up and strolled to the door. Laura slammed it behind her. Two steps down the stairs, she stopped. So many lies in such a short time. In sum, did they mean Kurt was the father? Had he persuaded her to come back—and to bring Matthew?

She strained to hear what Laura was saying. But all she heard was the sound of the corner window slamming shut.

9

Hannah stared at the pink message slip as Vera let it flutter into her palm. The secretary arched an eyebrow.

"Don't even start, Vera. I've heard all the tiger jokes I ever want to hear." Hannah knew she shouldn't snap, particularly given the news Vera had just given her, but she hadn't slept well. Coffee hadn't improved her mood. And then the mail came.

Guillermo's postcard was a view of aspens turning color, the leaves flaming before they fell. The message on the back was terse: *I need time to think, Hannah.* Then his signature. No *Love.* Not even *Sincerely.* She felt like her face had been slapped.

She leaned into Bobby's office. He didn't look any better than she did. The days since she returned from San Francisco had been a mixture of tension and tedium. There wasn't much to do with the Drummonds but wait—for the results of Kurt's blood test, for the hearing, for the next turn of Laura, the human weather vane. It took a toll on both lawyers, but more so on Bobby. It would be nice to give him some good news.

"What?" He winced like a well-kicked cur.

She handed him the slip. Vera's printing was as good as anything WordPerfect could spit out:

Some guy who calls himself "Tiger" called. Call him back at eleven. There was a number in the 415 area code. And it was ten-thirty now.

"We snared us a big cat," she said.

• • •

At eleven, Hannah dialed the number. The phone rang three times, and Hannah heard a soft but impatient baritone voice. There was a trace of Southern accent in it.

"Jerome Hoskins."

Hannah scribbled the name on a notepad. "Mr. Hoskins, this is Hannah Barlow. My law partner, Robert Terry, is here with me. Can I put you on the speaker?"

"I suppose. What's this about? All I know is what my friend said. That you were trying to reach me."

"If you'll answer a couple questions, we'll know right away if you're the person we're looking for."

"Fire away," he said. "But I think I know where this is going."

Yes, he was blond. Yes, he sometimes frequented financial-district bars. He was a broker. He was single. He'd donned the tiger outfit on a whim, after seeing it in a place in the Castro. And of course he remembered Laura.

"She was quite pretty. And pretty drunk."

"Yes," Hannah said neutrally.

But there was a pause, the sound of Hoskins weighing his comment. "It was Halloween. That's practically New Year's Eve up here. Everyone was drinking. She wasn't in a coma or anything, if that's what you're implying."

"I didn't imply anything, Mr. Hoskins, I just was—"

"I prefer my partners conscious."

"I guess that means you had sex," Hannah said.

"Look, this isn't some kind of date-rape thing is it? Because—"

"Mr. Hoskins, it isn't anything like that."

"Because if you want to know the truth, the only reason I'm calling you is that I spent three months wishing she'd left a phone number. Or even her last name. She was great. A great person, I mean. There's nothing wrong, is there? Because I've never had any kind of—"

"Mr. Hoskins, it's nothing like that." Christ, Hannah thought, this guy is skittish. "Mr. Hoskins, Laura had a baby. She thinks you're the father."

"Oh, my God."

"You can say that again," Bobby whispered.

"I'm the father?"

"She thinks so," Hannah said.

"Well, it could be. I hate condoms, and we didn't really talk about what she might be using." It sounded like he gulped.

Hannah heard the hurly-burly of a trader's office in the background. She imagined Hoskins staring at his computer terminal, watching the markets, realizing that his fatherhood futures were suddenly on the uptick.

"Look," he said weakly. "If it's child support, I completely—"

"No," Hannah said. "It's not that. Laura's placed the child for adoption with a wonderful couple. He's been there nine months."

"A boy?" There was a shimmer of amazed joy in his voice.

Bobby dropped his head to his knees, groaning. Hannah shook her head. What was it about producing sons that turned men to jelly?

"Yes, a boy," she said. "His adoptive parents love him very much. But there's a slight complication. Laura's married. She was when she got pregnant."

"She says she's married? To me?"

"No. Another man, her husband, claims to be the baby's father, and he wants custody."

"But the baby's not his. He's mine."

Hannah and Bobby looked at each other. The temperature seemed to drop ten degrees.

"I mean," he said, "I'm the father, right?"

"We'd like you to take a blood test," Hannah said. "That will clarify who the father is. And if it's you, which we believe to be the case, we'd like you to sign a consent for adoption. This little boy has never known any parents but the ones he has now. Laura thinks it's the right thing. She doesn't want his world disrupted. I'm sure you don't, either."

"Well, jeez. This is all happening kind of fast, you know?

I mean I just find out I have a son and now you want to cut me off? It's all a little . . ." His voice caught.

Hannah and Bobby looked at each other. She could understand Hoskins's emotions. But they scared her. Two men already laid claim to Matthew. They didn't need a third.

"Look," Hoskins said at last. "Can I call you back in a little while? I'm at work, and this is sort of a lot for me to deal with right now."

"Of course," Hannah said. She repeated her office number, and added the one for home. Hoskins mumbled a good-bye and hung up.

Bobby sank in his chair. "We're doomed," he said.

Two hours later Hoskins called back. Hannah put him on hold and called Bobby. He arrived clutching his bottle of Maalox. He'd begun to buy it by the case.

"Okay," Hoskins said, "It was a one-night stand, after all. I don't really know Laura. The last thing I want to do is upset this little guy's life. I'm getting married in six months, and this would totally—I mean completely—mess up my life. I don't want my fiancée to find out about this. How do we handle that?"

Hannah sighed. Thank God.

"I'm going to let Mr. Terry explain the process."

Bobby straightened. "Mr. Hoskins, if you'll just take a flight down here, we'll set up an appointment at GenType Lab—"

"No," Hoskins said.

"You just . . ." Bobby blanched, and it was Hannah's turn to despair.

"I told you, I don't want to draw attention to this thing. I can't just duck out of town without my fiancée knowing about it. We live together."

Bobby fanned his face and smiled. He had a plan. "It's no problem. GenType can send a draw kit to your doctor. Everything that's needed is in there. There's a disposable camera, and you have your doctor snap your picture. He takes your thumbprint—"

"What's that all about?"

"It's to ensure that the blood sample is really yours. Most of the time people going through paternity testing are trying to be ruled out as the father, so they won't have to pay support, you see? Some guys will take steps to evade that responsibility."

"Right. I see."

"Anyway, the doctor draws some blood. He seals the tube, initials it. There's instructions for packing and mailing. Once GenType has it, they'll run the sample."

Hannah listened and made notes. In a smooth, casual voice, Bobby went through the rest of it: the visit the state Department of Social Services worker would make to Hoskins, the consent document itself, the time it would take for test results. He might have been a tailor, talking about delivery of a suit.

"All we need is your doctor's name and address, and we're set to start," Bobby said.

"Fine." They heard the rustle of papers. Hoskins reeled off a name and address.

They hung up. Bobby threw the Maalox bottle in an arc and it hit the trash can with a thud. But Hannah had a strange sense of unease. She picked up the phone and punched in Hoskins's number.

"What are you doing?" Bobby said.

The phone was ringing, almost endlessly. Why didn't someone pickup? Finally someone did.

"Hoskins."

"Mr. Hoskins, do you have any objection to meeting Mr. Terry and me, if we come up to San Francisco?"

"Well, no. As long as my fiancée doesn't—"

"We can meet for lunch, if you like."

"That's fine, then."

No hesitation. No hedging. Good. They agreed to meet the next day at the Sheraton Palace Hotel on Market Street.

"Should I wear a white carnation or something?" Hoskins asked with a nervous laugh.

"No," Hannah said. "We'll just keep an eye out for the guy who would look good in orange-and-black stripes."

• • •

Hoskins sat in bar of the hotel's restaurant, Maxfield's, in front of the mural that gave the place its name. He gazed at the painted scene with unfocused, glazed eyes. Hannah recognized the story depicted at once: the artist, Maxfield Parrish, had dressed the Pied Piper in cobalt, fern, and churned-butter yellow. He led a line of children along a stony ridge. Their eyes were wide, but unseeing. They moved like dreamers, bound up in the breathy spell of the piper's music.

Hoskins was tossing back an amber drink in a lead-cut glass. He was nearly six feet tall, with slick, straw-colored hair. His eyes were slate blue, with flecks of yellow. He was the sort of blond who would normally be pale, but his cheeks were flushed red now. The gray suit, stiff white shirt, and burgundy silk tie looked new, and expensive.

"Drink?" He beckoned to the waiter as they sat down. He led off, ordering himself another single-malt Scotch. Auch-something, the sound a pebble-choked crow would make.

"No thanks." Bobby shook his head and stole a look at his watch. It wasn't quite eleven-thirty.

Hoskins saw and laughed tightly. "I'm nervous, I guess."

"I hope you don't mind," Hannah said, "but could I see some identification? Our clients are a little shell-shocked by the appearance of this other purported father, and we'd like to give them as much reassurance as we can."

"No problem," he said. He pulled out his wallet, flipped it to his California driver's license. Jerome Horace Hoskins. Thirty-two years old. Address in the 1000 block of Vallejo Street. Hannah made a mental note of the left-slanted handwriting and the final *s,* which looked like a treble clef.

"My turn," he said. "How do I know you two are who you say you are?"

"Fair enough," Hannah said. They showed him their driver's licenses and state-bar cards.

"Pretty chintzy," he said, examining her bar card. "This is all you get for five-hundred-dollar-a-year dues?"

"Well, there's the great front-row seats in the courtroom," Bobby said.

Hoskins chuckled. Bobby offered to see if their table was ready.

Hoskins shook his head. "I really can't stay for lunch," he said. "I've got loads of work waiting for me at the office."

"I didn't have anything else," Bobby said. "Hannah?"

Hannah didn't answer right away. She held Hoskins's gaze.

"I thing we've taken up enough of your time," Hannah said finally. "You're probably losing money on coffee futures right now."

"I try to stick to investments that can't be wiped out by freak weather events," he said. "But the high-tech stocks are wobbly today. I have to go."

They shook hands outside on Market Street. Hoskins disappeared in the lunchtime crowd. Bobby flagged a cab.

"We can catch a twelve-thirty flight if we hurry." He glanced at her and frowned as she started to walk away. "Hannah?"

"I've got a couple things to do. Have some lunch. I'll meet you back here."

She caught sight of Hoskins, walking faster as it started to rain. He turned on Battery Street, strolled into a high-rise, and stepped into an elevator as the doors were closing. Hannah watched it stop at the twenty-first floor. The building's directory listed the tenant there as a financial-services company, Rowan & Luana.

She dialed the office from a pay phone and asked for Hoskins. A receptionist said he was still at lunch and offered Hannah his voice mail. She declined, hung up, and checked in the phone book for the address of the Registrar of Voters. It was temporarily housed in the Superior Court building on Folsom Street. Only a few blocks away. Good. It was such a pleasure to be in a city where you didn't have to drive a half hour to get anywhere.

She knew what she needed: Hoskins's voter-registration card would have his occupation, address, even his signature. But asking for it got her a firm no from the clerk. He couldn't have been more than twenty-five. Black hair and goatee. Oversized gray sweater-vest and thick, so-square-they're-re-hip black glasses.

"Unless you're a journalist, or some other kind of bona fide researcher, you're out of luck," he said.

She understood. It began when a wacko used DMV information to get the home address of an actress at the center of his obsessive fantasies. And then he killed her.

"I'm not a stalker. Just a conscientious attorney."

"Not good enough," he said, shrugging. "Sorry."

Hannah tried to size him up. Money would probably offend his neo-hippie sensibilities. She didn't have much else to work with. But then she saw the wedding ring.

"You have any kids?"

He smiled. "A girl. Nearly two."

Hannah told him the story, heavy on the frantic-parent details.

"I don't know," he said. But he was coming close to the line. Hannah was pretty sure he wouldn't go over it. Not by much.

"Let's try this," she said. "I'll tell you what I already know: this guy's home address, his job, and how he signs the last letter of his name. Just confirm that, and I'm gone."

He looked at her, weighing the credible-to-crazy quotient. Hannah put on her best sane face.

"Write that stuff down for me and come back in about ten minutes."

It all checked out. The occupation, the address. The clerk confirmed the back-slanted hand and the treble-clef *s* at the end of Hoskins's name.

"I think you'll find that he's listed in the phone book," he added helpfully. "Same number as on his voter-reg card."

Hannah thanked him for trusting her and walked back to the Palace. Bobby was standing outside in the drizzle, arms crossed in annoyance.

"Are we finished here? Are you reassured?"

"Sort of."

He huffed at her and wouldn't speak all the way to the airport. They had, of course, missed the twelve-thirty flight. In the airport lounge, Bobby sulked over a cappuccino and a copy of the *Chronicle,* leaving Hannah to check with Vera for messages. Cleve Gibbons wanted Hannah to call him, but wouldn't say why. A caseworker from the state Department of Social Services had talked to Laura, who had agreed to acknowledge in writing that Jerome Hoskins was her child's father. The worker would go by Laura's in the morning to bring her the papers.

"What did Laura have to say about us finding the father?" Hannah said.

Although Vera hated recounting phone calls, she seemed to be enjoying this. "I told her his name, and she said it didn't matter to her. She said 'To me, he'll always be the big pussycat.'"

10

Hannah heard the nasal voice as soon as she opened the office door. Gibbons was waiting for her.

He was sitting next to Vera's desk, sipping a cup of tea and talking in peppy, overanxious tones about an absolutely great vegan newsgroup on the Internet. Vera nodded, wide-eyed.

Gibbons's cup clattered to the table when he saw Hannah.

"I think he hit her," he said, drawing his handkerchief from the pocket of his rough-woven tan pants and blowing his nose. "They were yelling, and someone was pounding on the furniture, and in the middle of it, I think he hit her."

Kurt and Laura. Maybe Cleve's snooping was worth something. She ushered him into her office and made him start again. "Where was this pounding? At Laura's?"

"Yes."

"And you know it was Kurt?"

He nodded. "I recognized him from the pictures she has."

Jesus, Hannah though, she keeps pictures of Kurt? "And you saw this?"

Gibbons shook his head. "Not the hitting, no. I was downstairs. I just heard a lot of yelling and thumping, and then I heard Laura crying. When I got outside, she was standing on the landing, screaming at him. I could see where he'd hit her, on her left cheek. All purple. We sell Peruvian potatoes that color. It was horrible."

Hannah pulled out a pad and started writing.

"Did Laura say anything to you? Ask you to call the police?"

Gibbons swallowed hard and plucked at the knees of his peasant pants.

"No. I started to, but she . . . she told me to mind my own business. Actually, she said I should mind my own fucking business."

"But you aren't doing that."

He glanced warily at her, as though she were going to scold him, too.

"It's okay," Hannah said. "I think you probably should have called the police."

"I can't stand to think of anyone hurting Laura," he said. "But she'd have been furious if the police showed up. I decided I had to do something. I though maybe you could talk to her. Make sure she's okay." His face had taken on the plaintive, needy look of every spurned guy Hannah had ever known.

"This all happened yesterday?"

He nodded. "In the morning."

"And what about Kurt? Did he talk to you?"

"No. He came down the stairs real fast, swearing and very agitated. He gave me a really dirty look and got in his car. He drove for about a block before it gave out. He kicked it and then took off. It's probably still sitting there."

Hannah thought about what the fight meant. Had she invited Kurt over or did he show up just to scare her? Was she keeping crack away from him, or luring him with it? What had they argued about?

Hannah chided herself for thinking it, but Kurt's attack on Laura was good news—good for the Drummonds, anyway. She might be less likely to go back to him. For the moment, anyway. But Hannah wasn't making any long-term bets on Laura's loyalties.

The fight also offered the Drummonds a chance to end Kurt's visitations with Matthew. Once Judge Baxter heard that he'd smacked Laura, she would be less impressed with his Sunday-school manners and spiffy clothes.

"I'll give her a call and make sure she's all right," Hannah said.

"Be casual, okay? If she thinks I put you up to this . . ."

"I'll do my best," Hannah said. "Laura's lucky to have a friend like you."

Gibbons smiled and blew his nose again. Hannah felt sorry for him. All his chivalry would never get him anywhere with a woman like Laura.

Hannah called Laura twice that morning, but got no answer. Around eleven, Bobby told her the firm's settlement negotiations in the Landry case—their client, a retired gardener, had his persistent cough diagnosed by an HMO as an allergy, but it turned out to be cancer—were threatening to go belly-up. She and Bobby were on the speakerphone with six other lawyers, clipping the ends of each other's sentences, when Vera slid into the room with a message from Jim Pabst.

Hannah had met Kurt's lawyer at an Orange County Bar lunch and didn't think he was the clueless bleeding heart that Drummond imagined. She wondered if Kurt was trying to turn the slapping incident to his advantage, though she couldn't see how that would work. She excused herself from Bobby's office to return the call.

Pabst, affable as ever, sprang no surprises on her. He just wanted to change the hearing date. It was a minor thing, a scheduling conflict, and the judge didn't care. Hannah saw no tactical reason to disagree. She thought of hinting at his client's recent outbursts, just to tweak him, but decided she'd better check out Gibbons's story first. She told Pabst she'd have to run the change by the Drummonds.

The answering machine was picking up when Rebecca came on the line. She sounded out of breath.

"The machine's supposed to save you from running for the phone," Hannah said.

Rebecca laughed breathlessly. "After nine months at home with a baby, I'll gladly sprint to hear a live human voice."

She agonized about the date change. Hannah imagined

her biting her fingernails, fearful of doing something to set a match to Stephen's short fuse.

"It's not a big deal," Hannah said. "A few days won't make a difference."

"Okay," Rebecca said. "Go ahead. I'll tell Stephen you don't think it's a problem."

Fine, Hannah thought, put the blame on me. The Drummonds were good at that.

Rebecca put down the phone and fought back the sob rising in her throat. Stephen was so hard to talk to these days.

He was short with her, angry at small things. She waited for moments when he seemed more amiable to tell him something that might upset him—the recurring problem with the Land Rover's ignition, the gardener's fee going up, the dinner invitation from her parents. She never knew what was going to set him off.

She had decided on her own to say no to dinner at her parents' house. Stephen was uncomfortable there. It wasn't that he didn't like Frank and Maura, but their worlds were far apart, and her father's endless, prying chitchat made Stephen cranky.

She didn't like spending time there, either. She thought at first it was her imagination, but now she knew it was real. Her mother didn't like Matthew. It took a mother to see it, but Maura didn't treat him like the other grandchildren. She would watch him cry instead of rushing to pick him up, as she did with Eileen's son or Frank Jr.'s daughter. She bought him fewer gifts.

She knew what it was. Matthew was adopted. Maura couldn't see the Malone cleft chin or the O'Neill eyes, dark green as seaweed. Rebecca's baby was a changeling, and she didn't trust him. Didn't love him. It made her sick at heart. She had only left Matthew there today because her father was home. He thought Matthew was wonderful.

"A right keeper," he said to her when he saw him for the first time, the day they brought him home. Maura had said nothing.

A keeper. The sob strained at the back of her throat, and

Rebecca let it out. She was alone, and that was her only time to cry. Her tears angered Stephen, too. A wet weapon, he called them. So she would cry, and maybe take a nap. And when she was done, she would bring her baby home and love him. Love him always, the keeper.

11

Hannah fumed about Rebecca for a moment more and then went back to the cacophony in Bobby's office. She emerged four hours later, with a jaw aching both from talking, and from holding back the insults a Century City lawyer so richly deserved. It was only six, but she felt drained.

"I'll do the loose ends," Bobby said. "Take off."

She nodded, got up, and felt the stiffness in her joints. She craved a glass of cold white wine and the restorative powers of a huge take-out bowl of *pho ga* from the Vietnamese soup restaurant near home. She was halfway there, imagining the scent of cilantro, basil, and chicken soup, when she remembered her promise to visit Laura.

She got the *pho* to go, slurped half of it in the restaurant parking lot, and washed it down with a *ca phe sua da,* murderously strong Vietnamese iced coffee, sweet and thick with evaporated milk. The wine would have to wait until she'd seen Laura. She would need it doubly by then.

The last traffic light before the ÜberMall turned from yellow to red. "Grand Opening" signs plastered the windows now.

She was headed west, looking over the tops of her sunglasses at the Rothko sunset: red, blocked at the bottom by a gray mass of storm clouds blown up from Mexico. The air was slightly humid, with a hint of summer in it.

The lights were on in Gibbons's store. She imagined him in his storeroom, mixing up a wheat-grass-and-bee-pollen frappé for Laura. What would he do when she moved? How would he fill that Laura-shaped hole in his life? She scanned the parking lot, and saw that her car wasn't there. Damm it. A trip for nothing.

A particularly annoying angst-and eyeliner band was on the radio, and that irritated her even more that the wasted drive to the outskirts of town. She pressed the tuner. And the world exploded.

Everything came at once. A deafening blast. A shock wave that lifted the Integra and slammed down again. Glass from the imploding windshield showered down on her, stinging like hail on her cheeks and forehead. She scrambled from the driver's seat and crouched on the street. Her ears throbbed. The air smelled of smoke.

She was shaking, still unsure what had happened. Cautiously, she looked back at the mall. Every window had been blown out.

Now a half-dozen other drivers were standing or kneeling in the street, as shaken as she was. A van had run up on the mall's new sidewalk and smashed into a light pole.

"Jesus Christ!" a man shouted. He was pointing to the column of smoke across the street.

The packing house looked like a ruptured tin can. Its roof was blasted away. Siding hung in twisted shreds. Corrugated-metal panels lay in the parking lot, the river channel, and the street. The palms that lined the path behind the building were blazing like oil-soaked torches. Hannah took off at a dead run toward the devastation. Cellular phones chirped as a half-dozen drivers punched 911 in unison. But for the sound of those beeps and the pounding of her heart, it was eerily quiet.

Cleve Gibbons was lying on his back at the bottom of the stairs. The side of his face was sooty, scraped, and bleeding. His right leg was bent at an ugly, unnatural angle. Dozens of cuts had been opened on his thin white arms. He was breathing though, thank God for that. His eyes were open, staring up at the maw that had been the door to Laura's apartment. Black smoke poured from it. She knelt on the grass next to him.

"Are you okay?"

He nodded.

"Where's Laura?"

He winced. "Dead. She must be dead. And the baby." His voice trembled. "She couldn't hold on to him."

Hannah felt her breath catch. "Matthew?"

"The light went on, and then we were falling and she couldn't hold him. I could hear her screaming, but I couldn't see anything. We were falling and they were screaming, both of them. They hit and I tried to get to them, but it hurt too much to move." He waved to his right, and Hannah saw two other bodies lying on the pathway, their backs toward her.

Rebecca's white shirt and jeans were scorched and torn. Like Gibbons, her exposed skin was covered with cuts. A long, jagged gash, running from jaw to eye, bled on the left side of her face. Matthew lay motionless in the crook of her arm. Blood enveloped his face and matted his fine blond hair. As though he'd just been born again.

Hannah fought down the feeling of panic and fear that was forming inside her. She put an ear to the boy's chest. But if his heart was beating, its small sound was lost in the noise—the wail of sirens, the throb of diesel engines, and the scuffle of boots as firefighters and med techs clambered through the rubble to the wounded, and to the ashes and smoke at the top of the stairs.

12

The phone was on its tenth ring when Hannah impatiently cut the call off and dialed the number again. Her finger shook.

"You're sure you're okay?" The battalion chief was in his forties. He had a bushy black mustache and calm gray eyes. He had loaned her his cellular phone and offered her a stick of Blackjack gum, which she refused. He crammed three sticks in his cheek and sat down next to her on the bumper of his truck. He was watching her for symptoms of shock.

"I'm fine," she said. Her face stung from the pelting glass. Her head pounded and everything sounded dim, as though it were coming to her through closed windows. It took effort to think straight. But she wasn't going to tell him that. He'd already tried to make her go to the hospital.

Finally, the call connected. Stephen Drummond's greeting was almost a drawl. The television was on in the background. Hannah could hear an ecstatic crowd and the corny, exultant piping of a baseball-stadium organ.

"Stephen, this is Hannah Barlow. There's—"

"Hannah, I was just gonna call." The words sloshed. "Somebody keeps calling here. Hanging up. It's that prick Kurt trying to—"

"Stephen, forget Kurt and listen to me. There's been an accident. Rebecca and Matthew—"

"*Matthew?* Where is he?"

"Stephen—"

"Goddammit, what hospital?"

"St. Luke's. Rebecca has a bad cut on her face. Her wrist might be broken. The paramedic said Matthew's scalp cut looks worse than it is, but his left arm has an open fracture. He's going to need surgery."

"Oh God, oh God, oh God," Drummond was chanting, his voice suddenly sober, and tight with panic. Hannah heard a clunk as the receiver hit the tabletop. His voice was fainter now. "Jesus, let me get there in time."

"Stephen?"

A door slammed. He was gone.

Hannah called Bobby next. He took in the news of the injuries to Rebecca and Matthew with a calm steadiness that soothed her. He would meet Stephen at the ER and stay with him.

She checked her watch. Seven o'clock. Less than twenty minutes had passed since the explosion. At her feet lay a singed poster—the builder's advertisement of store spaces for lease. There was certainly a lot of space, but nothing you could call a store, not now. She hoped the Malone Group had plenty of insurance.

Malone. She knew that name: Rebecca's family company was Malone Construction.

The battalion chief was back at her side, handing her a thermos cup of black coffee.

"The arson investigators will be here in a couple minutes," he said. "I expect they'll want to talk to you. Do you know the woman upstairs?"

So there was someone up there. "Blond? In her twenties?"

He nodded. "Sorry. She's dead."

Hannah absorbed the news and tried not to imagine Laura's last minutes. The air smelled of wet ash.

"Her name is Laura Benson," she said. "Her car's gone, and I thought that might meant she was safe. What happened?"

"That'll be up to the arson guys to say for sure."

Hannah knew that was a dodge. She nodded and let a few seconds pass. "You didn't tell me your name."

"Dan Feuer. And yes, it does mean 'fire' in German. I've heard every joke you can imagine about that."

The name brought up a memory that took her away from the smoke and worry for a moment. "Was your dad a firefighter, too?" she said. "Active in the union?"

"Now, how did you know that?"

"My dad is Jimmy Barlow, he was Las Almas PD. I think your dad and mine were on a negotiating team together. Do you remember walking a picket line with your dad in about 1971? You unmercifully harassed a kid about her freckles."

His face lit up. "That was you? You turned out less splotchy than I would have thought."

"I suppose that's a compliment. How long have you been at this?"

"Christ. Since I was eighteen. Twenty-five years now."

"So what do you think happened?"

Hannah could see the transformation. Their mutual history entitled her to hear his educated guess. "Looks to me like a gas explosion."

Hannah nodded. Short of a bomb, she couldn't imagine what else could have done it. She wondered if Rebecca knew her family's company had outfitted the apartment with a faulty stove. Had Laura complained about it? Or would that have seemed ungrateful, somehow, for a tenant who lived there rent-free?

"Laura told me the stove was screwed up. The pilots didn't work," Hannah said. "She had to light the burners with a match."

Feuer shrugged. "The arson guys will check it out. It would have to be quite a gas leak to do this much damage."

"Was she lighting the burner when it happened?"

"Don't think so. We didn't find her in the kitchen."

"How did the explosion kill her?"

"I don't think it did. She was cut up, burned some, hit by some debris."

"What killed her, if not the explosion or the fire?"

"Well, my guess would be she decided to kill herself."

Hannah tried to take that in. Why would Laura kill herself? And why this way? "I know people put their heads in ovens to kill themselves," she said, "but how often do they blow themselves up?"

"They don't do it intentionally," he said. "They turn on the gas and lie down, thinking they'll just never wake up again. But sometimes, they do wake up. And sometimes, they're so damned happy they're not dead that they celebrate— have a cigarette, light up a joint, and then it's the Fourth of July."

"Where was she when you found her?"

"On the bed. She'd never gotten dressed."

Hannah thought about the Baggie of crack she thought she'd seen Laura sweep into the drawer. She imagined the pipe in her hand, and the trembling ignition of a match.

"People who decide to kill themselves and then wake up—don't they smell the gas?"

"No." He proffered another stick of gum, and this time she took it. "It's like any other odor. After a while you get used to it."

Hannah looked at the ruined building, at the spot where she'd found Gibbons. He'd said they were falling. Were they on the stairs when the gas exploded? Why had Rebecca and Matthew been there in the first place? She handed Feuer his cup. "So if she never woke up, then what caused the explosion?"

"It doesn't take much," Feuer said. "Any open flame. A single spark, even."

Hannah imagined the scene again. Laura on her bed, the long, cavernous room filling with gas as she slept deeper, her breathing slow, slower, stopped. The paramedics opened the ambulance door to load Gibbons's stretcher. A light clicked on inside the van.

The light went on. That's what Gibbons said happened before he and Rebecca and the baby started falling. Presumably, what happened right before the explosion. She looked up. Feuer was watching her.

"If someone turned on a light in an apartment full of gas—would that do it?"

"Hell yes. Electricity arcs when you turn on a light switch. That would certainly do the trick."

• • •

A few minutes later Hannah gave a statement to the Mutt-and-Jeff arson investigation team: a squat, affable guy in a gray polyester suit and a lanky blond surfer type in jeans and an old rayon Hawaiian shirt. When they asked about the victim's next of kin, she told them where to find Gerald Lawrence, Laura's father. She also told them about his premonition.

"If that's what it was," she added.

"You think he's involved?" The plump guy scribbled Lawrence's address in a notebook. Was it a coincidence that Lawrence had been expecting someone to tell him his daughter was dead.

"I don't know. Maybe he knew she was depressed. He wouldn't say much to me."

"We'll get him talking," the surfer said. "Anything else?"

She looked back at the blown-out windows of the shopping center, and the street where a few windowless cars still stood, including Kurt's disabled Maverick. "She had a fight with her estranged husband yesterday. He smacked her. That's his car, over there. It broke down as he was leaving. Her car is gone."

The squat guy lifted his eyebrows, hearing what Hannah had left unsaid. She told him Kurt's name, and where to find him.

"And do you think he'll be surprised to hear of his wife's untimely demise?"

Hannah shrugged. "Set your bullshit detector on high. If he isn't surprised, I think he'll do a good job faking it."

Feuer, who was standing nearby, smiled at her. It made his gray eyes crinkle, and she realized Guillermo's scintillating conversation wasn't all that she missed.

The arson investigators left them. Feuer still was smiling at her. "You a cop like your dad? You sound like one."

"Not anymore. A lawyer. Laura was my client." She started walking back to her car, trying to avoid any contact with those eyes.

"So you get paid more for your suspicions now."

She nodded. "And we're even better than cops at seeing the worst in people."

Including our faithless selves, she thought.

Once she'd knocked out the remains of her windshield, Hannah could drive, at least as far as St. Luke's. Bobby met her in the lobby. Stephen was already there—in the operating room with Matthew, Bobby said. Hannah couldn't imagine watching your own son being cut and stitched and pinned, even if you were a doctor.

"How is Matthew?"

"Okay, I think," Bobby said. "The nurse said they set his arm, stitched his scalp. He's in recovery now. Stephen's with him."

"What about Rebecca?"

"The docs said the cut on her face is deep, and later she might have to have some plastic surgery if she doesn't want to carry around a nasty scar. Her right wrist is only sprained. She's bruised from the fall, but there's nothing internal. She could probably go home, but they want to be sure she doesn't have a concussion. Plus, I don't think she'd get any rest there. She was close to hysterical about Matthew."

Hannah nodded. "I don't blame her."

Bobby frowned at her. "Laura's not here. So I guess that means she wasn't home?"

"She's dead," Hannah said.

Bobby paled. "Jesus."

"The fire guys think she died from the gas." She told him about the faulty stove and the Malone Group sign.

"It's Rebecca's family, all right. And she supervised the rehab," Bobby said. "It was a place Laura could stay that didn't cost the Drummonds anything."

"Why didn't they do something about the stove?"

"Who says the Drummonds knew?"

"Why wouldn't she tell them?"

"Shit, Hannah, why did Laura do or not do anything?"

They were silent for a moment, feeling almost guilty that they'd brought up Laura's unpredictability now that she was dead.

They were waiting for the elevator when they saw Stephen coming down the hall. His face was ashen, red around the eyes.

"I'm sorry about the way I was on the phone." He stammered a bit, something Hannah couldn't have imagined him doing. Stephen was the sort who'd keep silent rather than fumble for a word. "You were trying to tell me about Matthew." His lips shook, and he stopped before his composure crumbled.

"There's nothing to be sorry about," she said. "Matthew's going to be all right?"

He nodded.

"Stephen, Laura's dead."

He closed his eyes, took in a long breath, and let it out again, and that seemed to revive him. He was the steady surgeon again. "What happened?"

"The gas, probably," Hannah said.

He shook his head. "Does Rebecca know?"

"No," Hannah said.

"Let me tell her."

They took the elevator to Rebecca's floor. Stephen pushed open the door and Hannah saw Rebecca, half out of bed. Stephen eased her back into the sheets.

"Jesus, honey, what are you doing?"

She shook her head. "Bathroom." The voice was soft, syrupy with sedation. Her eyes settled on Hannah. "Hannah?"

"Yes. I'm glad you're okay."

Rebecca sagged against the pillows, exhausted by the effort of shuffling to the bathroom. Her eyes were closed, but her face and body stayed stiff with tension. The cut across her face had been closed with a picket fence of tiny stitches. Drummond took his wife's hand. She slowly opened her eyes and focused on him.

"How's Matthew?" she whispered, squeezing his hand tight.

"He's fine, Becca. Just fine." He brought her bruised fingers to his lips.

"I'm so sorry, Stephen," she said. "I couldn't hold on to him."

Bobby poked Hannah in the back, signaling her to leave. But Rebecca turned to her.

"You were there, at Laura's, weren't you? I saw you helping Matthew."

Hannah nodded. "Cleve Gibbons had asked me to come by and make sure Laura was all right. She'd had a fight with Kurt. He was worried about her."

"She called me," Rebecca said. "That's why I was there."

"Laura called you?" Stephen said.

Rebecca nodded. "I had just come home from picking up Matthew at my mother's and—"

"Honey." Stephen softened the interruption by stroking her hair. "You should rest. We can talk about this later."

Rebecca shook her head. "No. I want to tell you what happened. I didn't know what was wrong with her." Her voice was rising, raw-edged. "If I'd known what was happening, I wouldn't have taken Matthew."

"Okay, okay," Stephen said. "Take it easy now."

"The answering machine picked up her message. I almost didn't recognize her voice. She was talking like she was drunk. But then I realized it was Laura."

"What did she say?" Hannah said.

"I can't remember exactly. She sounded sick, weak. So I went, and I took Matthew." She looked to Stephen, as if for his forgiveness. He kissed her forehead.

"What time was it?" Hannah heard Bobby click his tongue in exasperation behind her. She didn't want to turn it into an interrogation, but Rebecca seemed inclined to talk. The guests sat down, on the straight-backed plastic-and-metal chairs, and at the foot of her bed. Stephen stood, holding Rebecca's hand and gazing at her face.

"It was after six," Rebecca said. "Stephen was at a meeting. My mother's house was too far to take Matthew there and get to Laura, if she needed help. When we got to her place, I knocked, but there was no answer.

"I have a key. Laura gave it to me, just in case anything was wrong when she was pregnant. I was unlocking the door when that guy from downstairs came running up the stairs behind me. He said he'd heard some noises earlier, and was worried about Laura. He'd gone up, but she didn't come to the door.

"It all happened so fast. The apartment was dark. I knew where the light switch was—right inside the door. I put it there during the rehab, so you could turn it on, first thing. I was flipping the switch—and then I smelled it. The gas. But it was too late. Everything blew up.

"I was falling, and all I could think of was holding on to Matthew. I heard glass breaking, and I hit the stairs over and over. I realized that I didn't have Matthew.

"He was gone." Her voice choked. "I must have passed out. When I woke up, I saw him. The blood." She clenched her eyes shut and the tears there flooded her cheeks.

Bobby tugged on Hannah's elbow again. This time she nodded. She was ready to leave.

"No," Rebecca said, seeing them turn to go. "Laura. What about Laura?"

"Sweetheart," Stephen said, his voice almost a whisper, "Laura's dead."

She closed her eyes and turned her head on the pillow. "If I hadn't turned on the light, she wouldn't be." Her voice was flat, matter-of-fact. "It's my fault."

"No," Hannah said. "It wasn't the explosion. They think she died from the gas. There probably wasn't anything you could have done."

"It was the gas? From the stove?"

Hannah nodded. "They think so."

"She told me the stove was messed up. Christ, it is all my fault."

"Honey, no." Stephen put his arms around her and she burrowed in them. Bobby left quietly, and as Hannah followed him she looked over her shoulder at Rebecca. She was clenched tight in Stephen's grasp, softly beating his back with her scraped fists and bandaged wrist. Hannah pulled the door shut.

Across the hall at the nurses' station, Bobby was asking about Gibbons. The nurse pointed him down the hall.

"He's sleeping. He was in a lot of pain from the broken leg and the doctor gave him a good-sized dose."

The sheet was pulled up to his chin, the black beard laid smoothly over fabric. Although his eyes were slightly open, his chest rose and fell in a steady rhythm of sleep. He looked like a tranced prophet. He stirred and the eyes widened.

"Rebecca?"

Hannah came closer. "No. Hannah Barlow. Try to rest now."

The eyes closed and he sank into sleep. She didn't think anyone else would be this restful. Not for quite a while.

13

The answering machine was blinking at her when she got home. From the echo and buzz in the recording, she could tell that Feuer was calling from his cellular. She could see him in the truck, steering with one hand, holding the phone and yet somehow managing to cram a stick of Blackjack into his mouth.

"Hope you don't mind the call at home." The gum snapped. "Bill Summers gave me your number." One of the arson guys, she thought.

"Thought you might want to know this. They found a note upstairs, under the pillow. It was addressed to someone named Rebecca. I figure you know who she is."

A note for Rebecca alone?

"Here's what it said: 'I'm sorry for how this turned out. I never meant to hurt you. I'll never forget what you did for me, and for our little boy.' It's signed Laura. So I guess I was right about the suicide."

"I guess so," Hannah said to herself.

On the tape, Feuer wished her a good night and hung up. Hannah jotted down the wording of Laura's note, erased the tape, and stripped off her clothes for a shower. She reeked of smoke. The hot water felt good on her back and shoulders, but stung where pebbles of glass had struck her cheeks.

In bed, sleep was slow in coming. She sent up a prayer for Laura. A trace of the old Catholic thought—suicides don't go to heaven—was rattling in her head. Surely those who despaired needed God's comfort most of all. She thought about the gas, the explosion, and now Laura's note. Why the apology? And why only to Rebecca? Maybe she didn't give a damn what Stephen thought. Hannah had always sensed tension between them. The bond was with the other mother, with Rebecca.

Maybe Laura knew that the blood test would show Kurt to be the father. Maybe she foresaw the battle the Drummonds would have to fight to keep Matthew. It could have been enough to send her over the edge. When Hannah finally did dream, it was of falling into an ash-filled night where palm trees etched the sky with fire.

The weekend dropped her back into an unexpected normalcy. She called Stephen to see how Matthew and Rebecca were, but got only his answering machine. Feuer left another message for her while she was at the grocery store. Hannah had long ago sworn off uniformed lovers, but she found she didn't want to discourage Feuer from calling. He can get information I can't, she thought. But then she realized that wasn't the only reason for her interest in him.

She remembered his scent, a smokiness that she imagined never quite went away. She tried not to think about Guillermo. And as the days passed without a word from him—he must be very deep in thought—that was getting easier.

She spent most of her time in Emma Snow's dining room. There, she hoped, a couple gallons of a thick pink stripping goop would reveal the quarter-sawn oak paneling that hid under the years of accumulated paint. After the layers softened, she could begin peeling. Her plan was to work hard enough to exhaust herself into sleep each night.

On Sunday night, as she slathered remover on the door frame, the portable phone she'd brought from her apartment rang. Stephen Drummond.

"Sorry I missed your call. I had to get some groceries," he said. "Rebecca and Matthew are fine. She's home now. We're picking up Matthew tomorrow."

"Good," Hannah said.

"Listen, if you aren't too busy, could you drop by? Tonight?"

Hannah looked at Mrs. Snow's mantel clock, which her father had insisted on taking apart and refurbishing. It was still a little slow, and it said ten-thirty.

"It's so late. I'm sure Rebecca's tired."

"It's important." Drummond seemed slightly annoyed that she hadn't jumped at his command. Then, as though he remembered some manners, his voice softened. "Please?"

The house that Rebecca built was almost more beautiful at night. Soft lights played shadows over the muted walls. Deep darkness crept up toward it from the hillsides; there were no houses nearby. The streets in this part of Las Almas Acres were unlit, too. For the first time she realized how isolated the Drummonds were.

Stephen led her to the formal living room, one of the adult rooms Rebecca had designed. The kid-proofers had done their work: there was a portable plastic-and-mesh barrier at the threshold, meant to keep Matthew away from the metal, glass, and leather on the other side. Rebecca had filled the low, long white space with pieces Hannah recognized from the twentieth-century design books she collected once Arts and Crafts furnishings became her pastime.

Rebecca acquired the best work of the 1950s industrial-design geniuses: the sofa, low-slung wooden lounging chairs, and plywood wall unit were the work of Charles Eames. The black-and-maple bench under the window — George Nelson. The effect was one that Hannah admired aesthetically, but would never think of putting in her own house. Glass, black leather, and molded plywood didn't mix well with the fumed woods of the 1910s. In Rebecca's home, though, it worked.

Rebecca was standing by the sliding-glass door, looking back into the darkness. Her wrist still was bandaged. The cut along the side of her face would heal, in time. She walked in a narrow zigzag toward one last masterpiece: Eero Saarinen's deep, high-backed, enveloping Womb Chair, upholstered in cherry-red wool crepe. She sat down slowly and draped her legs over the wide padded arms. Her tan had faded, and her skin looked slightly chalky against the black tunic and leggings she wore.

"I'd offer you some coffee," she said. "But we seem to be out. Stephen was supposed to get it. And some wine."

Drummond nodded impatiently. "Sorry. I'll get it in the morning." He turned to Hannah. "This arson investigator called Rebecca—about the stove. He said something about the police? About a homicide investigator talking to Rebecca?"

"I wouldn't be surprised," Hannah said. "Either Bobby or I should be there."

"But why would they need Rebecca? You told me that they thought gas in the apartment killed her. It was some kind of accident."

"There's a possibility that Laura killed herself," Hannah said.

"Oh, Laura," Rebecca said, as though scolding the dead woman for the awful choice she'd made.

"There was a note, apparently. Addressed to you, Rebecca."

"Me?" Rebecca frowned. "What did it say?"

"That she was sorry. That she didn't mean to hurt you. That she'd always remember what you did for her and Matthew."

"Well, that settles it," Stephen said. "That's a suicide note."

"If the handwriting is Laura's, it probably is. But things that look like accidents and suicides aren't always. Good investigators like to make sure they've covered all the bases." If Hannah had been given the case, that's what she'd do. She found it hard to imagine that Laura would kill herself, despite the note.

"You're talking about someone killing her?" Stephen said.

Hannah nodded. "It's something they'd look at."

"She could make you angry enough to kill her," Stephen said.

"That's a sentiment you might not want to volunteer to

the police," Hannah said. "*Could* has a funny way of turning into *did* in some cops' minds."

"But they won't want to talk to me, surely."

"They might."

"I wasn't there. And besides, the note tells them it's suicide."

"That's just one thing. It's not everything," Hannah said. "They'll find out about Kurt claiming to be Matthew's father, and about the paternity hearing. Any good investigator will want to know whether that was a motive for suicide, or if it was a motive for something else."

"So it's Kurt they'll want to know about? Do they think he killed her?" Stephen said.

"I don't know. They had a fight the day before. He hit her. It's certainly a possibility. They won't view it as the only one."

"But this stuff about what I've thought about Laura—are you saying they'll think I killed her? It's ridiculous."

"I'm just telling you that cops are not priests. If they want to talk to you, you might keep in mind that you're not required to confess every bad thought you ever had. And I'd like to be there."

"What will they want to know?"

"About Kurt and Laura, and the paternity case, probably, but let them bring it up. They'll want to know what you were doing that day."

Stephen shrugged. "Easy. It was a busy day. I had a surgery, a gallbladder, at seven A.M. I did rounds after that, had lunch with Dr. Villarreal."

Hannah fished a notepad out of her purse. "What time was that?"

"About eleven-thirty. I was back at the office at one, doing some paperwork. I worked out from three until about four-thirty with Ricky."

"And who is Ricky?"

"My trainer. It's the only way I can get myself to do it. Rebecca's more disciplined than I am."

"So you were here?" She had seen Rebecca on the stairclimber, and wouldn't have been surprised if the Drummonds kept an array of other equipment in the upstairs room.

"No. At Ricky's gym. It's near the hospital. O So Strong."

"Then what did you do?"

"I was back at the hospital at four-thirty. The county medical association had a reception at six-fifteen. I stopped by, had a drink or two, and got home at seven. You called right after that. Rebecca?"

She glanced up, as though she'd been called out of a dream, and shook her head. "Sorry. What did you say?"

"Tell Hannah what you did that day, before . . ."

A wave of pain passed over Rebecca's face. She seemed to shrink into the chair.

"Honey, tell Hannah," he said. "I don't want some ham-fisted cops to have the first crack at you."

"I'm not an invalid or an idiot, Stephen," Rebecca said wearily. "I don't need to be rehearsed by my lawyer."

His brow tightened. He doesn't like it when she contradicts him, Hannah thought. And he's not used to it.

"I didn't mean it like that, Hannah," Rebecca said.

"It's okay. We can do this later. Just call me if the police contact you."

"I'll tell you now. I'm sorry." Her eyes were distant, as though she were behind a thick pane of glass. Hannah wondered if she still was taking painkillers. "I spent the morning alone here with Matthew, and then took him to my parents'. That was about noon. I stayed for an hour or so."

"But you left him there?"

She nodded. "My dad wanted to spend some time with him. Then I came home and puttered around. I made a sauce for pasta, and while it cooked I worked on the fort."

"The fort?"

She nodded. "I'm building a fort for Matthew, in the backyard."

Hannah remembered the pile of poles she had seen on her first visit to the house, and Rebecca's breathlessness when she called.

"It looks like a lot of work."

Rebecca smiled dimly. "At the rate I'm going, I figure

he'll be about five . . ." The specter of losing him surfaced again. She brushed harshly at her eyes. "When it's finished. I was working on it when you called. Was that at two?"

Hannah nodded. They'd talked for five minutes or so.

"At about six, I picked up Matthew. Then, about six-fifteen, I went upstairs to work out."

"That's why you didn't answer the phone?"

Rebecca looked at her blankly.

"Laura's call."

"Oh." Her face went red. "I had earphones on. I didn't hear the phone."

"We've saved the message. Do you want to hear it?" Stephen was already on his feet.

"Yes, please," Hannah said.

He motioned for her to follow him to the kitchen. A prerecorded voice announced the date and time of the call: Friday, 6:17 P.M.

Laura's voice was weak, slurred, barely audible. "Becca?" She mumbled, something they couldn't make out. Then, she said: "Help me." The receiver hit the floor with a clunk.

"I can't understand the middle part," Hannah said.

"Something about not being able to leave?" Stephen said.

Hannah turned up the volume. The words were garbled, but Hannah understood this time.

"I think she said 'couldn't breathe.' What does that mean?"

Stephen shrugged. "God, I don't know. Did she have an asthma attack? Had she choked on something?"

Hannah didn't know. Had she panicked when she felt her air supply dwindling, and managed to dial the phone and speak, only to lose the fight? It would be awful to decide you wanted to live, but not be able to stop the death you'd already set in motion.

"Any ideas about this, Rebecca?"

Rebecca was staring at the machine as the tape rewound. She seemed to start at the sound of Hannah's voice. "No. When I listened to it that night, I didn't understand what she was saying."

"What time did you pick up the message?"

"About six twenty-five. She sounded so terrible. I just wanted to get there quickly. I tried her phone, but the line was busy. I should have called 911. There might have been time to save her. And then Matthew wouldn't . . ."

She was about to cry again. She muttered an apology and left the room. Hannah could hear her footsteps in the slate foyer, and then moving faster and faster until she reached the stairs.

14

"Funerals are awful," Bobby said. "Do you think we really have to be there?"

Hannah gave him an amazed stare, but Bobby was too busy watching the road to appreciate it. Las Almas Acres was threaded with steep curving streets and hairpin turns, and the winding trip up to the Drummonds' house reminded her of mountain treks she'd made to Big Bear and Mammoth.

"Yes." She felt as though she owed it to Laura. Was there some way for Hannah to have known she was depressed— or that someone meant to kill her? If so, Hannah missed the cues, and that bothered her. But the reason she gave Bobby was another, also the truth. "I want to see if Churnin turns up."

Ivan Churnin was one of Las Almas's senior homicide investigators. He and Hannah had tangled once, when she was in law school. He had gone from mocking her as a burned-out, possibly unbalanced ex-cop to respecting her tenacity and investigative abilities. She hadn't seen him in more than a year, but she knew Laura's death was the kind of case that would wind up on his desk.

"I suppose we should go, then," Bobby said as they pulled up to the Drummonds' house. "But Catholic funerals are the worst. Incense, Latin. Bleah."

"They don't do Latin anymore," Hannah said. "The incense you just have to live with."

They didn't recognize the woman who opened the Drummonds' door. She was in her later twenties, with wide blue eyes, a determined, jutting little chin, and frizzy blond hair that had been tamed into a demure ponytail. She was holding Matthew in the crook of her arm. She smiled as Stephen Drummond came in from the living room.

"Hannah, Bobby, meet Anneke Vanden Raadt. She's here to help us with Matthew for a while." He slid his arm around her shoulder. "Anneke is an RN. We've known each other for a couple years and she's worked in surgery with me for, what, is it more than a year?"

"Yes. Sixteen months now," she said, shaking Hannah's hand with a businesslike grip without dislodging Matthew.

"We've asked her to live with us for a few months, until Matthew's all well."

Hannah nodded politely and saw the rapt gaze Anneke wore as Stephen talked. Drummond asked her to take Matthew upstairs. He dropped his voice as Anneke turned and left.

"Our doctor has told Rebecca that Matthew will be fine, but she's being . . . overly protective," Stephen said. "She's been sleeping in the nursery—actually, sleeping isn't the right word. She just stays in there, watching Matthew. She's a wreck, frankly. Anneke is here to take the strain off, since Rebecca's medication isn't exactly doing the job. Why don't you go into the living room. My brother, Martin, is there." He strolled to the kitchen, where a phone was ringing. As the door swung open, Hannah saw Rebecca at the sink. Water ran over her hands. She stared out the window.

In the living room, a shorter, overstuffed version of Stephen—in black jeans, a black shirt, and black wool vest—poured coffee for Bobby. Martin Drummond had a softness that would turn into a health problem on day, but at the moment it made him seem comforting and approachable. He and Hannah were shaking hands when voices erupted in the kitchen.

The three guests stopped talking, as though they were the ones being overheard. No, Rebecca was saying. She wasn't going anywhere without Matthew. And he was in no condition to be carted around to a church and cemetery. It didn't sound as if she were crying. Her voice was strong, determined. She just wouldn't leave Matthew, she said. It didn't matter that Anneke was here.

"It's about me needing him, Stephen, not vice versa."

They couldn't hear his reply. The kitchen door slammed open, and they watched Rebecca march out the front door. She didn't give them a glance or a word. Stephen started after her, stopped in the foyer, and went upstairs, cursing under his breath.

"Another fight," Martin said.

"Another?" Bobby said. But Hannah wasn't surprised. She imagined Anneke's presence alone was good for six or seven arguments.

Martin sighed. "Stephen's a good guy. He just doesn't know how to back off sometimes. And he isn't very good at saying he's sorry. I ran interference for him last night. He'd have me do it full-time if he could."

"But you have a life," Hannah said.

He smiled. "I live in Vancouver now, and it just doesn't have the same effect when I send a fax from the theater."

"What do you do?"

"Lighting design for the Vancouver Playhouse. About five years now."

Hannah heard the hint of a prolonged *ooh* his vowels. "You're catching the local accent."

He smiled. "Pleasant change from Orange County surf-speak, eh?" Then he frowned, obviously worried about his brother and the turmoil in his life.

"It seems like a lousy time to be fighting with Rebecca, after what she's gone through," Bobby said.

"Well, timing is not Stephen's strong suit. But he's all right."

Hannah had her doubts. Stringing together his behavior

since Laura's death, she liked him less with each incident: Stephen hadn't asked about Rebecca's injuries—just Matthew's; he'd hired a pretty, young nurse-nanny who idolized him; he was arm-twisting his wife to spend less time with Matthew, oblivious to her feelings.

"You don't agree?" Martin said. He must be used to watching faces, Hannah thought. He'd read hers, so it wasn't worth pretending.

"He loves his family, I'm sure of that."

"But you think that's as far as it goes. And you're wrong." He was smiling. Barely.

She wondered if they'd been like this as kids. Had Martin tagged behind his brother, putting him in his best light, blotting out his shadows? She didn't want Martin carrying back stories of her dislike. Stephen would take it for disloyalty.

"I don't think that at all," she said. "Anyone who goes into medicine cares about relieving pain, curing the sick."

"Exactly. He's always been that way."

"Splinting bird wings, stuff like that?" Bobby was trying to help, but it came out sarcastic. No one could think of Stephen as some sort of super Boy Scout.

Martin shook his head. "For you to understand, I have to set this up a little."

"We've got time," Bobby said. They could see Rebecca again. She'd gone around the back, and was pacing the deck. "They could use a few minutes to cool off."

"We had a couple roommates when we lived together. One was a medical resident, just as uptight as Stephen. The other was an actor. An actor manqué, actually, not as serious about the theater as I was. But he liked the lifestyle and the women. He and Stephen nearly came to blows once when this guy decided to have a party while Stephen was sleeping, after pulling about a million hours in the ER. But when our roommate made a bad mix of drugs and booze and almost died, Stephen was the one who saved him."

"That's what doctors do." No matter what Hannah said, it came out cooler than she meant it.

"Well, of course. But Stephen kept track of him. Got him in touch with AA. Tried to make sure he was okay, although there wasn't much Stephen could do once he moved out. The point is that Stephen talks tough. But he cares about people, and has loyal friends and patients because of that. And he cares about Rebecca most of all. He doesn't want to lose her."

Rebecca had walked down the hill where the half-built fort sat. Martin excused himself and went to her. Hannah watched the rise and fall of his shoulders as he gestured and cajoled to her. She actually laughed at one point. They fell into a hug. Then she came in and went upstairs.

Ten minutes later, she was back, dressed in black, purse in hand. She said nothing about the fight. Stephen did a less credible job of pretending nothing was wrong. Hannah rode with the Drummonds and Martin in Stephen's Land Rover, and Bobby followed in his Saturn. During the forty-minute ride to Long Beach, Martin prattled on about his adopted city, trying hard to lessen the tension. Rebecca smiled and joked with him, but didn't say a word to her husband.

The church, in a postwar neighborhood on Long Beach's east side, was as chilly and soulless a place as Hannah had ever seen. It was pale as the Virgin: blond wood pews, ocher brick wall, floors set with pink mosaic tile. An organist played in the loft, all stops pulled for a bombastic rendition of "Panis Angelicus."

None of the arrangements reflected Laura's tastes. Gerald Lawrence probably made them. But he wasn't there. The mourners—Hannah, Bobby, Martin, and the Drummonds—barely filled a pew. No one who'd seen Laura Benson come into this world was there to usher her out. They had known her for a couple years or a few months. Martin didn't know her at all. Hannah thought he wasn't alone in that category. She felt as if Laura was a projection, a shadow thrown up on a screen.

Someone who loved her wasn't here. Gibbons had been

released from the hospital on the same day as Rebecca, but
then he'd disappeared. The day before the funeral, a note
arrived at the office. It was addressed to Hannah with a
return address in Point Reyes Station, a town north of San
Francisco.

*I appreciate everything you tried to do for Laura. The
store was a complete loss. The insurance will let me start
over, but that will take a while. Healing must come first. I
am with my friends here, and will return when I can. If I
can.*

*Please give my condolences to Rebecca and Stephen on
the loss of their son's birth mother. And tell Rebecca that she
cannot blame herself.*

According to a card in the vestibule, Gibbons had sent the
spray of purple, pink, and yellow wildflowers that lay on
Laura's walnut coffin.

Jerome Hoskins was another no-show. Hannah left two
discreet messages with his secretary, but heard nothing in
the days before the funeral. She didn't blame him, in a way.
He was about to be married. He'd given up his rights to
Matthew. There wasn't much reason to further entangle himself.

Then, the morning of the funeral, he called her at home.
He was brusque at first, until she told him about the
explosion, Matthew's injuries and recovery, and Laura's
death.

"It might have been a suicide. There was a note."

"Christ," he said, his voice slight and distant now. "But if
you're asking me to come down there, I really can't."

"I don't think anyone expects that, Mr. Hoskins. We
understand your situation."

"Thanks!" Exaggerated bonhomie. Someone was walking by his desk. Then his voice fell to a whisper. "I met the
social worker for lunch, and I signed the consent. Did you
get the blood okay?"

"The lab got it Monday. Everything's going as Bobby
said it would."

"Good. Well, I'm sorry about all this—about Laura, I
mean. You do understand why I won't be there?"

"The fiancée. Sure," Hannah said.

"And my—the little boy is really okay?"

Hannah hoped the use of the possessive was nothing. "He's fine. His adoptive mother's okay, too."

"I'll keep a good thought for them all." He hung up.

Hannah glanced down the row at Rebecca. The effort of holding herself together was exhausting her. Hannah thought of the thin glass that Drummond had squeezed into shards. That was Rebecca. The pressure bore down, harder and harder. A little more, and she would shatter, too.

The priest began mass before the tiny congregation. She prayed for Laura. The father of her child didn't know her well enough to come. The man who honored her with casseroles and herb teas was too broken and devastated to be there. Here own father had planned his child's last rites and then decided not to attend them. It was a sad way to finish a life.

During Communion, Hannah heard the doors at the back of the church open. Kurt stood there, peeling off a pair of wraparound sunglasses. He wore black jeans and a black T-shirt on which a grinning Day of the Dead skeleton strummed a guitar. If this was Kurt's idea of respect for his wife, Hannah wasn't impressed.

His hair was a greasy shock and stubble covered his face. Their eyes met. Kurt looked dazed to her. Drugs, grief, guilt? She couldn't tell. He stumbled into a pew near the door, kicked down the riser, and fell to his knees in a melodramatic attitude of prayer.

Now Stephen was watching him, too. The corner of his mouth twitched. He started to get up, but Hannah put her hand on his arm and pressed hard.

"That's what he wants," she murmured. "Don't."

He pulled his arm away. But he did sit down, reaching for his wife's hand. Rebecca let it lie limply in his palm for a minute or two. Then, as though any sudden moves would spring a trap, she slid it free.

• • •

At the interment, Kurt decided to claim his place among the mourners. He fell in step beside Hannah as they walked to the grave site. This close, Hannah could smell the stale beer that hung around him. Stephen, Martin, Bobby, and three men from the mortuary carried the coffin. Rebecca followed, staring off at the far corner of All Souls' Cemetery, a place of mounded dirt and a sagging wire fence. The mourners didn't seem to notice the bald man in a baggy-kneed suit walking behind Rebecca. But Hannah saw him, and gave a nod. Ivan Churnin seldom missed the funeral of someone whose death under suspicious circumstances wound up as a case on his desk. Suspects so often came to them. And, as he'd once told Hannah, it was sometimes the only quiet time he'd have in a day.

Kurt leaned closer to Hannah as they walked. "You sent the cops after me."

"It was a notification. You're next of kin. And you had Laura's car."

"Had it—that's right," he said. "Cops impounded it. I told them she'd loaned it to me when mine broke down. They didn't believe me. You probably told them I stole it."

"I didn't know. But this isn't the time to talk about it."

They reached the canopy, the grave, and its welcome mat of artificial grass. Kurt slumped into a folding chair and put his hands to his face. "I can't believe she's dead." His voice cracked.

The pallbearers put down the casket, and the priest invited the mourners to join him in prayer.

"Bullshit," Kurt said under his breath. "All this is a bunch of bullshit."

Hannah could have kicked herself for not anticipating this from him. She grabbed for him, but he shook her off and stumbled forward. He threw himself onto the casket and tried to wrap his arms round it. In a croaking baritone, he sang a minor-key waltz:

> *"Perfect mother, full of me*
> *A belly full of living*

*Take back life—it's yours, you see?
Throw back the scraps they're giving."*

Drummond swore under his breath and went after him, showing every intention of depositing him in the fresh hole. To Hannah's relief, Martin tugged his brother back with a few words. Rebecca didn't react at all. The withdrawn, vacant expression reminded Hannah of a sleepwalker's.

As Kurt finished the first awful verse and gathered breath for a chorus, Hannah took him by the arm and whispered in his ear. She looked up to see Churnin, who had taken a chair in the last row, watching impassively.

When Hannah was done talking, Kurt nodded, lifted himself out of the crushed lupines and Queen Anne's lace, and took his seat. He kept a respectful silence for the rest of the service, and on the way back to the cars, he stopped Hannah.

"If the Drummonds, you know, don't feel like he's up to it, it's okay."

Hannah took in the unshaven, pasty face and the swollen eyes. If this was an act, it was a good one.

"What's okay?"

"The visit we're supposed to have Friday. It's okay if we don't. Matthew's kind of shook up, right?"

"It's been hard on him, yes. If you're serious, have Jim Pabst call me, confirm it's okay."

He nodded and slouched away.

Bobby and Churnin were waiting for her. "How'd you get him to back off?" Churnin said. "Threats of bodily harm?"

No. I told him I understood his loss. I understood his need to be here."

"You gave him a lot of sentimental crap, in other words," Bobby said.

Hannah glared. Bobby, surprised, shut up.

Churnin let a moment pass. "So this guy thinks he's the father of the Drummonds' baby?"

Hannah nodded. "You've been prepping."

"I put in a call to Kurt Sundstrom's lawyer. When's the paternity hearing?"

"In a week or so. They're running everybody's DNA now."

"You'll call me if anything useful comes of that little bonding moment you had with the grunge Pavarotti?"

"Sure," Hannah said.

Bobby drove her home. As they headed south on the freeway Hannah looked out at the neighborhoods below them, discouraging conversation. Bobby irritated her sometimes. He called on her to file off the rough emotional edges with the Drummonds and this hellish adoption, and then dismissed her peacekeeping as "sentimental crap." Let's see you keep this three-ring circus running smoothly through the paternity hearing, she thought.

She couldn't decide if Kurt's outpouring was staged. He could have guessed that a cop might show up. A few tears, genuine grief—that might be helpful to a suspect. But histrionic behavior drew suspicion. And singing bad lyrics definitely didn't help. Either he didn't know how to exonerate himself subtly, or that elegy in three-quarter time was real. But even if the emotion was real, it didn't mean he hadn't killed her. It just might mean he regretted it now.

They left the freeway, and in a few minutes they pulled up at her house. My house, Hannah thought. It still didn't sound right.

"You okay?" Bobby could see that she was angry. She decided to let him off the hook. Maybe what she told Kurt had been crap, but it kept the funeral from tilting out of control.

"Just a headache. Funerals do that to me."

Bobby beamed. He couldn't stand to have her mad at him.

Inside, her answering machine held another of Feuer's tidbits: the pilot of Laura's stove might have been faulty, but that wasn't what caused the gas leak. The line from the stove to the wall had been twisted off. A very fast, effective way to fill an apartment with gas. A classic suicide maneuver.

If Laura was so determined to die, Hannah wondered why she called Rebecca. If she'd changed her mind, why didn't she just leave the apartment, or call 911? Hannah remembered how Laura's voice sounded: slow and mushy, as though she'd taken steps to ensure that she wouldn't wake up. The autopsy would show if she'd swallowed pills or downed the half bottle of Bombay gin Hannah watched her hide during her visit.

Feuer's message continued: he'd heard a crack pipe was found in the apartment, in Laura's beside table. But the cops and the arson guys still were betting on natural-gas poisoning as the cause of death. The explosion came after Laura's death. From what the investigators had gathered from talking to Rebecca and Gibbons at the hospital, it happened when Rebecca turned on the light.

Hannah let her mind follow the chronology, and something shook her. Maybe Laura hadn't called Rebecca for help. Maybe she called because she didn't intend to die alone. Hannah wondered how Laura could have known that Rebecca would rush in, turn on a light, and trigger an explosion. And what would have turned her against Rebecca that way? Finally, if Laura was determined to kill herself and Rebecca, Hannah couldn't imagine Laura killing Matthew, too. Unless Laura decided that if she couldn't have Matthew in life, she'd take him in death.

For the rest of the evening, she tried to shut out thought like that. But as she fixed a dinner of scrambled eggs and onions, as she tired to read, one question kept surfacing. Who benefits from this death? She told herself to stop it. It was cop thinking. Prosecutor thinking.

But the questions nagged at her. She decided to let herself dwell on it for an hour while she did something productive. Downstairs in Mrs. Snow's dining room, the pink stripping goop had softened the paint on the built-in sideboard—there had to be oak under all those layers of enamel. With a flat-bladed scraper and a gentle hand, she began peeling back the ages. Let the questioning begin: who was better off without Laura?

Kurt would be, if Matthew turned out to be his. With Laura gone, there would be no birth mother to fight him for custody. But if Matthew wasn't his baby, then who came out ahead?

The Drummonds. My clients. Laura lied to them. She put their adoption in jeopardy. It seemed like a breach of faith to think of clients as murder suspects. But any decent cop would. Ivan Churnin certainly would.

But was the motive strong enough? The couple had a finalized adoption. If Laura had meant to change her mind, she had ninety days after signing the adoption consent to do it. And she hadn't. There was an agreement with Laura for visitation, and that seemed to be working. Until Kurt showed up, they were one happy family.

So Kurt was the wild card. Had he wooed Laura into changing her mind about the adoption? If he had, and the two of them intended to fight to keep Matthew, that would certainly have been a problem for the Drummonds. Courts like married birth parents. It would be an easier job to fight Kurt alone if he turned out to be the biological father. If he wasn't, the Drummonds had nothing to worry about.

Hannah stopped working for a moment. Her wrist ached.

She rubbed it and went back to work, inner and outer: Stephen's job and meticulous nature made him easy to track on that day. And he never was alone. He was in an office, at a meeting, in a gym. He was accounted for. But Rebecca was a different matter. Between two and five, she was alone. From six on, only Matthew was with her. So she had plenty of time, in either slot, to go to Laura's apartment and twist off the gas line. But Laura would have tried to stop her, if she were able. Maybe she wasn't. But Hannah couldn't imagine how Rebecca could have convinced or forced Laura to swallow pills and gin.

And if Rebecca had done those things, she wouldn't come back, baby in her arms, and turn on a light in an apartment she'd filled with gas. She spent her life around construction sites. She knew what would happen. The explosion exonerated her. She flicked on that light because she knew nothing about the gas. She was in a panic, worried about Laura. She'd hit the light switch, just inside the door, before she had a whiff of gas.

Hannah stepped back to look at the work she had done. The sideboard was indeed oak—very nice quarter-sawn red oak at that. But it had taken an hour to reveal a small section of it. It would take dental instruments to tease out some of the softened paint that had worked its way into the crevices. Now her fingers were numb from the constant pressure. Testing her clients' capacity for murder hadn't made the time pass any more pleasantly. But it had been necessary, and she had quieted her own doubts.

She tidied the dining room, turned off the lights, and let herself out through the front door. Eventually, she would move into the main house. Perhaps when Guillermo came back. If he came back to her. As she climbed the stairs to her apartment she could hear the phone ringing, and she ran for it. He'd been thinking—and now he called. If he was calling, it was good news. Another letter would be the way to end it. She caught the call before the machine picked up.

"So you do come home." Feuer. Not Guillermo. Guillermo still was thinking. Did Feuer think much?

"Sometimes," she said. "Thanks for letting me know what you found out about Laura."

"Well, since you were her lawyer. So after being a detective for Las Almas PD, you bailed out for law school?"

"That's what I did, all right."

"Bet that freaked out your dad."

Hannah preferred not to talk about Jimmy Barlow. Since Michael's death, she hadn't seen him much, except for the time he came by for an unannounced visit, saw Mrs. Snow's clock and decided it was his next fix-it project. When he was done, he'd sent it back, without a note. Hannah knew her stepmother, Estelle, didn't like him visiting. She also didn't want Hannah in her house. But there was no reason to get into any of that with Feuer.

"Nothing I do surprises my dad anymore."

"I thought you might like to know about this thing I heard. You told the arson guys Laura was smacked around by her husband the day before?"

Apparently entrusting information to anyone in the Las Almas Fire Department was like pouring sand into a sieve. But since Hannah was the beneficiary of the leaks, she wouldn't complain.

"Right."

"Well, I heard that during the autopsy, the coroner found semen. You know."

Inside her?"

"Yes. I'm sure Las Almas PD will be very interested in finding who that belongs to. But the husband would be a natural, don't you think?"

Hannah did think so. By now, Churnin was probably poised to subpoena Kurt's DNA results from the paternity hearing. It would be an investigative godsend for the police: a suspect's DNA on file, and a semen sample to match against it.

"Dan, did they also find that she'd taken anything?"

"Some kind of sedative, and plenty of booze."

She was mulling that, and almost missed what Feuer was saying. Something about getting together sometime, for coffee, maybe? Christ, she thought, a date. Cloaked in the innocuous guise of coffee, which was supposed to be even more casual than lunch. It made her uneasy. She knew he was bringing these tidbits as token of devotion. She didn't want to create a debit, to make him think she'd pay him back with mocha java, drinks, dinner, or any other, more personal, currency.

After a few seconds of silence Feuer cleared his throat.

"So there's a boyfriend?"

She could have said yes. That would have been the end of it. But she didn't. "I'm not sure. We had a sort of fight."

"He lives in?"

"Not yet. He might. I don't know."

"But you want him to?"

She didn't answer right away, and he took her hesitation for his last best chance. "If you're not sure, then maybe you shouldn't. That's what led to my first marriage, and divorce. We played house before we were ready."

It was the kind of encouragement she shouldn't take. She knew that. But maybe he was right about the dangers of hasty cohabitation. Maybe that's what Guillermo thought, too. That's why he was thinking. Remembering his note, its uncertain tone, her face burned.

"Coffee only," she said to Feuer. "No dinner, no dancing."

"Fine. I've got two left feet anyway."

They would meet the next afternoon, when his shift ended. Later, lying in bed, she thought about his eyes, gray as a winter sea at dawn. The smell of burned ash. Make up your mind, she told Guillermo. Before I change mine.

At her desk the next morning, she downed two cups of coffee and started a WESTLAW search on a new case. That would put Feuer out of her thoughts. She heard the slam of a door and shouting in the reception area. Simultaneously, her computer beeped at her. She called up the message, written in capitals. Vera's silent scream:

DEFCON ONE. DR. DRUMMOND JUST ZOOMED IN, AND HE'S GOING BALLISTIC IN BOBBY'S OFFICE. GET READY FOR THE SHOCK WAVES. . . .

In Bobby's office, Stephen was flinging a piece of paper onto the desk. He acknowledged Hannah with a nod and then resumed his rant.

"Rebecca found this in the mail this morning and called me at the hospital. She's a basket case, and I don't blame her. It's a fucking threat against me and my family. There is no way on God's earth I'm handing my son over to that maniac after this."

Bobby handed the page to Hannah. Someone had made a color photocopy of a Polaroid picture that showed Laura and Matthew sitting on a park bench, laughing. There was a playground behind them. Someone had typed beneath the picture: GIVE HIM BACK.

"You think this came from Kurt?" Hannah said.

"Who else, Hannah, for Christ's sake?" Drummond's face was vermilion, and his voice shook. "He's killed Laura and now he's threatening us. We won't stand for it. I expect you two to tell Judge Baxter that Kurt is not getting his hands on my son ever again. I don't care if I have to go to jail, or take him to Canada. . . ."

Bobby walked around the desk and put his hands on Drummond's shoulders. "Stephen, you're not going to jail, and you're not going to Canada. You're angry and you're worried about your son. We understand your concern, right, Hannah?"

"Yes," she said. "I'd be furious, too." She just wouldn't work up to a stroke, she hoped. But she wasn't a parent who had nearly lost a son in an explosion less than a week before. She wasn't the one who could lose him in court two weeks from now.

Bobby released Drummond's shoulders. The doctor sat down hard on the sofa. Pressing his palms to his forehead, he took a deep breath.

"I'm just so damn afraid."

"We are going to handle this, starting now," Bobby said soothingly. He raised his eyebrows at Hannah, encouraging her to elaborate.

"I'll start putting an affidavit together, telling the court what you told us about receiving the letter," Hannah said. "Vera can take down your statement, and have it ready for your review and signature in just a few minutes. We'll attach a copy of the letter. Did you keep the envelope?"

Stephen nodded and motioned to Bobby's desk. No return address, of course. The address and the Drummonds' names—Dr. and Mrs. Stephen Drummond—had been typed. It had been mailed from Huntington Beach the day before Laura's funeral.

"I want Ivan Churnin to have a look at this," she said.

"Who's he?" Stephen asked.

"The homicide investigator. The bald guy at the funeral."

"That's who that was? He could have said something to us."

"He likes to lie low at first. That will change."

Bobby sat down next to Stephen. "Now, I want you to promise me that you'll go home and reassure Rebecca that everything is going to be fine. And I don't want you calling your travel agent checking on the next flight to Alberta. That's not going to be necessary. All right?"

Stephen nodded impatiently. "Okay, okay."

"Hannah and I need to talk for a minute. Will you excuse us?"

When Stephen had shut the door behind him, Bobby sat down at his desk and ran his hands through his hair. He looked up at Hannah.

"He's losing it."

"What do you expect?" As angry as she had been at Drummond on the day of Laura's funeral, Hannah now felt a glimmer of compassion for him. It must be hard to live with a temperament like that. In his calmer moments, Stephen surely knew what his short fuse was doing to his marriage, his career, and even his health. Divorce, heart attack, and stroke loomed in his future.

"You don't get it," Bobby said. "It's this thing about Canada."

"What about Canada?"

He sighed. "There have been a couple of adoption cases where the birth fathers were butting into an adoption and lawyers figured a way to get around it: they spirited the kids off to Canada for adoption. It's a way to put everything out of reach of the birth fathers and the courts here."

Hannah shrugged. "So? That might work for Canadians who are adopting, but not for Rebecca and Stephen. Not unless they're planning to give up their citizenship."

"I know. But it tells me Stephen is reading up on train wrecks—these really bad adoptions. He's expecting something to go terribly wrong. He's looking at worst-case scenarios, working himself into a frenzy. Why else would he know about Canada?"

Hannah felt her sympathy for Drummond begin to dry up, like a puddle in the sun.

"Maybe he's not wondering if something's going to go wrong," she said. "Maybe he knows it *will* go wrong. Maybe he knows Kurt *is* the birth father. That's why he's working on extra-judicial ways to keep Matthew away from him."

Like moving to Canada?"

"Or sending himself a threatening letter."

Bobby gaped at her. "Come on."

"Well, why would Kurt do something like this? The hearing is just a couple weeks away and he's left a good impression with Bitsy. He's got to be careful: he's already on the cops' radar because of his fight with Laura, so he wouldn't want to make things worse by sending something like this. And then there's the way it's addressed."

Bobby looked at the envelope again. "You're going to tell me Kurt can't type?"

"No. But I doubt that Kurt would bother with a form of address as precise as 'Dr. and Mrs. Stephen Drummond.' I think Kurt would be more likely to address it to 'You Assholes.' "

"That's not much to go on."

Hannah shrugged. "I'm not going anywhere with it. I'll present what Drummond alleges to the court. I just have a feeling Kurt didn't do this."

She got to Rutabegorz late. Feuer was sitting at one of the window tables, framed by a variegated pothos. He sipped coffee from a glass mug and thumbed through a little stack of used paperbacks. She paused at the door to take him in. He'd had a haircut. The leather jacket looked suspiciously new. He turned a page. His hands were not big, but the fingers were finely shaped. Hannah touched her palms. They were damp.

He smiled when he saw her, swept his eyes down the black cashmere sweater and black wool pants, which would have been fine on an evening a month ago, but were too hot for a May afternoon. He stood, held out his left hand to guide her to the chair, and leaned in to kiss her cheek. Hannah turned her face at the last second, concentrating on the books. Feuer's lips grazed her cheekbone.

"Let's see: *Fahrenheit 451, The Man in the High Castle,* and *Dhalgren*. Science fiction's your favorite?" She knew she sounded a little breathless. Christ, she thought, he'll think your fuse is lit. Calm down.

She could see that he'd already sensed her nervousness. He sat back in his chair and looked at her for a moment. She pushed her hair away from her face. She'd taken it down after work and run out of time to braid it. The curls followed their own wild course.

He shrugged finally, ready to answer her question. "I read anything. Cereal boxes, if there's nothing else. How are you?"

"It was a weird day at work. And I think I had a little too much coffee."

"Well, we don't have to stay here and drink more of it, if you'd rather go somewhere else."

She started to say no, but found she didn't really want to. "No dancing, remember?"

Feuer smiled. "We don't even have to stand up, if you don't want to."

She followed him, and parked her car in front of a minuscule white stucco box with blue shutters. They were in a neighbor hood where half the people cared how their lawns looked. Feuer's was rousing itself from choking, weedy death. His marriage was finished and the ex got the kids and the three-bedroom home. But Feuer wasn't willing to give up the tax break that came with a mortgage, and he'd found himself a fixer-upper. He stood waiting for her at the front door, keys in hand.

He touched her back as she stepped inside. The living room was dim in the dusk. The furniture was second chance, too. IKEA sofa, Pier 1 pillows, Cost Plus rug.

"Nice place," she said. Her voice sounded hoarse.

He didn't answer. He stood behind her and his hand slid

up, the fingertips cool as they rested on her neck. He gathered up the strands of hair with one hand and bent to kiss her, just below the ear. The other hand stroked her waist, shaped itself to her breast. She didn't pull away this time. It was too dim to read the book titles on the shelf across the room. She tried to suppress the shiver, but couldn't.

15

The Orange County Courthouse might have seemed a gleaming palace of purest justice when it opened in 1966. But the rub and weight of cases—civil and criminal, bogus and heinous—had erased the veneer, exposed its true nature: an eleven-story box of pain and suffering—with a cafeteria.

Hannah held the door for her clients, but Rebecca stopped at the reflecting pool at the courthouse entrance. The wind drew circles and eddies in it, pushing the foam plates, bits of paper, and the jurors' cigarette butts like toy boats.

"Richard Neutra and Ramberg Lowrey designed this building," Rebecca said. "The trash makes it look like hell."

Hannah nodded and followed Rebecca into the lobby—still without a metal detector, she saw. The judges and the county supervisors were duking it out over court funding, and she had to wonder whether it would take a homicide to accomplish the upgrade. Rebecca stiffened as the crowds buffeted her. Hannah understood her unease. Courthouses were a second home for lawyers. The hallways, elevators, lobby, and cafeteria were theirs, where they tried gambits and made deals.

Litigants, defendants, witnesses, and victims were outsiders. To them, the courthouse was a little like Vegas—they came knowing they would either win or lose. But here there was nothing to soften the throw of the dice. No comped rooms, free drinks, or white-tiger shows. Here, you watched the cards flip in a sickening state of total comprehension.

Hannah took stock of her entourage: Stephen was appropriately stoic in dark gray. Rebecca looked older in a staid navy suit and high-necked cream silk blouse. Anneke broke the conservative fashion mold with her slithery black rayon blouse, pleated black miniskirt and knee-high Doc Martens. More Road Warrior than Mary Poppins, but since she carried Matthew like a priceless treasure, Hannah didn't care what she wore. Anneke was there because Rebecca had refused to leave the baby at home. No amount of pleading dissuaded her. Bobby, in his lucky blue pinstripe, brought up the rear of the parade behind their blood-typing expert, Bennett Thewlis, laboratory director at GenType, a thick man whose brown suit made him even more bovine.

Like Rebecca, Hannah had gone with navy, knowing that Bitsy Baxter sneered at women lawyers in jewel-tone Chanel suits. The judge was set in her ways, refusing to take her family-court caseload to the new juvenile justice center in Orange. She always spent lunchtimes in the civic center's Japanese Garden, and she wasn't going to give that up. The presiding judge decided humoring her was easier than dislodging her.

They sat outside Baxter's courtroom, waiting for the bailiff to open it. All of them were nervous, and trying not to show it. The last time they'd been there, for the hearing about the anonymous letter, Kurt turned into a man teetering on the edge of violence.

As promised, Hannah had kept her doubts about Kurt's authorship to herself. And during the hearing, Judge Baxter seemed skeptical. The Las Almas police were no help. The letter had no fingerprints except Stephen's. They couldn't find among Kurt's belongings a typewriter that matched the message. And of course he denied sending it. But Baxter decided that the upheaval the letter had caused, coupled with Matthew's injuries, were reason enough to cancel Kurt's two visits before the paternity hearing. He turned purpled with rage at this, and only Jim Pabst's hand on his shoulder kept him in his chair. Baxter did decline the Drummonds' request for a temporary restraining order against Kurt, but that didn't seem to soothe him.

The intervening week passed without any more letters. There were no more anonymous phone calls like the one Stephen got the night of Laura's death. They heard from Kurt only through his lawyer. And as Hannah thought that, there Kurt was, at the end of the corridor, glowering at her.

They heard a jangle of keys, and the bailiff came around the corner, coffee and sweet roll in hand. He unlocked the door. Rebecca nodded when Hannah reminded her that Matthew would have to stay outside with Anneke.

"As long as he's nearby, I'm fine," Rebecca said.

Kurt and Pabst were coming toward them. Hannah let them pass her into the courtroom. Kurt's suit hung on him. Hannah saw that he had missed one spot under his chin while shaving, and nicked two others. His eyes locked on hers for a moment as they sat down, and then he paid his undivided attention to a yellow legal pad. This was going to be a bad day for him.

If Kurt hadn't been a drug-using, wife-beating, possibly wife-killing lowlife, Hannah could have felt sorry for him. Civil matters cost money. The Drummonds had plenty of it, and were writing checks weekly without complaint. The testing at GenType cost them $1,200, with results ready in less than two weeks. Kurt could have run his own test at another lab, but hadn't. It was a question of money, Hannah was sure of that. Kurt had subpoenaed Jerome Hoskins to testify. She and Bobby were able to quash it: Kurt didn't have the funds to pay for Hoskins's travel. If she were in Kurt's place, she would have hired an expert witness, at a hundred dollars an hour, and had him ready to challenge GenType's lab results. She saw no such witness in the hallway. Money, again.

Just in case it was necessary, she and Bobby had found a child psychologist who had prepared a report and was ready to testify to the grave psychological damage that Matthew would undergo if he was removed from the only parents he knew. She didn't see anyone around who looked like he was ready to testify to Kurt's blood ties and their importance. Money, she decided, might not be able to buy justice, but it sure gave rich people a hell of a down payment on it.

The Drummonds sat down at the counsel table and twined hands. Somehow, the threat letter seemed to have bonded them. Hannah hadn't seen or heard of a squabble since it arrived.

She and Bobby shook hands with Pabst. Bobby knew him from an all-lawyer baseball league. The two wandered together to a far corner of the courtroom, making polite small talk about the fortunes of Pabst's team, the Bad News Barristers. Kurt looked on in stunned amazement. Some clients were utterly appalled when their lawyers didn't treat opposing counsel like pond scum. But the legal community in Orange County was small enough that paths often crossed again. They would have to deal with each other long after this case was over and this client was gone. Civility paid off, in the long run.

Hannah looked over the results from GenType again. She knew what Thewlis would say on the stand about DNA and paternity testing.

Like all children, half of Matthew's DNA came from Laura and the other half from his father. Thewlis would describe how the DNA extracted from the specimens provided by Matthew, Laura, Hoskins, and Kurt was processed in the lab: "cut" with enzymes, separated by electrophoresis through slab gel, converted to single-strand form, transferred to a nylon membrane, labeled with a radioactive isotope probe that binds itself to a specific fragment, washed, and finally exposed to X-ray film to yield an autoradiograph. That film displays the distinctive DNA banding patterns.

The contribution of the mother's and father's genes would be plain in the child's band pattern. The DNA of an unrelated man who claimed to be the father would not match. Now Hannah looked at the autoradiograph that showed the results of one probe. There were six lanes across the sheet. Laura's bands, vertical black stripes like bar codes, occupied the second and fifth lanes. Below that sample was Hoskins's DNA, in bands in lanes one and six. Then came Matthew's bands, in lanes one and two. The band in lane two was the DNA he inherited from Laura. The DNA from his father was the band in lane one.

Finally, below that, there was the sample from the "unrelated" father—Kurt—with its bands in lanes three and four. No match, in other words, to Matthew. The lab had produced two other probes, with identical results. Matthew's paternity was beyond question.

A door behind the clerk's desk opened. Judge Baxter, a woman in her seventies whose thin face and immense brown eyes made her look like an underfed cat in a Keane painting, peered out to see if the parties had arrived. As she made her entrance Hannah stood up, took a deep breath, and closed the folder. She knew it was a jinx to think it, but she felt they were going to win.

Thewlis took the stand. The lab director nodded and rocked like a kindergartner who needed a bathroom break, but his answers were succinct and jargon-free. Hannah glanced at Kurt. He already knew the results—his lawyer had the report, just as she and Bobby did. As Thewlis answered Bobby, Kurt's expression didn't change. But he gripped his pencil until his nails were white.

In the cross-examination, Kurt's lawyer tried the standard approaches, attacking GenType's procedures, the training of its employees, the conditions of the lab, and the accuracy of DNA testing itself. Thewlis easily swatted down each challenge without losing his clockwork rhythm.

Bobby tidied up with a few questions in his redirect. Then he paused for a moment.

"Do you have complete confidence in your laboratory, Dr. Thewlis?"

"I certainly do."

"And in the DNA-typing test itself?"

"Yes."

"And do you have any doubt whatsoever as to the outcome of the test your lab did in this case?"

Thewlis shook his head. "No, counselor, Mr. Hoskins is Matthew Drummond's father. Mr. Sundstrom is not."

Hannah looked to Kurt for a reaction. He glared at Thewlis and soundlessly mouthed a stream of obscenities.

Judge Baxter was watching Kurt, too. "Even an unpracticed lip-reader can understand what you're saying, Mr. Sundstrom. Stop it or I'll find you in contempt."

"Your Honor, he's lying. He's—"

"Enough, Mr. Sundstrom. Anything further, Mr. Pabst?"

"Judge, there have been some very strange events surrounding this adoption, not the least of which is the death of Laura Benson, Matthew's mother. In light of that, I would ask that the court order another test, utilizing a laboratory selected by the court. I think that would remove any lingering shadow of doubt."

Bobby stood up, ready to object. Baxter waved him down, put on her half glasses, and silently reviewed a stack of papers in front of her.

Bobby and Hannah exchanged glances. Pabst sat down and studiously avoided looking at the notes Kurt was scribbling to him. Rebecca ran her fingertips down her cheek—it was becoming a nervous habit. Stephen stared at the ceiling.

Baxter looked up and took off her glasses. "I don't have a lingering shadow of doubt," she said. "The court has been presented with test results that show Mr. Sundstrom isn't the father. The tests show that Mr. Hoskins is. Furthermore, I have Mr. Hoskins's acknowledgment of paternity, along with a consent to adoption that he has signed and the state Department of Social Services has accepted. And while I agree that it is a tragedy that Matthew's mother has died, I have in the report a relinquishment signed by her, so that part of this adoption is completely in order.

"Although Mr. Sundstrom was married to Matthew's mother at the time of his conception and birth, he was not residing with her. The presumption that he is the father has been adequately rebutted. And in the absence of any evidence upon which to overturn this adoption and upend Matthew Drummond's life, I decline to do so."

Hannah had been ready for an outburst—a shout of joy from Rebecca and Stephen, a scream of fury from Kurt. But there was only silence. Rebecca and Stephen hugged each other and began rocking in a slow, comforting Thewlian rhythm. Kurt stared straight, burning a hole in the state seal's grizzly bear.

Pabst got to his feet. "Judge, may I be heard? The issue of Mr. Sundstrom's paternity is far from settled. The DNA testing was highly—"

"You may take it up with the Court of Appeal if you wish, Mr. Pabst," she said. "I've made my ruling. We stand adjourned."

"Come on," Bobby said to the Drummonds. "Let's take your son home."

"That sounds great," Stephen said. Rebecca, on the edge of tears, just nodded.

Bobby hustled them out, leaving Hannah to thank Thewlis and pack up their papers. Pabst was talking softly to Kurt, who still hadn't blinked. Bobby caught Pabst's eye before he left, and the men nodded silently at each other. I get it now, Hannah thought. Their pretrial chat hadn't been just about baseball. They had agreed to keep Kurt in the courtroom until the Drummonds were long gone.

When Hannah got outside, Anneke and Matthew were gone. The hall echoed with the frantic click of Rebecca's heels. Stephen padded behind, trying to calm her.

"They're gone," she said, her voice rising into panic. "Stephen, where are they?"

Hannah looked down the corridor. It was a slow morning. No one milled outside the courtroom doors. She walked past the elevators, checked the nook that held two pay phones, and then pushed open the door to the women's room.

Anneke was there, singing to Matthew as she finished changing his diaper. Hannah slumped against the door, feeling relief flood her limbs.

Anneke blinked at her. "What's wrong?"

Hannah shook her head. "Nothing."

They were on the escalator. Bobby led the party this time, followed by Rebecca, who was holding Matthew. Anneke, Stephen, and Thewlis formed the middle part of the parade. Hannah was last. It was five minutes after noon, and people crammed the narrow, slow-moving escalator down to the lobby. She heard several annoyed voices above her, cautioning someone to watch it, stop shoving, cut it out.

Kurt was four steps behind her, shoving people out of his way. His eyes were locked on Matthew. Pabst was nowhere in sight. So much for the plan.

She glanced down at the marshal's security desk. Empty. One marshal was inside the glass-windowed office. He talked on the phone, his back to the lobby.

"Bobby!" Hannah shouted.

He looked back, just as Kurt bodychecked a woman, almost sending her over the escalator's rail. Bobby pulled Rebecca and Matthew in front of him. Anneke slipped in behind them. But then the trio was trapped. A crowd jammed the lower steps. Rebecca and Anneke couldn't push through.

Hannah faced Kurt and tried to block him.

"You don't want to do this," she said.

He didn't seem to hear or see her. His eyes stayed riveted on Matthew as he slammed her out of his way. She toppled against Thewlis's broad back. He stumbled against Stephen. Kurt passed the lab man and threw an uppercut that caught Bobby on the jaw. He fell to one side and Kurt squeezed past him. Now he was within two steps of Rebecca and Matthew.

Hannah struggled to her feet and searched the crowd that crammed the lobby. The litigants, witnesses, and court personnel filled it with a chattering, rising column of noise. Then she saw the security-desk marshal turning. Two more marshals in beige uniforms came down the hall, probably bringing back burritos from Los Panchos. The din and bustle of the lunch rush made them oblivious to the scene on the escalator.

"Bailiffs!" She screamed the word. They turned. "Kidnap!" She pointed to Kurt. "Stop him!"

She looked down. Rebecca and Anneke were off the escalator and running for the door. The bailiffs cut in from the right, pushing people out of their way. Hannah helped an indignant Thewlis to his feet. They were still three steps from the lobby floor.

Rebecca was outside, clutching Matthew to her chest. She ran with long strides, dodging people as she made for the parking lot across the street. But Anneke had stopped on the covered walkway next to the pool. She stood her ground as Kurt strode toward her. If he'd heard Hannah's scream to the bailiffs, it hadn't fazed him. And as he closed in on Anneke he seemed to look through her, seeing only Rebecca and Matthew. That proved to be a mistake. With a soccer player's aim, she launched a kick. The steel toe of her black boot connected squarely with Kurt's groin. He fell wordlessly, toppling into the reflecting pool. He splashed and writhed in pain. The bailiff's arrived a second later, hauled him to his feet, and dragged him, dripping, back into the courthouse. As they handcuffed him Stephen helped Bobby sit down on the edge of a lobby planter. Bobby muttered that he was all right, but he didn't look it.

"You fucks!" Kurt gasped as he passed the men. "Matthew's mine. And goddammit, I'm going to get him back."

Behind her, Hannah heard someone groan. Pabst was there, holding his head as though it might fall off.

"Hell of a client you've got, Jim," she said.

"He's not my client anymore. He decked me outside Bitsy's courtroom. That's all the bono he's getting out of me."

They watched as the bailiff frog-marched Kurt Sundstrom to the courthouse lockup. Hannah was losing her doubts about his innocence. Not only had he sent the threat letter to the Drummonds, he'd probably killed Laura, too.

Given the day's injuries, a celebratory lunch was canceled. Hannah worked at the office for a few hours, until the pain in her knees welled up. At home, she poured a glass of brandy, dumped a carton of Epsom salts into the claw-footed tub's steaming water, and eased herself in. The heat seared her legs and hip. Ugly blue bruises would blossom there by tomorrow. Kurt certainly had made an impression on everyone.

She lolled in the steaming water until it turned tepid. Then she wrapped herself in a robe and went through the mail. Amid the bills and junk, she found a thin white envelope with a Durango return address. She sat down on the sofa and held it for a moment. She was afraid to slit it open. She could barely think about Guillermo. Or Feuer. Especially Feuer. Especially after what she'd done.

Hannah felt herself toppling. The free fall began with Feuer's lips on her throat. His hands spanned her waist, paused on her breasts, and caressed her face. Half carrying her, Feuer found the way to the sofa. With one motion, her black sweater was off, falling on the leather jacket he'd draped on the sofa's arm. She slid off her pants, let them pool on the floor. She heard the crinkle and rip of plastic. The moment of condom fumbling almost gave her enough time to reconsider. But then Feuer sank his hands into her hair as though it were a pool of water, deep and warm and enveloping. She felt the tug on her scalp with each of his slow, deliberate moves inside her. As she tilted her head back, eyes tight shut, she could smell the newness of the leather jacket, almost feel the grain in the hide as it slid across her cheek. Then a whiff of Blackjack. And then she couldn't smell anything, hear anything. Everything swirled away in aching shudder that moved out in rings. Pebble in water.

After, he wanted her to stay for dinner, spend the night. She wouldn't. She was already feeling disconnected from herself. What the hell was she thinking? Not thinking. Just reacting, diving into this obliteration of her life with Guillermo.

Feuer could see she was distracted, but he didn't seem to take offense. Would she like to have dinner later in the week? She said she would call him after the hearing. He wound a tendril of her hair around his finger and pulled her close for a good-bye kiss. It seared.

She turned Guillermo's letter over. Maybe there was no need to worry about what she'd done. Or what she might do again. The long delay in the arrival of this featherweight envelope might mean that Guillermo's thinking brought him to the briefest reply of all: no.

Fast was best. She ripped the short end of the envelope and shook it. There was no letter inside. Just a photocopy of a form that had been completed in Guillermo's handwriting. He had asked *American Lawyer* to start sending his subscription to her address. Her face felt hot, and the brandy surged in her stomach.

She brushed her teeth, sat on the sofa, and stared at the form, filled out in his neat, crisp hand. It would be easy enough to end it. Wait for Guillermo's call and then tell him the truth, brutal as a slap. Then it would be his choice to reject her. Maybe that's what she wanted. Not to make the decision. Maybe she had hoped that Guillermo's leaving was a prelude to permanent separation. That his postcard was the first step to the end. But he'd called her bluff.

She tried to make herself call Feuer, right then. If she put it off, for even a day, it would be a worse betrayal of Guillermo. She was done with that. She would, at least, try to be done with that. But didn't that mean telling him what she'd done? It made her wince to think about it. She found she couldn't pick up the phone. Couldn't dial Feuer's number. It took another glass of brandy before she could sleep.

16

Ivan Churnin was in cat-and-mouse mode. Hannah knew it from the sound of his voice: a silky, feline purr of secrets kept from puny, lawyerly rodents.

"So your clients won custody? They said they were nervous about the hearing. Certain that Kurt wasn't the daddy, but nervous anyway."

"You talked to my clients?"

"Nice people. Tough time for them."

"Nice of you to be so sensitive." Hannah could barely constrain her sarcasm. The brandy had left her with a pounding headache. "You should have let me know you wanted to interview them." But why hadn't they called her?

"Oh, it was very informal. Nothing for you to fret about. They think the world of you."

"That's very gratifying, thanks for passing it on." If Ivan was trying to smoke her out, sniffing for defensiveness and alibis, she wasn't going for it. Still, if the Drummonds thought so much of her, why did they take on Churnin by themselves? Maybe they decided that having their lawyer present would make him unduly suspicious. It was a weakness that cops preyed on. Innocent people like you have no reason to have a lawyer around for questioning, they'd say. She'd said it herself, when she had a job like Churnin's. And they'd fallen for it.

"Will you be calling the Drummonds again, Ivan?"

"Hannah, it's an unpredictable world."

"It is that."

"Want to have lunch sometime, counselor?"

"Are you still vegan?"

"Firmly. But I know places that cater to you flesh-eaters."

"Then it would be my pleasure."

Thoughts of the Drummonds and Churnin nagged at her as she worked. She arrived at the point of uselessness about ten-thirty that night, went home, and fell into bed.

And at eleven-thirty, she was wide-awake, wondering why. As exhausted as she was, she should have slept straight through the night. She punched the pillow and faced away from the glowing clock face. But sleep didn't return. She kept imagining Churnin as various clever animal predators. Then it was the Drummonds as shivering rabbits, helpless voles. Were there voles in California? The Drummonds doubtless told themselves they had nothing to hide, so there was no harm in talking to Churnin. Hannah groaned to herself as she contemplated the ways a good cop could have gently worked them over.

Then, in the stillness, she heard it. The step just below the top landing always creaked under weight. But Hannah didn't want it fixed. It was a cheap early-warning system. So that was what woke her. Someone was outside.

She threw on a sweatshirt and jeans and crept into the living room. The streetlights cast a man's shadow on the shaded window next to the front door. The form was too thin for Bobby. Feuer didn't strike her as the stalker type, even though she'd broken her promise to call. The doorknob turned. The form pushed against the door, which was of course locked and dead-bolted. Hannah dialed 911. The shadow figure hovered, turned, and left.

"Nine-one-one operator." She sounded exhausted, over-worked.

"Someone just tried my door. Attempted break-in. But he's gone now."

"This is H. Barlow?" She read off Hannah's address.

"Yes."

"Okay, ma'am. We'll have a unit there in a couple minutes. Call back right away if he returns."

Hannah hung up the phone and waited, eyes closed. She

knew it would be more like ten minutes, at the earliest, before someone showed up. A bond issue for fire-and-police emergency services had failed in the fall, and response times were spinning out toward the two-hours-more-or-less of cable installers. She listened to the night—silent except for a dog's yipping bark, blocks away.

And then someone was knocking on her door. Not trying to break the glass, just announcing a visit. She opened her eyes and saw the figure again. Home-invasion robbers wouldn't give up the element of surprise by knocking. Would a rapist?

"Hannah? Miss Barlow?" The voice outside was tentative and too polite for Kurt Sundstrom, but that's who it was. "I know you're there. I need to talk to you."

Hannah had already redialed 911. "This is Hannah Barlow. You told me to call back. That someone who tried my door? He's a felon who tried to attack me earlier today. He's back."

"Shit, why'd you have to do that?" Kurt sounded hurt.

"Cops are on their way, Kurt," she called to him. Kurt wouldn't know about the bad response times. "You'd better split."

"But I need to talk to you." His voice was annoyingly whiny.

"Come by the office in about nine hours," she said.

The doorknob rattled.

"I have a gun, Kurt, and I know how to use it." She was pulling the lockbox down from the closet shelf as she spoke. Adrenaline made her hands shake.

Kurt groaned, and she saw the shadow slump. There was a dull thump, the sound of his forehead hitting the door in despair. "I just made bail an hour ago. Look, I'm sorry about what happened in the courthouse."

"You tell that to Jim Pabst and Bobby Terry. They're the ones you decked."

"I went crazy. It wasn't just the hearing. That would have been enough, but there's this other thing. I just wish you would get them to stop."

Despite herself, Hannah was curious. She stood next to

the door, the heavy revolver in hand. She almost never handled it anymore. Not since Michael.

"Who am I supposed to stop?"

"There's this Las Almas PD detective, Churnin? You know him, right?"

"Yes."

"He said you did. He showed up when I was in jail. He started hinting around that he knows I had something to do with Laura's death. Something about my DNA? Now, what does that have to do with Laura being dead?"

This had to be an act. Could Kurt really not know that blood wasn't the only source of DNA? Maybe. He wasn't a cop or a lawyer. He didn't have any record of sex crimes that would have heightened his awareness about semen as a DNA source.

"Hello? Awake in there?" The sneering sarcasm was working its way back into his voice. "Did you tell him something about my blood? My genes aren't any of his business."

Ivan Churnin, she thought, you work so very fast. He had done just what she expected him to do: he got a court order and, with it, access to the paternity hearing's DNA test results. The semen found in Laura's body had to be a match to it, or Churnin wouldn't be taunting Kurt.

"I didn't tell him anything," she said. "Take off."

"Swear to God?" He didn't seem to care about the police showing up. "You've been straight with me and that's why I'm here. What's going on?"

"I'm not the police, Kurt. I don't know what they're up to. I can't help you."

"Oh, you can."

"How?"

"You can tell this detective friend of yours that I didn't kill Laura. You know I didn't."

His voice piped with confidence. How had he decided she was his ally?

"Kurt, I don't know that. You used to beat Laura. You hit her the day before she died. You had her car. And it sounds like the police have some other evidence that implicates you. Why would I tell them you couldn't have done it?"

"But you know how I felt about her." He was sitting on her doorstep now—the voice came from somewhere around the knob. "I'd been looking for her for months because I loved her. We did have a fight, but I only hit her because she said we were through, and she started throwing stuff at me. And anyway, I love Matthew. You saw that for yourself."

She didn't answer him. His relationship with Laura was too ambiguous for her to read. But he probably did love Matthew, and the boy seemed to like him. She had no intention of telling Kurt that. It would only encourage his fixation.

"I've got a temper," he said. "And Laura does . . . did get me riled sometimes. But I loved her. And if I loved her and Matthew, how could I have killed them? How could I have put my baby's life in danger like that? Matthew is my flesh and blood." His voice caught on the words.

What could she say to someone who thought that wishing would make it so? Laura's denial of it, the discovery of Jerome Hoskins, and the outcome of the DNA test had done nothing to weaken his belief in his paternity. He seemed to have burrowed deeper than ever into his obsession. Hannah clicked off the gun's safety.

"Okay, I'm going." He'd heard the sound of the gun being readied. "But I'm telling you, that DNA test was a fake. You might not have been in on it, but I know someone screwed with the results. I know Matthew is mine. And now they've decided taking him away isn't enough. Now they're trying to pin a murder on me. I'm broke, you know? I spent what I had on making a home for Matthew, and that lawyer and bail. If I get arrested now, it's the public defender, and then I'm dead for sure. Nobody listens once you're charged and in jailhouse orange. Nobody believes you're not a killer."

"You want me to convince the cops you're not?"

"Yes."

"So you think it was suicide—"

"Laura wouldn't kill herself. I don't believe that."

"Then who killed her, Kurt? Who had more reason to hate her than you did?"

He was silent for a moment.

"Laura made some enemies," he said. "We both did. We needed money, and when you think about it, nobody got hurt. Not really. They could afford it. If they hadn't been so stupid, they wouldn't have fallen for it anyway."

"Fallen for what?"

Silence. He wasn't going to explain. "For a while now I've been thinking that someone was following me. I think it could be these people we—" He stopped himself. "But it's not just Laura, or me that I'm worried about. Not now."

Hannah felt a cool sliver of fear glide down her back.

"What are you talking about?"

"I worry about Matthew."

"What do these people want with him? Who are they? Did they send that letter to the Drummonds?"

He didn't answer. And then she heard the car coming around the corner. The doors opened, and closed. She caught a burst of radio chatter.

"You tell your cop friend that I'm a straight-up guy on this. Then I'll tell you more. You know the Palm Motel?"

"On Glassell."

"Be there tomorrow afternoon, after you've talked to Churnin. Then, depending on what you tell me, maybe we'll talk some more."

She heard a thud as he vaulted the rail and hit the ground. Then the doorbell of Mrs. Snow's house rang. The officers hadn't seen the stairs leading up to her apartment, and missed the "½" after the address—it happened all the time. Hannah put the gun away and went downstairs.

In the morning, she called Churnin. She usually tried to meet him on neutral ground—at his favorite vegetarian restaurants or one of the coffeehouses that had sprung up near the Douglas Law School campus. Las Almas Police headquarters made her uneasy. The building was so thick with memories that the walls seemed to pulse with them.

Hannah worked out of the low, white-stucco headquarters

building for twelve years, moving up from patrol officer to detective, her career on a good track until it derailed on the twist that was Janie Meister's case.

All in all, Hannah didn't enjoy trips to her former professional home. But on this day she had no choice. Churnin told her that if she wanted to see him that morning, she'd have to play in his yard.

"I'm so fucking busy I can't see straight," he told her.

Churnin's cubicle in the detective squad room was, as always, neat as grandmother's parlor. His dedication to law and order extended to his desktop. There were no untidy stacks of paper there, or Post-its scrawled in an incomprehensible hand. She fully expected that one day, she would come here and see antimacassars on the two guest chairs. There usually was a framed picture of a woman on the desk—Churnin's wife, she always had supposed—but today it was missing.

Churnin stood up as she stepped into his perfect sanctum and gestured for her to sit down. She sniffed at something.

"Do I smell lemon?"

Churnin nodded and pulled an aerosol can out of the desk drawer. "Air freshener. Guy next to me goes out for a cigarette about every fifteen minutes. But he brings the smell back in with him. It stinks the place up."

"You wouldn't have lasted a minute in here when I started. Smoking was practically a religion then."

Churning smiled, lips tight at the teasing. "So, counselor, what's up? You want to know what your clients had to say?"

"You should have called me."

"Hey, they're adults. It's not up to me to control them. But since you came all the way over here . . ." He pivoted in his chair, unlocked the credenza, and took out a file. "We talked about the paternity case and the threatening note, allegedly sent by Kurt. Dr. D talked about what he was doing the day Ms. Benson died—at the hospital, working out at the gym, going to a meeting. And Mrs. D, meanwhile, is cooking, building a fort—that's nice, huh?—exercising, and then there's the phone call. She's lucky she and the little boy didn't get hurt worse than they did."

Hannah nodded. "And?"

"And she's feeling guilty."

"She said that?"

"Not in so many words. But who wouldn't feel bad?"

"She turned on the light. That's what Gibbons said, too. Right?"

Churnin didn't answer her. He wasn't about to tell her someone had corroborated her client's account. "I know that's what Gibbons said," Hannah told him. "He was behind her when she opened the door and turned on the light."

"Then everyone is ass over elbows down the stairs. So she feels responsible."

"Do you think she's 'responsible'?"

"I don't think I have anything else to say about that. Are we done?"

Hannah smiled at him. "No, Ivan. I wouldn't have bothered coming down here for you to play coy with me. We could do that over the phone. As you demonstrated yesterday."

"Okay, so what's on your agenda?"

"Kurt Sundstrom paid me a visit. About eleven-thirty last night."

Churnin sat back in his chair and closed the file. "Really? And what did Mr. Sundstrom want?"

Hannah recounted the conversation, ending with Kurt's hints about Laura's enemies, who now might be a threat to Matthew.

Churnin shrugged. "From what I've heard, Laura and Matthew's worst enemy is Kurt. He wanted that baby just to screw her over. Another torture, only slightly more subtle than the beatings and that nasty phone call."

"Cleve Gibbons told you he'd heard that? Someone arguing on the phone to Laura?"

Churnin didn't raise an eyebrow. "I didn't say that."

"But you think what Gibbons overheard was Kurt and Laura."

"We're looking into it." He turned some pages in the file and stopped to read one.

Hannah thought for a moment. Laura's angry reply to her caller—*Why would I do this to you?*—certainly applied. Kurt felt aggrieved by what Laura had done. But the rest of it didn't fit: *Think what you did to me. And then you try to pay me off? You can't buy people.* How could Kurt, spending his last dollars on his paternity case, have tried to buy Laura?

"Why would she have let Kurt in the apartment anyway, the day she died?" Hannah said.

Churnin looked up sharply but didn't answer.

"Was it because she was drunk? And had popped some pills?"

"I really couldn't comment," he said.

"Ivan, I heard the message she left Rebecca. Her voice was slurred. Alcohol and drugs, right?"

He shrugged. "Maybe."

"So, a day after Kurt hits her, he shows up again and she eagerly invites him in for drinks, pops some pills he's brought, and then goes to take a nap while he spews gas into the loft? It doesn't really make sense."

"Well, speaking hypothetically, she might have been drunk and taken the pills before he got there. If she already was impaired, it was no trick for him to get in. One shove on that door would be all that was necessary."

"So you have some evidence of a struggle?"

"In this hypothetical thing we're talking about, no, we don't have much one way or the other. Half the apartment was blown out."

"But you have semen, with a DNA match to Kurt."

He smiled slightly. "If we had something like that, it would be a good foundation for a death-penalty case. Rape, and then murder. That paves the way to lethal injection."

"So you have something to indicate sex wasn't consensual?"

"She said she couldn't breathe. What does that suggest to you?"

Hannah got it. Kurt had choked her, maybe into unconsciousness, before he raped her. "So there was bruising on her neck? Fingernail marks? Petechial hemorrhaging?"

His eyes narrowed suspiciously. Oh, Hannah thought, there was no bruising, no gouges, no bleeding in the tiny blood vessels in Laura's eyes. Churnin's death-penalty charge was melting away. "Get to the point."

"It could have been seduction. These two have a complicated relationship. He beats her up in Seattle, she runs away, he turns up in Las Almas, she wavers and won't say bad things about him to a judge. Maybe it's fear of him, or maybe it's a sick kind of love, and she can't quite cut herself loose from him. So this time he was nice to her, and made her think that everything was going to be good between them. They got high, he got her a lot higher. They're in bed, and she's out. Then Kurt pulls the gas line. Maybe for Kurt, it's not about possessing Laura, or showing her who's boss anymore. It's about Matthew. If she's dead, and he's the father, he can get Matthew back. He thinks."

"But he's not the father," Churnin said.

"He didn't know that then. He was convinced Matthew is his. He still is."

Churnin shrugged. "I'd say that's a deluded person capable of violence."

"What about the suicide note? Is it Laura's handwriting?" He sighed. "Yes, it is."

"But you don't think it's suicide?"

Instead of answering, Churnin sniffed. Hannah smelled the faint smoke in the air, too. Her first thought was of Feuer. Goddammit, she thought, what have I done?

Churnin pulled out the air freshener and spritzed the cubicle until a plaintive voice on the other side pleaded with him to stop with the Martha Stewart act, already.

"So you don't think she killed herself." Hannah wasn't falling for any spray-can diversionary tactics.

"You don't rule anything out, Hannah. You know that."

"You're including my clients in that 'anything,' too?"

"That's right."

"So what you're saying is that Dr. Drummond checks out. His whereabouts are established for the day. But Rebecca Drummond was alone most of the day, so she doesn't have that luxury. She could have gone to Laura Benson's house and twisted off the gas line. That's the thinking, right?"

Working from two shallow glass dishes, Churnin began making a chain of paper clips, alternating plastic-coated white ones with links of plain metal. "Go on, Hannah. But I'm just an audience for your theorizing here. I'm neither confirming or denying."

She watched the chain making, and went on. "If Rebecca did twist off the gas line, why would she endanger her son by coming back and turning on the light? And how did she get Laura to write a note?"

After a pause Churnin began undoing the chain, link by link.

"Tell me, Hannah, is this just you being a good lawyer, or is there something else going on? Your clients don't have much to sweat now. They have their baby, who's safe and sound, Kurt's bullshit notwithstanding. Kurt, from what you tell me, is not the child's father, so he doesn't have a rat's-ass chance of messing up the adoption. And the way things are going for Kurt, I see him at San Quentin, snugly strapped down in the little room, waiting for a potassium-chloride nightcap. Maybe, if he's lucky, he'll remain the guest of the state of California for twenty-five to life."

He swept a little dust off the blotter. "The unstable Ms. Benson, who apparently did not always tell the truth, is no longer among us, no longer a source of worry. And you could just have called me and told me Sundstrom was bugging you. So why are you really here?"

Churnin had good instincts. It wasn't just Kurt's visit, or the Drummonds' position as potential suspects that had brought her to him. It was a deeper feeling, an uneasiness that she couldn't shake.

"It's Matthew. He's my client, just as much as the Drummonds are, as much as Laura was. You make it sound like Laura's dying was the end of something. I don't think it was."

"So what did her death start?"

"I don't know. She kept secrets. She lied, as you said. I'm

afraid that whoever killed her—or whatever made her kill herself—isn't finished. I'm worried about Matthew."

"You shouldn't let Kurt spook you. He's blowing smoke, Hannah. The adoption's wrapped up. Let us handle the rest. It's our specialty."

If there was a criticism there, she decided to let it pass. "If this was another kind of case, I could do that. But Matthew doesn't go into the closed file. If something Kurt and Laura did threatens him, I'm not going to ignore it. And anyway, even if Kurt is just blowing smoke, Matthew is going to wonder someday what I did when his mother died, in the middle of his very messy adoption. Did I stay with it? Look out for him? Or did I just cash the check and move on to the next matter?"

Churnin grunted. "Waxing heroical again. Kids bring it out in you."

"They're defenseless."

"He has his parents, Hannah. Besides, you can't tell me babies are defenseless. Ever change a diaper?"

"You must have. You're such an expert at giving me shit," she said. "Have you talked to Laura's father?"

"Lawrence? We asked him to do the ID, but he wouldn't. He wouldn't even look at a picture. He said his daughter told him that he wasn't her father anymore, and he took that seriously. Dr. Drummond made the identification."

Something else the Drummonds hadn't shared with her. Why did people bother with lawyers if they were going to treat them like potted plants?

"When?"

"The Saturday after the explosion. As much as people hate identifications, I think I hate them more. They're necessary, sure. But you never know how people are going to react. Doctors have seen a lot, so they're pretty stoical. I wasn't worried about Dr. Drummond."

"So you showed him Laura's body?"

"It wasn't that bad. But even for doctors, I guess it's different when it's someone you know."

He could have shown him the picture. He'd taken him into the viewing room—which could never be purged of its

faint smell of chemicals and decay—on purpose. Churnin
wanted to see how he'd react.

"He left the coroner's, sat in his car in the lot for a minute,
just staring at nothing. What do you make of that?"

"Before the shit hit the fan, the Drummonds and Laura
were close," she said. "For all the problems they had after
Kurt Sundstrom showed up, they had been a family, really."

He shook his head and smiled sarcastically. "Marriage.
Family. Great little boats on a sea of trouble, huh? Till they
sink."

Hannah looked at him quizzically. Did he know something about Guillermo? Was the gossip membrane filtering
stories of Hannah and Feuer back to him? And if not, then
what was wrong with him? "And what about Laura's father?
Where's he in your thinking?"

Churnin chewed his lip for a moment. "Since we've come
this far down the theoretical trail, I'll tell you. If we were
discussing the case, I'd tell you Lawrence is out. He said
he was at his yacht club at noon for lunch. Had a drink. The
busboy said it was three. Then he said he had a meeting with
some shipping-container lobbyists in Long Beach. We
verified that. If you put that together with how long it took
for the gas to fill Laura's apartment, there wasn't time for
him to drive to Las Almas, pull the line, and get back in time
for his meeting."

"What about these enemies Kurt talked about? It sounded
like someone from their Seattle days. Did Laura make any
long-distance calls up there?"

"This is information that Matthew will want in eighteen
years, is that right?"

"Look, you're not even really talking about this case. So
what's the difference?"

"There was one toll call to Long Beach. Someone named
Bill Beckett. We just got an answering machine when we
called."

"That name sounds familiar." She thought for a few
minutes, and then had it: the same last name as on the sign
in Gerald Lawrence's lawn. Susan Beckett, candidate for
Congress. She told Churnin.

"Thanks. We'll ask Mr. Lawrence about his daughter and the Becketts," he said. "Now I've got a theoretical question for you."

"Go on."

"Was Laura Benson some kind of genealogy buff? Looking for long-lost relatives?"

Hannah shook her head. "Not that I know of. She and her father were estranged. She told the Drummonds she'd had a lousy childhood. That's the only family talk I heard. What's going on?"

"Nothing, probably."

The detective next door stood up and cleared his throat. "That meeting's just about to start." A faint trail of smoke issued from his nostrils. He was sneaking puffs in the office.

Churnin looked at his watch. "I'll be right there. And goddammit, don't think you can get away with smoking right under my nose." He put the case file back in the credenza and locked it before turning to Hannah. "Home-invasion robberies are way up this year. We've got a special tactical meeting. So . . ."

"Thanks for seeing me, Ivan."

"Lunch on me next time." He reached for the air freshener. The can brushed a stack of files in the corner, and Hannah saw a plastic sleeve that contained a burned paper. Churnin was too busy shooting the spray at the cigarette addict to see she'd noticed it. Some kind of report, she thought.

"I'm going to use the rest room here before I go," she said. "Okay?"

"Ladies' is down the hall." Churnin double-timed it in the other direction, shrugging on a brown sport coat and hammering the Marlboro man with data on secondhand smoke. Hannah waited in the bathroom for a count of eighty and then strolled back into the squad room. It was empty now. She figured she had five minutes of privacy. No more. Someone was bound to wander in. She sat in Churnin's chair and opened the file that Churnin had forgotten about. If this was about the Drummonds, some evidence against them, she would eventually see it, but by then they'd have been arrested and on their way to trial. She didn't intend to wait around for that.

Most of the charred pages in the folder were typed. One was handwritten. A forensics report, stapled to the back of the file, described where the fragments were found: a singed envelope was under Laura's bed. The pages came from the apartment's bathroom sink. The envelope had been post-marked in Huntington Beach, a few weeks before Laura died. The second time someone had sent a letter from there, Hannah thought. The pages themselves were half-destroyed. Only some of writing, coaxed out by chemical treatment and examined under ultraviolet light, was decipherable.

She could make out a few of the handwritten words on the curled black pages. But the lab techs had more success: . . . *hard to believe. But read what he has to say. He's found the truth. You said that if you knew, things would be different. I hope that you'll keep your promise, and give us* . . . Later in that line, the sentence ended: *late to make this right.*

From the typed pages, very little could be reconstructed, the report said. Only two fragments were readable: *Laura Benson's father remained away, in Ge.* Educated guesswork suggested that an *o* and possibly an *r* followed the letters. Someone had scribbled *Georgia?* in the margin. Another page contained one sentence, and part of another: *Burden came to Paraclete on May 13. She stayed there un* . . . The rest was seared into oblivion.

Hannah heard laughter down the hall, and the sound of men's voices. She put the file back and grabbed her purse. Telling herself not to look guilty only ensured she would. Her best hope was that the two approaching cops didn't know her. They were young ones, freshly turned out from the academy, judging from the brush-cut hair, buff biceps, and spit-polished shoes. They didn't give her a second glance.

In the car, Hannah scribbled down the phrases that had been reclaimed from the fire. Someone was indeed giving Laura Benson family history. But who? They hadn't recovered a signature on what must have been a cover letter. And no prints were found.

The letter talked of promises made and broken, and debts to be paid. What was Laura supposed to give the writer in return for the information? Was the letter from one of the enemies Kurt talked about? Perhaps Kurt himself was the writer, and Matthew was what he wanted Laura to give him. Had Kurt killed Laura and then burned the letter to cover something incriminating in it? If he had any idea of what the cops had on him, he would check out of the Palm Motel in a flash. She decided to see if that had happened yet.

17

The last time Hannah had been at the Palm was years before, when a schizoid father locked his small children in the bathroom and stabbed their mother to death on the double bed. It was the home of last resort for people who sifted down from the saner, safer strata of Orange County. There were only two stops after the Palm: the shelters, and the streets.

The blacktop parking lot held only two cars, including Kurt's Maverick. It was parked at the room farthest from the office, but so close to an all-night drive-through restaurant that Kurt would hear the shouts for fries and shakes in his dreams. A white Crown Victoria was parked in the restaurant's lot, facing away from the motel. Even from the back, the two men in it had the unmistakable look of plainclothes cops. Kurt couldn't have missed them.

There was a gap in the closed drapes in Room 11. Through it, Hannah caught glimpses of Kurt, pacing through the disorder of the place. Kurt bit at this cuticles. She knocked. After a few moments he opened the door a fraction, leaving the chain up.

"Well, I talked to Churnin," she said. "I told him what you told me."

"And now what?"

"You're going to tell me why you think Matthew might be in danger."

"But Churnin's not backing off." He nodded to the white car.

"I never said he would. I can't tell him what to do about you. Cops are always hearing stories from suspects about the other shady people who are really the guilty ones. It's a cliché, frankly."

"It's not a fucking cliché, it's the truth."

"Fine. Then who are these people, and what did you do to them? Where do they live? What do they want with Matthew?"

Kurt fiddled with the chain and flicked his eyes over Hannah's face. "It was something . . . I never knew exactly what was going on, or if they were even pissed at Laura and me, you know?"

"You don't know if they were angry?"

"Right. It was no big deal."

"You said last night that these people were pissed off."

"No. I didn't say that."

"And what about Matthew?"

"He's a good kid."

This was another reason Hannah didn't miss police work. She enjoyed a fresh and spicy tale from a gifted fabulist. But mostly what you got as a cop were people like Kurt. Their feeble lies sat there, sad and slimy and dull as a pile of day-old salad.

"So you didn't have anything to do with making anyone angry enough to kill Laura."

"Right." He stared down at this feet.

"So you don't have any enemies yourself?"

"Steve Drummond hates my guts. That's about it."

"And you don't have the slightest clue as to who might have killed Laura. You don't know if anyone is a threat to Matthew."

"No. Look, I've gotta go now."

She could feel a flicker of anger warming her face. "Just remember that you were the one who showed up at my house in the middle of the night, pleading for help. I don't appreciate being jacked around. If anything happens to Matthew, you'll have more than Churnin to worry about."

"Don't you fucking threaten me." But Kurt's mumbled threat held no menace. The chain slid into place.

Hannah went back to her car and stared at the door to Kurt's room. Something made him come running to her apartment. Now something else pulled him back. Perhaps he only wanted to hear what Churnin had on him. But he hadn't pumped Hannah for information. Maybe after talking to her, he realized the enemy story was a fairy tale that wouldn't hold up.

She started driving back to the office. Kurt was lying to her. She knew that. Who else was holding out? She began to wonder if the Drummonds were. She called Vera and let her know she'd be out for a while.

It took a few hours to retrace the Drummonds' steps on the day Laura died. But it was as they'd said: Stephen was accounted for at his office, lunch, rounds, and meeting. She found Drummond's gym, O So Strong, in a rehabbed brick building with a neon logo of a bulging bicep. Hannah tried the door, but it was locked. Then she saw the sign taped to the door: FAMILY EMERGENCY—SORRY! She scribbled a message—call me— on a business cared and slid it under the door.

She found a listing for Rebecca's parents in the phone book. Maura and Frank Malone lived on Las Almas' flatland, in a two-story house that Rebecca could probably spot from her stair-climbing aerie. There were rosebushes bordering the lawn and a Cadillac parked at the curb. Maura used the car to advertise her industrious womb: the license plate read MOM OF 10.

When Maura Malone answered the door, Hannah saw where Rebecca got her looks. The mother had the same thin face and well-formed mouth. Maura's hair was straight and blunt-cut, an expensive styling but not a flattering one. She was wearing corduroy pants, a white cotton shirt, and a tiny cross on a chain. She put her hand on her hip and eyed Hannah up and down, as she would one of her children who'd been sent home from school. There was a sturdiness in her posture, and a kind of roughness to her, despite her preppy-grandmother clothes. She looked capable of every chore from canning tomatoes to caning children.

Hannah introduced herself. The woman's eyes—a sharp

blue that missed very little, including Hannah's reasons for standing on her doorstep—darkened.

"Well?" She had a rising lilt to her voice, the ghost of the brogue that marked her parents as immigrants.

Hannah hoped to have this talk inside the house, but Maura Malone made no move to admit her. "I wanted to ask you about Rebecca's visit, on the day Laura Benson died."

"What about it?" She closed the screen door a little.

"Well, what time it was, how long Rebecca stayed."

"You don't believe what she told you?"

"I wanted to verify her recollection of it."

"For what purpose? Are you saying my daughter's a liar?"

Hannah had no idea what she'd done, if anything, to make Rebecca's mother so hostile. "I'm not saying anything of the sort. Do you suppose I could come in for a moment?"

"No. I'm on my way out."

This was clearly not the case, but Hannah nodded. "I'm sorry I've inconvenienced you."

"No bother." And the door was shut.

In the car, Hannah decided she was an idiot. If Rebecca hadn't been at her mother's house that day, wouldn't her mother lie for her? Isn't that what mothers did?

It was after three. She decided to go back to the Palm before returning to the office. Kurt's artless about-face bothered her. He knew something. She was sure of it, and she was going to make him tell her what it was.

At the motel, the unmarked car had moved out of its surveillance position and now idled in line at the drive-through. From there, Hannah didn't think they could see, as she could, that the drapes to Kurt's room were open. She parked and peered in the window.

The room was clean. The bathroom door was shut. She called Kurt's name and hammered on Room 11's door. No one answered.

The cops had just ordered two double-double chili burgers when she tapped on the Crown Victoria's passenger window.

They told Hannah to stay outside as the manager let them

into Kurt's room. The bathroom door was locked. Over the manager's protests about the cost of doors, the beefier of the officers slammed his shoulder against it. On the second try, it crashed open. The cop was silent for a moment, and Hannah felt her heart bump as she envisioned Kurt in the bathtub, wrists slit. But then he started swearing, the sons-of-bitches and Jesus-Christ-goddamns bouncing off the cheap prefabbed shower enclosure. As the manager shoved his way through the splintered door, Hannah had a glimpse of a pried-out screen and a neatly removed window. It was too small for burger-eating plainclothes guys but big enough for a stringy specimen like Kurt. The cops probably wished he had killed himself. It would have been less embarrassing.

18

Hannah hadn't heard Guillermo's voice in more than a month. And between the blasts of static and rumbling crowd noise, she could barely hear it now. She'd gone back to the office after Kurt's disappearing act, worked until seven, come home, and dozed off on the sofa. The phone woke her, and it took a moment before she knew that his call wasn't part of a dream.

"Where in God's name are you? The connection is awful."

"The airport in Mexico City," he said. "I've got a few minutes before my flight."

An intercom-garbled voice made whatever Guillermo had just said to her unintelligible.

"What was that?"

"I said I'm going to Guatemala for a while. Two families of . . ." A burst of noise crackled through the line and made her wince.

"Did you say something about families of beavers?"

"Weavers." He was laughing. "There's some kind of problem in the village near Todos Santos Cuchumatán, where my mother gets the *huipiles,* those Frida Kahlo blouse things that you like. We can't figure out what's going on. The shipments just stopped. The phones are worse than these, so it's best to go in person. Did you get what I sent? I hope—"

The line went dead.

Hannah hung up and waited for him to try again. Limping

technology could be annoying, but it sometimes forced people to cut to the chase. When he called back, she would tell him: yes, she got the subscription change. She missed him. She was afraid to talk to him.

Because of Feuer. She had been avoiding his calls. Three of them now. The phone trilled and Hannah picked it up halfway through the first ring.

"Guillermo, before we lose the connection again, I just wanted to—hello?"

There was silence at the other end. No static, no tumult of travelers. Just silence. Hannah's back stiffened. "Who is this?" Then she knew. "The Palm was too fancy for you?"

"I couldn't talk to you before. The cops were making me nervous."

"I don't think the Las Almas police have the budget for parabolic microphones, Kurt."

"They were going to bust me."

"Then you should think about going by and talking to them. Running isn't something an innocent person usually does."

"I didn't kill Laura. I told them that, just like I told you."

"If that's true, you don't need to run."

"You don't understand. It looks bad."

The call-waiting tone beeped on Hannah's phone. It had to be Guillermo, but if she tried to make Kurt hold, he'd think she was scheming with the police. She ignored it.

"What looks bad?"

She heard him swallow. "I was at Laura's apartment that day."

"The day she died."

"Yes, but you've got to believe me. I didn't kill her."

"Okay. Tell the police that."

"You don't have any idea of the shit she was up to. She did piss off a lot of people."

"Who?"

"These people in Seattle—they went crazy. And then there's this thing with Laura's mother. That could have blown up. Or the father. It could have been him."

"All right." It was simultaneously too much information

and not enough. "Did she tell you about all this that day?"

"No, no. I knew about it from before. But that morning, she called me." His voice caught. "She invited me over. She said she was sorry she'd made me mad. She said she had something for me."

"And what was that?"

"A couple rocks. She knows I like the stuff. I'm okay with a little, and that's all she had."

Hannah nodded to herself. She knew she'd been right about the crack cocaine. It was in the plastic bag that Laura had swept into a drawer the day she visited her. She had it for Kurt, the way other people kept their friends' favorite Scotch on hand.

"Then what?"

"We talked, about us, and Matthew. And we made love. It wasn't rape, not the way the cop is saying, which makes me sick, goddamn son-of-a—"

"I get it. You'd never do that."

"I never had to force a woman in my life."

Hannah bit her lip at this ridiculous brag. "Go on."

"She told me the truth. She said Hoskins isn't Matthew's father."

"What?" Hannah felt a sickening twist in her stomach. She had known something was wrong with Hoskins.

"We were lying in bed, you know, after, and I was holding her. We'd been talking about Matthew, and I was trying to find out about this Hoskins guy. Did she love him? How long did she know him, and she told me, exactly these words: 'He isn't the one.' And I knew what that meant. She was telling me that I was the one. I'm Matthew's father. That's how I know the test results were a fake."

It didn't necessarily mean anything like that, Hannah thought. It could have meant Hoskins wasn't the one she loved. Or a dozen other things. She was about to correct Kurt's misapprehensions when she stopped herself. What if Laura told him the truth? What if Hoskins *wasn't* the father?

"And then what did she say?"

"Nothing else about that. There was nothing more to say. I was so happy. She let me use her car 'cause mine had croaked, and we were going to talk the next day. And then, the next day, she was dead. It nearly killed me to hear it. I really, really loved her. It was going to be okay. She told me so."

"Kurt, where are you? I'd like to—"

"I can't. You'll have to tell the cops if I do, and I'm not ready to talk to them yet. I've gotta get my head straight."

"What will help you do that?"

"I need a lawyer."

"I hope you don't mean me."

"I know you can't, but if I had some money . . . if the Drummonds really cared about Laura . . ."

"You want the Drummonds to pay for your lawyer?"

"Show some goodwill, you know?" Hannah heard a commotion in the background, a pounding noise and then a blast of music and noise. Now she could picture where Kurt might be: a phone in some bar. He was hogging it, pissing someone off. "Look, I gotta go. I'll call you back about this." And before she could name a time, he hung up.

She took the phone into the living room, in case Guillermo tried again. After an hour, she went to bed, sure he wouldn't. He was on a plane by now, probably a DC-3, and therefore phoneless. She lay awake, wondering why Laura would tell Kurt a bald-faced lie about Matthew's paternity. The tests were valid. They had to be. There was no way a lab would have come up with a result that showed Kurt to be the father and then somehow converted it to become Hoskins.

What Kurt said about a blowup with Laura's mother worried her. There was no sign of a wife at Gerald Lawrence's house. She couldn't remember Laura or Lawrence ever mentioning her.

She got up and left a voice-mail message about Kurt for Churnin. She would have to tell the Drummonds about his proposal in the morning, but she doubted they'd consider it. It smacked of blackmail. But what did Kurt have to use against them?

Kurt had talked about Laura's mother, but when he described the other parent, he'd said *the* father. Not Laura's father—not Gerald Lawrence, necessarily. So whose father, then? Matthew's father? The one who was not Hoskins?

She went back to bed, tossed for another hour, then got up, dressed in a sweater and jeans, and drove to the office. The building was white and somber as a tombstone, the lobby and hallways hot and still. She shook off a shiver of apprehension as she faced the elevators and opted for the stairs to the third floor.

Vera's recordkeeping was impeccable, and in a moment she had Jerome Hoskins's file, including the home number. Four in the morning would be too early for most people to be up, but not a broker whose work was dictated by New York. He wouldn't be happy, but he'd be awake. She dialed the number.

After three rings, a recording clicked on. The number was not in service. No new number. A wave of panic lapped at her. Had Laura convinced Hoskins to say he was the father when he wasn't? She was about to dial the direct-line office number Hoskins gave her, but stopped and instead called San Francisco information. She got the number for Rowan & Luana. In a moment she found herself listening to a voice-mail announcement. She spelled out Hoskins's name on the telephone keypad. A recorded voice announced that this was Jerome Hoskins's line, and she could leave a message. She did, and then waited.

She stretched out on the sofa but couldn't relax enough to sleep. Laura's lies, as profuse and fast-growing as kudzu, wound their way around her thoughts. When they were pushed out of the way, she found herself thinking about Feuer. She couldn't go on avoiding his calls. He didn't deserve that kind of treatment. She went to her desk and dialed his number. She knew he wouldn't be asleep. He would be reading. She could see him in his second-chance living room, with Heinlein or Asimov, living in the future.

When she said she was sorry for not returning his calls, he didn't say anything for a moment. She liked that about him. He not only listened to what she said, but what she didn't say.

"So you've patched things up with this man you weren't sure about."

"I hope it's more than a patch."

"And now you're sure about having him live with you?"

"No. But I want to do it anyway. Leap of faith."

"You must have been running a little short of faith the other afternoon, when you were here."

"I'm not proud of that. I'm sorry, Dan. I didn't mean to hurt you."

"Didn't hurt. I sort of liked it."

She didn't say anything.

"So," he said. "You're not interested in keeping a safety net, just in case this leap doesn't work out?"

"It's not fair to you, or him."

He was quiet again. "You're fighting yourself. You know that."

She had to laugh. "But I'm determined to win this time."

There was another pause. "Well, I think that means I'm the loser. I'm sorry I didn't get to you before this other guy. I've got the worst timing."

"It wasn't your timing. It was me. Listen, I appreciate what you did. Telling me what you heard about Laura Benson."

"I could have used a little more appreciation."

She had to smile. An honest acknowledgment of the *quid pro quo* they'd been dancing around. "Is that what you were doing when you called me? Tossing out screw bait?"

He sighed. "No. A little, maybe. Anyway, I hope you can do something for the poor girl. And for God's sake, don't rat me out."

"You either."

"Never. Does this guy know how lucky he is?"

"I'm not sure he's lucky."

"Be sure. He's damned lucky." He hung up.

She went back to the sofa, and started to doze. But then she thought of what she could say to Guillermo to make him understand and forgive her. Had he ever done something like that? She didn't know. She thought of all the things she didn't know about Guillermo, and—worse yet—the things she did know: He was an obsessive tidier. He was a bit of a pedant, particularly when you got him started on copyright infringement. He had timidly mentioned a liking for cats. He knew all the words to the *Partridge Family* theme song. What the hell was she doing?

At seven, Hoskins's secretary called back. He had recently moved, and had not forwarded his home number for personal reasons, she said. No, Hannah couldn't speak to him right now. He was vacationing. No, she couldn't say where. Exasperation lurked behind the secretary's professional-perfect phone voice. She had passed on Ms. Barlow's other calls, and would do so with this one.

So Hoskins hadn't disappeared off the fact of the earth. He had merely moved—the marriage, of course. The vacation probably was his honeymoon. Hannah slouched in the chair and touched her back—cold and clammy. Sleepless, sweaty, stomach in knots—all in anticipation of some awful discovery about Hoskins. She should have known not to get worked up about anything Laura told Kurt. Laura lied, fluently and without provocation. So did Kurt. Maybe, after making love, she'd told him, once and for all, that he was not Matthew's father. And hearing that, he killed her.

Vera, arriving at nine, tactfully offered no comment on Hannah's dishevelment. She went home, took a shower, and dressed for the rest of the workday. With any luck, Guillermo might find a working telephone in the weavers' village. Hearing his voice would go a long way toward calming her.

19

The Drummonds were waiting when she went back to work. Vera caught Hannah's eye and raised her brows—they'd been there awhile. Hannah shook their hands: Stephen's warm and dry, Rebecca's chilled, shaking slightly. She looked terrible: dull skin, eyes gray with sleeplessness. She was wearing a straight-cut burgundy knit dress, which rode on knees that seemed bonier than ever to Hannah.

"I didn't expect you," Hannah said. She was furious with them for talking to Churnin without her. She would have liked a few minutes to prepare a stern lecture.

Rebecca ventured a smile. "No reason you would. Can you spare us some time?"

"Yes. I need to talk to you, too."

In Hannah's office, Rebecca chose the chair next to Hannah's desk and skimmed her fingers through her hair and along her scarred cheek. Stephen sat on the sofa and unbuttoned his suit jacket. Most men had developed a bit of paunch by his age, but Drummond's fitted shirt was snug over a flat stomach. His trips to the gym were obviously paying off. He glanced at Rebecca as they sat there, and Hannah saw his concern for her, as well as her refusal to acknowledge it.

"You didn't tell me you talked to Ivan Churnin," Hannah said.

Rebecca's face colored. Drummond shrugged.

"No big deal," he said. "We've got nothing to hide."

"I didn't say you did. But what point is there in having a

lawyer if you're not going to consult her? In case you haven't noticed, Ivan Churnin considers you prime suspects."

Rebecca's eyes slid closed. "I told you, Stephen."

"Not now." Drummond sat back in his chair and folded his arms. "We didn't do anything. We're innocent people. Innocent people don't go trooping into police stations with lawyers in tow. Maybe guilty people do."

"And you identified Laura's body, I understand."

"Yes. Someone had to, and her father wouldn't. It was me, or Rebecca. I didn't think she should have to do that. It was bad enough for someone who's been around death."

"What about Kurt? Why didn't you let him do it?"

"Kurt told them to fuck off. Pretty cold, I'd say. Her father and husband left her lying there, unclaimed. Like a suitcase."

Hannah put her pen down and regarded them: Stephen, blustering, cocky, but with an obvious tenderness for Rebecca, as well as a somewhat clinical, but real, compassion for Laura. Rebecca, as she had been since the explosion, seemed slightly glazed, still trying to piece together her shattered world.

"Let's understand something, Stephen. If you get another phone call from Detective Churnin, I want you to refer him to me or Bobby. If you can't do that, I think you'd better find some other lawyers."

"We're sorry," Rebecca said. "This is all new to us. And I'm sorry about my mother. She—"

"Your mother?" Stephen turned to her. "What's she got to do with this?"

"I went to talk to her," Hannah said.

"What for?"

Hannah didn't answer him.

"Now you're checking up on us?"

"If you want to put it that way."

"So our word isn't good enought for you?" He was glaring at her, enjoying the turned tables of trust.

Rebecca interrupted before Hannah could say anything. "It's her job, Stephen. It wouldn't have done her much good if she told us in advance she was going to do it. You'd have told her not to."

"You can get another lawyer, Stephen." Hannah almost relished the idea of never seeing him again. But there was Matthew. "I have to do what I think is necessary, just in case Churnin comes after you."

He sighed. "I understand what you're doing, Hannah, but I'm sure all of this is moot. Churnin won't—"

"He might, And if he does, what's going to happen?"

"I'm going to call you or Bobby."

"Fine." She felt like she'd mended a dam with chewing gum. "Now, what can I do for you?"

Stephen cleared his throat, a hint of nervousness, and began.

"Through friends, I've heard some things I wanted to ask you about."

"Go on."

"The handwriting in her suicide note has been authenticated. Is that correct?"

"I don't know. You have friends in the police department?"

Stephen's face colored. "My family has been here a long time. My mother knew a lot of people. There are relationships that—" He stopped and looked at her, as though asking if he needed to go on.

He didn't. Hannah heard that Mary Catherine Drummond had pull—she'd used her influence to keep out of Las Almas what she saw as unsavory elements: strip clubs, public housing. She didn't know that the woman had juice from beyond the grave. She was surprised Stephen was willing to trade on it.

"What else have your sources told you?"

"That the flex line from the stove had been pulled out, typically a method of suicide. She died of asphyxiation."

She. He wouldn't even say Laura's name. "I've heard about the same thing," Hannah said. "I'm not sure the police are completely satisfied with suicide as an explanation."

"They shouldn't be," he said.

"You were so sure it was, not long ago."

"I was wrong." The phrase wasn't typically in his repertoire.

"We got another phone call," Stephen said. "Like the one I got that night."

He meant the night Laura died. "A hang-up call?"

He nodded. "It had to be Kurt. He called back a few minutes later. He had the guts to say who it was, this time. He told this incoherent story about enemies she had made."

"Laura?"

He nodded. "He said she'd threatened her mother, and there was something about her father, too."

"Her father? He didn't say 'the father'?"

"He could have. I don't remember. He wasn't making much sense."

"Did he say anything else about Laura? Anything that hinted at him killing her?"

"No. But I'm afraid we're next on his list."

"Did he threaten you?"

"Not in so many words."

"Did he ask you for money?"

"Money? Why would he?"

Hannah told them about Kurt's plea for legal help. When she had finished, Rebecca sighed and shook her head. Stephen snorted dismissively.

"We wouldn't spend a penny to keep Kurt out of jail. That's where he belongs. I think he did kill her."

"And the note?"

"Maybe he made her write it to cover himself. In any event, I'm afraid of what he might do. He's likely to show up and try to take Matthew by force."

"Maybe. Do you want to get a restraining order?"

"How much use is that?" Rebecca said.

Hannah shrugged. "It's what the law has to offer."

"For people who care about the law, that's fine," Stephen said. "I don't think Kurt is anyone's idea of a model citizen."

"But it's what we should do, right? If there's a restraining order, and he violates it, he goes to jail?" That's what Rebecca wanted.

"That's how it works," Hannah said.

"Then do it," Stephen said.

"What's bothering us is the part about Laura having enemies," Rebecca said. "Who are these enemies?"

"I don't know," Hannah said. "Kurt could be bluffing, trying to divert the police's attention to someone else."

"That's just what he's doing," Stephen said.

Rebecca shook her head. "But what if it's not? What if Laura's mother, or her father, or whoever Kurt is talking about, really did kill her? What does that mean for Matthew?"

"You're getting worked up for no reason," Stephen said. "That's what Kurt wants."

"You wanted me to find out what things Laura hadn't told you?" Hannah said. "I could still do that. We could lay those fears to rest. Either Kurt is bluffing or he's not."

"We could help you," Rebecca said. "We'll give you whatever help we can in reconstructing her life before we met her."

"Rebecca, I don't . . ." Stephen looked uneasy.

"It's completely up to you two," Hannah said. Rebecca wanted to know what Laura had been covering up. Stephen seemed to prefer letting all her secrets rot with her.

"Okay," he said finally.

"We can give you some things to start with," Rebecca said. "A letter we wrote, the ads that ran. A message she left us. Come to dinner, you and Bobby. We've taken a lot out of you lately."

Hannah wondered if Vera had mailed out the client bills. Once they got their latest statement, they'd be the ones feeling drained. Matthew's security hadn't come cheap.

"We'd be happy to come," Hannah said. "If you're not sick of us."

Rebecca shook her head. "Never that. You're godsends, both of you."

Stephen was looking at his watch. He tapped his fingernail against the crystal.

"One last thing." Hannah said to him. "Tell me again what Kurt said about Laura."

He repeated it: there was some kind of mess with Laura's

mother. And then there was her father. Or the father. Kurt had used almost the same words with Hannah. Only God knew where the path of Laura's life would lead. She wondered if the Drummonds had considered that.

"I don't know why Laura lied so much about her life," Hannah said. "She could have had good reasons for keeping her secrets. Are you and Stephen sure you want to know what they are? You might not like what I find out about her."

Rebecca nodded fiercely. Stephen was looking out the window. She was driving this, Hannah thought. Stephen had already eradicated Laura's name from his vocabulary, a step toward erasing her completely.

"Stephen, you want to know everything?"

He seemed to be minutely examining the leaves and branches of the jacaranda outside.

"I don't ever want to go through what we did that day here, when Kurt showed up," he said finally. His jaw was tight, the way it had been when Hannah told them about Kurt's first visit with Matthew. "I don't want to know, but I think I have to. It's the only way to make sure that our son doesn't have any shadows hanging over his life."

"Okay, Hannah said. "What kind of wine should we bring to dinner?"

Stephen Drummond favored her with a smile—the warmest one he'd ever given her.

"Something good—you can afford it. We just paid your bill."

20

The Rebecca Drummond who opened the door to Hannah and Bobby two nights later, wearing a loose raw-silk tunic and pants in a shade of coral, was a woman transformed. She seemed rested, peaceful. A portable phone was in her hand.

"Stephen will be down in a minute. And my parents have invited themselves, but they won't stay late." She took the bottle of 1995 Château Mouton Rothschild that Hannah had pried out of Bobby's oenophilic grasp. "Help yourselves to a drink." She gestured to a collection of bottles on a sideboard in the living room. "I'm just finishing up a phone call with my construction supervisor. Crisis at a house in Monarch Bay."

Bobby sized up the offerings and picked one out. "Want to try this one? Condrieu."

Hannah nodded. She could hear snatches of the supervisor's tinny, panicked voice as Rebecca walked by. She was trying to calm him.

"Okay, so there's a little creek under there. Yes, the soils test was a crock. We know that now." Rebecca mouthed an apology to Hannah and pointed to a plate of smoked-salmon appetizers. "We'll deal with it. I told you how. The Kappe house in Pacific Palisades turned out to be a masterpiece. The same system will work for us. You get so rattled when things don't go the way you expect. Sometimes you have to think on your feet. Okay? Good. Call me if you need me." She hung up and shook her head. "Sorry."

"No problem," Hannah said. "It sounds like you've gone back to work."

Rebecca smiled. "Part-time. But it's good to be on a project again."

"Hey, give me a hand with this little project." Stephen was standing in the entryway. Anneke was next to him, balancing a giggling Matthew on her shoulders. The baby saw Rebecca and chattered to her, finishing the unintelligible patter with an aria: Mama, mama, mama, on a rising note. Rebecca went to him and tickled his feet. He let out a shrill, delighted laugh. Anneke watched, a look of professional approval on her face.

This is how it should have been from the beginning, Hannah thought. A baby, a mother, and a father. A tight weave of family and love.

Stephen lifted Matthew from Anneke's shoulders and handed him to Rebecca. "We're just going to put him down for the night," he said. "You'll excuse us?"

Matthew's gurgles faded as his parents carried him up the stairs. Anneke trailed them.

"Looks like Anneke is fitting right in," Bobby said.

"I've had a good feeling about her since she placekicked Kurt's privates into the courthouse pool," Hannah said.

"The Drummonds are pretty lucky, really." Bobby got up from the sofa to examine a picture of the three on a side table.

Hannah laughed. "Let's see: a nearly botched adoption, a crazed would-be birth father, explosion injuries, dead birth mother, threatening letter, anonymous phone calls. That's your notion of luck?"

He put down the picture, collected her glass, and poured more wine. "It hasn't been easy, but now they have what they've always wanted. You think we'll ever have that? Be that happy?"

Hannah shrugged. "Maybe. Aren't you happy now?"

"Oh, I suppose. But I'm not getting any younger. I'd like a family, I think." Bobby smiled. "Are you still avoiding permanent pair bonding?"

She thought about Guillermo, who at that moment

probably was praying for dear life as a bus swayed around a mountain curve in the Guatemalan highlands. There would be adjustments she'd have to make when he came back. It would take practice to break her habits of solitude and selfishness. The panic that took her to Dan Feuer still worried her. She thought it possible that she was using Guillermo, that he was the body and the voice and patient spirit she needed to fill up the hollow core of her heart. That notion—of using him up to salve her wounds—bothered her. But maybe it was what everyone did, to some degree.

"Hannah?"

"I'm reconsidering my position."

Bobby nodded enthusiastically. "That's good. What brought about this epiphany?"

"I'm not sure that's what it is. I'm just trying to keep an open mind. Be flexible, like Rebecca said."

He offered a toast. "To flexibility."

Rebecca's parents arrived just before eight. Hannah and Bobby heard them talking over each other in the foyer. An older man's voice demanded to see Matthew, if only to kiss his dear forehead. They went up, and came down a few minutes later. Maura was first, followed by her husband. She was talking over her shoulder at her daughter about diapers and teething. And was a nanny really necessary? She of course meant that she hadn't been overwhelmed by her brood.

Frank Malone clomped into the living room. He showed his age more than Maura did and was tanned to mahogany from work on construction sites—his was not a generation for sunscreen. Thin white hair fringed his skull. His short-sleeved plaid shirt had a pocket over either breast: one for eyeglasses, the other for a tobacco pouch. He and Stephen barely looked at each other as they took up chairs at opposite ends of the room.

Maura smiled a hello to Bobby, with a slightly chillier nod to Hannah. Frank was more gallant. He got up and took Hannah's hand.

"Tough job you've got with this crew," he said.

"I don't mind," Hannah said. He was so much friendlier than Maura, who had taken her place in the womb chair and declined a glass of wine. Hannah could see her disapproval of Rebecca's decorating scheme. Some nice Laura Ashley print would have suited her. Hannah turned her attention back to Frank.

"Rebecca's been through a lot."

"Haven't seen her really happy since the last time she stopped by the house," he said.

"When was that?"

"That very day, when little Matthew's mom died. She brought him over for a visit."

"How long?"

He shrugged. "An hour? Not long enough." Then he pulled out a yellowed meerschaum pipe. When Rebecca gently told him he couldn't smoke inside, he held it clamped, unlit, in his teeth and sulked.

Maura had watched Hannah talking to Frank. Now she turned to her daughter and squinted. "Becky, where's your medal?"

Rebecca's face colored. "I don't know, Mom."

"I don't see the statue, either."

The references went over Bobby's head, but Hannah understood. They were talking about the medal and statue of Saint Gerard, patron of mothers and childbirth. Gifts from Maura, apparently.

Stephen gleefully turned to Maura. "She got rid of the damn things."

But Rebecca hadn't gotten rid of the medal, not until recently, anyway. She'd been wearing it the day of Kurt's first visitation with Matthew. Had Rebecca put it on thinking it would guard her baby? Maybe she was so sure of losing him that she had begun praying for another child to take his place. Hannah wondered what made her stop wearing it.

Maura drew herself up and cocked an eyebrow at her son-in-law. "It's a wonder God gave you a child at all. You wouldn't think to ask for his help. Too proud to even offer up a prayer."

"Praying to a statue and wearing a medal didn't bring us Matthew, nor did the stork, Maura. I don't believe in any that stuff."

Family fights, Hannah thought, should not be served to guests before dinner. Or after, for that matter. Bobby was suddenly interested in a coffee-table book on mid-century furnishings.

"Rebecca believes," Maura said. "And you should thank God for her faith. You were granted a child, even if wasn't one of your own."

Frank Malone locked his eyes on Stephen. "A little prayer wouldn't hurt, son. Wouldn't you like a little fellow who looks like you, no offense to young Matthew." He spoke in what he thought was a whisper and gestured with his pipe. Flakes of tobacco fell on the pristine carpet. "My nephew went through this. Unable, you know, for years. But now, thanks be to God, there's three children. And another on the way. You should . . ."

Rebecca was on her feet then, trying to stop whatever advice was coming next. "I think dinner's probably ready. Shall we?" Not a minute too soon, Hannah thought. Stephen looked like he wanted to stuff the pipe down the old man's throat.

Rebecca arranged it so that her father was far away from Stephen. Maura was at Hannah's left, and even if she hated her daughter's lawyer, she made polite-enough conversation. But she threw Rebecca steely maternal glances every now and then. More fertility-producing religious artifacts would be arriving soon, Hannah felt sure.

Bobby steered the talk onto safe topics. He drew Stephen into a discussion about the best Japanese restaurants in Orange County, laughed appreciatively as Frank shared his naked horror of raw fish, and nudged Maura into a description of her mother's quirky Galway relatives, a bunch of hapless fishermen. Impotence and infertility, Laura and Kurt, Saint Gerard and God—all were left behind, thanks to Bobby's deft conversation.

It was Frank who ventured back to family, with his love of Matthew. He compared the boy favorably with his other grandchildren in height, humor, and intelligence. Unlike Stephen's mother, adoption didn't seem to bother him. But Maura offered nothing but a forced smile. An odd time for a grandparent to go silent, Hannah thought.

As Frank chattered on, oiled by Bobby's expensive wine, Hannah had a hard time keeping track of all the sons, daughters, and grandchildren. For the first time she realized how difficult it must have been for the childless Drummonds to endure Christmases and suffer through birthdays. It would have felt like being pressed with a hot brand, every time. *B,* for barren.

The Malones obviously hoped that prayer and manly resolve might produce a Malone-Drummond grandchild for them. But that didn't matter to the Drummonds. Rebecca could finally laugh and listen as her son was named in her father's proud litanies. Matthew was just as loved as any of them. And finally, she belonged to that sisterhood, that charmed circle: the tribe of mothers.

Hannah watched as Rebecca's eyes fell on the snapshots of her son on the sideboard. The pictures were set in tiny silver frames, shapes from the history of architecture. In one, Matthew became a caryatid, holding up his share of the Parthenon. He stood on the dome of the Hagia Sophia, scuffed leaves on the stairs at Monticello, and splashed in the stream at Fallingwater. Boy as foundation and keystone.

The conversation ebbed as the Malones wolfed down the strawberry shortcake Rebecca served. They declined the invitation to stay for coffee in the living room. They had to be up early for a grandson's stage debut as a caterpillar. As Rebecca walked them to the door Stephen collapsed in the Eames lounge chair and rubbed the heels of his hands into his eyes.

"I could just barely handle them at Christmas and Thanksgiving. Now we see them at least twice a month."

Bobby shrugged. "I suppose they mean well."

"And I suppose they could keep their speculation about my sexual functioning to themselves."

Rebecca overheard that, and suddenly the good humor of the dinner seeped away. She sat in the red Saarinen chair.

Her finger danced along her scar, as if to reassure herself that it was still there. She stopped when she saw Hannah watching her.

"They seem very fond of Matthew," Hannah said, stretching Frank's fondness to encompass Maura's meager reaction to the boy. "Do you still want to tell us about finding him, and Laura?"

Rebecca nodded. "What happened is our own fault. Laura duped us, but only because we let her. We told Barkin to look into her background, but I think he knew how much we wanted the adoption to happen."

"It's no excuse," Stephen said. "When he gets back, I'm going to—"

"Stephen. Litigation is beside the point. We were ultimately responsible, not Barkin. We let our need for a baby cloud our thinking. That was a mistake. We realize now that we didn't know Laura at all. Everything was a lie, except how much she loved Matthew."

"How did you meet her?" Hannah asked.

Stephen handed her a photo album. "This started out as something we'd show potential birth mothers. Later, after we found her—"

"Laura?" Hannah said. She was determined to make him use her name.

"Yes. We turned it into a kind of scrapbook after that. A record of the journey to Matthew, I guess."

"Is this everything?" Hannah hefted it, and it seemed a skimpy archive.

"God no. That's just up to the point of meeting Laura. We have a file cabinet full of stuff, out in Rebecca's office."

Hannah and Bobby sat down on the sofa next to each other and opened the book. On the first page was a letter, handwritten on pale yellow paper with a floral watermark. In a picture at the top right, Stephen and Rebecca sat on the lawn in their backyard, holding hands and smiling.

> Hello!
> We are Stephen and Rebecca, both native Californians from happy families. We live in a beautiful house

with lots of room in the backyard for a child to run, play, and keep a pet—a dog or maybe even a pony! Unfortunately, our infertility has prevented us from having children of our own.

We have successful professional lives, but more than anything, we want to bring a child into our home. Your baby would grow up in a family that loves to go hiking, skiing, and camping. Each summer Stephen's family takes a cottage on the beach, where we spend the days swimming and beachcombing. At night we sing around the campfire. Your baby would grow up in a warm, loving environment, receive a wonderful education, and enjoy the results of our hard work as a doctor (Stephen) and an architect (Rebecca).

If we can help you, please call us, collect if you like, at the number we've listed. We want to talk to you.

"We sent out hundreds of these," Rebecca said. "Stephen got a national list of OB/GYNS and sent one, with a cover letter, to every one on it, right?"

He nodded.

"Was that how Laura came to you? She called you here after getting one of these letters?" Hannah said.

"Not here." Stephen got up and poured himself a glass of wine. "I had a second line installed at the office. I didn't want to run the risk of someone being able to trace the number to this house. We could have been robbed. You never—"

"Stephen, just tell Hannah what happened." Rebecca's patience seemed strained. Hannah had a glimpse of how resistant he must have been to the adoption. Reaching out to strangers, owing them, trusting them—it was not in his nature.

"We got a few nibbles, even one woman who said her daughter was pregnant and wanted to meet us," he said. "But nothing panned out. If any mother had shown up, we would have given her the book."

Hannah nodded. On the next page, there were pictures of the Drummonds' house and photographs of people Hannah guessed to be their families. Bobby was right about the Sears-Armani split between the Malones and the Drummonds. On another page, there stood Stephen, dressed in the height of early-eighties fashion. Hannah recognized his brother, Martin, despite the full head of shaggy hair and the drooping mustache.

"Martin was working at ACT then," Stephen said.

"That's when you lived together?"

"The Animal House, south of Market, before the neighborhood was trendy," Stephen said. "Marty was always bringing home stray would-be actors. What a bunch."

Next to the snapshot was a photograph of Rebecca, standing in front of a church, surrounded by men and women. All of them looked like her.

"The Malone clan," she said.

"What was the occasion?" Bobby said.

"Um. My penance?" She gave a halfhearted smile. "When we found out we couldn't . . ." She looked to Stephen, who stared at his hands. "I thought that we were being punished somehow."

"Rebecca," he said. "You know it's not your—"

"That's not what I mean. I'm not talking about who . . . malfunctioned." The word hung there like spider.

"I'll get more coffee." He picked up the carafe from the table and went into the kitchen. With a muttered apology to the guests, Rebecca went after him.

Stephen refused to tell Barkin which of them was infertile, but between Frank Malone's comments, Rebecca's remark, and Stephen's reaction, Hannah thought she could guess. As Rebecca artlessly put it, Stephen's equipment had broken down.

Hannah and Bobby exchanged a glance. They could hear the couple's voices, hushed but intense. So much for perfect happiness, Hannah thought. Matthew hadn't cured the wound of infertility. He could only soothe it, put a layer of relief over his parents' loss. He was their son in spirit, but in skin, blood, and gene, he wasn't. Rebecca would never see her father in Matthew's eyes. Stephen would never catch the shadow of Mary Catherine Drummond's haughtiness on his son's lips. She wondered if they had come to terms with that.

The Drummonds were back. Rebecca slid into her chair, and Stephen sat next to her on the ottoman. She tenderly took his hand. Stephen was so cocky and short-tempered sometimes that it was easy to overlook his pain. People made a fuss over women who couldn't conceive, mourning the tragedy of a womb unfilled. They didn't offer men the same solace. No one lamented sickly sperm, or wept over a kink in testicular ductwork. Frank Malone probably wasn't the only one who'd offered Stephen unsolicited advice. There had undoubtedly been the usual jokes about Stephen shooting blanks. And even Rebecca had found a word to wound him.

"This is always hard for us," Rebecca said, as though she knew what Hannah was thinking. "No one really knows what it's like for people who can't have children. You start to avoid couples who do. Baby showers are terrible. At one point I'd rather have walked through fire than go to one."

"Rebecca, no apologies are necessary," Bobby said.

"Anyway, this picture. I started going to church again. Praying, asking God to let us have a baby. My family didn't know then, about our problem. So they were just ecstatic I was going to mass. They surprised me that Sunday. I put the picture in because our first lawyer told us that some birth mothers like a couple to have a faith, go to church."

She swallowed before going on. "I should have taken it out of the book. I was just going to church to make a deal with God. My faith wasn't real. You have to be real with birth mothers, so they'll be real with you. Jennifer's mother . . ."

Stephen stiffened. From his reaction, Hannah knew that Jennifer was the baby they adopted, and lost. Another taboo topic, another name, like Laura's, that shouldn't be spoken.

"Rebecca," he said. "We don't have to go into all this."

"It's okay. You know we tried to adopt once before?"

Hannah nodded. "That's about all I know."

Stephen shifted in his chair. "I don't think—"

"No," Rebecca said. "Let me tell them what happened." My God, Hannah thought, she is determined to flay herself. "The girl, the birth mother, the one our first lawyer found for us, she was very young. And desperate."

"She was sixteen," Stephen said. "Lived in a trailer park in Cudahy. Which is about as bad as it sounds. She swore up and down that she wanted to do the adoption. And she wanted to 'cut it off clean.'"

Hannah felt a shiver, hearing her own thoughts about adoption echoed.

"She told us she didn't want any contact with the baby," Rebecca said. "Didn't even want to see it after the delivery. She wanted to get on with her life. And that was just what we wanted to hear. What a fantasy: suddenly there's a baby, and she's ours. Our Jennifer was perfect."

She had been steady up until then. But now her face crumpled.

"Rebecca, it's okay. You don't have to go on," Bobby said.

"No. I want to. Two months after Jennifer was born, her mother changed her mind. Just like that, no explanation. She wanted Jennifer back. She was marrying her boyfriend, and they wanted to raise their baby together. God knows how they're doing it on McDonald's wages." The expression on her face told Hannah that Rebecca could see them: scraping by with a crappy car and living in a cheap apartment that smelled of rancid frying oil.

"It was within the ninety-day window?" Bobby asked.

Stephen nodded. "The Slug—that's what we called our first lawyer—had told us not to worry about those three months. It's scary, sure, he said, but most birth moms didn't change their minds. It was a very, very slight risk, at best. But he didn't know this girl. The Slug told us to give it up. We could spend a fortune, try to win her back, but it would be brutal. We would have to show her mother was unfit, showing that the father was degenerate."

"Which could have been true," Rebecca said.

"Which would have entailed thousands of dollars in legal

fees for the Slug, and not much hope for us," Stephen said. "We had gambled. We lost. We gave Jennifer back."

Rebecca only glanced at her husband. But it was enough for Hannah to see that she would have been willing to spend every dime for Jennifer. A part of Rebecca hated Stephen for not going along. But the fight would have sapped them financially and turned Jennifer's infancy into a bloody battlefield. In the end they would have lost. Courts tended to favor biological families.

She felt a pang for the Drummonds. They weren't easy to know, and now she understood why. They were riddled with loss. Fine threads of hope had frayed and snapped and been rewoven. They only wanted a child of their own. And look what it got them so far.

"I can't imagine what that was like for you," Hannah said.

"I was a wreck, no matter what Stephen did for me. We blamed the lawyer, we blamed Jennifer's mother. We blamed each other." She didn't mention the separation. Nor did Stephen.

"It's the worst thing I'd ever been through," he said. "But Kurt topped it, that day in your office."

Rebecca sighed. "I'm just telling you this because Jennifer's mother wasn't honest with herself, or us. She never wanted to give Jennifer up. We pretended we didn't know that. That was why that adoption failed. We decided, when we tried again, not to make those mistakes again."

"Amen," Stephen said.

There was a silence. Hannah watched as Bobby turned to the next pages, which held columns of classified advertising from different newspapers. On each clip, one ad had been circled—Rebecca and Stephen's ad, a variation on their letter:

ADOPTION

Are you worried about your unborn child's future? We are a loving couple who can offer your baby a home full of joy and warmth. We love the outdoors, fresh air, and trips to the

mountains and seashore. We can give a child a
wonderful home and an excellent education, but
more than anything, we can give your baby a
secure and loving future. Please call us collect if
we can help you.

"It's a different number," Hannah said.

"We had a second line put in here," Rebecca said. "I think
having them call an office was a bad idea."

Stephen got up and poured himself some wine. If it was
a rebuke, he didn't seem bothered by it.

They had placed the ad in *USA Today,* and a scattering of
smaller out-of-state newspapers. Their ad wasn't the only
one, Hannah saw. All around it were similar entreaties.
There were advertisements for fertility clinics and invitations for women to consider surrogacy. The science and
strategy of being a parent, Hannah thought. Out of the
bedroom and into the classifieds.

"That's about it," Stephen said as she began to flip to the
empty back pages. "Is there still a cassette in the back
pocket of the album?"

There was. Stephen put it into the Nakamichi tape player.
After a high-pitched beep, Laura Benson's voice filled the
room.

"Hello? Umm. I saw your ad, about adoption? And . . .
God, this is weird. Sorry. I'd like to talk to you about . . .
what you said? About helping? I could come down
and . . ."

The sounds of a bar—clinking glasses and a call for a
Red Hook Rye Beer—masked what Laura said next. There
was music in the background, too. But not bar music.
Something with a piano and cello.

"Sorry. It's loud here," Laura said. "I could be there
tomorrow, if that's okay? Okay. Bye. Oh, God. My name is
Laura. Laura Benson. I'll call back in an hour or so to see
if you're there? Okay? Bye."

"Did you send her the book?" Bobby hefted the album.

"No," Stephen said. "She said she didn't need to see it.
We never even had a number for her. Now I know why. We

would have known she was in Seattle, not San Francisco. She called back and said she'd like to come meet us. She was at Barkin's office the next day at noon. Took a cab from John Wayne Airport. She said she didn't want to inconvenience us."

"She didn't want you to see her getting off a Seattle flight," Hannah said.

"That's right. And so there she was, about six months pregnant. We went out to lunch."

"She was nice," Rebecca said.

"She was an actress, and we bought her performance," Stephen said.

"What did you talk about?" Bobby asked.

"Well, Barkin thought it was a bad idea to hit her with hardball questions right off, so we just let her tell us about herself, kind of the way she wanted to," Rebecca said. "She told us that she expected us to check on her background. We told her we trusted her, of course, but we'd do what was necessary.

"She mentioned a place she'd worked while she was in Seattle for a couple months. It was a restaurant where a friend of mine had done some interior redesign. So I called up there." She paused, frowning. "I should have known, right then. The manager had never heard of Laura Benson. It was like I'd imagined her. I thought for a second I'd dialed the wrong restaurant, but I hadn't. The manager just didn't know any Laura Benson."

"What did you do?" Hannah said.

"Nothing," Stephen said. "Rebecca didn't have the nerve to confront her."

"I didn't want to make her think I'd been skulking around behind her back," Rebecca said.

"Rebecca didn't want to make a big deal, as she put it. But I insisted, and Barkin took care of it," Stephen said. "Laura said she'd worked there under another name. It was a messy situation: a guy had been stalking her at another job, and she felt like she had to change her name, keep different hours at a different place, to keep away from him."

Laura Lawrence to Laura Benson to someone else,

Hannah thought. Who was she, really, when you peeled back the lies?

"Laura was really apologetic, when we talked to her about it," Rebecca said. "She told me that if I'd only asked her before I called, she could have explained everything."

"Was Kurt stalking her?"

"She didn't say who it was. Just a guy, and not the baby's father. She told Barkin the name she'd used, he called the place back, and the manager confirmed it," Stephen said. "She worked there as Claudia Bengstrom."

"So we thought it was just a misunderstanding," Rebecca said. "We didn't worry."

Hannah thought she saw how it was for them: despite the loss of Jennifer, they were once again caught up in baby fever. There was a child in Laura, and that baby could be theirs. They couldn't let themselves distrust her.

"What else did Laura tell you?"

"Something I wouldn't have ever guessed," Rebecca said. "We went to lunch one day, after she moved down here. We wanted to have her nearby, with our doctor. We were at Piret's, giggling and laughing like kids, talking about when we were little. She already told us about her parents: that her father, Gerry, was a drunk. That her mom, Evelyn, was sort of a bitch. She looked right at me and said: 'Sometimes I wondered how much worse my real parents could have been.'"

Hannah nodded. Somehow the news didn't surprise her. "So Laura was adopted."

"She wouldn't talk much about it. She said her adoptive parents were cold and secretive. They thought she was boy-crazy, from the age of eleven. They didn't trust her, kept thinking she was in the back of a car with some pimply guy.

"She didn't understand the reason until she found out by accident that she was adopted. She was fifteen then. That's why they treated her as though she were a slut—they were afraid she'd turn out like her birth mother. She asked—"

"She demanded, she said," Stephen interjected. "She

demanded their help in finding her birth parents, but they wouldn't."

But someone had decided to help: the author of the burned letter apparently knew who Laura's family was. Maybe when Kurt talked about Laura's relationship with her mother and father, he meant her birth parents, not the Lawrences. Maybe Laura found the birth parents. Had she wound up dead as a result? Hannah considered telling the Drummonds about the charred letter. But she wasn't ready to explain to them—or Bobby—that she'd found it by rifling Churnin's files.

"Did Laura say if she found her parents?"

"I don't think she did," Rebecca said. "She had this illusion—that they were warm and loving. Everything she thought her adoptive parents weren't."

"It's a pretty typical fantasy," Stephen said. "Every adopted kid thinks his parents were famous and perfect. Laura probably thought she was the result of a one-nighter between Marilyn Monroe and JFK. Or, given Laura's age, maybe Bill Clinton and Madonna."

Bobby started to chuckle, but swallowed it in a gulp of wine when he saw how Rebecca's expression had soured.

"Laura suffered from not knowing who she was," she said. "That's hardly a matter for cheap shots."

Stephen's face flushed, and Hannah thought a fight was going to erupt. Instead, he reached over and stroked her hair.

"Sorry. Too much wine. More coffee for anyone?"

"I'll help," Bobby said.

When they were gone, Rebecca continued. "We were concerned about Laura being adopted because of any possible medical problems she might not know about. We told her that. But her parents had a blind medical history, from the adoption agency that placed her. She gave us that, and records from her family doctor until she was sixteen."

"May I see that history?" Hannah said. "There might be something in it that we can use."

Stephen was back with coffee. "It's in Rebecca's office. I'll get it."

"Laura said she managed to get one piece of information

from her mother, but it wasn't much use," Rebecca said after he left. "Her birth mother's name was Ellen. She couldn't get very far with just a first name. She had nothing about her birth father. Her parentage was a hole in her life that she didn't think she could fill, and that's why she was so glad when we agreed to an open adoption."

Bobby arrived with cream and sugar. "Why did you agree to it, Rebecca? It seems like a complication most people would want to avoid, if they could."

"That's how we looked at it, at first. We did it because of what Laura went through. She told us how it felt to be lied to for all those years. Her adoptive parents kept up an illusion that she was theirs, but she had this feeling she didn't belong in that house. And then, to find out when you're fifteen? It undercut all the trust. You couldn't hear her story and not be affected."

Stephen came back with the file and handed it to Hannah.

"Laura had a bad time, no question. But I thought open adoption was a bad idea from the start," he said. "You can share a kid's background with them without keeping the birth mother in the middle of your life. I should have been more emphatic."

It came perilously close to blaming Rebecca for everything that had happened. She stared at him, but said nothing. Hannah concentrated on Laura's file.

Laura's parents, whoever they were, had been blessed with good health. There were none of the serious illnesses that coursed through successive generations, the fear of every adoptive parent. Laura had the usual maladies: measles, mumps, and chicken pox, but nothing serious. Not even a tonsillectomy.

"We said we'd consider some openness in the adoption. It was important to her," Rebecca said when Hannah was done reading. "We studied some books about it. I wanted to go to classes, some counseling, and get some counseling for Laura, too, but Stephen . . ."

Stephen shrugged. "The Slug was a jerky lawyer in lots of ways, but he said something that made sense to me: 'The problem's not in your head, or the mom's. It's in your plumbing, and her tummy.' He was right. We didn't need a lot of psychological mumbo jumbo. We needed Matthew."

"Well, anyway, I began to see why we should keep the lines of communication open with Matthew's birth family," Rebecca said. "Why do you think Laura turned out to be someone who lied, who couldn't connect, who picked the wrong husband? We had the chance to make sure that wasn't going to happen to Matthew."

"Was it a deal breaker?" Hannah said, as gently as she could.

Rebecca frowned at her. "What do you mean?"

"I mean, did Laura say that if she couldn't stay in touch with Matthew, she wouldn't go ahead with the adoption?"

"She never said that."

But, Hannah thought, it was implied. She was almost sure the message was there, running through all of Laura's dealings with the Drummonds. Rebecca had talked herself into believing it was the right thing to do. And Stephen, for all his second-guessing now, had gone along, rather than risk losing the child.

"I'd like to go to Seattle, and see what I can find out in a day or so," Hannah said. "That's where Laura and Kurt supposedly made some enemies. I'm also curious about where she called you from, that first time. Could I hear that tape again?"

"Sure."

She sat on the floor by a speaker and strained to hear the music in the background. Before Guillermo left, he had been force-feeding her his latest musical passion: twentieth-century Russian composers. Listen to this, he'd said, putting on a sonata for cello and piano. The composer, who saw his career rise and fall at the whim of Communist-party chiefs, had captured the small-minded brutality of the apparatchiks in every icy, precise note. Hannah was certain she was listening to that Shostakovich sonata now—the background music to Laura's first appearance in the Drummonds' lives.

21

Hannah booked a Seattle flight for the next afternoon. In the morning, she went again to see Gerald Lawrence. Déjà vu: he glared at her, started to slam the door. Hannah pushed her hand against it and started talking.

"I'm sorry about your loss, Mr. Lawrence. You didn't give me the chance to tell you why I was here that day, when Laura still was alive. She was my client."

"I don't give a—"

"I still represent the couple that adopted her baby—your grandson."

Lawrence was as gnarled as the first time she had seen him, but seemed weaker. His face was flavescent, the color of eggy, uncooked dough. And whether it was illness or curiosity about his grandson, she saw his resistance wavering.

"Go on," he said.

"When Laura died, she left a lot of questions about her background. The people who adopted Laura's baby want the answers, for his sake. She didn't tell them everything."

He stopped trying to wrestle the door shut. "I doubt she told them anything that was the truth."

"The police don't really know what happened at her apartment, Mr. Lawrence. The lies she told could be the reason she's dead. I know you weren't close."

He made a disgusted noise.

"But even if you were at odds when she died, you did raise her. You didn't bring her up to have her killed."

The fight went out of him at that. He gaped at Hannah. "It was suicide."

"My clients are concerned that it might have been murder, and that it involves Laura's son. Their son, now."

"When they told me suicide, I couldn't see it." He let the door swing open. "You might as well come in."

He led her into a narrow, low-ceilinged room with teak paneling and built-in bookcases. Only the picture window onto the little yard ruined the illusion of a yacht's cabin.

"Killing other people with her cruelty, that was Laura's style." Lawrence sat down. His eyes worked their way across one of the bookshelves. Pictures of a woman were enshrined there, along with a low glass bowl in which a white gardenia floated. As an altar, it lacked only burning candles. So Laura's mother was dead. That's why no one talked about her.

"Laura and her mother didn't get along?"

He shook his head. "It's what killed her, Laura's running away, then promising to come back, then taking money and disappearing again. We gave her everything, hoping, every time, that it would be enough."

"That was where she got the car, then," Hannah said.

"What car?"

"The Fiat."

"A black one?"

Hannah nodded. "Laura told my associate that you bought it for her."

He wiped his mouth, and Hannah thought for a moment that he was going to vomit.

"Mr. Lawrence?"

"I didn't buy it for her. That was something my wife might have done."

"So she died recently?"

"No."

"Then how—"

"It was what Evelyn might have done, I said. But she's dead, so she couldn't have. I don't know how Laura got it, or why she said I bought it for her. I never understood why she did anything. She sat right there, where you are, the last time she was in this house, five years ago, and told Evelyn she never loved her and only loved her real mother. Real mother. As though she had any idea what being a mother meant." Lawrence got up unsteadily. "I don't want to talk about this anymore. Please, leave me alone."

Hannah brought the picture out of her jacket pocket. "This is Laura's son. His name is Matthew. Someday he might want to know you. Just as Laura went looking for her birth family, he might come to you."

Lawrence stared at the picture for a moment, and then gently took it from Hannah's fingers. He slowly closed his eyes and opened them again, as if expecting the picture to change somehow. He handed it back to her.

"It will be less painful for everyone if you will talk to me about Laura," Hannah said. "Matthew's parents can tell him, when the time's right."

Lawrence nodded. "I don't want to be hounded, do you understand?"

"Yes."

"I'll tell you, you tell his parents—because they are his parents now, no one else—and they can tell him what they want. But then I want to be left alone. I'm nothing to him."

He led Hannah upstairs and opened the door on a room that must have been Laura's: white canopy bed, wicker furniture, pom-poms, and a stuffed bear wearing a shirt that said WILSON HIGH. Lawrence stood at the door and pointed at the pictures on the dresser: Laura's prom. Her sailing-school graduation. The St. Mary's Auxiliary Ball. Hannah couldn't imagine Laura as a debutante, but here was the proof.

The woman in the shrine downstairs was in many of the photographs. She was big, with thick arms and a round face. Blond, with brown eyes, like Laura's. Except for their bodies, one lithe, one full, no one would have guessed they weren't related.

"You and Mrs. Lawrence have no other children?"

He shook his head. "We tried for years. It wasn't quite like it is now, so high-tech and all. When we heard about Laura, we were thrilled."

"How did you hear about her? Was it through friends, or—"

"No. We used Blessed Sacrament. An agency. It was in Santa Monica, but it's gone now. It's a dying business, now that girls have abortions all the time, or raffle off their babies to the highest bidder."

"Was Ellen Catholic?" She watched for the reaction to the birth mother's name, the only thing Evelyn had shared with Laura. There was a flicker in his eyes.

"You mean Evelyn? My wife?"

"Laura told my clients that her birth mother's name was Ellen. Your wife told her that much, she said."

He shook his head. "She couldn't have. We never knew the birth mother's name, or her religion."

Was that true? Was Ellen just a name Evelyn Lawrence made up, to make it seem that she was cooperating in Laura's quest? Hannah wondered why she would have bothered.

"She didn't know she was adopted until she was fifteen, my clients said. That she found out then." She tried not to make it sound like a criticism.

Lawrence looked around his daughter's room for a moment. "Are you finished here?"

Hannah nodded, and he led her back downstairs.

He settled into the chair next to Evelyn's pictures.

"It wasn't my idea, keeping it from her," he said. "But it wasn't as important to me as it was to Evelyn. Evelyn wanted a baby of her own. And when we got Laura, she wanted to pretend that Laura was really ours. I didn't see the harm in it. We didn't know who the birth mother was. We just knew she didn't want Laura. We did. We sat up nights with her when she was sick, and fed her and clothed her. She was ours, no one else's."

"What happened when Laura found out?"

He got up and shuffled into the kitchen, as though Evelyn shouldn't be subjected to this part of story. Hannah followed him and watched as he poured out two glasses of Glenmorangie. It was barely ten in the morning, so maybe Laura had told the truth about her father's problem with alcohol. But judging from the house, the furnishings, and his choice of Scotch, she could see that the rest of the poor-childhood story was a lie. Lawrence seemed to be retired, and Hannah wondered what he'd done to earn his expensive cottage. He slid the glass to her and sat down at the kitchen table.

"Laura was hurt and confused when she found out. We tried to tell her why we'd done it that way, not telling her, but she refused to understand. Didn't really make an effort to. Laura was wild. Headstrong. Always battling with her mother. I think in some way, it pleased her."

"Why?"

"It gave her a weapon. 'You can't tell me what to do. You're not my *real* mother. I'm going to go live with my *real* mother.' It cut Evelyn to the quick."

"Even though Laura didn't know who her mother was."

"She expected us to help her—we owed it to her, she said. That's all she talked about. We didn't know who the girl was, so we didn't see how we were supposed to help. The agency would only give out general information: how old the girl was, that she was white, and healthy. We told Laura she had been in a spot of trouble, probably, and she had probably gotten on with her life."

"That didn't wash with Laura, I suppose."

"No. Everything changed. Laura quit school when she was seventeen and moved out. She turned up every six months or so, usually asking for money. She was using it to find her mother, she told Evelyn. She wanted so much to have Laura back, she'd have done anything. She gave Laura whatever she wanted. God knows what Laura did with the money. It went up her nose, I imagine."

"The cocaine, you mean."

"She was thin as a rail the last time I saw her. Fast-talking, irritable."

"And did Laura ever find her mother?"

He drew himself up indignantly. "Her mother—both her parents—were right here, all the time."

Hannah blushed at her gaffe. "It was a stupid thing to say. I'm sorry. I should have asked if Laura found her birth mother."

"Said she did, but I don't know if it's true. Maybe she just said it to punish us."

• • •

Hannah was on her way out when she saw the stack of invitations on a hall table: Committee to Elect Susan Beckett, with Lawrence's return address. Laura said politics was a business that made her sick.

"Are you involved in the campaign, Mr. Lawrence?"

"I advise Susan, from time to time. I'm retired, officially, but I managed campaigns for years. Now I just give pointers to the young guys. I do some for Susan because of her dad."

"Her dad?"

"Bill Beckett. Senator Beckett."

Laura had called Bill Beckett. Hearing his title, Hannah remembered him: U.S. senator, now retired. He'd started as a sixties radical—a minor-league Abby Hoffman/Tom Hayden type—and matured into a lesser-rank liberal in the mold of Teddy Kennedy or Daniel Moynihan. Hannah remembered his daughter's slogan, painted on the sign in the lawn: Values Family, Family Values. That hardly sounded like second-generation Chicago Seven thinking.

"But his daughter's not a Democrat, is she?"

"God no. That would be the kiss of death in most of Orange County."

"That's where she's running, not here?"

"Right. I put the sign up to annoy my liberal neighbors. Susan's Republican. Neoconservative, with a feminist-libertarian twist."

"What does that mean?"

"She believes women are equal to men, but should make it on their own. No affirmative action, or whining sexual-harassment lawsuits. That's 'radical lesbian crap.' Her words, not mine."

She'd be a hit in some segments of Orange County, all right, Hannah thought. "Does it bother Bill Beckett that you're working for someone who's diametrically opposed to everything he stands for? Even if it is his daughter?"

"No. Bill's not the fire-breather he used to be. He's still liberal, of course, compared to Susan. But times have tempered him. It's what happens with age. But he still raises a lot of money for Democratic candidates. Susan helps."

"Why?"

"Reciprocity. Remember when Timothy Leary and G. Gordon Liddy debated? Or Rose Bird against Robert Bork? That's what the Becketts do. It's a political road show: right versus left, young versus old, man versus woman, daughter versus daddy."

"It sounds weird."

"No. People eat it up. Susan does a great riff on how her father sent her away to school for a classic liberal education and how she came back as a cross between Phyllis Schlafly and Arianna Huffington and bit him on his ideological butt. They get their points across, they each make money for their party's causes."

"Laura called him."

"That's what the police told me, but I can't believe it. Christ, the last time she saw him, she was only eleven or so. It was some party at Bill's house."

"Why would she call him, then? At his house? How did she even get the number?"

Lawrence shrugged and opened the door for her. "I don't know."

Outside, the wind had come up, turning the day unseasonably cold. It brimmed with the scent of salt and ocean. Hannah breathed deeply, expelling the air of regret and loneliness from Lawrence's house.

"She also said she hated politics," Hannah said. "That's why I wondered why she'd be calling Beckett, someone associated with you, if she——"

"She did hate the business, and me. As I said, I don't know why she called him." He put out his hand and smiled mildly at her, employing the expression she would have expected from someone who knew how to gracefully usher out a small-check contributor. "Thanks for coming."

"I know it can't be pleasant to talk about Laura and your wife. But it is important for my clients, and their son."

"It was my pleasure. Good-bye." The door shut, and she was alone on the canal's walkway.

She sat down on the bench opposite Lawrence's front door and looked at the color campaign poster stuck in the lawn. Susan Beckett was one of the cookie-cutter true-believer Republican women that could be found at any political gathering in Orange County. Hannah wondered if there was a training college for them at the Nixon Library. Susan Beckett was blond—maybe not a natural one, judging by her eyes and the color of her brows and lashes. Her hair was slightly teased, then heavily sprayed. An hommage perhaps to Pat Nixon, the mother of all California Republican women. Susan Beckett's makeup was professionally perfect, but overdone. There was too much eyebrow pencil, and the lipstick was bloodstain red, as if she'd just bit someone in the neck. Her red suit was the same shade. She smiled just enough to show she had very white, strong teeth. Hannah leaned forward to study the face. Had she ever met Susan Beckett?

The wind came up, shuddering the poster. The motion seemed to animate the face. There was something around the mouth, a tension there. Laughter would be a release of pressure, not an expression of joy.

Hannah knew then. She'd never met Susan, but she knew someone who had inherited those features, that same tense smile. It was an intuition only, but one that fit in with the other pieces she had.

Laura Benson was adopted. Her adoptive mother claimed to know nothing about the birth mother, but then gives Laura her first name. A fake one, obviously, to placate her. Years later, for no apparent reason, Laura calls the last number she probably had for Susan Beckett, the number at the senator's house. Suddenly Laura has a new car, a gift expensive enough to imply love—or a payoff. Then Laura tells Kurt something about her mother "that could have blown up." And that was the thing that didn't fit. Pinning a scarlet letter on a woman like Susan Beckett would be a disastrous political strategy. The only thing that could ruin her political career would be the revelation of an abortion. Adoption, on the other hand, was practically a sacrament in conservative circles. So why wasn't the selfless surrender of her daughter, Laura, the diamond-bright centerpiece of Susan Beckett's conservative political career?

22

The campaign worker clearly had been to Happy College. She'd be delighted to take Ms. Barlow's message, she announced cheerfully. And the reason for her call?

"Please tell her it's regarding Laura Benson," Hannah said. The Seattle flight was boarding, and since it was on an airline that eschewed reserved seats, Hannah would have to fight to find one on an aisle. She didn't feel like playing twenty questions.

"And that would be who?" A cheerleader at Happy College, Hannah decided. But the question showed that Laura hadn't been a fixture at her mother's campaign headquarters, stuffing envelopes or calling the faithful to remind them to vote.

"Ms. Beckett knows who it is. Would you ask her to call me as soon as possible?"

"Okay." The worker crooned the word, three notes of discouragement. "But Susan is extremely busy, as I'm sure you can understand. So if you could tell me what this is regarding . . ."

"Susan will know what it's regarding. If you'd ask her to call me, please."

"Of course." The perkiness was gone, replaced by a chilly facade of courtesy. Postgraduate courses at Icy-Bitch U. "I'll see that she gets the message."

Sure, Hannah thought. Hearing the final boarding call, she gave herself the satisfaction of hanging up first.

As the plane landed at Sea-Tac, Hannah was glad to see

that for once, Seattle wasn't blanketed in rain. The sun was shining, but to Hannah's thin California blood, the weather seemed more than a little brisk. The sun-deprived children of the Northwest, however, walked the streets near Pike Place Market in shirtsleeves and shorts. Hannah thought she recognized Pike Place Fish as the spot that had served as backdrop for Laura and Kurt's wedding picture. Hannah had some smoked salmon shipped to Bobby and showed the picture to the fishmongers while she waited for her change. But the happy couple was unknown to them.

Two blocks away, within sight of Elliott Bay, Hannah found the restaurant where Laura had worked, as Claudia Bengstrom.

Phuket was in the lull between lunch and dinner. And although the name and cuisine were Thai, the restaurant's decor crossed the border to the rest of Asia. A shakuhachi flute and koto moaned over the stereo system. The waitresses wore baggy black silk pants and diaphanous blouses in a bamboo print. Hannah asked to see the manager and glanced at the menu while she waited. This was no white-carton take-out joint. Laura might have made decent tip money here.

The manager met Hannah at the bar. He was in his fifties, his crag turning to sag. His appearance was not enhanced by the dirty-blond hair and undernourished ponytail that trailed down the back of his maroon silk tunic. He introduced himself as Philip, nodded recognition at Claudia's name, and showed an unbecoming coolness at the news of her death.

"She was a good employee. Pretty, nice with customers." Philip summoned a waiter. "I'm having some chicken satay before it gets too crazy in here. Care to join me? No? Some tea, then."

"You didn't know she was using a fake name?"

"Not at first, and I was not happy to find out. By the time that lawyer called, of course, she'd already split. What was the real name again?"

"Laura Benson. She told my clients that she used a fake

name because a guy was harassing her. Did you see anything like that while she was here?"

"No. Not with her husband around."

"So you knew Kurt?"

"Knew? No. Saw him enough times, though. He picked her up at closing, every night. If she had any scary ex-boyfriends around, Kurt would have handled it. Kind of a sour guy, if you ask me."

"Was Claudia—Laura—afraid of him?"

"Nah." A waiter brought the tea and Philip poured it out with a flourish. The scent of ginger and jasmine curled up from the glazed cups. "Seemed to me she had him tied up in knots for her."

Philip had rightly read half their relationship. She wondered what he knew about the other half. "He beat her up a couple times," she said. "Got arrested for it."

"Really." He contemplated that for a moment as the satay was set down before him. "She did come in one night with a bruise under her eye. I heard one of the girls asking her about it, and she said she'd fallen on some stairs."

Hannah sipped at the tea. He read her silence as a rebuke. "Look, I'm just the boss, not the den mother."

"Did Laura seem nervous about anyone else? Kurt has hinted that they had enemies."

"If she was running from somebody, it explains how she quit. If you want to call what she did tendering her resignation.

"It was a Friday. She was working as hostess, because the regular girl was sick. People were packed at the bar like a rush-hour ferry to Bainbridge Island, and what did she do? Bolted. Phone ringing, people calling for tables, and she bolted.

"Took off in the goddamn uniform, which costs more than two hundred bucks. She never called, never came back. Not even for her last check, in which I'd just given her a raise. Thankless little . . ." His voice trailed off.

"Do you have your reservation book for that night?"

He nodded. "I keep all that stuff. Just a minute."

He opened it to the day Laura walked out of Phuket for

the last time. Hannah ran her finger down the reservations for nine o'clock: Rogers, Huang, Serrano, Fiedler, and something starting Wester. . . . It was in pencil, and half-erased. She couldn't make out the rest of it.

"Do you recognize this last one?"

He shook his head. "It doesn't sound like anyone I know as a regular."

Hannah listened to the Japanese music in the background as it worked its way through a pentatonic cadence and faded to silence.

"Do you play classical music here?"

He blinked at the change of topic. "Classical Chinese, Balinese. World music that fits in with the ambience."

"Not Russian, though."

"We don't serve blini or caviar, so no. We have a theme going, as you may have noticed."

"No Stravinksy, Prokofiev, Shostakovich . . ."

"No. That's Tom's place."

"Who's Tom?"

"Esterhaz. From what you were describing, I thought you knew the place."

"No."

"It's supposed to be a kind of hip joke. Only a history major would name a place the 900 Days. And it would only make money in a city where the sun doesn't come out for months at a time."

"It's a restaurant?"

"God no. A bar. Who'd eat in a place named for the siege of Leningrad? You know what went on there, right? You look like an intelligent-type woman."

"People starved. They ate whatever they could, even . . ."

"Right. That's why Tom doesn't serve ribs. Stoli and slivovitz. And lattes, of course. Pseudo-intellectual student types like the place."

"And did Laura—Claudia—hang out there?"

"Don't know. Hang on. Mai?"

A wisp of a black-haired young woman in the Phuket uniform did a U-turn a few feet away and came to the table.

"You knew Claudia Bengstrom, before she ducked out of here?"

She nodded and fiddled with her tray. "Kind of. We worked the same shifts."

"Did she hang out at Esterhaz's place?"

She blinked at him in surprise. "It was her other job."

He shrugged. "Like I said, I'm only the boss." He reached for Mai's order pad and scribbled an address. "900 Days is up in Fremont. It's a kind of hippy, retro, groovy neighborhood, wouldn't you say, Mai?"

She nodded. "And a nuclear-free zone."

"That's a relief," Hannah said.

"Take a left after you cross Suicide Bridge," the manager said.

"It's really called that?"

"No. Aurora Bridge. But since it's a hundred thirty-five feet down to Lake Union and people jump off it fairly regularly . . ."

Hannah nodded. "You're not at all curious about how she died?"

"Who's dead?" Mai said.

"Claudia," Philip said.

Mai clapped her hand to her mouth. "My God. What happened?"

That was what Hannah would have expected from Philip. "She might have been murdered," Hannah said. "Maybe by Kurt."

"Jeez." Despite the bronzer Philip had slathered on his face, his pallor faded. "Guess I read him all wrong."

"It's not clear. There was a note. She might have killed herself." Hannah sketched the details of the explosion at the loft in Las Almas.

"She could have done it up here, a nice swan dive from Suicide Bridge. Saved herself the seventy-nine-dollar airfare."

Mai shook her head as he left. "He's still pissed that she wouldn't sleep with him. Told him she wasn't settling for scraps anymore. I don't think he liked that." She stopped before saying any more: Philip was staring at her.

• • •

Outside, it was clouding over. Hannah bought a plain coffee—probably a misdemeanor in Seattle—at SBC and found a pay phone. The proprietors of O So Strong had never called her back. She got the answering machine and left a message. Then she called the office. Vera had only one message for her: call Rebecca Drummond.

She answered on the first ring, letting a second pass before she said hello. Her voice was hushed, hesitant.

"Rebecca? Are you all right?"

"Hannah. I don't know what to do. It's the calls. They've started again. Now it's twice a night, at least."

"It's Kurt?"

"It has to be. He never says anything, though. Just hangs up."

"Haven't you changed your number?"

"Of course, but he got it somehow."

"Have you called Detective Churnin?"

"Yes, but Stephen's out of his mind with this. He doesn't want me to use my office at night."

Hannah nodded. The Bauhaus pavilion was isolated, too full of windows to be safe. She wasn't sure it was even on the alarm system.

"Stephen hired a new security company, with its own patrols and armed response," Rebecca said. "He listed you and Bobby as contacts, in case something happens. I hope that's okay."

"It's okay."

There was a pause, Rebecca grappling with her last piece of news. "He signed us up for a class, too.

Hannah knew what kind of class.

"He bought three guns, Hannah. For us, and for Anneke. We're learning to use them this weekend."

Some people were perfectly capable of having guns at home. Hannah's father was one of those. Hannah had been, for most of her life. She'd learned to shoot with her father and, as a cop, carried a gun daily for years and knew its value. She knew that no one in the Drummond household—particularly Rebecca—should have a loaded weapon at hand. Stephen was too angry, and Rebecca too frightened to use a gun safely.

But before she could say any of that, Rebecca's voice dropped to a whisper. "Stephen just came home. Please, call him when you get back. See what you can do."

The line went dead. Talk Stephen out of protecting his son and family? That wasn't likely, even if she could cite him statistics. The most she could hope for was a good shooting instructor. A coolheaded type would see Rebecca's tendency to panic and calm her down. Even the most macho NRA type would sense Stephen's rage and, maybe, scare some sense into him.

23

At dusk, the rain began. Hannah ducked inside the 900 Days and let her eyes adjust to a room as dim as winter on the steppes. Hannah was fairly sure she was in the right place, and the music on the stereo clinched it: Prokofiev, the final triumphal chorus from *Alexander Nevsky*.

The bartender raised an eyebrow at her request for decaf and told her that Tom Esterhaz was on his way in. She picked a table near the door and a few seconds later a slip of a young man—no more than a teenager—dripped past her. Five-ten, barely one hundred twenty-five pounds, Hannah guessed. A smooth, beardless face and, when he smiled, braces. The bartender didn't card him. He did point Hannah out. The kid grabbed a mug of coffee and came to her table.

"You're the boss?"

Esterhaz put out his hand. "I can't wait till I look my age."

"Someday you'll wish you never said that," Hannah replied.

Esterhaz draped his denim jacket over a chair and sat down. Hannah took out a picture of Laura and handed it to him.

"Claudia. You a cop?"

"No. A lawyer. I represent the people who adopted Claudia's baby. Claudia wasn't her real name, you know. And she's dead."

Esterhaz shrugged. "Listen, I'm sorry to hear that, but

nothing about Claudia surprises me, least of all the news that she didn't make it to Social Security. I just knew I'd wind up having a conversation like this."

"Why do you say that?"

"I should have pegged her as trouble right away, hearing she lived at the Bridge—what a rathole. Then there was the way she used the pay phone. Every damn minute, she was calling or getting called. I switched it to outgoing-only finally. And the last straw was that crazy-assed woman who came in here, screaming to see her. I was going to fire her. But she quit first."

"Slow down a bit. Who came in here after her?"

"She was in her forties, I'd guess. Looked like my mother the Deadhead—a touch of gray, but still tie-dyed, you know? She was just wild-eyed and shaking mad. She said Claudia gave our number as her home phone, and she'd been trying to call her, but with the outgoing-only, she couldn't get through. God knows how she found the address. She barreled in here, wanting to know where the hell her baby was. So there really was a baby?"

"Yes. She said 'her baby'?"

"Yeah. It made no sense to me. I figured it was some code for coke or something. Claudia, did she OD?"

Hannah shook her head. Kurt had been telling the truth: Laura had indeed made an enemy. She promised Matthew to someone else, and didn't deliver. Jesus.

"What happened with the woman?"

"I told her I didn't know nothin' about birthin' babies, but she didn't get the joke and really got whipped up in a lather. I told her to stop making a scene in my place. I was about to call the cops when she slapped a card on the bar and told me to call her if Claudia ever showed her lying face in here again.

"When Claudia came in for her shift, I told her to keep her druggie friends out of here, but she pretended not to know what I was talking about. The whole thing freaked me out, and the next day I was set to tell her not to come back. But she didn't show up, so that was that."

"Do you still have the card?" Hannah asked.

"Does a historian ever throw away primary source material? I kept it in case there was a hassle later."

Esterhaz brought a gray box out from behind the bar. He flipped through it and pulled out a rectangle of pink paper, crimped at the edges, with a teddy bear in the corner, a phone number, and a line of precious, curlicued script. *The Westerlands, waiting with open arms.* Wester-somebody had a reservation at Phuket on Laura's last night there. That was why she'd quit so abruptly. The Westerlands' arms were open, all right, and their fists clenched.

"Mind if I use your phone?"

"If it's to track down Claudia, it would be poetic justice," Esterhaz said.

Hannah fingered the raised outlines of the embossed teddy bear on the card as she waited for the call to connect. But the number was out of service.

"No good? Try the Bridge Motel." Esterhaz held out her coat for her. "I'll bet they remember her over there."

The Bridge was aptly, unimaginatively named. It sat on a busy street near Lake Union, the last in a string of sodden, sad buildings before Suicide Bridge. Its twin, a motel called the Daybreak—Tough Break would have been more like it—was on the other side of a parking lot that was mostly mud and potholes. Neither place was a motel you would pick for your out-of-town guests, unless you wanted them to be propositioned, harassed, or mugged.

They did remember Claudia at the Bridge. At least the night manager did. She introduced herself as Mrs. Odegaard—Hannah could call her Mrs. O, everyone did. It had been her dad's place. He died a month before, and now it was hers.

"I'm going to clean it up, make it respectable," she said. Hannah nodded. Had Mrs. O ever heard of the Augean stables?

She walked Hannah into a mildewy office without asking why she was there. Maybe, like Esterhaz, she just assumed Hannah was a cop. Hence the promised cleanup.

She offered Hannah a choice: cappuccino, coffee, latte? Hannah chose the last—there was no point arguing with

Seattle's caffeine-based lifeforms. She watched as Mrs. O bustled at the machine. Hannah guessed her to be in her late fifties. Her bike shorts and tank top showed a body that age was taking in the direction of skin and tendons, rather than soft fat. She had watery blue eyes and pale almond-colored hair stiff as cotton candy.

She put down Hannah's drink and looked at Laura's picture.

"Yup. Claudia Bengstrom."

"Laura Benson, actually. Or Laura Lawrence. She changed names fairly often."

Mrs. O just nodded. The initial friendliness faded slightly. She didn't seem to appreciate the implied criticism of Laura. Hannah ignored the chill in the air and explained: Matthew's adoption, Kurt's arrival, Laura's death. The news that Esterhaz had expected seemed to hit this woman like a freight train. She fingered the picture tenderly.

"The poor thing. She and Kurt lived here for about a year. Was Kurt involved?"

"Maybe. Did you hear them fight?"

She shook her head. "I worked days then, mostly. Went home to look after my son's kids at night. I knew they had problems, but I would have done something if I thought Kurt was hurting her. I didn't like Kurt much."

The two paid their rent more or less on time, she said. But then they were late, and Mrs. O discovered that Kurt was in jail. Claudia couldn't swing the rent on her own. Mrs. O cut Claudia the break she pleaded for—without telling her dad, who believed in rent by the tenth, slack for none.

Then, a little while later, this guy started paying for the room. She didn't get his name, but he was fortyish, burly, on the tall side, with thinning blond hair. Had him some nice wheels. American, not that foreign crap. The man came on the first of the month, for three months, and slapped the rent down. He seemed happy as hell about it, and wanted receipts. Why would that be?

Mrs. O seemed several watts short in the illumination department. But nice enough. Hannah waited for what else she might have seen.

"He could have been a relative of theirs, though," she offered.

"Why do you say that?"

"He brought groceries—milk and fresh fruit. And presents, in little-kid wrapping paper. Claudia didn't have any kids up there."

Not any that were detached from an umbilical cord, Hannah thought. If Mrs. O hadn't figured out what was going on, she was going to have a hell of a time clearing her motel of its dodgier guests.

"When she and Kurt left, all the presents were still in the room. I took them to my son's house. He said it wasn't anything he could use. Then the guy showed up. I told him they'd moved out, and he just lost it. Ran down to the room, kicked in the door. I had to threaten him with the cops to get him to cool down."

"You have no idea of his name, though?"

"Nope. Think he mighta been a short-order cook of some kind. Smelled like bacon sometimes."

Hannah filed that away. "Would you know his name if you heard it? Was it Westerland, maybe?"

"Dunno. Was he family?"

Hannah shook her head. "Only in the sense that he thought Laura was going to make him a dad." The stacks of clutter gave her an idea. "Do you have a phone book from a couple years ago around here?"

Mrs. O rifled the top of a filing cabinet and pulled one out. Then she clapped her hand to her mouth. The light dawns, Hannah thought.

"Claudia was pregnant? Christ, she didn't look it at all. She and Kurt were gonna give that guy their baby?"

Were they? It was a good question, Hannah thought. Laura and Kurt obviously offered a baby to the Westerlands as a way to get their rent and food bills paid. Then they disappeared. But was Matthew the baby in question? Did Laura and Kurt always intend to scam the Westerlands, or did they just get cold feet? She ran her finger down the pages of *W*s in the phone book, and found it. Connie and Edmund Westerland.

Mrs. O peered over her shoulder. "Up in Ballard. You want directions?"

Ballard was technically a suburb of Seattle, but it kept its own character—a slice of Scandinavia on Puget Sound. On Ballard Avenue, where Hannah looked for someplace that a short-order cook might have worked, she discovered she could have had herring a dozen ways, or crossed lutefisk off her list of foods to try before she died. On the third block she tried, there was a retro-looking coffee shop with a Norwegian flag. Connie's Cup. She asked a waitress if the owner was around.

"The new guy? Or did you want to see Ed?"

It didn't take long to hear the story: Ed Westerland's family had owned the place for years, and he'd just sold it. The new owner didn't know where Ed had gone—maybe to someplace down in Southern California? He wasn't sure. Ed didn't talk much after Connie left him.

She thanked him and went to the Westerlands' house.

The house had probably been nice once. But now the paint on the gutters was peeling off in strips, like sunburned skin. The For Sale sign was only marginally taller than the uncut, weedy lawn. The pungent smell of the local cats' markings hovered near the front door. As she'd expected, no one answered her knock. She peered in the narrow window next to the door. It looked as if the Westerlands had engaged in a furious argument and then just walked out. Newspapers cluttered the coffee table in the living room. In the dining room, the door to the sideboard swung open, and smashed plates and glasses lay on the floor beside it. It looked like the set of *Who's Afraid of Virginia Woolf?*

Hannah glanced across the street in time to see a curtain stir. God bless nosy neighbors.

A young mother answered her knock, a sleeping baby on her shoulder and a toddler tugging at her oversized T-shirt. The mother had the hungry look of someone for whom even a crumb of adult conversation would be a feast. She told Hannah what she knew about the Westerlands. Connie was an avionics technician at Boeing—had been, anyway, she didn't know what she was doing now. Ed inherited the house and the coffee shop from his folks. He was always quiet and standoffish, even when her husband tried the usual conversation openers: their trucks, hunting, or how the Sonics were doing that season. Connie was like that, too. Quiet. Sad, almost. But the Westerlands didn't tell the neighbors what the trouble was. Then, for a while, they seemed to brighten. A baby was on the way, Connie said. And then, a few months later, the house was vacant, the couple gone.

"Was it the baby?" The young woman's brow furrowed, and she pulled her infant closer. "Did they lose it?"

Hannah nodded. She wondered if the Westerlands had decided that Laura, the instrument of their loss, should pay the price for that.

24

Her flight didn't leave until ten that night, and she wondered if Mrs. O could reconstruct the time frame of Laura's pregnancy, now that the scales had fallen from her eyes. First, she got a salmon burger at a health-food restaurant's drive-through and sat in the rental car, eating it and watching the flow of people through the motel's parking lot.

Every community has a spiritual and geographic center, and in this simulacrum of a town square, the residents of the Bridge and the Daybreak mingled, shared beers, and smoked cigarettes. A few people aborted their handshakes when they saw Hannah. They would have to pass their goods later. Hannah dropped her eyes and wondered if she would ever stop looking like a cop. It was a drawback, sometimes. She feigned disinterest, finished her food, and walked to the motel office.

Mrs. O was there, pulling a double shift.

"Mrs. O, do you remember when Kurt went to jail? When he and Claudia stopped paying the rent?"

She pulled on her lip for a moment. "My dad kept records pretty good. Let's see."

She pulled down a ledger book. "Rent was due on the first. They always paid late, but Dad didn't start hassling people till the tenth. This says he gave Laura notice at the end of September. She told me Kurt had been arrested a couple weeks before. That would make it mid-September."

"And Kurt was gone for how long?"

"Came back around Christmas, seems to me."

Hannah did the math. Matthew was conceived in late October, by Laura's account. He was born, healthy and full-term, at the end of August. Even if you discounted the DNA—and that was quite a markdown—Kurt had a larger problem: the length of human gestation. Matthew was born too late to be conceived by Kurt before he went to jail. He came too early to be fathered by Kurt after his release.

So it was back to Hoskins. But now Hannah wondered: if Laura was so broke, how did she have money to traipse off to San Francisco for a Halloween fling? Maybe there was more to Laura's relationship with Jerome Hoskins than either had been willing to admit. Maybe he'd visited her in Seattle, then paid for her trip to see him. The waitress at Phuket said Laura turned down Philip, the manager, because she wasn't settling for scraps. A stock broker was definitely a five-course meal.

"Did you ever see Laura with this guy?" Hannah showed Mrs. O the picture Jerome Hoskins had supplied with his blood sample.

Mrs. O raised her eyebrows and pointed her finger toward the door. "I can see the cars parking and watch the stairs from right here, and I made it my business to keep an eye on Laura when Kurt was in jail. I'd have known if she brought some guy to her room."

Hannah's eyes followed the neon-polished nail. Mrs. O kept an eye on her own motel, but what about the Daybreak?

"One more thing," Hannah said. "When did the big guy start paying the rent?"

She screwed up her face in concentration, then snapped her fingers.

"I'm amazing, at my age. It was October fifteenth. My grandbaby's first birthday. He congratulated me on how cute she was."

So when Laura and Kurt promised Ed and Connie a baby, she probably wasn't even pregnant. It was a scam, the kind Bobby had described to Hannah: a mother fakes pregnancy, promises a naive couple a baby to adopt, takes them for as much money she can get, and then skips. Kurt had hinted that they'd run the scam before. The Westerlands were only the most recent victims. The most tenacious. What Kurt apparently didn't know was that this time the game had changed. Laura really had gotten pregnant—without telling him. This time she was running a scam of her own.

Hannah thanked Mrs. O and started to leave.

"Hey, wait a second," she said. "I've got some of the stuff Claudia—Laura—left in the room. I sort of hoped she might come back for it. I always liked her, you know? I never had a daughter."

Be grateful you never had a daughter like Laura, Hannah thought.

"Would her little boy want some of this, you know, someday?"

"Sure," Hannah said. Mrs. O brought back an envelope crammed with snapshots. Maybe there were pictures of the Westerlands inside. Hannah quickly flicked through the pictures. Nothing resembling the two as they were described to her. She should have asked the neighbor what kind of truck they had. But then she realized: Mrs. O knew.

"The big guy drove a truck. Do you remember the make or the color?"

She popped some kernels of caramel corn in her mouth and chewed noisily. "Mmm. It was American, old. A classic. A Dodge, maybe? But the color I remember for sure. Flame orange. A Waikiki sunset."

The truck that followed Laura on the day Kurt showed up at the law office. Kurt might be paranoid, but in this case, he was right. Somebody was after Laura.

At the Daybreak, the nodding-off clerk could barely rouse himself to look at the pictures of Laura and Hoskins. Here, Hannah thought, was the one person in Seattle who could actually benefit from a jolt of the local beverage.

He didn't recognize Hoskins. He thought Laura looked familiar. But he couldn't remember if Laura had stayed at the motel in October. Did Hannah think he was a fucking concierge? Hannah did not. She pulled out two twenties and a ten, and although his eyes didn't widen from slits, he produced a stack of guest register cards and shambled into the back office as Hannah skimmed them.

She was looking for Benson, Lawrence, Bengstom, Sundstrom, or Hoskins. But none of the names were there. Page, Backus, Romero, yes. She slapped them facedown on the counter. Grover, Svoboda, Glink. She was nearly through them all. The last card was a registration from October 25. She sighed as she read it. No link to Laura. But Maurice Anthony Dixon, who had checked into Room 19, had a personalized license plate that hit a chord with her: *IM MAD*. That was just how she felt. MAD, and frustrated.

25

In the envelope Mrs. O gave Hannah, there was a shot, faded with age, of a pale girl. She looked to be about fourteen. She turned away from the camera, shying from its gaze like a spooked colt. She wore a uniform of some kind: a white blouse with a Peter Pan collar and a plaid jumper. A moon-faced friend, whose jumper and black sweater did not hide her swollen belly, had her locked in a giddy, silly embrace. The girl's sweater had a crest on the pocket: a dove at the center of a cross-shaped beam of light. The Paraclete, the embodiment of the Holy Spirit. It was a link to a line in the letter that burned in Laura's apartment—the line that began *Burden came to Paraclete.*

So Paraclete was a Catholic home for pregnant girls. Hannah vaguely recalled that the Paraclete was often pictured hovering over the unmarried, about-to-be pregnant Virgin Mary. The irony probably was lost on a bunch of frightened teenagers.

She took a sip of the airline coffee and turned the picture over. *To Ellen B.—Thanks for getting me through freshman year. And for trusting me so much. I know everything's going to be fine.*

Ellen B. *B* for Burden, no doubt. Hannah looked at the pale girl's face again and knew that her hunch was right. Although Ellen Burden had a bumpy nose and mousy hair, her eyes and chin were those of the middle-aged politician Susan Beckett. As it turned out, Laura's adoptive mother didn't exactly lie when she said her birth mother's name was

Ellen. Susan Beckett's family apparently decided it was impolitic for their daughter to be listed on the Paraclete student roster, so they came up with an alter ego. Burden was an interesting choice.

Who sent Laura the letter with the clues to her mother's identity? The information let Laura make the connection between Ellen and Susan Beckett. Laura's possession of the picture suggested that mother and daughter might have met. The fact that Laura didn't take the picture with her when she left Seattle suggested the reunion was less than heart-warming.

Hannah wondered if the phone call Gibbons overhead was Laura screaming at Susan Beckett. The words had some resonance: *Why would I do this to you? Think what you did to me. And then try to pay me off? You can't buy people.*

The Fiat might have been what Laura was talking about. Susan could also have thrown in some cash to make amends for abandoning her. Or perhaps it was an incentive for Laura's cooperation in the spin her mother would give the story. Because it would come out, somehow. It was only a matter of who would reveal it, and how it would be shaded.

Pictures of mother and daughter, tearfully reunited, prob-ably were impossible now. But maybe Laura's death might still be of some use to her mother's campaign. Hannah imagined the commercial: in soft focus, accompanied by dripping strings and piano, the story of the long-lost daughter, dead at the hands of her violent husband, would be told. Brilliant, Hannah thought. Pro-life and anticrime at the same time.

In Las Almas, the Drummonds listened, unruffled, as Hannah told them about Laura's sleazy life in Seattle. They had ex-pected the worst. But the identity of Laura's mother raised their eyebrows.

They were in the family room, where Matthew's toys had been corralled in one corner. The morning sun came weakly through the clouds, dappling the room in pools of light and shadow. The local weather people called it June gloom.

"Laura is Susan Beckett's daughter? I loathe that woman,"

Rebecca said. "I wish she was running in this district. I'd vote against her."

Stephen nodded. "All that moralizing she does. She was an unwed mother?"

"It's not inconsistent," Hannah said. "She'd have more political problems if she'd had an abortion."

"But she's a hypocrite. She's always talking about how destructive premarital sex is," Stephen said.

"Maybe that's something she and I agree on," Rebecca said, almost to herself.

"She was very young. She could be speaking from experience," Hannah said.

"I don't really care what she did when she was a teenager," Stephen said. "But as an adult, she's been out there with those wackos, trying to tell women what to do with their bodies. Picketing doctors' houses. It's disgusting."

"There's more about Laura you should know." Hannah would have preferred not to tell them, but she had to.

Stephen's ironbound jaw began to clench as she described Laura's deception of the Westerlands and the devastation it caused them. Rebecca looked more horrified with each detail.

"She could have done that to us. She could have given Matthew to someone else."

"Jesus, Rebecca, are you out of your mind? There was no way that would have happened. These people were idiots."

"No, they weren't. They're just like us. They did what we did—trusted her, cared about her, believed her because they wanted a baby. We were just lucky. That's all."

Hannah, who tended to agree, watched as Stephen's face worked. He was grinding down the anger and swallowing it. "I'm going to be late for my first appointment. Excuse me."

Rebecca made no move to follow him. She sipped at her coffee and thoughtfully turned the cup in her hand. Hannah thought she was reacting less and less to his rages. Probably better for the collective sanity of the household.

"He hates to think about things like that," she said. "Chance, luck, fate. He doesn't believe in it."

"Do you?"

"In a way. I believe you can't control everything in life. When good things happen, you rejoice. When they're bad, you deal with them." Rebecca saw Hannah checking the time and got up to show her to the door. "Does Laura's mother know about Matthew?"

Hannah had stepped outside. The weather was colder than it had been when she arrived. "I think Gerald Lawrence has told her everything by now. I thought I'd go talk to her, if that's all right with you both."

"There's something I want to make sure she understands." The voice had an icy, imperious edge that Hannah hadn't heard before. Like the shift in the weather, Rebecca's personality seemed to be cooling. Hannah nodded for her to continue.

"Tell her Matthew already has a grandmother. He doesn't need another one."

26

The stream of cars on Country Club Drive stopped in front of a pillared antebellum mansion. The pause gave Hannah a good view of her destination: a scaled-down version of Hampton Court, swarming with breathless valets instead of courtiers. It would take hours to be parked, at this rate. She pulled out of the queue and drove through the neighborhood in which Susan Beckett had been raised.

Virginia Country Club was an old-money enclave, with an adobe rancho of the last century at its heart. Wealth spread onto wide, quiet streets and solid houses that copied stately homes but otherwise eschewed too much showiness. A white private-security car followed Hannah for a block or so, apparently uneasy with her slow-motion tour of the streets and alleys.

She tried to imagine how Susan Beckett might have felt: a wealthy politician's daughter, pregnant at thirteen. Had she stayed, the disgrace would have spread like an oil slick, the result to her life just as damaging. In this slice of Long Beach society, a daughter going off to boarding school wouldn't raise any flags—as long as the name wasn't mentioned. Perhaps Paraclete was more of a refuge than Hannah imagined.

She drove the neighborhood from edge to edge, beginning at a wall of hedge on the east. The Los Angeles River bounded the area on the west. To the south was the San Diego Freeway, and the northern boundary was a sort of commercial DMZ. The neighborhood took a step demographic plunge just beyond a barbecue hut called Johnny Reb's. The smell of grilling meat lured her, but the invitation on the passenger seat indicated that the Bill and Susan Show started at eight.

It had taken some work at Susan Beckett's campaign headquarters to wrangle the ticket. Happy College receptionist pretended not to remember Hannah's phone call. Hannah finally demanded an audience with a more elevated minion. He turned out to be a gangly young Aryan, but he had enough authority to be reasonable. He also was susceptible to the hundred-dollar campaign check she wrote. The primary was over, and Susan had handily beaten a too-moderate former county supervisor. But the November race must not be completely cinched if the campaign office was humming this way in mid-June. To her check she added a note for Susan. She let the puny aide read it first.

" 'Does Ellen Burden have five minutes for someone who knew her daughter?' That's your message? Who's Ellen Burden?"

"Someone Susan knows. She'll understand."

He shrugged and headed to a cubicle festooned with patriotic bunting. A minute later he returned with an engraved card. "Susan will see you after the event."

"This says it's fifteen hundred dollars a person."

"Don't worry. We'll comp you. Treat you like press."

"God forbid."

Finally, a sweaty valet took her car and Hannah joined the line of entering guests. From the front hall, Hannah saw that the living room, to her left, had been cleared of furniture and outfitted with two blocks of folding chairs, separated by a middle aisle. In a cavernous study to Hannah's right, people milled in front of a fireplace's huge maw, which was roaring away despite the eighty-degree evening outside. The air-conditioning had been cranked up to compensate. A squadron of waiters passed drinks and canapés. Hannah snagged a few bites of food and tried a quick head count of both rooms—two hundred and fifty people at least. A nice take for one night.

At the living room's entrance, a young woman with a walkie-talkie and a severe hairstyle motioned for Hannah's invitation. She wore a suit in Susan Beckett's shade of red, but had gussied it up with buttons and braid until she looked like a Bijou ticket taker.

The usherette looked at the card closely. "Are you with Susan or Bill?"

"I don't know either, really."

The usherette rolled her eyes. "Look, you don't want to be booing when everybody around you is cheering, do you? Who do you side with—Bill or Susan? It's pretty clear-cut."

"Put me with Susan's people."

She smirked. "Susan really puts the old guy through his paces."

From her seat in the first row, Hannah was close enough to catch a whiff of the politicians' cologne. There were two Queen Anne chairs on the raised dais, each flanked by a side table with the requisite cut-glass water pitcher and glass. A podium stood between the chairs. Hannah glanced back and saw the room filling. Susan's side held more people, and they were younger and more extravagantly dressed than Bill's. The seats on either side of Hannah were taken by college-age men in navy and women wearing jackets or shirts in Susan's peculiar shade of scarlet. To her relief, none had the glassy-eyed stare of the fanatic. She didn't feel like being elbowed for insufficient enthusiasm.

The usherette stepped up to the microphone and lavished the crowd with praise for its "support of the democratic process." Right, Hannah thought. But the truth—thanks for shelling out $1,500 to ensure that your particular pork barrel stays filled to the brim—was so much less melodious and uplifting.

Accompanied by the usherette's blandishments, Susan Beckett and her father took the stage, entering from opposite ends. They glanced at each other as they sat down. The usherette produced a coin—a Susan B. Anthony, as agreed upon by the Becketts—and flipped it. Tails. Bill Beckett would go first.

Hannah knew Beckett only from the newspapers and TV, and he hadn't been in either much since his retirement. He was under six feet tall, and had a bureaucrat's body, wide in the seat and soft in the belly. But his charm lay in his face. He had a good strong chin, and very blue, intelligent eyes. His smile began as a grin and grew huge from there—it was a prop to be expected in his line of work. He had a medium tan, which suggested weekends usefully spent outdoors— Habitat for Humanity, for example. Any shade darker implied vain hours idling by the pool. The wrinkles on his face had confined themselves to the corners of his eyes, showcasing a look of warmth and compassion, and to his mouth, setting off the geniality of his smile. His hair was still brown, but graying at the temples. He was aging gracefully, in that way that irks the hell out of women.

Hannah had read rumors of a drinking problem. He certainly wouldn't have been the only politician to battle that demon. But if he was an alcoholic, he seemed to be a recovering one. There was no sign of the habitual drunk's broken veins and bloated face.

Beckett waved and acknowledged the applause that came most vociferously from the right side of the room. Of course, from his standpoint, they had been put on the left. The usherette's doing, Hannah concluded.

"My daughter and I are delighted that you've come tonight, to an event that we're very proud of." His voice was a perfect politician's instrument: baritone, free of regional flavor, full of bonhomie, and touched with just enough imperfect grammar to keep him from sounding like a snooty intellectual.

"Most fund-raisers are partisan outings—you have some drinks and bash the other guy as the Antichrist. We do something different in these little get-togethers. We ask you to listen to the side you don't believe in. Susan and I are here to remind you that America is a family. We may disagree politically, but that does not break the bonds that bind us. Your attendance here tonight benefits both our parties and, more importantly, the political process that makes this nation great."

The speech that followed was slightly better than standard political boilerplate. Hannah sensed it had been pulled from a file, freshened with new anecdotes, and delivered with the required amount of sincerity, but no more.

Toward the end of his time Susan's partisans began to squirm. Every few sentences, someone behind Hannah let out a cackling, derisive laugh or exaggerated groan. When Beckett finished, the applause of his claque couldn't drown out the cat calls that coalesced into a chant among Susan's faithful: "Seven, six, five, four, you're a commie dinosaur!" From his chair, Beckett toasted them with his water glass. His daughter stood up with a look of amusement.

In person, she looked less like the archetypal ultraconservative harpy of her campaign poster. Her hair was softer, her lipstick less harsh. She seemed at home before the crowd, even though half of them probably considered her a consummate traitor to her liberal family.

Susan Beckett had identified and emphasized her best features—the large, serious brown eyes and the apple-round cheeks that must have come from her mother. Susan's nose had been reworked. And the fine brown hair that looked so distinguished on her father had been lightened to an ashen blond.

She might have distanced herself from her father's politics, but she had picked up one of his mannerisms: the instant, high-wattage smile. Hannah tried to imagine what Laura had done when Susan tried it on her. Maybe she mirrored it back, for Susan to see in all its grating artificiality. She motioned for the noise to stop, and when it did, she sighed melodramatically.

"Look, I'm going to have to ask you people to stop haranguing my father," she said with mock sternness. "He told me that if my friends misbehave in his house, he'll throw them right out and ground me for three weeks. Let me tell you, it's tough to campaign when you're locked in your room and all you've got to work with is a one-line pink Princess phone. So please, no dissing Dad, okay?"

A sense of humor. The last thing Hannah had expected. And as Susan Beckett began speaking, Hannah found herself actually listening.

"I have to tell you that it wasn't easy growing up in a liberal household," she said. "Other girls got in trouble for breaking curfew, or using bad language. Well, in our house, there wasn't a curfew. That was an outmoded notion. Children had to grow, experience life, taste the forbidden fruit. They'd decide what was best for them. Punishment for bad language? That would be a brake on free expression. Dad had the complete Lenny Bruce collection for everyone to enjoy. We were liberals, after all.

"So what got me in trouble? Ideology, that's what. My parents wanted Caroline Kennedy. What they got was Tricia Nixon. A political changeling. Drove them nuts. Do you want to know why I wasn't allowed to attend the first dance of my junior year? Dad caught me cheering Gerald Ford for pardoning—rightly, I might add—Richard Nixon. So much for free speech.

"Now, you might wonder how a nice, union-loving, welfare-spending, liberal-apologist family got somebody like me. It's genetic, believe it or not. The skeleton in my father's closet was—"

"Jack Daniel's!" It was a well-scrubbed college boy down the row from Hannah. A snicker rippled through the section. Susan Beckett stopped. Her eyes bored in on the boy until he looked away, his face coloring to match his jacket.

"My grandmother. Geneva Beckett was a rock-ribbed Republican. Dad managed to keep his mom away from the press by getting her a nice ocean-view apartment with an unlisted number in Miami Beach. But in return, he had to let me spend two weeks with her in the summer. She took it as her personal responsibility to talk some sense into me. So the way I look at it, my family isn't really liberal. We just had a one-generation Democratic aberration."

She turned to her father, beaming. "It's not too late, Father. Repent!"

He flashed the family grin and shook his head. "I've got nothing to be sorry about, sweetheart."

Her smile curdled. "Really?"

For the next five minutes Susan Beckett savaged her father and his party, quoting from his early speeches and picking out his far-left positions on everything from the arms race to penal reform. By the time she was done, even Hannah, who had voted Democrat for most of her life, wondered how she'd been so misled.

"So there's nothing to be sorry for, Mr. Senator?" Susan Beckett's voice was thick with disdain. "That's only because you won't look back, or take responsibility. Nothing to be sorry about? Nothing but the whole sorry state of our country. Men won't work, because they believe it's our job to support them. Women don't know the meaning of self-respect, thanks to the filth you say the First Amendment protects. People think the color of their skin earns them the right to a better job than the rest of us. Children can't read, but can tear down a Uzi in record time. That's quite a legacy. What a mess you've left me, Dad, and everyone else who has a shred of decency and an ounce of concern about this country."

She sat down to wild cheers and applause from her half of the room. Her father's supporters sulked. But his expression was only slightly pained. With a knife plunged so deeply into his back, it seemed to Hannah he would react with something other than a wince.

He got to his feet slowly, and held on to the podium for a few seconds, as if centering himself after his child's salvo.

"To borrow a line from someone in your pantheon, Susan, there you go again." He waited for the laugh, which came on cue. "It's not easy, as a parent, to realize how far astray your child has gone. So I guess maybe I do have something to be sorry for. I'm sorry that I raised a daughter who has so little compassion for anyone who isn't as lucky as she is.

"Susan doesn't understand that not everyone in this country is born to wealth and privilege and a Princess telephone. She has never spent a week hungry because her mother couldn't get a job. She doesn't know what it means to be hated for the color of her skin, or the language she speaks. My daughter had a cosseted existence, a life where she got everything she wanted. She was showered with gifts, she got everything she ever asked for—and more."

If anything that her father was saying struck home, Susan Beckett's face didn't show it. She sat straight as a Citadel knob, her gaze unswervingly locked on a point somewhere in the farthest reaches of the house.

"Susan was a studious girl, and a shy one," Beckett was saying. "She would spend hours in the library at our home in Georgetown, reading *Foreign Policy*. Or she'd cuddle up with her idol's latest tome on international affairs. Mind you, all of Nixon's books she read in the university library, not ours."

A bubble of liberal laughter floated up.

"Regardless of what Susan would have you think, we weren't limousine liberals. We put our money where the need was, and our labor, too. We worked at soup kitchens. We helped Jimmy Carter build houses for the poor. Susan didn't want to be a part of that—something about handouts, I think she said. And I let her make that choice. So maybe she's right about me being a permissive parent. I indulged my only daughter, and in the process, she grew up to be a narrow-minded, judgmental woman. I don't intend to sit back and let a petulant brat, who has never suffered as the poor of this nation suffer, shape a national policy to grind them even further into blight and deprivation. I'll fight her and her fat-cat sponsors until the day I die."

There were cheers from his gallery. Susan Beckett continued her expressionless stare. It was as if she had already left the room.

Hannah wished she weren't there, either. Gerald Lawrence said that the Becketts took this act on the road. Hannah couldn't imagine how they could do it more than once. Each of them had crossed the line, taking the debate down into the family's basement of scraped feelings and unhealed resentments. This wasn't good-natured sparring. It was the first round of blood sport.

Susan stood to respond, but was stopped by a sloshing voice from the back of the room. It crooned "How Dry I Am," with new verses. The usherette ran down the aisle, hissing into her walkie-talkie, but the singer did a few steps of broken-field maneuvering to avoid her and capered to the dais.

A giant chicken tortured George Bush on the campaign trail. Bob Dole was pursued by a man dressed as a cigarette. Mr. Martini obviously was there to embarrass Bill Beckett.

The costume was impressive: someone was hidden in a tube of white cardboard that made the stem of a glass. The bowl was clear plastic, and although it held no fluid, it did contain a basketball painted to look like a pimento-stuffed olive.

As the security squad raced to tackle him, Mr. Martini began a last refrain: "Old drunken Bill, by God that's me! What did I do? No memoreeee."

Bill Beckett looked at Mr. Martini impassively. If this was Susan's attempt at humiliating her father, it didn't seem to be working. He took a sip of water and got up to leave, condescendingly patting his daughter on the shoulder as he passed her. She shrugged his hand off and shot to the microphone. "Get that thing out of here," she snarled. The grotesque mascot tottered toward Beckett.

A security crew converged, tackling the stemware at the ankles. Mr. Martini crashed to the ground. The plastic bowl crumpled. The olive rolled into the audience. The scrubbed boy who sat next to Hannah retrieved it, tucked it under his arm, and disappeared into the crowd.

Hannah watched as Susan grabbed her notes and left the

dais. For a moment, as though a match had struck and then guttered, a look of rage flared on her face.

Hannah followed her across the hall and into the study, toward the double door through which Bill Beckett had just passed. The usherette was in hot pursuit, but Hannah outpaced her. In the narrow passageway, Susan Beckett turned to see who had the nerve to follow her.

27

She scanned Hannah briefly and apparently sensed no danger. "Sorry, but I'm on my way to a private meeting. A little cooldown we do after the main event. We'll be out in a second." She flashed the smile and kept walking. Hannah was instantly forgotten.

She had to admire Susan Beckett's aplomb. Whatever had rattled her out there had been swallowed whole, to be digested or spat out later.

"Actually, it would be better if we could talk now. I'm Hannah Barlow. I sent you a note about Ellen Burden's daughter."

The politician stopped and turned, her attention completely reengaged now. Susan Beckett must do it dozens of times a day—switch guises, turn a particularly interesting facet to the right person. The pleasantly distant candidate became the tough insider, right before Hannah's eyes.

"Five minutes, your note said."

"You can have more, if you want it."

Susan Beckett shook her head. "I doubt that will be necessary."

She opened a door onto a room paneled in fumed oak. Its two club chairs and sofa were covered in oxblood leather. French doors opened onto a bricked terrace, which led to a carriage house and garage. Beyond them was a meticulously trimmed floodlit lawn, where a sprinkler thwacked lazily. Inside, the room lacked only some hunting prints and a golden retriever on the carpet to complete the image of a country gentleman's retreat.

But instead of engravings, press releases and schedules dangled from bulletin boards on the walls. A fax was spitting paper onto the dogless rug and the phone rang insistently. No one moved to answer it.

Bill Beckett sat on the sofa, opening a can of Orange Crush. A blond, very white man—perhaps the whitest person Hannah had ever seen—sat on the floor at the open doors, playing jacks with a little girl in a petal-pink party dress. The girl looked up as Susan Beckett entered and waved at her.

"Mom! I'm winning."

"Good, Amy sweetheart, but your dad's game is terrible, so don't get too carried away. Why don't you two come away from the door now, before you both catch cold."

Hannah should have known that Susan would have a family. It was a virtual requirement for an Orange County Republican woman. But why had Susan kept the Beckett name?

The little girl favored her father: white-blond hair, long limbs, fair skin. She slid into the chair across from her grandfather and made a game of balancing the rubber ball on the back of her hand. The girl's father sat down at the desk, answered the phone, and began scribbling notes.

Bill Beckett slipped out of his loafers and stretched across the sofa. "Susan, I thought I'd taught you that if you're going to trot out some papier-mâché bogeyman to embarrass your opponent at an event, make sure you're not up there with him when the creature barges in. The blow-back potential is considerable."

Susan dropped into the chair next to her daughter and sighed. "I didn't know anything about it."

Hannah stood at the doorway, wondering if Susan would introduce her or at least ask her to sit down. She didn't seem to care if Hannah listened to a couple of pols deconstructing their dark arts.

"You have to say that, of course," Beckett said, nodding. "Most of the time nobody buys it, but that God Squad of yours is so fanatical that somebody might be willing to accept that it was unauthorized, as opposed to being simply unacknowledged."

"If it was one of my people, I'd have heard. I swear I don't—"

"Yes, of course, swear. I would, too, if I were in your position. I also wouldn't do it again if I couldn't do it right." He glanced up at Hannah. "Who's our guest?"

Susan motioned for Hannah to close the door. "Hannah Barlow, this my father, and my husband, Drew Fails."

Beckett nodded and let his smile illuminate the room. Fails looked wary. Hannah understood now why Susan hadn't changed her name. A politician wouldn't get far with Fails trailing her through the headlines.

"Miss Barlow wants to talk to me about Ellen Burden," Susan said.

Beckett put down the can and turned a smoothly perplexed countenance to Hannah.

"Who?"

"That was going to be my first question," Susan said. "But Miss Barlow made a contribution, so I thought I'd give her the courtesy of five minutes."

He nodded. "Seems fair."

Amy looked up at Hannah and gave her a bored, polite smile. She slouched in the chair, dangled her thin legs, and yawned. Her grandfather softly said her name and gestured for her to toss him the ball. She ignored him.

Hannah knew what Susan was doing: betting that Hannah would fold, refuse to talk about the adoption in front of her family, particularly the girl, who was no more than ten. Hannah thought about it for a moment. If Susan was callous enough to use Amy as a shield, that wasn't Hannah's problem. But she paused and chose her words carefully.

"Paraclete School," she said. "You were Ellen Burden there. When Laura was born, she was placed with Gerald Lawrence and his wife. When she got older, she changed her name from Lawrence to Benson. She was also looking for her birth mother by then, but no one thought it was a good idea to tell Laura who that was. Laura either figured it out, or someone told her. I think you saw her recently." She took out the picture of Ellen and handed it to Susan.

Susan glanced at it, but said nothing. Amy was staring down at her black patent-leather shoes, watching the changing reflections. She pretended not to listen. Hannah thought she probably did that a lot.

At the desk, Susan's husband muttered into the phone that he had to go. Yes, now. He got up and put his face about four inches from Hannah's. His eyes were brown and moist, thickly lashed. Hannah felt she was being confronted by a spindly bleached-white poodle.

"Look, I don't know who you are, but you have no right—"

"Drew, I can handle this," Susan's voice sounded wrung out. She put the picture in her jacket pocket. "Go ahead, Miss Barlow. Laura Benson found her birth mother, you think."

"Did she?"

"You wanted to talk to me for five minutes. I didn't consent to an interview."

"Laura Benson is dead. She had a son, whom she placed for adoption. I'm an attorney, and I represent his parents. They are trying to piece together their son's background. Laura was less than forthcoming about it. But I suppose Gerald Lawrence already told you all of this."

Susan didn't answer right away. She pushed her fingers through her hair, then dropped her hand onto her daughter's head. Amy wriggled like a happy puppy at her mother's touch.

"Sweetie, why don't you and your dad go see if they've got dinner for you, okay? We'll go after you eat." Her voice had lost its brittle edge.

Amy slid out of the chair and took her father's outstretched hand. She looked up at Hannah as she passed and arched an eyebrow.

"I was somebody else at my school, too," she said. She'd picked up on the tension in the room. "Alice, in Wonderland. Our spring play."

"You look like Alice," Hannah said. She also looked like Susan. And, a little, like Laura.

"Amy, go on." Susan, watching them leave, tugged in two short breaths, like someone getting ready for the shot put. Beckett, who had been flipping through a magazine, dropped it. He was staring at Hannah.

"I knew Laura was dead," Susan said. "Gerald and I tried not to talk about her. She's a sore subject for both of us. It's a shock. I hardly know what else to say."

"I know what to say," Beckett said. "What do you want? If you think you can use this, somehow . . ." Behind the bluster, Hannah could see the pain in his eyes. He was defending his daughter's political future, but there was more to it than that. Laura was his granddaughter. The news must have hit him, too.

"Dad, please," Susan said. "I said I could handle this. I heard suicide, but that's all I know."

Hannah told her about the pills and alcohol in Laura's body, and the explosion.

"My God," Beckett said. "You didn't tell me that, Susan. She blew herself up?"

"You didn't want to hear about Laura when she was alive, Dad. I didn't think you'd care about the details of her death."

"Susan, you know that whatever—"

"I don't want to hear it."

Beckett got up and poured a shot of Scotch for her. She took the glass, but didn't drink. Beckett, his solace spurned, returned to the sofa and sat down heavily.

"How is Gerald taking the news?" Susan said.

"It's hard to say," Hannah said. "My sense was that he was expecting it, somehow."

"That's because Laura was like someone out on a ledge."

"So you saw her?"

She nodded. "She was scared. She was up there, and couldn't get down."

"How did she find you?"

Susan shook her head. "No. You have it backward. I found her, and told her I was her mother."

• • •

"I loved Laura from the minute I saw her. That was about as long as I had with her. It's how they did things then. I never even held her."

Susan was standing at the French doors, looking into the dark at the edge of the lawn. She had put down the drink, shucked off her jacket, and lit a cigarette. Hannah expected Beckett to leave them alone, but he stayed, saying nothing.

"I was fourteen. Too young to raise a child. I knew that. Giving her up was the right thing to do." She inhaled hard and blew a stream of smoke toward her father. "My parents, of course, would have preferred an abortion, but I wouldn't do it. They tried to pressure me, but my grandmother threatened to leak it. She knew people on the right—the hard-core ones—who'd find ways to use it against Dad. That's what finally did it. My feelings weren't really a consideration."

Hannah glanced over at Beckett. His arms were folded and he stared down at his lap. Without an audience, he was apparently unwilling to paw over the past.

"I'm not ashamed of giving Laura up. I never was," Susan said. "I was told that she shouldn't know about me. She had a family—the Lawrences." She tapped some ash onto the oak floor and smeared it with the toe of her shoe. "So I did what I was told. I tried to forget about her."

This was aimed at Beckett. He didn't look up, but slowly shook his head. "For God's sake. We did what we thought was best for her, and you."

"And I believed that crap for a long time."

The silence thickened until Hannah felt she couldn't breathe. Wait, she thought. Just wait, let them keep pushing each other.

"Of course, forgetting her was really not possible. I saw her, a couple times a year. It was horrible, not being able to say anything. It was worse when I saw how much she struggled in that family. She never fit there. They didn't even tell her she was adopted. They let her think it was all her fault that she didn't belong. What about that, Dad?"

"We couldn't tell the Lawrences how to raise a child."

"No," she snapped. "You certainly couldn't."

Beckett hauled himself off the sofa and left the study, shutting the door softly behind him.

Susan lit another cigarette, sat down in one of the chairs, and shook her head in apology to Hannah.

"We're not good at plastering over our arguments. The Becketts battle. It's part of the family dynamic."

"So what happened? One day you just called Laura?" Hannah said. " 'Hi, Laura, I'm your mother'?"

She chortled through another suck of smoke. "No. It didn't happen quite that way. Someone at the adoption agency called me. She'd been in there, trying to get information. Ineptly, apparently. It seemed to me it was only a matter of time until she perfected her method, found the right person—a greedy one, probably—and got my name."

"And what about politics? It played no part in your decision?"

Susan trained her eyes on Hannah, who could almost hear her weighing the choice: acknowledge the realpolitik or stick with the selfless-mother routine.

"It played a part," she said. "I wanted to be in control of how it came out, if it was going to come out."

"Was it?"

"Probably. When you run for office, people start rummaging through your life. They usually find something they think they can use against you."

"You didn't want them to use Laura."

"I thought I could make it less likely."

"So your meeting didn't go well."

She shook her head. "No, it did. Better than I thought it would. Gerald told me she was down here from Seattle, visiting friends. I called and invited her to lunch, just being the family friend she thought I was. She was suspicious, I think. She thought I was going to play Kissinger for her and Gerald.

"I hadn't seen her in a long time, since she dropped out of high school. We drove to Laguna, and she didn't say two words the whole way down. I was very nervous."

"We got to the restaurant, and she picked at a salad. I told her that she should try to eat something, she was too thin.

She smirked and said, 'Please, Susan, you're not my mother.'"

Susan smiled, reading Hannah's reaction before she could say anything. "I know. But it's what she said. And I just put down my fork and told her: Yes, I am your mother. It was a lot for her to take in. She said she needed time, and she'd call me. But . . ."

"You didn't talk to her again?"

"Only once, after she moved down here."

"And you gave her the picture?"

Susan nodded. "That first lunch, yes."

"Why did she leave it in Seattle? It seems like something she would have wanted to keep."

"I don't know. Maybe she misplaced it when she was moving." Susan stubbed out her cigarette and rummaged through a stack of papers on the desk. She handed two sheets to Hannah. "This is going out next week."

The press release headline read: THE COURAGE TO LOVE AND LET GO: SUSAN BECKETT'S BRAVE DECISION. The paragraphs below quoted Laura, Susan, Bill Beckett, and Gerald Lawrence on the story Hannah had just been told. There was even a quote from Amy: *"I'm sorry I couldn't have spent time with my big sister. I talk to her in my prayers."*

Hannah looked up from the release. "Why didn't Laura tell anyone about your reunion?"

"I asked her not to. I didn't want it leaked."

"I thought Amy didn't know, either."

"She will, tomorrow," Susan said.

The press release wasn't quite the soft-focus anticrime commercial Hannah imagined, but it was just about that smarmy. Laura wasn't there to contradict any of her mother's story. She couldn't protest if, like Amy, words had been put in her mouth. She wasn't around to say how she felt about her mother's use of their relationship as a family-values theme of the day. Hannah wondered if their meeting had been anything remotely like the one Susan described.

"So, as a gift for all that lost time, you gave Laura a car?"

Susan shook her head. "A car? No."

"No? Laura had a black Fiat. She told people her father had given it to her. Gerald says he didn't. I thought it might be from you, or from Laura's birth father? A reunion gift?"

A look of something like revulsion crossed the woman's face. She recovered quickly.

"Laura's father died, years ago. I never had the chance to give Laura anything. I came into her life too late. But I don't intend to make that mistake with my grandson."

There it was. This was how Susan was going to salve her guilt about Laura. She'd start over, with another child.

"I'd like the opportunity to meet him," Susan said. "I haven't even seen a picture."

"I'd have to talk to my clients. I'm not sure how they'll react."

"Laura didn't tell me much about them, except that she cared for them very much." From the desk drawer, she pulled out a half sheet of parchment-colored writing paper and scribbled a number on it.

"This is my private line at home. Let your clients know that I'm anxious to build a bridge to them. They can call me, anytime."

"I hope you understand how sensitive this is."

"Of course." Susan flashed the family smile. Now Hannah saw a glimmer of menace in it. "That's why we didn't mention Matthew in the press release."

On the way out, Hannah found Amy sitting on an elaborately carved Black Forest bench in the entry hall. Wooden bears hovered at either end, making the child look like a kidnapped Brothers Grimm princess. Her father talked into a cellular phone as Amy stared at the door, apparently trying to will herself home. She glanced up at Hannah and fluttered a smile.

"Adult parties are sort of boring for you?" Hannah said.

Amy shrugged. "I wish I could just go play someplace."

"There must be a million places to play in a house like this. My grandfather's house wasn't a quarter this big, and I loved it there."

Amy sighed. "Well, Mom told me I'm not supposed to

let . . ." She glanced back at her father, who had finished his call and was motioning for her to get up.

"Come on honey, let's scoot. Mommy will meet us at home." He pointedly avoided speaking to Hannah. But his daughter's manners were better. She gravely reached for Hannah's hand.

"It was a pleasure meeting you," she said. She followed her father outside.

28

The blue envelope—crumpled, mangled, just short of destroyed—was on Hannah's desk when she got to the office Monday. The letter inside had been scribbled on the sheets of paper so thin that even the thought of breath fluttered them. She ignored the blinking message light on her phone and read the pages twice.

Querida Hannah:
The skirmish that had broken out here apparently is a Romeo-and-Juliet situation—rival weaver families, two stubborn old women who've hated each other from childhood—and the kids' elopement brought work to a complete halt. These two bickering ladies may well have given my mother her heart attack. How do you say *yenta* in Spanish?
Up until now, the talks have not gone well. But this morning I invoked the specter of my mother's profound sadness, how it will pull her toward death, if they don't cut it out. That seems to be working. I think a breakthrough is imminent.
I miss you terribly. I'll be back, I hope, soon. First, it's back to Durango, to debrief mother, take care of some things that I'm sure are going awry in shipping and receiving, and then I'll be home. I'll call from Colorado.

All love,
Guillermo

He had enclosed a Polaroid picture—mutilated on its journey and shot with film so old that faces were tinged a sickly green. He crouched next to a table, gesturing with such intensity that Hannah almost could hear him cajoling cooperation from two glowering, wrinkled women who seemed determined not to look at each other.

She slid her finger along Guillermo's jawline. She wanted him back, right then. It didn't surprise her that he could bring together two angry rivals. He as a healer, a go-between, a resonant sounding board. If he were here, he would listen to her ramble about Laura's death without picking her suspicions apart like so much carrion.

Talking to him, it would perhaps make more sense. She propped the picture up on her desk and silently addressed herself to him. Take a look at these people, she asked him. Tell me what you think.

He would agree that although Kurt was capable of smashing up some sedatives and feeding them to Laura in a gin-and-juice cocktail, he wasn't the sort to plan on a suicide note and a well-timed explosion. A rage, followed by a stabbing, or a bludgeoning—that was more his style.

Susan Beckett was obviously not telling everything about her relationship with Laura. Hannah very much doubted that the reunion had gone smoothly. There was her reaction to the Fiat. Why had it unnerved her?

Bobby had talked to Laura about the car. Maybe he would know.

He was sitting at his desk, feet atop it, reading the *Daily Journal.*

"Hey," he said. "I was beginning to think you didn't work here anymore. Rebecca told me what you found out in Seattle. Is Susan Beckett really Laura's mother?"

"Yes. And now the problem is that she wants to be Matthew's grandma."

"Great. How are the Drummonds going to feel about that?"

"Rebecca told me in no uncertain terms that she didn't want another grandmother for Matthew. I don't think Susan's got any legal grounds to visitation, but she can certainly make the Drummonds' lives messy, if she puts her mind to it."

"As though we needed more mess," Bobby said. He tossed the newspaper to the floor.

"How did Laura get that car again?"

"The Fiat? She said her father gave it to her."

"Gave her the car? Or the money for it?"

"The car, I think."

"Gerald Lawrence said he didn't give it to her. But he guessed what color it was. I thought maybe Laura lied, and the car came from Susan—a sop for all the years she ignored Laura. She said it didn't come from her, and when she heard that it was a black Fiat, she was shaken."

"Over a car?"

Hannah nodded. "Weird, isn't it?"

"I'll see what I can find out about it."

"Good. Thanks."

Hannah went back to her office, tucked the picture of Guillermo into the edge of frame on her desk, and dialed up the voice mail, where the mommy-voiced automated attendant told her there were two messages. The first was from Kurt:

"Tonight at ten, come to Terry's Coffee Shop. It's near your office. I've been in touch with some friends in Seattle, and I found out why Laura's dead. Bring me some cash, and I'll tell you more. Her dying has nothing to do with me. It's about the father, like she said. You're not there right at ten, with money, I'm gone, okay?"

Those words, again, Hannah thought. Whose father?

The second message was Kurt, again.

"And no cops. But you knew that."

Sure, Hannah thought. She was already dialing Churnin's number.

At nine-thirty, Hannah was at Terry's, a drive-in trying to recapture its glory days. She had ten one-hundred dollar bills for Kurt, but it wasn't from the Drummonds. She hadn't even bothered calling them. The money came from the office account. She would show it to him, but hold on to it until she heard his information. Churnin had agreed to let her talk to Kurt before he hauled his ass to jail.

As she parked she saw Churnin and another detective sitting in a baby-blue Volvo. Churnin, who was about to place his order with a roller-skating carhop, nodded to her as she went inside. Hannah wondered what a vegan would possibly find on the menu here.

From her booth, she could see Churnin slouched at the wheel of the Volvo, his eyes fixed on the restaurant's door. He picked up a cellular phone and dialed it. The phone in Hannah's purse trilled in reply.

"We've got to stop meeting like this," Churnin said.

"Sad that it takes someone like Kurt Sundstrom to bring us together," Hannah said.

"We've got a pretty good case on him now, regardless of what he tells you. I think once he's in custody, your clients will be able to relax and put down their weapons."

"So Rebecca told you about the guns?"

"Yeah. At least they took a class. Most people don't even bother."

"Ivan, there's one thing about Laura that you should know. She and Kurt pulled an adoption scam on a couple in Seattle. Connie and Edmund Westerland."

"What kind of scam?"

"Laura and Kurt told the Westerlands they would give them their baby—in return for rent, food, probably some money under the table. But Laura and Kurt didn't give them a baby. I don't think Laura was even pregnant then. The Westerlands' house in Seattle is deserted, no one knows for sure where they've gone, but maybe Southern California. I know it's not likely but—"

"You think maybe they had something to do with Laura's death? Jesus, Hannah, aren't things complicated enough?"

"I'm just trying to be a good citizen." She saw him shake his head and check his watch. "Yeah, well, I'll call you for details if Kurt goes south as a suspect, okay? Look, it's ten minutes until ten now. I'll talk to you after this is over."

The phone rang a minute later, and as she answered it she saw that Churnin was on his phone, too.

"The name is Westerland," she said. "Spelled just like it sounds. Connie and—"

"It's Bobby, Hannah. Thank God I got you." Bobby's voice was urgent and shaking. "I just got a call from the security company. There's been a shooting at the Drummonds' house."

She looked out into the parking lot. The Volvo was already gone.

Only one light was on at the Drummonds' house. The gate to the yard was open, and voices came from down the slope. Light bars flickered in blue, red, white, and yellow from an ambulance, patrol cars, and the security company's Jeep. She spotted Bobby's Saturn. Ivan had run the Volvo off onto the grass and left it there. Hannah did the same.

She ran down the path and saw that whatever had happened had taken place in Rebecca's office. The door was open, and she could see the vague outline of a body under a sheet on the floor. Jesus, she thought. Stephen?

Hannah was stopped by a uniformed cop before she could get close. But she saw a figure she recognized coming out of the inner office. Stephen, barefoot, walked out onto the office's deck. He held a glass of water with shaking hands. His white sweatshirt was bloodstained. Hannah felt her heart race. The draped body was too big to be Matthew. Rebecca, then? Anneke?

A bulky, impassive security guard followed Stephen. Then Churnin emerged, arms folded. She could tell by his posture that he already had begun asking questions. Hannah shouted to him, and he motioned for the cop to let her come down.

"So you weren't here, is that right?" Churnin was standing close to Stephen, head lowered, like a priest in a confessional. "What was he doing here?"

Stephen shook his head, started to answer. He stopped when he saw her. "Hannah, thank God."

"Who is it?" She put the question to Churnin.

"Kurt Sundstrom."

Hannah understood. Kurt had tried to break in. And

Stephen had shot him. And now Churnin was questioning him. "It would have been nice if you'd waited for a couple minutes," she said to Churnin. "You knew I was on my way."

Churnin shrugged. "I'm just trying to do my job."

"Me, too. May I have a moment with my client, please?"

"Okay, but I think you'll want to go in the house. Mrs. Drummond was the one who shot him."

"That's about all I could get out of her, that she shot him." Stephen led Hannah into the family room. Churnin was making coffee in the kitchen.

"Where is she now?" Hannah said.

"Upstairs. Bobby's with her."

Hannah glanced up. She wondered how much more Rebecca could take. When she looked back at Stephen, he was cramming something into a humidor next to his chair. It looked like a stack of cash.

"What's that?"

He started. "Oh. Poker money."

"It looked like quite a wad of bills."

He nodded. "I play with a couple plastic surgeons. High stakes."

"Do you always keep a lot of cash here?" She wondered if somehow Laura might have told Kurt about such a habit.

"No. Not really."

"It's not a good idea."

"You're right."

"Where's Matthew? Anneke? Hannah found the house uneasily quiet. No baby noises, none of Anneke's fast, purposeful footsteps overhead.

"Anneke's out somewhere, which is something else I don't understand. It's not her night off. But the baby's fine."

"We'll worry about Anneke in a minute," Churnin said, setting down two mugs of coffee. "Now that your attorney is here, let's talk about what happened."

"I have a poker game every month with some other docs," Drummond said. "It was in Newport Beach this time, but I left early. I was tired. Everything that's been going on is wearing me out, I guess. When I got home, I went upstairs and got ready for bed."

"What about your wife?"

"Rebecca was at some city meeting. She said she'd be home after eleven. I thought Anneke and Matthew were already asleep. She turns in early so she can get up early with him in the morning."

"What time was this, when you got home?" Churnin said.

"About nine forty-five."

"You didn't see anybody out there in back? Didn't notice that the lights were on?"

"I didn't look. Rebecca had promised me she wouldn't work down in the office at night, so I didn't even consider it. I was taking my shoes off when I heard a gunshot. I ran down here and found him. Shot in the chest."

"Was Sundstrom still alive when you got to him?"

Drummond nodded. "Trying to talk, but I couldn't make anything out. I called 911 and started CPR, but he was gone before the paramedics got here. The security company's guy came in while I was working on him."

"Who called the security company?" Hannah said.

"Mrs. Drummond," Churnin said. "She said a prowler was in her office. That was nine forty-two. Where was your wife, Dr. Drummond, when you came in?"

"On the floor. She still had the gun in her hand."

"What did she say?"

"Absolutely nothing, at first. She was frozen. After I called the paramedics and saw that Kurt was gone, I tried to hold her. All she said was: 'I had to. Kurt was coming after Matthew, and he wouldn't stop.' "

Churnin nodded. "We're going to see if she can talk to me now. We'll be back down in a few minutes."

"I'd like to give her something to calm her down."

"Later."

Upstairs, Rebecca was sitting in a rocker in Anneke's room, holding the baby gently against her chest and stroking his forehead. Bobby sat on the bed. Rebecca seemed composed enough without Stephen's tranquilizers. But her face was flushed, as though she'd sat too long by a fireplace.

"Hannah," she said quietly. "It's good of you and Bobby to be here." She nodded to Churnin. "You want to know what happened, I guess."

"If you please, ma'am."

Rebecca looked to Hannah, who nodded assent. She handed Matthew to Bobby, who cradled him expertly and took him to his room.

"The planning-commission meeting I went to was supposed to go late," she said. "New hillside construction limitations—it's got everyone up in arms. But the item was tabled, so I came home early."

"And Anneke, was she here then?" Churnin pitched his voice low. Hannah hated the act, hated the fact that she had done it herself to gain the trust of a witness or suspect.

"Of course. She works very hard. She hasn't really had a night off since she got here. She had talked about going to a club where friends from Holland were playing. Since I was back, I told her to go. That's probably where she is now. Linda's Doll Hut in Anaheim."

"We'll call over there, see if she's still around." Churnin stepped into the hallway and was back in a moment. "My guys will know something shortly. So you came home at what time?"

"It was about nine-fifteen, I think. Anneke was having trouble getting Matthew to settle down, but I told her not to worry about it. I had some papers I had to get in the office, and I took him down there with me."

"Your husband says he told you not to work down there at night."

Rebecca's eyes flared with resentment, but the anger died there. She nodded. Stephen had been right.

"I just went to get some papers," she said. "I didn't mean to stay long. But I couldn't find what I was looking for. Then I thought I heard something in the outer office. I opened the door a little and I saw Kurt."

"What was he doing?"

"Handling things. He picked up a picture of Matthew.

And then he started going through the files. I closed the door and hit the first number on speed dial. It was the security service, and they said they'd call the police."

"When was that?"

"I don't know. They told me someone would be on the way. But I was scared. I thought he'd start searching my office any minute. Matthew was with me. He was sleeping, but I was afraid he'd wake up."

"What about the gun?"

A uniformed officer appeared at the doorway before Rebecca could answer. "Linda's Doll Hut doesn't know anybody named Anneke. Some Dutch group called Kraai was there. But they took off early. Slow night."

Churnin nodded. "Sorry. Please go ahead. The gun?"

"It was in the desk drawer. We decided to keep one of them there. I took it out and made sure it was loaded. Then I waited. That's all I could do."

"But he came in? Why?"

"Matthew woke up, and he cried a little." Rebecca's voice was losing its steadiness. "I picked him up, and he didn't make another noise, but Kurt heard him. I sat down on the floor, next to the desk, and waited. He opened the door, and he saw us. He reached for his waist, and I saw the gun. All I could think was that he was there to take Matthew."

"And you shot him?"

She nodded. Her hands were shaking, and she fought back tears.

Churnin crouched next to the chair. "We'll talk more later. In the meantime you take it easy. The main thing is Matthew's okay, right?"

She smiled, her eyes flooded. "Right."

Hannah and Churnin didn't speak until they were downstairs.

Churnin shook his head. "What was Kurt doing here?"

"It doesn't sound like kidnapping to me," Hannah said. "He could have had no way of knowing Matthew and Rebecca were in that office."

"Unless he followed them."

"But what was he planning on doing then? Bringing Matthew to the meeting he set up with me?"

Churnin shrugged. "I'm going to take a look around the office before they take Kurt out."

"I'd like to join you."

He scowled at her. "Just don't touch anything."

In the office, crime-scene investigators were photographing Kurt's body. A gun lay on the floor beside him, and from his front pocket, Hannah saw a glimpse of silver. She pointed it out to Churnin.

"Is that what Rebecca was talking about?"

At Churnin's instruction, the technician eased the silver thing out of Kurt's pocket. A tiny framed picture of Matthew.

"What else had he got on him?" Churnin said.

From the other pocket, the technician slid out a folded scrap of tan paper.

"Phone number." He held it up for Churnin to see. Hannah peered at it, too. Why did it seem so familiar? She reached into her purse and, after some digging, found what she wanted. She asked Churnin to step outside and handed him the piece of parchment-colored paper.

"This number's the same as the one Kurt has. Same paper, too. And the handwriting looks the same."

"Okay, so?"

"That's Susan Beckett's home phone number, written by her."

His eyes went wide, and then he gave a barking, derisive laugh. "Susan Beckett? The next congresswoman and this petty crook are phone pals? Come on."

"Susan Beckett is Laura's birth mother. Susan had her when she was fourteen, and it's been a big family secret, until recently, when Laura found out. Matthew is Susan Beckett's grandson."

Churnin's face lost its amusement. "Go on."

"I talked to Susan recently, and she is very interested in Matthew. The Drummonds don't want her in their lives right now, particularly after all the problems they'd had with

Laura. It bothers Susan that someone has the nerve not to go along with her demands."

"So you're saying she put Kurt up to this?"

"Politicians don't direct break-ins?"

He winced. "I'll follow up with Susan Beckett in the morning."

29

Just before dawn, Hannah was back at the Drummonds' house. She picked up the newspaper from the driveway and paged through it. The story was inside the local-news section—only a brief, thank God. It had been too late for the nightside cop reporters to get much detail. The headline brought even more relief.

HOME-INVASION ROBBERY FOILED. If that's what the police were telling the media, then the Drummonds had little to fear. Had the police said that "details were sketchy," it would have been different. That phrase often meant the police hadn't decided who was telling the truth.

The story didn't mention Rebecca or Stephen by name. It said only that the "homeowner" did the shooting. A nice neuter noun. Kurt's name, however, was in print. *A suspect with an out-of-state felony conviction.* Good again. Churnin thought the Drummonds were telling the truth. So did she. The evidence backed it up: Kurt was armed, and had Matthew's picture in his pocket, as Rebecca said. The security guard's story jibed with Rebecca's. There was a notation of her call to the security firm, and probably a recording, too, in which Rebecca's terror would be evident.

The Drummonds had answered all the questions police put to them. Even when they were taken, hands wrapped in paper bags, to Las Almas PD's crime lab for a gunshot residue test, they barely blinked. Rebecca's sense of guilt was obvious—she felt she deserved to be treated like a criminal. Stephen's usual bluster and bad attitude were absent, and Hannah couldn't decide if it was shock, or if he was holding it all back in deference to Rebecca. After going downtown with them and bringing them home around two in the morning, she went home for a few hours of sleep.

Now she rang the doorbell and waited, listening to the silence. She hoped that Stephen hadn't prescribed a sleeping pill for himself, or she'd be on the doorstep all day. Rebecca had definitely needed a sedative, and with any luck, she would be in a clean, dreamless sleep. Anneke, on the other hand, would likely be waking up with a hangover.

It was just after midnight when she finally appeared at the house, narrow-eyed and redolent of pot, with a tall, black haired, kohl-eyed Dutch friend on her arm. He was a shade more sober and dejected at seeing his intimate evening ruined by the death of a stranger. And yet he also seemed fascinated, as though a violent California killing was being performed just for him, like it was one of the attractions at Universal Studios.

She rang the bell again. A moment later Drummond appeared, tousled and red-eyed.

"No sleep?" Hannah said.

"Not much. Every time I started to doze off, I dreamed about Kurt. Rebecca shouldn't have had to do that."

Now she understood his earlier mood. He'd put a ring of defenses around his family and trained himself to shoot, but had been absent at the crucial moment. Stephen had failed as family guardian.

"No one is to blame but Kurt."

"What did he want here? Was it Matthew?"

Hannah shook her head. Whatever he was after, it was clear that he intended to be done by ten, when he would be sipping coffee with Hannah, and telling her why Laura had been killed. But if he hadn't come for Matthew, what was he doing there? Had Susan sent him? Why did he have a gun?

She handed the local-news section to Stephen. "You made the papers."

Stephen read the brief. "That's not so bad."

"That's just the start. Some reporter will weasel more information out of the police and come looking for an interview. People defending their homes—that's a surefire story for tomorrow. If they find out Rebecca pulled the trigger, they'll be here in droves. Something about women shooting guns drives the media crazy."

"Can we do something to stop it?"

"The story will die out if we stall them, I think. So if it's all right with you, I'll hang around awhile, and tell them no comment. How's that?"

"Great. I'd like Rebecca to get some uninterrupted rest."

"You could use a little, too."

He went back upstairs. Hannah made a pot of coffee, checked her voice-mail messages, spoke to Bobby, and waited for the first enterprising journalist to show up.

One did, just before noon: a newspaper reporter in her forties, with black hair, dead-grape lipstick, and a grating East Coast attitude. After working her way through a menu of approaches, beginning with sympathy and ending with threats, she realized Hannah—whom she'd assumed to be a relative—wasn't going to budge. She stamped down the driveway, vowing, in MacArthuresque tones, to return.

She was followed by a tabloid-TV outfit posing as a local news crew. They nearly got into a fistfight with the real local crew when it showed up. Hannah decided she wasn't answering the doorbell for an hour or so.

Instead, she called Churnin. "What did Susan Beckett have to say?"

"Hannah, are you back in my police department and nobody told me?"

"I helped you out, and it would be nice if you'd return the favor. It's my clients who had their home invaded, and if Susan Beckett is a threat to them or Matthew, they deserve to know about it."

Silence. Hannah wondered if she'd pushed him too hard.

"Susan Beckett denies knowing anyone named Kurt Sundstrom," he said at last. "She doesn't have any idea how he came into possession of her phone number, on her stationery, in her handwriting. She conceded all that, by the way."

"Did you tell her what Sundstrom did?"

"No. Just that I was conducting some inquiries in connection with a crime."

"She'll know, soon enough. Reporters have been clawing at the door all morning. What about the Westerlands?"

"Jesus, Hannah, you're worse than my boss. I'll get to it, all right?"

In late afternoon, Drummond came downstairs. Hannah had fended off three more waves of journalists and was scanning the late-afternoon local new shows to see if they'd managed to work up a story without interviews.

"Shit," Stephen said as tape of the house's distinctive facade rolled on two different stations. The stories that followed were sketchy, but by now the reporters had the Drummonds' names and occupations.

"In a couple days it'll die down," Hannah said. "Some other story will have replaced you. Rebecca still sleeping?"

"No. She's in the shower. Anneke and Matthew are playing. I'm glad neither one of them saw anything."

"There's something I haven't had the chance to tell you. Susan Beckett wants to see Matthew."

"Tell her no. She doesn't know who we are, so that'll be the end of that."

"I'm not sure she doesn't know." She told him about the phone number in Kurt's pocket.

"Kurt knew Susan Beckett? What the hell's going on?"

"I think Laura told Kurt about her. And I wouldn't be surprised if he told Susan Beckett everything about you and Rebecca, out of sheer malice, if nothing else."

"Well, that completely settles it. If she's on Kurt's side, she's not getting anywhere near Matthew. You can tell her that in no uncertain terms."

Susan Beckett lived in a low-slung ranch house built sometime in the sixties. Hannah entered through a gate into a central atrium, where dozens of coddled fuchsias bloomed.

Gardenias scented the humid air. The debate's usherette—released from her epauletted getup in favor of a plain navy dress—directed Hannah to a wrought-iron chair and brought her a cup of tea.

The house had sliding-glass doors and glass walls that faced into the atrium. Hannah looked through the walls at rooms as neat as a furniture-store display. From behind a closed door, she could hear someone at the piano, first playing scales, and then banging out the notes of "Für Elise" with what sounded like a blunt instrument. Amy, she supposed, still shackled to her mother's expectations.

After ten minutes had passed, Susan Beckett emerged, wearing a pair of khaki pants and a rose-colored striped shirt. She stood with her arms folded, impatient and excited at the same time.

"I've blocked out two hours on Sunday. The parents can bring him here and my aide will—"

Hannah was certain that Susan Beckett had no plans for a quiet afternoon with her grandbaby. She'd probably already picked out a backdrop, had a cute T-shirt printed (MY GRANDMA'S HOUSE IS IN WASHINGTON, DC), and planned the photo op. Hannah tried not to enjoy interrupting.

"Ms. Beckett, my clients don't feel it would be appropriate to introduce you into Matthew's life. Laura never made any mention of wanting him to have a relationship with her birth family. If she had, my clients certainly would have honored her wishes."

"How do I know any of that's true? My daughter is dead." Susan's words were clipped, her voice higher than usual. "There's only your clients' word that's how she felt."

"Actually, they had a written agreement, and you're not in it," Hannah said. "On the other hand, they only have your word that you had a good relationship with Laura. If you two were so close, why didn't she ever mention you?"

"You seem to think this ends it."

"It does."

"It doesn't. I've made a few inquires. I know who adopted Matthew. Dr. Stephen Drummond and his wife."

If Laura had given her their names, she would have contacted the Drummonds directly long ago, Hannah thought. So it probably was Kurt who told her.

"When Matthew was adopted by my clients, regardless of who they are, all his ties with his birth family were legally severed," Hannah said. "They chose to have a relationship with Laura. They choose not to have one with you."

Susan got up and plucked out the dead, browning blossoms in the baskets that hung overhead. With each angry pinch, her face tightened.

"You tell Dr. and Mrs. Drummond this, Miss Barlow: I exist as a part of Matthew's life. That's the starting point. They can't wish me away, or write me out of his life with a legal document. I saw how that loss—that blank space where a birth parent was—hurt Laura, and I won't let it happen to Matthew. I'm the only link to her that he has left." Her red-painted nail bit through a browned stem. She threw the dead flowers into the dirt. "We can do this one of two ways: it can be cooperative and quiet, or contentious and public."

"What are you going to do, picket their house?"

She favored Hannah with a cold smile. "I can run a campaign for anything, Miss Barlow, whether it's Congress, or a relationship with my grandson. It's really all up to the Drummonds. You tell them that." She brushed flakes of dead petals from her hands.

"Do you really think you should be making threats like this? Have you read the paper today? I brought a copy, in case you were too busy with the campaign."

She had folded it back to the story of the break-in at the Drummonds. Susan read it, and Hannah saw how her eyes froze halfway through the story, where Kurt's name appeared.

"So how will this play, when it comes out?" Hannah said. "This felon, who beat your daughter on more than one occasion and might well have killed her, terrorized the Drummonds. He was rifling an office—armed, I might add—and had your phone number, on your stationery, in your handwriting, in his pocket. How are you going to spin that?"

Susan threw the paper into Hannah's lap. "I don't have to answer any of that. You're not the police." She went into the house and pulled the sliding door shut with a thump. One by one, she pulled the drapes across the glass walls. Hannah waited for a minute, looking at the wrong side of Susan Beckett's life. She finished the tea the aide had so graciously brought, and let herself out.

30

Hannah tried to break Vera of a bad computer habit: She sometimes typed her E-mail messages in capitals. It was like hearing Vera shout, and it didn't fit her bride-of-silence personality. But as Hannah read this message, she decided a yell was appropriate:

IVAN CHURNIN IN RECEPTION. EXTREMELY PISSED OFF— PARTICULARLY FOR A VEGAN.

Regardless of what he'd eaten recently, Hannah couldn't imagine what upset Churnin. A week had passed quietly since Kurt's death. Churnin had called Rebecca twice, but only to check minor details. There would be no charges, Hannah thought.

The hang-up phone calls to the Drummonds also had stopped, confirming who had been making them. And Susan Beckett had gone silent. There was a Republican-party retreat in Ojai, and Hannah guessed that accounted for it. For the first time in weeks the Drummonds' life almost seemed normal. And Hannah got seven nights of undisturbed sleep, which she savored.

Nap time was over now: Churnin, sitting on the edge of the waiting room's leather sofa, tore through a *People* magazine with undisguised fury. He jumped up when he saw her.

"Goddamm it Hannah, what have you done now?"

"I don't know what you're talking about. Let's go to my office."

With a snarl, Churnin got up and followed her. Hannah enjoyed seeing his behavior on her turf. Her cluttered office bothered him. He sat on the edge of the guest chair as though it would swallow him. She sat behind her desk and coolly took out a notepad. That annoyed him even more.

"What have I supposedly done?"

"I'm wrapping things up on this shooting at the Drummonds' house. Things have checked out—ballistics, the residue test, the security company's logs, and the recording of her call. Kurt's fingerprints were all over the picture of Matthew. They were on the gun, too. Which was stolen several years ago in Washington. So the stuff wasn't planted, in other words."

"Did you think it was?"

"I didn't think anything. I let the evidence tell me the story. And this is what's bothering me. Why, on this night, was everybody someplace other than where they were supposed to be? Dr. and Mrs. Drummond were supposed to be gone. Anneke was supposed to be home. So how is it that they both came home early, and she wasn't there?"

"Coincidence?"

"Coincidence gives me a pain in the gut."

Hannah understood. It would have bothered her, too, if she were Churnin. "So that's why you're pissed at me? Because my clients came home early, and Anneke went out to get laid?"

"No. The problem is, before I got a chance to finish my work and forward my recommendation—justifiable homicide—to the DA, I got preempted. I'm told that the DA already has decided he isn't going to file charges. I'm told that Mrs. Drummond is a good citizen who faced down an armed scumbag burglar and stalker, a guy who probably murdered Laura. I'm told it isn't relevant that Kurt had Susan Beckett's number in his pocket. I'm told she probably gives it out to lots of people."

"Bullshit."

"Bullshit is right. I think Susan Beckett is behind the hustle to shut this case. But it benefits the Drummonds, so I want to know what kind of deal you cut with Susan Beckett."

Hannah hadn't expected that. She laughed. "There's no deal. The woman hates me, and the Drummonds. They decided Matthew doesn't need another grandmother. She didn't want to hear that. She actually implied she'd make thing difficult for them."

"An open investigation would have served that purpose."

"Absolutely."

Churnin chewed the inside of his lip for a minute, mumbled what might have been an apology for taking her time, and left. He didn't quite believe Hannah had nothing to do with the hasty closing of his case.

The no-charges decision should have made Hannah happy. But the way it happened bothered her. Susan Beckett shouldn't be doing favors for the Drummonds—she should be carrying out her threat to make their lives miserable. Maybe Susan was a more refined player than Hannah imagined. Maybe this was a marker she thought she could pick up later—in return for time with Matthew. More likely: she had a personal reason for wanting to the case closed— quickly.

Hannah went back to work, but she couldn't concentrate. The WESTLAW prompt blinked insistently at her, but she ignored it. Stephen Drummond said Kurt was trying to talk—something so important that he spent his last breath trying to say it. Kurt had told Hannah that Laura's murder had nothing to do with him, but everything to do with the father. She mulled the stubborn ambiguity of the words. The father—that might mean Matthew's father, who was Hoskins. Or perhaps Kurt meant Laura's father. But not Gerald Lawrence, Hannah decided. Laura refused to even call him her father. That left the biological father. The one Susan said was long dead. Was there something about him in the Drummonds' files, somehow? Was Kurt getting it for himself—or for Susan Beckett?

She logged off the computer. She needed to walk. She volunteered to get lunch for the office, and Vera shrugged assent. She scribbled her order: eggless tofu salad and a mango shake.

The health-food store was a block away. Hannah barely saw the passing storefronts as she walked. What could Susan want from the Drummonds' files? Just hearing about Laura's Fiat made Susan Beckett flinch—dead men didn't go auto shopping. Maybe she just thought Laura's father was dead. But perhaps Laura actually had found him. Was that discovery enough to get Laura killed? She wondered where Susan Beckett had been when the gas line in Laura's apartment was pulled.

Hannah was about to call Lawrence and try to get him to talk about the Becketts when her intercom buzzed. It was Bobby, and he didn't sound happy.

"Hannah, will you come to my office, please. Someone who claims to be Jerome Hoskins is on the line."

Claims to be? "I'll be right there," she said.

On the speakerphone, the caller was swearing, very creatively, in a gravelly voice at full volume. It didn't sound anything like Jerome Hoskins. Bobby stared at the phone as if it were a snake about to strike him.

"I never talked to anybody named Hannah Barlow," the voice said. "Drinks at Maxfield's? I don't drink anymore. Blood sample? What the fuck would I do that for?"

Hannah sat on the edge of the desk. "Mr. Hoskins? This is Hannah Barlow. You're saying we've never met?"

"Exactly. I've just come back from vacation, and I'm returning calls, including this one from you and your—"

"My law partner."

"He starts in with a story about how some guy named Kurt is dead, but Matthew is all right. I don't have any idea what he's talking about, and then he tells me I'm this Matthew's father? I don't think so. Not unless my vasectomy did a spontaneous reversal, and my luck isn't that bad, my history in Vegas notwithstanding. Is this some kind of joke?"

Hannah and Bobby looked at each other. She knew what he was thinking—goddamn lying Laura.

"Mr. Hoskins, I called you at your office. We spoke on the phone and in person."

"No, we didn't. What is going on here? Is this one of those deals where someone has stolen my identity? Is someone at Bally right now, running up my American Express?"

"No. But I think someone might have impersonated you," Hannah said. "Could we impose upon you—could you fax us a copy of your driver's license?"

"I'll do that, and one better. What's the number?"

They watched the pages inch out of the fax. On the first was a copy of the license. There was the Vallejo Street address they'd seen before, but not the same picture, or the same statistics. This Jerome Hoskins was squat, with straight black hair and brown eyes. He was not the man whose photo came with a vial of blood. Not the man they met at Maxfield's bar.

"Jesus God," Bobby said. "What's happened here?"

The second page was a clipping from the *San Francisco Business Times*, and there was Jerome Hoskins—the short, porky one—gazing superciliously at the camera.

"That could be a fake. People can cobble together a newspaper on the computer," Bobby said.

"Maybe." Hannah called the *Business Times's* library and had them fax the story from the archives. Again, the image of the dark-haired, portly Hoskins slid out of the machine. Now he seemed to be mocking Hannah and Bobby.

Bobby dropped into a chair. "Who is the guy who gave us the blood sample? I mean, I know he's Matthew's father, but who is he?"

"I don't know," Hannah said. "Laura went to a lot of trouble to make sure we couldn't find out." And she apparently told Kurt the truth—Hoskins wasn't the father. The phony Hoskins had faked a good bogus driver's license, complete with accurate information about the real Hoskins, right down to the final, musically shaped *s* in Hoskins's name.

"Where's the picture of the fake?" Hannah said. Vera got it, Hannah dialed Hoskins's number, and fed the photograph through the fax.

"I don't know this guy," Hoskins said when she called him five minutes later.

"But when I called your office, he answered your phone."

"Hang on." Hoskins shouted for someone to find Jan. Hannah heard them talking.

"Christ almighty," Hoskins said to Hannah "I'm putting my secretary, Jan, on the line with us."

"This guy worked for us," Jan said, her voice tinny in the speaker phone. "He was a messenger. Tom something. He was a charmer, did a mean Bill Clinton impression. I caught him using Mr. Hoskins's line a couple times. He just grinned, said it was a local call, no problem. Then I noticed that he'd turned off the voice mail."

Hannah had called back after their first conversation with the fake Hoskins. He had guessed that she might do that. He turned off voice mail and hovered around the office, waiting for the phone to ring. When Hannah had left messages with Hoskins's secretary, he intercepted and returned calls. But he hadn't been able to keep it up forever.

"We'll get you the dates he called us," Hannah said. "I think you'll find our number on your bill. You said he was a messenger?"

"Right," Jan said. "I haven't seen him in a few weeks. Want me to find out what happened?"

"If your boss doesn't mind."

"Hell, no," Hoskins said. "I want to confront the son-of-a-bitch who's pretending to be me. The last thing I need is another paternity suit."

Bobby shook his head. "Another one?" Hannah couldn't help but ask.

"Hell yes. Why do you think I got a vasectomy? God-damn women lie about being on the Pill. They're just looking to snag some guy, get a free ride."

They waited in Bobby's office for Hoskins's call. Hannah thought about breaking the news to the Drummonds. That made her sick to her stomach. Bobby seemed to read her mood.

"Want some good news? I found out where Laura got her car."

"And who bought it for her?"

"She bought it herself. With cash. The salesman remembered her."

"Of course he did."

"He said she came in, asked for a black Fiat Spider, and wouldn't consider anything else. She said if she couldn't get that model and color, the deal was off."

"With the dealership?"

"No. With the person who was paying for it."

"Who was that?"

"You're not going to like this."

"Just tell me, Bobby."

"Her father."

"Was this father dead or alive?"

"What?"

"Was this some kind of inheritance, with very particular rules? Laura's real father, whoever he is, is supposedly dead."

Bobby shrugged. "I don't know. The guy was trying to sell a car and ogle Laura's breasts, that was the impression I got. He didn't care about her father."

Hannah felt the beginning of a headache. Trying to straighten out Laura's past was like riding an off-kilter merry-go-round: she never got anywhere, and the trip just made her sicker and sicker.

"You're going to love this," Hoskins said when he called back, two excruciatingly long hours later. "The guy is named Tom Streeter. My incredibly naive company, in the name of civic-mindedness, hired him through a Parole Department work program—can you beat that? All we do is deal with highly sensitive client information, and their money, and they hire an ex-con."

"Was he fired?"

"Jan says he quit."

"That was a parole violation, I'll bet."

"Anything I can do to put this bastard back in prison, I'll do it," Hoskins said. "Imagine that lowlife, trying to be me."

"Just imagine," Hannah said.

Late that afternoon, Bobby and Hannah sipped diet Cokes on ice and fought the urge to break into the office's cache of Scotch.

"So Streeter was Laura's idea of a fantasy date," Bobby said. "She wanted everyone to think he was a nice, upscale guy. But he was an ex-con. She had lousy taste in men."

"She went to a lot of trouble to hide who he really was," Hannah said.

"I wonder if the Drummonds would have gone ahead, if they knew the father was a criminal?"

Hannah shrugged. "I don't know. Maybe that wasn't why she had this guy lie to us."

"Then what was the reason?" Bobby's hand was inching toward the drawer that held the Lagavulin—the Scotch they saved for Friday nights after particularly grueling weeks. She slapped his hand away. She needed him sober.

"It could be that Laura and Streeter planned to set up the Drummonds for one more fall. Streeter shows up with a blood test that declares him the real father. He argues that Laura put him up to the lies . . . he didn't know what she was really doing. But now he wants his son."

"And if the Drummonds want him to go away—they pay?"

Hannah nodded. "Maybe he got cold feet, now that she's dead. It's too messy for him to show up now."

"Because no one would be more suspect of her murder than an ex-con?" Bobby crunched a cube of ice.

"That could be it," Hannah said.

Bobby nodded. "Are you going to call the Drummonds with this good news, or am I?"

"We should do it in person."

"I think I'd rather be fired over the phone."

Hannah shook her head. "Let's take a drive over there. We owe them a face-to-face explanation."

Drummond answered the door. His expression was wary, and Hannah understood. Two lawyers on your doorstep? It wouldn't be good news.

"Is Rebecca here?" Bobby's voice was softer than usual.

"She's out shopping with Matthew and Anneke. What's wrong?"

"We need to tell you something," Bobby said. "And you're not going to be happy."

He wasn't. His face darkened as they told him about Tom Streeter and the real Jerome Hoskins. Hannah waited for the eruption of rage with a surreal feeling of calm.

"Well," he said at last. "She's dead, but she's not gone, right?"

Hannah and Bobby glanced at each other. "Laura?" Hannah said.

"She's fucked us over again. What do we do?"

"We?"

"Look," he said. "You're as much victims in this as we are. You're not responsible for Laura's machinations. How do we fix this?"

"I think at the very least we have to notify the court that Tom Streeter perpetrated a fraud by pretending to be Jerome Hoskins," she said.

"We don't have to track Streeter down, do we? The notice was published in San Francisco. If he lived there, we're covered."

Hannah was impressed at Stephen's grasp of legal detail. "Usually, that's right. In this case, I'm not sure that's how it works," she said.

"Why not?" Drummond was frowning at her challenge.

"What worries us is the lengths to which Laura and this guy went to hide his paternity," Bobby said.

Drummond nodded. "Okay, so she's devious. That's not news."

"It could have been a setup for some kind of scam,"

Hannah said. "I think it's unlikely now, but Streeter could still turn up and claim that it was all Laura's idea, but now he's seen the light."

"The light?"

"Matthew."

"That's not going to happen," Stephen said.

"I don't want to recite the cases to you," Hannah said.

"Some court would let a total stranger, a con, take Matthew away from us? Impossible."

"I don't know if it is. It's risky to predict what judges will do."

"So what does that mean? Now I'm supposed to pony up money to find this guy, in addition to everything else? It never ends."

Bobby caught Hannah's eye. Something dangerous was brewing here.

"Stephen, we're not trying to make work for ourselves," Hannah said. "If he's violated parole, I imagine the state Department of Corrections will look for him. When they can."

"When they can? You ride herd on them, okay? And do whatever you have to do with the court to make it happy. I just want this crap over with."

"Okay," Bobby said. "Shall we wait for Rebecca?"

"I'll handle that," he growled. Hannah decided she couldn't blame him for snapping. Laura was gone, but her lies remained, trickling into his family's life like a slow poison.

In the car, Bobby doled out aspirin for himself and for Hannah.

"It's like a bad dream coming true," Hannah said.

"What?"

"Laura was telling the truth when she told Kurt that Hoskins wasn't 'the one.' Kurt just didn't get it. He thought that proved he was Matthew's father."

"Thank God you kept trying to call Hoskins. We could have found out about this when Tom Streeter showed up demanding custody."

Hannah nodded. "There are too many fathers around. Kurt told me that Laura had done something to 'the father,' and that's what got her killed. I can't figure out which father that meant. Laura's father? Or now that we know Matthew's father is not Hoskins, maybe it meant Streeter."

"Why would Streeter kill Laura?"

"I don't know." She slouched in the seat and tried not to look at the curving road that Bobby was taking too fast. "Laura obviously told Kurt a lot that he didn't share with us. And it all died with him."

For a few days Hannah tried to put Laura out of her mind. It was necessary for her own well-being, to say nothing of the health of the office bank account. And it worked, after a fashion. Bobby tried to get the Department of Corrections to actively look for Streeter. He had not only quit his job, but also had failed to show up for a meeting with his parole officer. He'd moved, without leaving a forwarding address. But he had no history as a violent felon. Hannah knew his case was at the end of a very long line.

Hannah hadn't talked to Rebecca, but she'd left a message, apologizing for Stephen's hint that Hannah and Bobby were milking him for money. They both knew better, she said.

On Independence Day, Hannah begin thinking about Guillermo again. He was supposed to be back in Colorado, but he hadn't called. She was afraid to phone him. What would she say? Yes, please come live with me and share my bed, but while you were gone for a few paltry weeks, I slept with someone else?

To the sound of M-80s being set off by the neighborhood kids, she tried to put the thoughts aside. She immersed herself in a new, seemingly uncomplicated recipe. Coquilles St. Jacques. If Guillermo was moving in, she would probably have to cook dinner from time to time. She didn't mind eating her own bad cooking, but she didn't think she could inflict it on anyone else without facing criminal charges.

She made a botch of it—lumpy sauce, undercooked scallops. She threw it down the garbage disposal, and pitched out the shells in sheer disgust.

Finally, she grabbed the phone and dialed the Durango number. Amelia Agustin answered. Her son was still in Guatemala.

"You miss him?" Amelia said, the sound of a matchmaker in her voice.

"More than I can even say." Hannah didn't want to stay on the line. Amelia was uncannily perceptive. She might hear the timbre of infidelity and shame in Hannah's voice. Hannah told her she had another call. Amelia promised to have Guillermo phone the minute he got home.

"He misses you very much, *mija*," she said. Hannah cringed and poured herself a glass of brandy. What was she going to do?

The phone rang. Stephen's voice was tense, but not angry. Fearful, she decided.

"What's wrong?"

"Hannah, you're going to think I'm crazy, but it's started again. The calls."

"That's not possible."

"I know. It can't be Kurt."

Hannah knew then: the Westerlands. They'd all made the wrong assumption. Some calls might have been from Kurt, but not all. They'd been from the people he and Laura had cheated out of a son.

"You didn't change your number again after the shooting?"

"No. The new number we had was unlisted, and no reporters called, so we thought we were okay. But there were three hang-ups last night. Two more around nine this morning. Rebecca is going crazy."

"You called Churnin?"

"Yes. He won't say it, but he thinks I'm nuts."

"All right. Ask the security company to do some extra patrols. Make sure the alarms are on. And stay out of Rebecca's office. I'll see what I can do."

"You know who's doing this?"

"The Westerlands."

"The people who think they're supposed to get Matthew? Jesus Christ."

"Stephen? Let the police handle this, okay?" She was sure he knew what she meant: keep the guns locked up.

She had Churnin's home number—not directly from him, of course. She'd always made it a point of honor not to call him there, not until it was a true emergency. Even this situation didn't warrant that. Instead, she beeped him, and he called her back within a half hour.

"The Westerlands may have been doing it all along," Hannah said. "They terrified the Drummonds, and Kurt would up dead as a result. You can find them a lot quicker than I can."

Churnin grunted assent. "We'll see if we can scare them up."

He called back on Saturday. She was in the office, typing notes for a deposition while trying to keep leftover mock-egg salad out of her keyboard.

"Would you like to meet me for lunch?"

"I'm having lunch. What's up?"

"I thought you might like to meet Connie Westerland."

Churnin told Hannah he'd found her in Kerrville, Texas, and asked her if she could pay Las Almas a visit. She'd agreed at once. She was worried about Ed, she told him. She and Churnin met Hannah at a Denny's near the police station.

She was as the bartender at the 900 Days described her: very thin and nervous, ready to jump out of her skin. Her frizzy black hair hung to her shoulders. She wore baggy black pants and a thick chenille sweater. These softened her bony figure, but the magenta sweater made her careworn skin look even more pale. Her smile was a faint wash over a face haunted by loss. She plucked at her necklace, a double strand of glass beads, spaced with bits of shell and carved dancing-bear fetish charms, as Churnin introduced her. A faint scent of patchouli came from her wrist as she shook hands. She'd also been smoking clove cigarettes. Hannah wondered if she also had a Grateful Dead CD in her embroidered backpack.

At a back table, Connie Westerland told them how she and Ed were duped by Kurt and the woman they knew as Claudia.

"She called us after we put an ad in the paper," Connie said. There was a sagey twang in her voice: Texas was obviously home. "We were so happy. She needed our help, and we gave it. We knew there were risks, but we thought we'd bonded with her." Her face crumpled and she didn't speak for a moment. Churnin slid the pot of tea closer to her, and she poured a half cup before she resumed.

"When Claudia disappeared with our baby, I think I went a little crazy. I blamed Ed. I shouldn't have. I just hurt so much, and somebody was responsible for me losing my baby, and I just couldn't face that it was my fault as much as his."

"It was Laura who did this—and Kurt," Hannah said. "I think that's where the blame really belongs."

She nodded. "But they were gone, and we just had each other. Pretty soon we didn't have anything. I couldn't stay in that house anymore. I quit Boeing and went to my mama's in Kerrville. Then these started coming."

She pulled a thick pile of letters out of her bag.

"From Ed?"

She nodded, and pushed the stack toward Hannah and Churnin. "You won't really understand until you read them. I'm going outside for a smoke."

They were not meant to be read by strangers. In schoolboy printing, Ed Westerland pleaded and wept and prayed for Connie to take him back. He invoked their love, their pain, their deepest secrets—anything that he thought would work.

A few letters later, apparently reacting to Connie's silence, he told her he could get the baby. He'd learned Laura's real name and found her. Laura was sorry. It was all Kurt's doing. Some other people had the baby—he was almost walking now, could Connie believe it?—but Laura could get him back.

In the envelope was a picture. Hannah stared at it: Laura and Matthew, sitting on a park bench, laughing. There was a playground behind them. The last time she saw the picture, it was in black-and-white, and carried a message: GIVE HIM BACK. It came in an envelope with a Huntington Beach postmark. Just like this one. She handed the picture to Churnin, who recognized it.

"You think Westerland sent the threat to the Drummonds? Where did he get the picture?"

Hannah looked at it again. It could have been taken the day the adoption was finalized—in the picture, Matthew and Laura were wearing the clothes they wore on the day of the hearing—ducky white and yellow, and Day-Glo orange. Hannah saw a stack of Polaroids on Laura's coffee table during her visit.

"Maybe he got it from Laura's apartment."

"After he drugged her and before he pulled the gas line? Christ."

Connie came back and sat down, averting her eyes from the picture of Laura and Matthew. "The letters just got crazier and crazier, until I couldn't read them anymore," she said. "I didn't trust Claudia, Laura, whatever she called herself. Not after what she did. If someone else adopted the baby, then that was it. I wouldn't have done anything to take him away from his family. Mama opened the letters after that, made sure they weren't suicide notes, and then put them with the others."

Churnin addressed himself to Hannah. "I've told Connie that Laura is dead."

Connie's breath caught, and Hannah knew what Churnin would say next.

"Connie, do you think Ed would have killed her? As part of a plan to get back the baby?"

Tears welled in her eyes. "No." the voice was no more than a whisper. As she reached for her teacup her hand shook like an arrow just hitting its mark. She said what she wanted to believe. But her trembling body told what she felt.

Churnin promised to call Hannah the next day. It came and went without a word from him. She beeped him, but he didn't call back. Finally, after two more days of silence, Hannah broke her rule and called him at home, early enough in the morning to catch him before he went to work. He sounded anxious to get off the phone.

"This is not my only case, Hannah. Your clients are not the only people who need attention."

"I never said so. I take it you haven't found Ed Westerland."

"I haven't looked."

"And why is that?"

His voice was thick with sarcasm. "Laura Benson's off my desk. Open cases are my priority, the lieutenant says. Get it?"

She did. Kurt's death had closed Laura's file. The dominoes had fallen just right. The DA and Las Almas PD weren't interested in setting them back up. But Ivan Churnin was an honest cop; he didn't like being shoved around. Hannah played to that.

"Do you have any problem with me trying to find him?"

In the pause she heard ice clink, and then the sound of a drink being chugged. Hannah hoped it was an idiosyncrasy— orange juice on the rocks—and nothing more.

"Go ahead. And call me—here, not at the office—if you find something you can use. How long have you had this number, anyway?"

"Years. Don't bother changing it."

The return address on Ed Westerland's letters led Hannah not to a house, but to a mini-mall on a landlocked street in Huntington Beach, a city that hadn't managed to claim its share of Orange County's Gold Coast cachet. Certainly, there were miles of sand and good surf here. The pier had been rebuilt after a churning storm destroyed it in the mid-eighties. The downtown had been redeveloped, but the behemoth pink-stucco mall with a multiplex wasn't much of an improvement over the scuzzy beach-town main street it replaced.

The worst part was that skinheads regarded the city as their Orange County capital. More than once, a brown-skinned man had found himself beaten or stabbed for nothing more than taking a walk on the pier. Independence Day was once the occasion for a cute hometown parade, but after dark, the city saw riots two years in a row—burning sofas and bottles upside the head. Since then, the police—well-known throughout the county as hard-asses—locked up anyone who so much as stepped outside with a sparkler and a beer to celebrate. This year the holiday had been observed with all the wild exuberance of an algebra final.

The return address on Westerland's letters had a unit number, but Hannah couldn't match it to any of the businesses: Nguyen's Dry Cleaners, Touch Me Pagers, Holey Moley Doughnuts, and finally, Big Buddy's Breakfasts. If Ed knew how to flip eggs and bacon, maybe he'd worked there and used the place as a mail drop, too. She parked, ignoring the pair of skinheads who lolled on the curb with a forty-ounce malt liquor between them.

Big Buddy said Ed was good with short orders but quit after a month and never came back to get his last paycheck. Next door, Touch Me's counterman didn't know anything about Westerland, but took the opportunity to pitch a great cellular-phone deal. Sau Nguyen was more helpful, and less sales-oriented. He was a thin man, deep in middle age, and half a head shorter than Hannah. He looked to her like someone who might have been an army officer at home in Saigon, but now his lot was getting butter stains out of silk blouses. His hand hovered near a panic button behind the counter as the skinheads sauntered by, one pausing to grind half a Holey Moley cruller into the welcome mat at the door.

"Trash," he muttered as they turned the corner. He shook the mat into the garbage, and nodded when Hannah asked about Westerland.

"He only was here a month, and then no more," he said.
"Do you know where he is?

He hesitated. "Maybe he's dead? Like Connie."

"Connie's not dead," Hannah said. "Did he tell you she was?"

It was a struggle for both of them. Nguyen's English was sketchy, and Hannah didn't speak French or Vietnamese. But after a few minutes the story emerged: Nguyen and Westerland took coffee and cigarette breaks together when business was slow. They talked about family, and Westerland said he'd lost his wife. Just after they lost their baby.

Nguyen was frowning, frustrated at the slipperiness of English. "It means dying, right? When you say you lose someone?"

Hannah nodded. "It can. But this time it means that she left him."

He gave a regretful shrug. "As bad as dead."

Nguyen asked her to wait for a moment, and then returned with an address scribbled on a claim ticket. "But I think he is gone," Nguyen said. "Lost."

The apartment house was three squat units, two blocks from the Huntington Beach pier and across the street from one of the squeaky oil-pumping rigs that dotted the city, bobbing their grasshopper heads and sucking the earth's wealth. The manager showed her a drab, unfurnished single with an orange-countered kitchen that overlooked a tireless pumping insect. Ed had moved out on short notice. Hadn't bothered to leave an address for his security deposit's return. The manager asked Hannah to lock up when she was done. "Place was cleaner than when he moved in," the woman said. "And that's a first."

Hannah opened the kitchen drawers and ran her hand around the back of the cabinets. Next was the bathroom, where the faucet dripped just enough to be annoying. The mirror on the medicine cabinet was losing its silver. Inside, it was empty. Nothing in the toilet tank. She opened the cupboard under the sink, and found a Chock full o' Nuts can catching drips. As she pulled it out it erupted in cockroaches. They scuttled out, several using Hannah's bare arms as off-ramps. The flurry startled her, and she dropped the can. Rusty water spilled across the floor, and with the last splash came an amber plastic vial, which rolled into a corner behind the last retreating roach. Hannah retrieved the bottle.

The pharmacy label was half off, except for the first letters of the medication: Xan. She wrapped it in a piece of toilet paper and put it in her purse.

At seven that night, Churnin answered his home phone on the fourth ring and grudgingly agreed to a visit. Hannah had never been to his house, but it was easy to pick out. The lawn was as green as a celery stalk, and so weed-free that she had a picture of how Churnin spent his weekends: on his knees, armed with an infomercial garden gadget. The tan house's chocolate trim looked freshly painted. There was a For Sale sign out front, adorned with pictures of a Barbie-and-Ken real-estate team.

Churnin came to the door with a glass in his hand, his heavy eyelids suggesting that this wasn't the first aperitif of the evening. He waved her into a small living room, done in peach paint and pale floral-print furniture. A woman's choices, clearly, and made without the husband's consultation. Her mother had done the same thing once, in a rage. But Jimmy was so overworked that it took weeks for him to notice the new sofa, or the glass coffee table.

From Churnin's kitchen came the scent of baking apple pie. But there was no sign of Churnin's wife, whose picture until lately had sat on his desk.

He jiggled the glass at Hannah. "Small-batch bourbon. Want some?"

"No thanks." She hadn't had anything since the coconut doughnut she grabbed at Holey Moley, on the way to Westerland's apartment. Churnin seemed to take the refusal as a rebuke. He stretched out on a recliner and picked up the TV remote.

"No lectures on drink, all right? Had enough of that from *her*."

Hannah didn't say anything to that. But now she understood why the picture was gone. And why the house was freshly painted and filled with an aroma meant to evoke happy-family images. Potpourri, curb appeal, and a cut-rate price: the recipe for a fast divorce sale.

"Sorry, Ivan. I didn't know."

He shrugged. "Occupational hazard. You know that— your boyfriend's MIA. Now, what's up?"

She let the comment about Guillermo pass. "What kind of sedative did the coroner's toxicological people find in Laura's body?"

He looked at her suspiciously. "The metabolite? Why?"

"Come on, Ivan. I'm not trying to trip you up. What was it?"

He considered her for a moment, then motioned for her to wait as he went down a hallway. On television, Lawrence Welk's Champagne Music Makers worked their way through a truly perverse version of "Lucy in the Sky with Diamonds." Hannah had been subjected to nearly all of it by the time Churnin came back with a report in his hand.

"Alpha hydroxy alprazolam."

"And what pills would those have been when she took them?"

He consulted the report again. "Xanax. She'd also swigged quite a bit of alcohol. And there was something else."

"What?"

"We wanted to know if she'd been drinking something that could have been spiked with the Xanax without her seeing it. The tox guru in Santa Ana was thrilled when he tracked it down."

"Let me guess: carrot juice."

Churnin gaped at her. "You got the tox guru to tell you that? He barely talks to me."

"No. Carrot juice was something she liked—particularly mixed with gin." The opaque juice would hide the cloudiness of the crushed pills which would have been obvious in a glass of Bombay gin. If the pills came after the first drink, her tongue, numbed by alcohol, would be less likely to taste the bitterness in the second one.

Hannah held up the prescription bottle with its ragged label. Churnin's eyes locked on the three letters: XAN. "I found this in Westerland's former apartment," she said. "The PDR will tell you if the pills inside are Xanax. I'll bet they are. You might also be able to lift some prints."

Churnin took it from her and was silent for a moment as he looked at the bottle. The bourbon miasma seemed to be lifting. "Xanax is pretty common."

"That's true."

"It's not like you found curare-dipped darts or something."

"Also true. But Westerland moved out without a forward for his security money. He quit his job and didn't come back for his last check. Put those things together with the threatening letter to the Drummonds and his promise to Connie to get Matthew back. What does that tell you?"

"That I can probably kiss my job good-bye." Then he brightened. "Diana's never going to get her alimony now."

Hannah took Churnin to his favorite Indonesian haunt, where he ate two sobering servings of yellow curried vegetables and pretended the divorce from Diana ("princess of wails," he called her) was fine by him. Hannah went home feeling unsettled. What did Churnin mean when he said that Guillermo was missing in action? Did he see something weak in their relationship? She poured a brandy and told herself Churnin was hardly a qualified relationship critic. Then she decided she was drinking too much brandy and poured it back. She was turning back the sheets when the phone rang.

Connie Westerland haltingly asked if there was any news about Ed. Hannah could only imagine how she felt. She loved her husband but had left him. Left him bereft and crazy—maybe crazy enough to kill, from the sound of the letters.

"No one's found Ed," Hannah said. "But Detective Churnin is working on it." She hoped that would be true, come morning. She thought about mentioning Ed's pills, but didn't. Maybe they were actually Connie's pills. The thought made her uneasy.

"I know it's pretty late, but can I come over?" Connie's voice was small and plaintive. "I'd like to talk to you about something. About Matthew."

31

Connie couldn't talk without one of her vile clove cigarettes, so she and Hannah sat outside on the porch. Hannah had started stripping the paint from the columns there, but abandoned the task the week Kurt died. In the dark, they could have been dead trees with sick, scabrous bark.

Connie sucked one cigarette to stubby death and began on a second one. The match trembled on its way to the tip. Hannah sipped at the herb tea she'd made and waited for Connie to complete the ritual that would let her talk.

"This is so hard," she said. "I know I shouldn't even bring it up."

Hannah considered Connie's worn face and sad, tired eyes. Women complained about the toll children took on their youth and beauty. It seemed to her that motherhood denied could do far worse things.

"It's okay, Connie. What about Matthew?"

She stubbed out the cigarette and pressed her hands between her knees.

"Could I see him?"

Hannah knew she must look stunned. Connie hurried into the silence.

"I just would like to look at him, only for a minute." Her hands mapped out the tiny territory of her request, her body tucked to show how little trouble she'd be. Her eyes were lively, for the first time, and they gave her face a tenuous

ight. "Those good people don't even have to meet me, and
won't intrude on their lives. I just . . ."

It was the worst idea Hannah could imagine. After what
the Drummonds had been through—Kurt's death, Susan
Beckett's bullying, and the calls from Connie's husband—
she couldn't imagine they would even entertain the idea.
And the Xanax, she thought, could have been Connie's. She
didn't know for a fact that Connie wasn't there, helping her
husband kill Laura.

"Connie, I don't think—" Hannah stopped. The caul of
loss enveloped Connie's face again. She struggled not to
cry, and her voice was husky with the effort.

"I need to see him," she said. "I promise I'll never bother
them again."

"But, Connie, but try to understand how it is for them."

She nodded, but an edge of defiance sharpened her
voice. "They should understand something, too: he was
mine first."

The tone—desperate, righteous, and angry—lifted the
hairs on the back of Hannah's neck. Maybe Connie wasn't
the sane half of the Westerlands.

"Not a good approach, Connie. I'm not going to do any
special pleading for someone who threatens my clients."
Hannah picked up her cup and headed for the door. Connie
scrambled to stop her.

"No, wait. God, I'm not threatening anyone. I just want
them to understand how much—" She stopped, worked to
keep from breaking down. "How much I lost. They'd
understand what I've gone through, wouldn't they? Weren't
they just like Ed and me, for a while?"

Desperation and contrition played across Connie's face.
Hannah thought of the night that Rebecca talked about
childlessness. Hannah pictured it as a desert, vast and empty
and dry. Rebecca and Stephen wandered it, desolate and
lost, separated even from each other by their pain. They
thought nothing could have been more devastating. Until
they lost Jennifer. And then childlessness—never having
had a child to lose—must have seemed like a garden.

"They were just like you." Hannah paused, looked away

from Connie's pleading eyes, and thought about how it could be done safely. She'd talk it over with Churnin and Bobby. They could make it work, if the Drummonds were willing. "I'll talk to them," she said.

Connie smiled, and then dissolved into a shower of tears. Hannah sat with her, waiting out the storm and praying to God that she would never want a child the way Connie Westerland did.

"If you do this, I think you should bring Matthew to my office," Hannah told the Drummonds the next night. "I don't think you should meet her here."

Drummond paced the length of the white living room before stopping in front of Hannah with his arms folded. "What do you think?"

"It's up to you. I don't think Connie is a threat to you. Ed is another story, but she says she's not in touch with him. She's cooperating with the police. Bobby and I will be there. I've asked Churnin, and he thinks there's a minimal risk."

"Minimal?" he said.

Rebecca, who had been silent during Hannah's description of the meeting with Connie, finally looked up. "Why can't we meet her?"

It was a response Hannah hadn't considered. "You can, if you want to. She doesn't want to intrude on your lives. She just wants to see Matthew. Once, in person."

"I'd like to meet her."

Drummond spun on his wife. "Are you nuts? You won't have anything to do with Susan Beckett, but you'll let this lunatic into our lives?"

"It's not the same."

"No, it's worse. I've had it with these fucking leeches—these people trying to attach themselves to our son. This woman's husband has threatened us, Rebecca. Don't you get it? She's probably as crazy as he is."

"They lost a baby, Stephen. Don't you remember how that feels?" She glared at him, as though daring him to make her bring it all up again. Stephen wavered, regained his self-righteous anger.

"I won't have any part of it." He turned to Hannah. "You should have just said no. What are we paying you for?" He threw open the door to the deck, stamped out onto it, and then down the hill to Rebecca's office.

Rebecca got up and gently closed the door. "When can we do this?"

Matthew had a cold. Snot trickled from his nose, and he was as cranky as Hannah had ever seen him. He writhed and sniffled as Rebecca sat with him in Hannah's office. Rebecca kissed the top of his head and made soft, cooing noises, but it didn't seem to do much good. He pulled his Winnie the Pooh T-shirt over his face and began a droning, miserable whine.

"Will she be here soon?" Rebecca tried to make the question sound casual, but Hannah could see her anxiety. Smudgy circles ringed her eyes, and without makeup, the scar on her face seemed more prominent. She had dressed in a check skirt and a white cotton blouse with fancy cutwork, but she wore no earrings, bracelets, or rings. Just her wedding band. Hannah wondered if she thought Connie might be a jewel thief in her spare time. But since Kurt and the phone calls, she had every reason to be edgy about strangers.

Hannah was surprised that Rebecca wanted to do this. But she no longer was taken aback by Rebecca acting against Stephen's wishes. She had disengaged from the need for his approval. All in all, Rebecca was far different from the woman who fetched tea for Hannah at Stephen's command.

"She'll be here any minute," Hannah said. "I told her ten-thirty."

Hannah's computer beeped. She turned the screen so Rebecca could read Vera's message: *connie westerland in reception.*

Vera had switched to lowercase, and now Hannah heard her voice as a confidential whisper.

"Oh, God," Rebecca said. Matthew tensed with her.

"You don't have to do this," Hannah said.

She took a breath. "But I want to."

Connie was decked out in what looked like her finest: a red rayon suit, matching shoes. Pearls. No patchouli. Her hair was cut, styled, and tamed by some antifrizz potion. She had pleaded to see the boy, but she was doing her best not to look pitiable.

She tried to focus on Rebecca, but her eyes strayed to Matthew, who sagged dispiritedly in Rebecca's arms and curled his lip at Connie.

"It's not personal. He has a cold," Rebecca said. She tried a smile.

"Oh, poor little guy." Connie waved at him. He buried his face in Rebecca's chest. "I could have done this another time."

"That's all right." Rebecca shifted Matthew and put out her hand. "I'm Rebecca. I'm so sorry for what you've gone through."

Connie's eyes misted. "Connie. Likewise."

Matthew grunted unhappily. For a minute Hannah thought all four of them would start to cry. It took guts for Rebecca to do this. Hannah wasn't sure she could have done it. But she realized the women had more in common that just Matthew. They shared the experience of Laura.

Despite everything Laura had done to Rebecca and Stephen, it was nothing compared with her deceit of the Westerlands. The Drummonds came out of it with a son. The Westerlands had nothing, not even a marriage.

Although Stephen refused to accept it, Rebecca saw that Matthew could have easily slipped through their fingers. She could be the one in a lawyer's office, pleading for a visit. Laura had never intended it, but she'd made allies out of two women who should have been wary, wounded enemies.

"He's a sweet boy," Connie said. "So blond."

"He looks like his mother," Rebecca said. "Laura, I mean."

Connie shook her head. "You're his mother. Don't you forget that."

• • •

The visit was coming up on the hour to which Rebecca had agreed. Hannah stepped out to answer a phone call and give Bobby a progress report.

"They've utterly bonded," Hannah said. "It's amazing."

"Nothing about this business surprises me anymore," he said.

"What's new on Tom Streeter?"

"Nothing. Department of Corrections can't find him. I'm going to court tomorrow to have a chat with Judge Baxter about the father problem."

"What do you think she's going to do?"

"I'd like to think she'll find that the ad we placed in the *Chronicle* was enough to put Streeter on notice that he had a kid. But she'll wonder what I still do: Why did he and Laura lie? Why was that so necessary?"

Hannah shook her head. "I wish I knew. Laura had us all dancing in circles. Maybe it just amused her to make this as complicated as possible."

Hannah returned to find the women embracing like long-parted sisters. Matthew was dozing on the sofa, his thumb in his mouth.

Connie separated from the hug first and wiped at her eyes. "Well, time to go." She cleared her throat, got herself under control. "I've tried for a long while to tell myself that things happen for the best. But this is the first time I've believed it. Whatever brought Matthew to you and your husband—it was the right thing."

"I only wish it hadn't hurt you so much," Rebecca said.

Connie nodded. "I'm going to be okay." She turned and glanced at Matthew, whose face now was scrunched against a cushion, his cheeks flushed red.

"Could I give him a little kiss good-bye?"

"If you don't mind risking a cold," Rebecca said.

She bent down and brushed her lips against an eyelid. He wrinkled his nose and sniffled in annoyance. "Bye, little guy," she said.

Hannah steeled herself against all the warm feelings the scene evoked. If Connie was going to make her play, she'd do it now. But she shouldered her purse, thanked Hannah, and turned to shake hands with Rebecca.

"Connie, if you'd like to visit us, that would be all right." Rebecca scribbled her address and phone number on Hannah's notepad and handed it to Connie, who stared at it, dumbfounded. Hannah thought about snatching it back, but didn't. This was Rebecca's choice.

"Really?" Connie looked as thought she might cry again. "That would be wonderful."

"Anytime."

"I'll be here in town for another week or so, before I go back to Kerrville."

"Then just call me." Rebecca hugged her and walked her to the door. Hannah sat down next to Matthew and wondered where that generous gesture would lead.

Rebecca came back and scooped Matthew into her arms. "Thank you, Hannah. She's wonderful."

"That was supposed to be closure," Hannah said. "You just opened everything up again."

Rebecca shrugged. "I felt sorry for her. And I got a good feeling about her. There's room for someone like her in Matthew's life."

"I can only imagine what Stephen's going to say about this."

Rebecca smiled coolly. "Maybe I'm not going to tell him."

Hannah hated working late, particularly on a Friday, but sometimes there was no getting around it. The mothers' meeting had cut two hours out of the day. She supposed she could get a laptop and tussle with her pleadings over the weekend, but that would ruin the sanctuary that Mrs. Snow's house had become.

She could walk through the front door and forget about hearings, filings—even the Drummonds, if she put her mind to it. There was only the house and its myriad refurbishing chores. The work was going well, and she finally could imagine how the rooms would look when everything was done.

She had begun to picture Guillermo not only in the study, as she had on the night she asked him to live with her, but in the dining room, kitchen, and bedroom. Why ruin that idyll by taking work to the upstairs apartment, where it would wait like a big, ugly, poisonous cane toad?

So she made herself stay at work for a while longer. It was bearable enough. She had fresh coffee, and Vera had left two unopened cartons of yogurt in the fridge. Hannah finished them off and left her an IOU. And, because the office observed the instant tradition of Casual Friday, she was comfortably dressed in jeans, a pair of old thick-soled boots, and a slate-gray cotton sweater. Of course, she and Bobby ran the place and they could wear what they wanted, whenever they wanted. But dressing down was really only fun when it was an antidote to suits, so they limited the practice to the end of the week.

It was nearing ten when the phone rang. Guillermo, she hoped. But the voice was Anneke's—jittery, breathless.

"Can you come here, please?" Anxiety had thickened her accent.

"Now?"

"Yes. There's . . . something wrong. Rebecca is going crazy."

Hannah heard Stephen and Rebecca shouting in the background. Matthew cried. Jesus, she thought, Stephen found out about Connie.

"I'm coming now. If anyone is likely to get hurt, call the police."

"My God," Anneke moaned. "I wish I'd never moved in here."

The two-lane road to the Drummonds' house was wreathed in fog. Hannah knew there were houses along the way, set back from the road and screened by trees and bushes. But there was no sign of them right now. Halfway up the hill, the layer deepened, and Hannah had to slow to a crawl so that she wouldn't miss the turn.

The lights bordering the driveway and around the entry were off. Hannah listened. There was no audible commotion now, at least not one loud enough to penetrate Rebecca's mauve stucco walls. Then one of the koi splashed. Silence again. And then the front door opened. Anneke must have heard her arrive. She let Hannah in and indicated she should go into the family room. Hannah turned to ask if the fight was over, but Anneke was already halfway up the stairs. Hannah wondered if she had started packing.

The Drummonds sat in silence, Rebecca on the sofa with Matthew asleep on her shoulder, clad only in a diaper. The baby's cheeks were red, his breath deep and noisy, like an old man's. Rebecca's arms sagged with his weight. Stephen sat in a chair, his head dropped, his hands resting over his ears as if to stop some incessant noise.

He looked up at Hannah, reached to the side of his chair, and tossed something to her. The object, round and furry, landed in her hands with a squeak. She was holding a teddy bear. There was a tiny paper envelope, run through with a ribbon, attached to its collar.

"Rebecca found that at the foot of the stairs. Read the card."

It was inscribed in a blocky hand that Hannah knew from Connie's stack of letters. FOR MY SON MATTHEW.

"It's from Ed Westerland," Hannah said. "How did it get inside?"

Stephen was instantly on his feet. Rebecca huddled over Matthew, as though Stephen was going to hit them both.

"We don't know." He hadn't raised his voice, but the words hit like thudding explosions. "Despite everything that has happened, someone apparently leaves doors unlocked." He stabbed his finger at Rebecca. "You're responsible for this. You're encouraging that loony woman and her crazed husband. Goddammit, I told you not to see her!"

Rebecca nuzzled her son's cheek. "Shut up, Stephen, you'll wake him."

"Well then, take him upstairs. Goddammit, it's too late for him to be down here anyway."

Rebecca lifted the boy and brushed past Hannah. "Anneke must have thought I was going to do something drastic. Sorry to ruin your evening." She looked back at Stephen with cold anger. Turned backs at best in their bed tonight,

Hannah thought. If he was less lucky, Stephen would find himself sleeping down here. At worst, he'd be bunking in a hotel.

Stephen slouched on the sofa, the bear on his chest. He stared at it, as though he expected it to speak. "Goddamn maniacs. I wish we'd caught them doing this."

Hannah knew what that meant. "You'd have liked Rebecca to shoot them, too?"

He shook his head, but then shrugged. "At least it would be over then."

Hannah hated him sometimes. "Why don't you try to get some sleep? Tomorrow I can draft a restraining order, and let Churnin know what's happened. Check the doors before you go to bed."

"Christ, I'm the only one who does."

Hannah heard the dead bolt click behind her. In the time she'd been inside, the fog had thickened. It pooled around the grass and shrubs, rising like a rain-swollen lake. As she got into the Integra the outdoor lights came on in a blaze that made her blink. Stephen was securing the perimeter. When she turned onto the road, she looked back, but could see only the blurred blue-white lights, not the house itself. The fog had swallowed it, and it was gobbling every inch of the road behind her.

She took the turns slowly. She couldn't tell when the road was flanked by a fence or when there was nothing to stop a steep fall into the canyon. For a few feet, the fog was thick as layered gauze. Then it frayed and floated back, revealing road, the shadows of trees, and the star-dotted night above.

But now she plunged into another thicket of blindness. She heard an engine race behind her, but she saw nothing. The engine screamed with a downshift. She knew the vehicle was closer, but she still couldn't make it out. On the next curve, the fog thinned. Hannah squinted at the rearview mirror. A truck. Headlights off. It was closing on her.

Hannah tapped the brake pedal, hoping the lights would remind the driver he didn't have the road to himself. Now his high beams blazed to life. She was blinded for a moment. She looked again. An orange truck, closing fast.

The same truck that followed Laura on the day of the finalization hearing. In the dark, behind the high beams, Hannah was sure the driver was a burly blond man, half-crazy with loss. Ed Westerland.

With a jerk, the truck swung out from behind her and sped into the uphill lane on her left. He pulled up even with her. Hannah glanced at Westerland. His hair, trimmed and clean in the picture Connie had given Churnin, was flat and lank. He wore what had once been a white T-shirt. His narrowed eyes were fused to the road. Hannah knew what would come next: one hard right on the Dodge's wheel and she'd plunge into the canyon. She floored the car, pulling away from him. For a few feet, the road was straight and empty. She could see the glow of downtown Las Almas below. She watched Westerland's headlights recede as she made a curving left. And then she descended into a maw of fog. Now the road snaked left, right, left, and Hannah had to slow down or risk missing a curve. It was like driving inside a sack of flour. Then the truck was on her again. She blinked in the glare of the lights.

As they came to a stretch of road bordered by a shoulder and hills on either side, he came at her from the right. Hannah clenched her teeth and swung the wheel toward him, hoping to force him onto the embankment. But he held his ground. The truck raked the right side of her car with a grating howl and she fought to keep control of the wheel. Their eyes met as she swung the wheel left, peeling away from the truck. Westerland's expression was flat, unreadable. If he wanted her dead, he wanted it with an icy detachment that frightened her more than rage would have.

From just behind her, Westerland veered left and rammed her rear bumper. The Integra shot across the road. She saw the hillside rush up. She pulled the wheel right. Now, ahead of her, the road curved. There was no shoulder—only a spindly wooden rail stood between her and a crash into the canyon. She slammed the brakes. The car skidded and then shuddered, dropping sharply on the right. Hannah felt her control on the wheel slip. One of the tires had gone flat—did he have gun? Had he shot it out? She turned with the skid, and had control again.

Hannah felt jangled, every nerve and muscle shaking so that she could barely undo the lap belt. But she had to get out. The Integra wasn't drivable. On foot, in the dark—that was her only chance now. She scrambled over the railing and made a few sliding steps down into the canyon. The truck screeched to a stop, popping gravel and rocks. Westerland fumbled with something inside the cab. The gun, she thought.

She huddled on a rocky shelf, breathing slowly, trying to stop shaking. Above her, she heard the truck's door open and slam shut. Footsteps shuffled in the dirt. She crept farther down the slope, knowing that the crunch of branches and leaves would give her away once he was close enough to hear. She told herself to be still.

The fog was lighter here, and darkness was not absolute. She looked for anything resembling a fire road or trail. There seemed to be a lighter-colored cut in the hillside below her, but only a controlled fall could get her to it fast enough. She heard more footsteps, and now she could see him, silhouetted in his truck's headlights, scanning the landscape. His hands were empty—no flashlight, no gun. He climbed over the rail and began inching his way down the slope, occasionally grabbing onto the scrubby brush to keep from sliding. Hannah picked her way to a U-shaped outcropping of rock that lay perpendicular to the hillside and huddled in its arms. She could hear Westerland's truck idling above her. He'd left the engine on. If she could get back to the road, she'd take his truck, leaving him stranded, at least for a little while.

Now Westerland came closer. He stopped twice, and Hannah imagined him squinting into the night, opening his nostrils to catch her scent. She could make him out against the straw-colored hill, several feet above her, but far to her right. He picked his way down until he was almost parallel with her hiding place. Then he cut across, trying for an easier path down the hill. She found a palm-sized stone and picked it up. Then she held herself motionless.

He angled up as he approached. Hannah could hear his panting breath. He sat down on a boulder just above Hannah's hiding place and let out a tired sigh. Hannah quieted her breathing and willed him to keep walking.

Instead, he sat, as stolid as the rocks around him. Hannah couldn't outwait him. And as soon as she moved, he would be on top of her. She fingered the stone.

He stood up, stretched, and gingerly stepped to a cluster of bushes. Hannah heard the zipper, a trickle, and then a gush. That was when she threw the rock. It hit the ground far below him, clinking against rocks and setting off a landslide of pebbles.

Westerland froze at the sound, zipped up, and raced toward the steep drop-off where he thought she must be hiding. When he passed, Hannah waited a few more moments, gathered a breath, and shot out, scrambling up the hill as fast as she could. Over the sound of her own frantic paces through the dirt and rocks, she heard him. He'd stopped. Turned. She cursed herself for not being patient for a few more seconds. She'd panicked.

Now, up the steep hill, both of them stumbled and slid in the loose rocks. As she grabbed at a branch to hoist herself around a boulder, he yanked her back by the waist of her jeans. She fell, and Westerland lost his footing, too. They tumbled through stinging branches and hard rocks. They were back where they began.

Hannah got to her feet first. She was breathless. Tiny cuts stung her hands. She gulped air and stumbled once again up the hill. Then Westerland was on her, tackling her from the side. They hit the ground hard, slid, and stopped. Hannah kicked out of Westerland's grip. They were at the lip of the canyon's next drop. He tried to get up, to scramble after her, but she could see he was exhausted, driven now by sheer rage that made him shake. Their eyes met, and she saw something in his: fear, maybe. And seeing it, she kicked him squarely in the forehead, once with the toe and then, as he started to slide, with the heel of her boot. He scrabbled for foothold, grabbed for a last handful of brush. His voice was panting, angry, frantic as he slid away: "Fucking bitch."

And then, nothing but his grunts and the sound of rock shaken loose.

She wondered if she should check to see if he'd broken his neck. Instead, she ran, stumbled, and crawled her way up the hill she had so carefully descended.

32

She swung open the door to the Dodge, jumped into the cab, and let off the brake. The truck, which had been idling rough, sputtered, stalled. She swore, turned the key. Nothing. And then she heard him.

Westerland leaped the railing and rushed her, his face scraped and filthy. She twisted the key again, but it was too late. The door swung open and he grabbed her by the hair.

He dragged her out and slammed her head against the truck's hood. He let out a little noise of primordial satisfaction as her forehead bounced off the metal. Through the spattered lights that danced through her eyes, Hannah saw Westerland pull a baby's car seat out of the cab and fling it into the truck bed. Then a wave of sickness surged through her and her ears roared.

When she woke up, she was next to him in the truck. He sped down the road, barely braking as he took the turns. On one curve, she slid into him and he shoved her against the passenger door.

"Goddamn lawyer. This is your fault." There was a vicious edge to his voice.

She didn't think any answer would improve the situation, so she said nothing. She wanted to sit up, but it hurt to raise her head. She tried to focus on where they were, where they were going, and what Westerland's intentions might be. Would he kill her up here in the hills and dump her somewhere? But then she saw they were nearing the bottom of the winding road, not far from downtown Las Almas. A few blocks more and they would be at her office.

They came to a light. Her hand was on the door handle, and when Westerland stopped, she pulled it, ready to tumble out and run. But the door wouldn't yield. Childproof locks: he'd outfitted the old truck for Matthew.

"It's not enough that a man has a decent job and a house that's paid for," Westerland said, ignoring her escape attempt and picking up the soliloquy where he'd left it miles ago. There was a red waffle, the imprint of Hannah's heel, tattooed on his forehead. His hands were scraped raw in a half-dozen places. They vibrated slightly as he pumped his grip on the steering wheel.

"It's all about money, isn't it? Your rich clients bought Matthew. Now they're buying off Connie. And there's nothing I can do about that, you think."

She swallowed. Her throat was dry and tight, but she felt as though she had to say something, or let her silence be understood as agreement. "It wasn't like that. The Drummonds didn't know anything about you."

He didn't answer her. His lips pulled into a tight, bloodless line as he wrenched the truck into a hard right that slammed Hannah against the door. They were on the San Diego Freeway, heading north. He jammed the accelerator and the truck was suddenly doing seventy-five. In any other county, that would attract attention from the CHP. But not here.

Westerland got off in Huntington Beach and headed toward the ocean. He turned into the driveway of a trailer park that was dwarfed by the Edison generating plant next to it. Yellow lights pooled in the darkness as they drove through the park. There were more empty concrete pads along the road than trailers. Nothing so grandiose as mobile homes here: only snail-shaped, rusting metal boxes surrounded by green-rock lawns. One pair of aging eyes watched through parted curtains as Westerland's truck drove by.

They stopped several aisles later. He pulled her out from the driver's side. The smell of ocean fought with something gassy that seemed to burp out of the plant next door. Between the smell and the dizziness, Hannah didn't know if she was going to vomit or faint. Westerland held her tight by the arm and marched her to an old trailer. In her swimming vision, it seemed better tended than the others.

Westerland unlocked the door and flicked on the light. Two yellow plaid sleeper sofas faced each other across a table. Butterscotch curtains in a pattern of chickens and eggs covered the windows. There was a tiny kitchen and sliding plastic divider that hid the bathroom. For its size and vintage, the trailer should have reeked. Instead, it smelled of spaghetti sauce and Lysol. Westerland motioned for Hannah to sit down on one of the pullout beds, and then locked the trailer door with a padlock.

He washed his hands, dabbed the bruise on his forehead with a paper towel, and then turned toward her. "How much money did it take to turn Connie against me?"

Hannah's head still felt as though it was being pounded with a ball penn hammer. A bump was rising on her forehead.

"I don't know what you're talking about."

"You paid her off. I saw her talking to you and that cop. I saw her coming to your office. So what did you pay her to forget about what your fucking clients did to us?"

She shook her head. And then he was on her, slapping her face until it burned. But as he pulled back she had a moment. She kicked him, this time in the groin. As he crumpled she lunged for the keys were on the counter. But he was faster. He threw her to the floor, facedown. He yanked her hair. She shrieked for him to stop. And, amazingly, he did.

"Goddammit, don't run. Don't make me hurt you. I don't want to hurt you."

She couldn't see him. But something in his voice had changed. "Then let me up," she said.

"No running?"

She nodded. He was too big for her to overpower. Once, when she was in fighting trim, she might have been able to do it. Not now.

He took her by the arm and helped her up. He couldn't quite stand up straight, and she was glad of that. He dumped her onto the sofa bed and stepped back.

Now that he wasn't trying to kill her, she could look at him. Somewhere, behind the grime and rage, she glimpsed another Ed—maybe the sane one. He blinked at her silence and stillness.

"Do you want some water?"

Before the loss of his wife and baby turned him into whatever he was now—Laura's killer, a would-be kidnapper, or just a stalker who wanted to scare the Drummonds out of their minds—he'd been a normal person. When normal people have guests, they offer hospitality. Maybe Ed Westerland was remembering who he'd been once, in a nice old house in Ballard.

"Thanks."

"Want coffee?"

That surprised her even more. "Okay."

"Don't try anything, all right?"

She shook her head. "I won't."

He pulled out a coffee can—Chock full o' Nuts—and a percolator. While he worked, Hannah looked around: there was no telephone. Her cellular was in her purse—which was in her car, on an unlit road in Las Almas. On a shelf behind her was a stack of letters, first addressed to Claudia Bengstrom, and then to Laura Benson, but all marked in Laura's looped handwriting *return to the sender*. A portable Royal typewriter sat next to the mail. The bed opposite Hannah held a milk crate full of stuffed animals, plastic pull-toys, and children's books. What looked like a collapsible playpen stood against the door. It seemed that Westerland was readying the trailer for the baby he regarded as his son. But it didn't make sense: if he was planning to kidnap Matthew, why did he drop messages, leave toys? Those things only made the Drummonds more edgy and vigilant.

Westerland put before her a glass of water and a mug of steaming coffee. He sat down across from her. Hannah started to reach the cup, but he suddenly slid it away from her.

"Christ. I'm fucking stupid. You'll splash me in the face with it."

Hannah picked up the water glass and offered no comment. Tossing the coffee had occurred to her, but she decided against it. It wouldn't disable him long enough for her to get out.

"You ran me off the road," she said. "You can't expect Miss Manners after that. What do you want?"

"You and your partner helped the Drummonds steal our baby. Now you're trying to turn Connie against me. I want my wife and my baby back." He reached into the lidded storage compartment behind the bed and pulled out the or-else: a crappy seventy-dollar Saturday-night special, a cheap metal-and-plastic semiautomatic pistol. The damned things jammed as often as they shot, but she couldn't rely on lousy firearms technology to save her. And at this range, one shot would be all he needed. Westerland's hand quivered as he tensed it around the grips.

Hannah didn't think Westerland would kill her. That wouldn't bring back Matthew and Connie. If the real Ed could be found, he would know that. But he was lost in someone else—the one who glared at her as he ran her off the road. The one who enjoyed bashing her face against the Dodge's hood. Rationality wasn't Ed's strong suit at this point.

"The Drummonds didn't know anything about you and Connie," she said. "They didn't steal Matthew. Neither did I. Neither did Bobby." She worked to keep her voice low and calm. Maybe the mood would catch. She considered reminding him that Laura wasn't even pregnant when she took his goodwill and money and hope. But if he'd ever figured Matthew's age, he knew that. He had disregarded the facts and held on to a shaky theorem: Laura promised them her baby. She had a baby. So the baby belonged to him and Connie.

She took another tack. "But now the Drummonds know what Laura did to you. They sympathize. They weren't paying Connie off. They let her see Matthew."

His eyes narrowed. "No way."

"You didn't see Rebecca Drummond come to my office with Matthew when Connie was there?"

His face reddened. "I might have dozed off for a minute."

"You're tired."

He shrugged. "I can't sleep at night."

"Connie saw Matthew. The Drummonds will let her see him again."

He said nothing.

"They did it because they understand how much Laura and Kurt hurt you and Connie."

"They couldn't know. But that doesn't matter. And I'm not worried about Laura and Kurt anymore. They got their comeuppance. That's a start."

Hannah felt a thread of rising panic. His ability to hear her—hear reality—faded in and out, like a weak radio signal. If she was going to get out of his tin-can prison, she had to get him to see the Drummonds as Laura's dupes, as victimized as he was.

"You want to see Matthew?"

"I want him back. I want you to tell them that. No cops, no static. Just you get my boy and then you won't die."

"Ed, if I'm going to tell Rebecca and Stephen about your request—"

"Demand." He pointed the little gun at her.

"Okay, your demand, then." He lowered the pistol. "So they'll understand, tell me what happened with Laura. Connie said Laura promised to get Matthew back for you."

He took a sip of her water and cleared his throat. "Laura said the Drummonds wouldn't do it, even though they knew he was ours." Thinking about that seemed to infuriate him. His face darkened. "Shit. I'm not bargaining. I'm telling you."

"I know. But unless you make them understand, they're not going to listen."

He glowered at her, trying to see the trick. "They'd better listen—if they don't want to see you dead."

"To tell you the truth, Ed, I think Matthew matters more to them."

He considered that. "Bullshit."

"If you try to swap him for me, they'll call the police, Ed."

He frowned, deciding whether she was telling the truth.

"Let me go back to them and tell them what's going on with you," she said. "Reason with them."

He still was doubtful. "You can't call the cops. I'll be watching you. I'll have this gun ready to kill you."

She nodded. "Okay. But Ed, I'm not going to do this until you tell me what happened with Laura. I can't be your advocate unless I know. Make sense?"

It was a stall, and he probably knew that. But Hannah thought he hadn't had a chance to talk much about the hell his life had become. He needed to tell someone how wronged he was. This was his chance.

"I'll tell you," he said. "But after that, we're going. And you'll tell the Drummonds to give our baby back to us."

"All right."

The dead-eyed look he gave her as he slammed into her car was back. "And you'd better be convincing."

Ed Westerland wasn't used to narratives. He stopped between sentences to drink his coffee, and then started in on Hannah's cup. He never let the scary, unpredictable pistol out of his hand.

"Makes me sick, what they did to us. It was so bad that Connie left. So I had nothing: no wife, no baby. I could have killed myself, right then. But then I decided that was wrong. I shouldn't pay. They should."

"They?"

"Claudia—Laura. All I had to do was find her, get her to change her mind."

"You thought you could do that?"

He nodded. "Kurt was the problem, all along. I liked Laura. She liked me. If I could just convince her, it would be okay. Then Connie would come back. I decided the way to do it was to give Laura something she wanted. Really wanted."

"What?"

"Tell her who her father was. The real one."

Hannah blinked at him. "You knew she was adopted?"

"She told me. She'd found her mother, but she didn't want anything to do with Laura. That really hurt her."

Hannah nodded. She had been right about Susan Beckett: she lied about the joyous reunion. "Susan told everyone the father was dead," Hannah said.

He shook his head. From the storage bin that held the gun, he took out an envelope and held it up for Hannah to see.

"I did okay when I sold the coffee shop. I hired a guy, used to be Seattle PD. I told him who Laura's mother was, and he went off to do his thing. It cost me most of what I'd put away for our baby's college. But there's no point in having the money if you don't have your son, right?"

It made sense to Hannah. "Go on."

He handed her something typed, stapled, folded in half. Hannah knew what it was. She'd seen fragments of this report in the file on Churnin's desk. She put the pages down on the table without looking at them.

"You wrote a letter and sent it to Laura with a copy of this report. You asked her to believe what it said, and you told her it wasn't too late to make amends to you, right?"

He nodded, surprised. "How did you know that?"

"The police found parts of the letter and the report. Burned, in Laura's apartment. Probably right before she died. Why would they have been burned, Ed?"

He frowned, missing the point of her question—that he'd burned the report to obliterate any trace of his contact with her. "Because of what's in there. Go on, read it."

Hannah didn't need to. The fragments were sifting into place: things said and unsaid, the way people behaved, the gifts they gave, the mistakes they swore they wouldn't make again.

Susan never used her teenage motherhood in a campaign. Susan Beckett's friend thanked her, on the back of the snapshot, *for trusting me so much*. It meant that Susan told her who the father was. Hannah knew now why that required trust. The fragment she'd seen said the father of Susan's baby went back to Geo . . . someplace. Not Geor-

gia, as the cops had guessed, but Georgetown, where the
Becketts lived for a time. Susan never left her own daughter
alone with Senator Bill Beckett. Even though the senator
didn't drink anymore.

Finally, the car. Laura had told the truth when she said her
father had given it to her. And Susan Beckett's revulsion
made sense, if Bill Beckett had given her just such a car
when she was a teenager. It was one of the gifts he said he
showered on her. He told the debate audience he'd spoiled
her. He had—but not in the way everyone thought.

"Bill Beckett is Laura's father."

Westerland looked at her, dumbfounded. "Jesus, you
could have saved me a lot of money. You psychic or
something?"

"I just pieced some things together. You told Laura about
him, on the promise she'd get Matthew back?"

He nodded.

"Why did you believe her?"

He shrugged sheepishly. "You never heard her talk about
what it would be like to know her real mother. She freaked
out when her mother wouldn't see her."

"And how did she act when you gave her the report?"

His face tightened into the anger-suppressing blank she'd
seen before, when he was about to slam her head against the
truck. "Well, how would you expect her to act? She was
upset, but goddamn grateful to know the truth."

He loomed over her and Hannah flinched, wondering
why that question had set him off. Westerland swore under
his breath and went to the kitchen for more coffee. She used
the moment to gather her thoughts. Westerland had given
Laura the perfect tool to destroy Susan Beckett's career. If
the truth came out, how would Susan Beckett explain her
continuing relationship with the father who violated her?
Instead of denouncing him, or quietly freezing him out of
her life, she bantered with him to raise money. Hannah was
sickened by it, and thought voters would be, too.

Susan surely told herself she was punishing her father in
her own way. Rather than let him off the hook by disappearing, or assuming a victim's wounded stance, she stayed

in his face, always reminding him of what he'd done. She played off her father's guilt, his shame, a desire to make amends as a way to make money for her political career. And she got to speak the deepest truth of her heart in public, over and over: she truly did hate him, and everything he'd done to her.

But Laura changed all that. If she confronted Susan, demanding money, love, and acknowledgment or a revelation of the truth, what would Susan have done? She was used to subtly blackmailing her father. She never expected anyone to dangle the threat of revelation over *her* head. Laura could have ruined Susan's life in the time it took to make a phone call.

Westerland was back, watching her, frowning at her silence.

"After Laura read the report," Hannah said quietly, hoping this question wouldn't set him off, "what did she say about getting Matthew back for you?"

"She wanted to think about it. She said it explained a lot of things to her. But she told me she could get Matthew back. She said it had to do with the father. That was her out, she said."

Please, Hannah thought, just one pronoun to make everything clear. "She didn't say whose father, did she? Her father? Matthew's father?"

"No. I hope the father—whoever she was talking about—wasn't anyone like Beckett. It made me sick. Who could do that to his kid?"

Hannah remembered the martini man's song at the fund-raising debate: What did I do? No memory. "Bill's an alcoholic. Or was," she said.

"The investigator said both parties might have suspected the thing with Susan for a long time. The rumor comes up every now and then, but nothing comes of it. They manage to hush it up."

Hannah nodded. If the Republicans tried to use the truth to ruin Beckett, they'd wind up hurting Susan. The problem was the same for the Democrats—there was no way to paint Susan as a hypocrite without tarring Beckett.

"My guy said I should be careful with what I did with this stuff," Westerland said. "It would be a slam-dunk slander case, unless you got proof, he said."

There was no proof, of course. There was a birth certificate with a dead teenage boy named as Laura's father. No one else would verify a thing. Particularly now that Laura was gone. The political considerations that had protected the Becketts for so long didn't apply to Laura. Slander threats? She was penniless—nothing to lose. All she had to do was make her allegation to the right tabloid, wait for the mainstream press to pick up the story, and watch the destruction of the mother who'd rejected her. Even if voters didn't wholly believe it, the stench would be enough to ruin Susan and Bill Beckett. If she ever got out of Westerland's trailer, she intended to find out where the Becketts had been on the day Laura died. But first, she needed to know where Ed had been.

"When did you find out that Laura had no intention of giving Matthew back to you?"

He blinked and shook his head. "She never said that. She needed more time."

"But she wouldn't see you anymore. She wouldn't respond to your letters."

Westerland looked sadly at the stack of returned mail. "I don't know why she wouldn't talk to me. The Drummonds scared her, I think."

"Ed, she never told them about you. She was using you." He started to protest, but she overrode him. "And when you figured that out, it made you mad. Anyone would have been."

He nodded, but then understood where she was leading him. "You're saying I had something to do with killing Laura? No way."

"I found the Xanax, Ed. In your old apartment, under the sink. You talked your way into Laura's place. You had some crushed pills. You doctored her drink, and when she passed out, you pulled the gas line. Then you were going to go grab Matthew. That's what was going on, right?"

"Shut up." He jammed the gun in her face.

Hannah shook her head. "No good threatening me, Ed. I gave the pills and the bottle to the police."

He blanched. "They'll think I killed her."

"That's right."

"But I didn't. I couldn't."

"Ed, everything you've done is suspicious. If there's another explanation, it would help. What was the Xanax for?"

"I got it from my doctor after Laura disappeared. We'd lost our baby. I was freaking out, panic attacks—my doctor could tell you."

"How did you get the picture of Matthew, the one you used with the anonymous letter?"

"I took it from Laura's apartment. When I gave her the report. She wouldn't miss it. She had tons of them."

"What about the calls to the Drummonds. How did you get their number? It was new, unlisted."

He shrugged. "The bill was in the mailbox. I took it. I thought I could just talk to them. Make them understand what happened. Then they'd do the right thing. But every time I called, I lost my nerve. And I was afraid they'd call the police."

"And the stuffed bear, what about that?"

"I wanted Matthew to have it. What's wrong with giving a baby a present?"

"Come on, Ed. I know better. You did it to scare the Drummonds. You wanted them to know they were vulnerable. You sat outside, listening to them argue. That's how you saw me—you were still there, gloating over the damage you'd done. Did you believe you'd make them think that Matthew was too much trouble?"

"No. I wanted them to know he didn't belong to them. Laura did what she did because she needed money. It wasn't her fault. They bought a baby. And that's wrong."

"Ed, Laura lied to you. And now the police are looking for you. Once someone finds my car, they'll really be after you."

He wet his lips. She was making him nervous. She had to be careful that he didn't see her as the threat.

"Listen, you've still got a chance to make it right," she said. "So far, you can explain everything you've done. It isn't all good, but it isn't murder. Even what happened with us tonight can be handled. I'd just say that you were distraught, and needed to talk to me. That should take care of the kidnapping charges."

"Kidnapping? Jesus." Good, she thought. Be scared.

"Yes. You ran me off the road, assaulted me, and dragged me here. The door's padlocked, and I'm being held against my will. That's kidnapping."

"I just wanted my boy back. Things have gotten out of hand."

"That's what you tell the police. If it's the truth, I think everything can be straightened out. There's one thing they'll definitely want to know."

"What?"

"Where were you on the day Laura died?"

"That's what I'm trying to tell you," he said. He smiled and Hannah saw that she'd been right: there was a decent, rational Ed Westerland. She was meeting him now.

"Tell me," she said.

"I was in Seattle. My sister was in the hospital. She's got cancer, and they thought she was going. But she's hanging on. When I came back, I heard what happened to Laura."

There would be plane reservations, Hannah thought. Doctors, nurses might have seen him. And the sister, too, though sisterly alibis could be suspect. It would be easy enough to check out.

"If you're telling the truth, there's no problem." She tried to smile. "I won't be a problem for you. And I think the Drummonds will understand, once I talk to them."

"What about Matthew? Will we get him back?"

He still had the pistol, although it lay slack in his palm. Hannah had to decide how to answer. Facile lies—the Drummonds will see your suffering and bring you Matthew in a golden cradle—would sound ridiculous to both of them. His delusions were receding, a fetid puddle drying up in the sun. She decided to give him a blinding ray of the truth and hope for the best.

"Ed, you can't have Matthew. The adoption is finalized. The Drummonds love their son—and he is their son. They've done nothing wrong. Matthew hasn't either. You don't want to disrupt the only home he's ever known, do you?"

"It's not home!" He slammed the gun down on the table. Hannah couldn't tell if he was going to punch her or collapse in tears.

She spoke as softly as she could. "It is. It's the only home he knows. Have you thought about what Matthew's been through? He was blasted out of Rebecca's arms when Laura's apartment exploded. You didn't see him there, bleeding on the sidewalk. I did."

Westerland looked up, stricken by the thought of it.

"He soaked up all the fear in the Drummonds house. You caused some of that, with the phone calls and pranks. He was right there when Kurt was shot. He *saw* that. I can see how all this has changed him. He shies at noises. His thumb is in his mouth—always. He is a frightened, traumatized baby, Ed, and you helped make him that way. And now you want to take away the only security he has. It would ruin Matthew's life, the way Laura ruined yours. You'd wreck innocent people, just the way Laura wrecked you and Connie. Do you really want that?"

His eyes were downcast. Hannah thought he might have been fighting tears. His mouth worked for a moment. "No."

Hannah let the word linger there. The Ed Westerland who mowed his lawn, worked hard, and loved his wife was coming back from a dark and dangerous place. She wanted him to see that word as a beacon, and follow it.

"There's someone you might be able to get back," she said.

He looked up at her.

"Connie would like to see you, I think. She's worried about you."

Tenderness lit his face. "I miss her."

"Work with me and this will turn out all right. But you've got to be straight—one hundred percent—when you talk to the police."

He nodded, dropped his head, and stared down at the gun for a few moments. "There is something else I have to tell you."

The story came out haltingly. Hannah offered to make more coffee, and he let her. She listened as he talked, and filled in the shadings and nuances of the husky, strained voice.

He came upon Matthew and Anneke by accident, the first time. He was sitting at the bottom of the hill, watching the road up to the Drummonds' place, trying to work up his courage to go talk to Stephen Drummond. He'd seen him in a picture Laura had, called his office once, and learned that he came home early on Wednesdays. He was waiting for him to drive by when he saw Matthew and the nanny in the park. The boy's hair was nearly white in the sun. The nanny pushed him in his stroller around the park's perimeter walkway, let him watch the ducks, laid out a blanket, and held his hand as he practiced some ambitiously huge steps. He forgot about talking to Drummond. The sight of his boy, teetering on his feet and giggling uproariously, was all he needed.

But one session of watching Matthew and Anneke wasn't enough. For the next three weeks he sat every day at the bottom of the hill, waiting for them to get out of the little red car and go into the park. He took up a place on a bench and watched them. The nanny didn't notice him. But he thought Matthew did. The boy frowned at him, as he would at any stranger. Ed understood. A relationship would take time.

A patrol car stopped him once, thinking that he might be a child molester, scouting for victims. But he held up the sack lunch he'd brought and said he was just there to eat and get some fresh air. The cop seemed satisfied with that.

As the weather grew warmer the nanny took Matthew to an ice-cream truck that parked at the far edge of the park. She bought a Popsicle for herself, and let Matthew try a few tentative licks. He was close enough to see the boy's delight at the cold and sweetness.

The next day, Anneke left Matthew with another sitter

while she went to the truck. The sitter's charges, a little girl and boy, got into a fight in the sandbox. As she rushed to break it up Ed found himself on his feet, moving closer to his baby. He crouched next to the stroller. Matthew was sleeping, his mouth lolling open. Ed could smell baby shampoo. Matthew shifted with a sigh, and his tiny arm fell free of the blanket that covered him. Ed didn't think twice about the bracelet on his son's wrist. He took it. The sitter began to turn. He ran.

Westerland put an envelope in Hannah's hand. "It's in there."

The silver bracelet had a caduceus on one side. Matthew's name, address, and date of birth were engraved beneath it. On the other side, the condition for which the medical-alert bracelet had been issued: malignant hyperthermia. Hannah had never heard of it, but if it was on a bracelet, she assumed it was serious.

"I saw it was a medical-bracelet thing as soon as I took it off," Westerland said. "But the nanny was coming. I didn't have time to put it on him again. You don't know how I worried about him. What if something was wrong, and no one knew what to do?"

Hannah nodded. "I'll take it back."

He nodded, pulled three twenties out of his pocket, and clinked a couple quarters atop it. "You can call a cab from the pay phone by the entrance. Tell the police where to find me. I won't go anywhere."

She motioned for the gun that sat beside him. "Give me that."

He guffawed. "Don't worry. I thought about killing myself. Plenty of times. But I don't think I will now."

"Good. So you don't need the gun."

He put on the safety and handed it to her, then undid the padlock on the trailer's door. "You really will help me? With the police, and Connie and all?"

"I promise."

"Sorry about everything." He nodded to her forehead and the bruises that were beginning to darken her arms. She smiled despite the pain that was beating double-four time just above her nose.

"Well, you look like you did time in a waffle iron," she said. "Your crotch probably aches. I'd say we're even."

Hannah glanced back at him as she walked to the park entrance. He was leaning against the railing, watching her. He raised his hand, an ambiguous gesture that could have been a farewell or a beckoning back. She waited for him to say something. But instead he went inside, and the lights of the trailer went out.

33

It was still dark when Hannah got to Churnin's house. He was waiting for her as the cab pulled up, wearing jeans and a T-shirt, holding a glass of water and a handful of aspirin. She took four pills and downed the water in a gulp. She had started to shake again.

"Tell me again why I shouldn't have Huntington Beach PD bust down on this guy for kidnapping and assault?" Churnin led her to the kitchen. Two cups of coffee and a bag of muffins from 7-Eleven were on the table.

"Because I told him you wouldn't."

"That was what you said to get out of there."

"That was what I said because I meant it. He was half out of his mind from what Laura did to him."

"So this guy was the one that killed Laura? Is that it?"

She shook her head, and told him about Westerland's explanation for his mostly used bottle of Xanax, and his alibi for the day of Laura's death.

"It's not him, you're saying? Then we're back to Kurt."

"No, we're not. There's Susan Beckett. Her father. Maybe both of them."

Churnin's face held steady for a moment, then he started to laugh, tears sliding out of his eyes. "Christ, Hannah," he said between hoots, "Westerland must have hit you pretty hard."

She pushed the coffee away to show she wasn't amused. "She had a good reason to want Laura dead. So did her father. If you'll shut up for a minute, I'll tell you."

She did, and Churnin's giggles faded. He looked slightly ill. "Pretty fucking *Chinatown,* if you ask me."

"So that means what? That incest only happens in movies? That would be comforting, wouldn't it?"

"I'm not saying there isn't incest in the real world, all right? But this is extremely creepy. Why didn't she ever tell anyone? Why is she still associating with him?"

"That's why she killed Laura. If Laura announced who her father was, people would sympathize with Susan for about fifteen seconds. She was a victim, as a teenager. But then they'd want to know why she stayed close to a man who molested her. Why the funny little debates? Why did she let him host parties for her?"

Churnin looked unhappy. "Do you have any idea what's going to happen if I pursue this?"

"What happens if you don't? Are you willing to pretend that Kurt killed Laura? You were never satisfied with that. And when he died, it irked you. You knew you could have found out what he was doing in Rebecca's office. And it would have taken you right to Susan Beckett."

She watched his face, and could see she'd hit the mark.

He shook his head. "You know, if I do take a shot at Susan Beckett's part in this, I'm going to look very hard at that shooting. That isn't necessarily a good thing for your clients, counselor."

"Rebecca shot him in self-defense. I'm sure of that. But go ahead and look hard. I think Kurt was there to find out for Susan how much the Drummonds knew about Laura's birth parents. How much Laura might have told them."

"Did Kurt know who Laura's parents really were?"

"He hinted that he did. And if he did, the Becketts were able to tie off another loose end. That's why you got the word to leave the shooting alone. It put everything back the way it had been, neat and pretty."

He was quiet for a few moments, thinking it over. He pushed the coffee back to her. A peace offering. "I'll do this on my time. The bosses don't need to know."

Hannah smiled, remembering that just a few years ago, he

nought she was a stress case who'd cracked, and she saw
im as a cocky jerk with an oversized ego.

"Thanks, Ivan."

He shrugged, cleared his throat. He started to say some-
ning, but stopped himself. The divorce had shaken him, she
as sure of that. Reaching out to a woman who expressed
armth, even of the most neutral variety, was a reflex. But
e knew about Guillermo and Hannah. He could see that
ven a hint of an overture to Hannah would sink their
riendship like a shallow, tippy skiff. And Hannah, recently
wakened to the perils of sexual attraction, knew better than
) put out any signals that could be misread.

"Thanks for the muffins. I was pretty hungry."

"Want a lift home?"

No way, she thought. "It's okay. I can catch a cab on
rove."

At the door, he took her by the shoulders and kissed her
heek. It was emphatically chaste, and over in an instant.
You be careful," he said. "I don't want to lose you."

The cab brought her back to her car. It hadn't been broken
nto or ticketed, and for that she was grateful. One tire was
at, and on the promise of a healthy tip, the cabbie helped
er change it.

t home, there was a message from Guillermo. If she could
o without him for a few more days, he was taking his
nother to see relatives in Glenwood Springs. It was a
urprise for Amelia.

"These are real rustic ranch folks," he said. "No phone.
Iama needs some peace and quiet."

Hannah groaned to herself. A conspiracy. That was the
nly explanation for Guillermo's continuous separation
rom a telephone. She took a long shower and considered
rying to sleep for part of the morning. But that was useless.
'he Becketts preyed on her mind, and thinking of them led
er to Gerald Lawrence. He knew much more than he ever
aid. He was the palace guard and the secret-keeper. He
new who fathered Susan's baby. He might have taken
ne infant Laura at Beckett's urging. She wondered what he

thought of Susan, and her allegiance to the parent who raped her. And what about his own allegiances?

She was knocking at his door an hour later.

"Down here." Lawrence's voice came from the canal. He stood on the deck of the sailboat and frowned when he saw who his visitor was. "I thought I told you to leave me alone."

"This will be the last time. It's important. It's about Matthew."

He said nothing as he coiled ropes and got ready to cast off.

"I know you must care about what happens to him," Hannah said. "I know you wonder about what happened to Laura."

He shrugged. "I'm going sailing. You want to come, fine."

Soon they had cleared the canals and were gliding along the coast. Lawrence sipped coffee from a thermos, but didn't offer her any. He glanced at the lump on her forehead.

"What the hell happened to you?"

"It has to do with Laura. I know who her birth father is."

Lawrence shrugged. "So? A boy Susan dated in high school. Jim something. He's dead now."

"The real father. Bill Beckett."

Lawrence shook his head. "I can't believe you fell for that story. Desperate, sniveling little liars let that rumor slither out like some kind of pit viper every few years. No one believes it, you know."

"Laura did. I do."

"Well, you repeat it and you'll be slapped with a lawsuit faster than you can say flat broke."

"Is that what Susan threatened Laura with? Or did she find another way to shut her up?"

He tipped his head and watched her for a minute. "I don't know what you're talking about."

"It was the car, I think, that must have set Susan off. When she realized that Beckett gave Laura the money for it, it was an ugly flashback for her. Do you think Bill ever realized what he was doing?"

"You're not making sense."

"He was about to give Laura the same car he gave Susan s a pathetic makeup gift for raping her."

"What are you planning on doing with all this . . . peculation?"

"I just want to get someone to start telling the truth. aura's dead because of lies. When they're undone, I think 1e police will have a better chance at figuring out who illed her."

"What happened to the suicide theory? That's what Susan inks happened."

"Laura was the least suicidal person I ever met. Tough as ails."

He nodded. "She was that."

"Like her parents."

Lawrence sighed. "We're not having this conversation. If ou repeat it to anyone, and it comes back to me, I swear to iod, you'll be on the receiving end of a very hefty lawsuit. 'd spend my last one hundred and eighty-two dollars for the leasure of filing it against you."

"Understood."

"Bill Beckett was a raging alcoholic. Everyone in that amily, on the staff, in the campaigns, worked like hell to eep him propped up when he lost it. He was a good olitician, and worth saving. But in his own house, in rivate, I couldn't help him, or anyone else. He went out of ontrol sometimes. Cynthia, his wife, was half-crazy with 1e strain of it, and she started drinking, too. In those days, vhat people saw—appearance, image—that's what was 1ost important. Bill Beckett's career was Job One. If he vent down, everybody went with him. So the whole amily—including Susan—pretended that everything was ine."

"Even when he started molesting her."

"Susan tried to tell, I gather. Cynthia wouldn't listen. Couldn't listen. She just drank more, accused Susan of rying to kill her with awful lies. Well, what was a hirteen-year-old supposed to say to that? I felt horrible for Susan. I would have taken her in myself." He looked away,

vaguely pointed at the ship moored to their left. *"Quee.
Mary."*

Hannah nodded at the diversion. Lawrence would hav
taken Susan in, but that would have signaled to the worl
that something was wrong in the Beckett household. Specu
lation would begin, and Beckett would see to it that hi
career ended before Susan finished unpacking.

"She wouldn't have an abortion. So they came up with
story about a Montana ranch vacation, just before Susa.
began to show."

"And did you know all this, from the start?"

He shook his head. "I found out when I went to the ranc}
and Susan wasn't there. Then Cynthia told me abou
Paraclete School, the place for pregnant girls. I told my wif
that Susan was pregnant. It was her idea to adopt. Bill an
Cynthia were happy to go along."

Because, Hannah thought, Lawrence and his wife wer
loyalists, inner circle. No scandal would seep out throug}
them.

"Bill made a big donation to the adoption agency an
everything went pretty smoothly."

"You knew that Beckett was the father, all along?"

He shrugged. "The story about the boy . . . it was s
vague. Susan told me the whole story, but that was much
much later."

"But you'd already guessed the truth. And you let Bi}
Beckett know that."

"It wasn't that way."

"Maybe not exactly that way, but close." It was clear t(
Hannah that Beckett knew Lawrence suspected the truth
And so Lawrence had assured himself campaign jobs fo
life.

"I'm going to come about," he said. "Keep your hea(
down."

Hannah ducked as the boom came across. Lawrence':
eyes narrowed in the sun. But his shoulders relaxed. Th
wind and the air seemed to do the old tortoise good. Sh
could almost see his carapace soften.

"Why has Susan stayed close to him?" Hannah said. "N(

one would blame her for what happened to her as a teenager. But what she's doing now doesn't make sense."

He didn't speak for a while. The waves slapped at the boat and the wind snapped the sails. "He's changed," Lawrence said finally. "He asked her to forgive him for what he did when he was drinking, and she did."

"And that's it?"

He shrugged. "What else?"

"How about power? She must have learned how it worked in that family. He had the control then. She has it now. And she's taking advantage of it."

He forced a cackle. "You're very cynical, Ms. Barlow. A typical lawyer."

"I'm just realistic. So is Susan. She holds the reins now. But what if Laura took the reins away?"

"If she told people, you mean?"

"She was furious at Susan for giving her up and refusing to acknowledge her. When she found out Susan's real secret, it gave her a weapon."

"What are you saying?"

"Do you know where Susan and Bill Beckett were on the day Laura was killed?"

"That's ridiculous. They're well-known, visible people. Bill Beckett was a senator, for God's sake. He's not a crim—" He stopped himself.

"That's exactly what he is. He just was never prosecuted. And Susan's capable of anything to save herself."

"This is ludicrous. I know exactly where they were, and I can prove it. Take the wheel for a minute."

She held the boat to the course Lawrence had set. She saw him rummaging in a briefcase belowdeck. He brought up a leather-bound appointment book and handed it to her. The page was open to the day of Laura's death.

"There. At five-thirty, they were with me, in a strategy-planning session. Just the three of us. We were together for a good three hours."

"That covers the time of the explosion, but the gas took hours to build. Where were they before your meeting?"

He stared down at the calendar, as if reconstructing the

day. "It was before the fund-raiser. They were alone, working out a new debate."

So the ugliness Hannah witnessed was rehearsed. She felt her skin crawl.

"I know they couldn't have been in Las Almas." Lawrence sounded almost desperate in his need to convince her.

"How do you know that?"

"I called them. They were at Bill's house here, in Long Beach."

"And you talked to them?"

"No. Drew—Susan's husband—took the call. He put the phone down, came back, and said he'd have to take a message. I said I'd call back."

"So you didn't talk to them."

He didn't say anything for a moment. Hannah went on. "Susan is the tough one in the marriage to Drew Fails, right? She calls the shots?"

He nodded.

"So that leaves him where? Message taker? Baby-sitter? What happens when he interrupts her important meetings?"

"She quietly glares. The yelling is later, I think, in private."

"So he never even bothered trying to talk to her. He just slipped your message under the door. They apparently weren't there to pick it up."

Lawrence sucked his cheeks. Hannah wondered how he really felt about Susan. He was the ally of her father, the ugliest figure in her life. But then Lawrence sided with her, stepped in, and raised her child. He saw the darkness that Beckett had created in Susan. He would make excuses for her. But this would be difficult. This was Laura's death—and Susan could have killed her. Susan had once again allied herself with her father—that drunken shadow that came to her bed when she was a child—to keep the truth buried.

Finally, Lawrence looked up. The color had seeped from his face. He looked worse than ever. "You saw Bill's office?"

Hannah nodded. The leather furniture, the hardwood floors, the French doors, and the lawn outside.

"So you saw the doors, and the lawn, and the carriage house on the other side? It's used as a garage now."

Hannah understood. The office was in the back of the house. You only had to cross the lawn to get to the garage. If it was like the arrangement of garages elsewhere in the neighborhood, the garage opened onto an alley. Lawrence meant that the Becketts could have left the house and driven to Las Almas without Drew knowing they were gone.

34

Hannah didn't know the man sitting on the hood of the white SAAB parked in the Drummonds' driveway. A porkpie hat topped unruly, damp-looking hair. He was finishing off a cigarette and looking over the skinny, spiral-topped notebook propped on his knee. The distinctive pad gave him away. It was as if he'd tatooed *reporter* on his forehead.

Hannah passed him and parked closer to the house. He stubbed out the cigarette and made himself ready to approach her. This was the work of Susan Beckett, Hannah thought. The press release is out, and she's tossed the tastiest bit—the grandson—to this guy. Susan might find herself in a less comfortable spotlight soon enough.

On the way to the Drummonds' house, she left a message for Churnin at home, letting him know about the vulnerability of the Becketts' alibi. She'd talked for more than fifteen minutes with Bobby, who'd made the mistake of asking how her weekend had been so far. She even tried calling Guillermo, but he and Amelia were already gone.

Now she picked up the cellular phone and dialed the Drummonds' number. Stephen answered.

"I'm about to ring your doorbell—I have something for you. Did you say anything to this guy who's camped out in your driveway?"

Stephen sighed. "Nothing, except to tell him to get lost, which he obviously hasn't done."

"Where's Rebecca?"

"Church. Anneke's with the baby."

"Good. I'll get rid of this guy now."

"Great. They you can make Susan Beckett disappear."

Maybe into prison, Hannah thought.

The reporter, who kept a respectful distance while she talked, put out his hand and smiled.

"Mrs. Drummond?"

Hannah smiled back. If he was going to jump to conclusions, she wasn't going to soften a bad landing. "Who's asking?"

"Jim Griffith. The *Register.*"

"We already subscribe." Stephen should be opening the door about now.

"Wait a minute," the reporter said. "I know you. You're Monsignor Barlow's sister—the lawyer, right? I knew Michael. Interviewed him a couple times. I'm sorry."

It never stopped hurting, hearing Michael's name like that. The reporter's tone of regret was enough to soften her attitude toward him. She put out her hand. "Hannah Barlow. I represent the Drummonds. What do you want?"

"It's about Susan Beckett, and Laura and the baby. You saw my story Saturday?"

"No. But let me guess: it was about Susan giving up her baby, and her regret at not having known her."

He frowned. "I thought you said—"

"I saw Susan's press release before it went out. My clients have nothing to add."

He chuckled. "She told me that the Drummonds' lawyer was sort of a bulldog. But I think she meant it as a compliment."

Hannah could imagine what Susan really said about her. "Why don't you tell me what you have in mind for this piece?"

He sketched it for her: a more featurized, in-depth story, talking not only about Susan Beckett's girlhood pregnancy and her pain at the death of the daughter she never knew, but the big news: the grandson, and her desire to know him.

"She said this is all she has." He held a photograph out. It was Matthew, sitting up in a faded flowered chair. She recognized the furniture—the picture was taken in Kurt's first motel room. More evidence of his collusion with Susan.

Hannah shrugged. "They're not going to talk to you right now. Susan made a promise of privacy that she hasn't kept. They're angry. You can understand that?"

He nodded. "And then there was that shooting here, and all. What's going on with that investigation, anyway?"

Hannah took another look at the man. The ridiculous hat and the disarming manner were just camouflage. He'd done his homework, guided by Susan.

"Ask the police."

"Right," he said. "They're more tight-lipped than you and your clients."

"Look, I'll tell you what: if you call off the vigil here, I'll talk to them for you. Maybe they'll reconsider."

His lip curled into a slightly weary smile. How many times had he been put off that way? It was on the tip of his tongue to say something smart-assed, but he stopped short and handed her a business card. "If you're anything like Michael, then you're a good person. So please just put it to them straight. I'm not here to do some hit piece, or try to embarrass them. I just want to tell this story about Susan, which is pretty amazing, after all."

"Okay, Jim," Hannah said. "I'll tell them that." If he knew the truth, he would find it more loathsome than amazing. She considered that for a moment. The more pressure on Susan, the better.

"Here's something I've wondered about, Jim. Who was Laura's father? Did Susan get into that at all?"

"She said it was a classmate. It sounded like a fumble in the backseat, actually."

"And what became of him?"

"Well, I don't know yet. She hasn't wanted to talk about it."

"I heard he died, when he was quite young."

"Really?"

"That's one version."

"Meaning what?"

"I don't know all the details. As you said, Susan doesn't want to talk about it." With that, she rang the doorbell. As Stephen let her in, she saw the reporter scribbling notes to himself. He nearly ran to his car. Good, she thought. It was no less than Susan deserved.

Stephen led her into the dining room. He sat down with a cup of coffee and closed the medical journal he'd been reading.

"He's going to make Susan Beckett's life miserable," Hannah said. "And I have something you've been missing."

He blinked at her. "What am I missing?"

She dropped Matthew's bracelet into his hand.

He let out a sigh. "It's been gone for weeks. Where did you find it?"

"Ed Westerland took it. He was watching Matthew in the park and decided he wanted something of his."

Drummond's face was turning crimson. "Jesus fucking Christ. I'll kill him."

"Let the police deal with Ed. He has information that might help them with Laura."

"What information?"

"About Laura. And who killed her. We'll just have to see if it pans out."

"And so that's why I'm not supposed to be upset that Westerland was pawing Matthew? Christ, I told Rebecca these people would—"

"Stephen, let it go. Believe or not, Ed and Connie are not the enemy."

His face hardened. "So now you're defining my enemies?"

She wasn't going to rise to this bait. "I'm trying to give you some perspective. I spent a lot of time listening to Ed Westerland this weekend, and I'm trying to convey my sense of that."

He sighed. "Whatever. Jesus. What a goddamned mess Laura left us."

"Matthew's okay?" She nodded at the bracelet in his hand.

He closed his fist over it. "Sure. It's just a precaution."

"What is malignant hyperthermia?"

"An allergic reaction. It only happens under circumstances that are so rare that . . . well, really it's not a big deal. Rebecca just worries so much. It's as much for her peace of mind as for Matthew's health." He smiled, a condescending comment on his wife's nerves.

"I can't remember Matthew ever wearing the bracelet. Not even on visits with Kurt."

"No? Well, I'm not sure we had it then."

"I don't remember it recently, either. Before it disappeared, I mean."

His smile seemed to freeze. "It was there. You must have missed it."

35

She found Anneke and Matthew where Ed Westerland watched them: in an emerald triangle of park, near the swings. The ice-cream truck was there. Anneke had a cone in hand, even though it was before lunch. She smiled at Hannah. Matthew mimicked her, raising a tiny fist in defiant salute. A bracelet, identical to the one she'd just given Stephen, dangled from his wrist. Hannah knelt next to him and touched it gingerly.

"So he had another one of these."

Anneke nodded. "He lost the first one."

"I never noticed it before."

"Oh, Dr. Drummond doesn't want him to wear it at home. I just put it on him when we go out."

So Hannah's memory wasn't murky. Stephen had lied to her. "Why is that? I thought these were supposed to be worn all the time."

Anneke took a long lick of strawberry ice cream. "Ideally. But Rebecca . . . She would worry."

Hannah noted that conditional description of Rebecca's emotions. She would worry. If she knew. "Is it something to worry about?"

"Sure. Malignant hyperthermia is very serious."

Another lie by Stephen. "What is it?"

Anneke straightened her back, suddenly looking very much like a nurse. Her hip clothes and semiwild ways could make someone forget that. "It's a syndrome triggered by general anesthetics. It's very scary in an OR. The patient's metabolism kicks into high gear. Muscles go rigid. Fever can go to one hundred and ten degrees or higher. People die from it, because of cardiac arrest, internal hemorrhaging. Scary."

The skin on Hannah's arms pricked as Anneke talked, as though it was winter, and the sun wasn't beaming down on this patch of grass. "Was Matthew just lucky that none of that happened when his arm was set, after the explosion?"

"It wasn't luck at all," Anneke said. "Dr. Drummond kept the anesthesiologist from administering one of the inhalation anesthetics that can trigger it. Got there just in time." Her eyes shone with pride for her hero. She had worked her way down to the cone, and she crunched into it before continuing. "If you know someone has MH, the anesthesiologist and the other doctors can deal with it. But if Dr. Drummond hadn't shown up, terrible things could have happened. Matthew could have died."

Matthew was playing with Hannah's fingers, pulling one and then another closer to her thumb. Hannah put her other hand on his head, and he looked up delightedly at her before cramming her index finger into his mouth. My God, she thought, this poor baby.

"Why haven't the Drummonds ever mentioned it?" Hannah said.

"Dr. Drummond doesn't want it brought up around Rebecca. He asked the pediatrician not to discuss it with her. It's too upsetting. He says it can be talked about later, when Rebecca is stronger."

There was a cozy medical superiority about this, the professionals determining what was best for the hysterical, invalid mother. "So Rebecca doesn't even know about this?"

"Well, I don't really . . ." Anneke's fair face turned red.

"You're keeping a secret about Matthew from his mother?"

Anneke glanced away from Hannah. She could have been looking for someplace to take shelter, but chose to throw away the remains of the cone instead. When she sat down, she still wouldn't look at Hannah.

"Anneke, was there something between you and Dr. Drummond?"

She stared down at the pavement. Finally, she nodded. "While they were separated. Not since."

Hannah doubted Rebecca knew. Suspected, maybe. And Stephen probably made her think she was paranoid, cooking up a jealous notion in her explosion-addled head. She hated him for that.

"I like Rebecca," Anneke said, twisting a napkin in her hand. "I just wanted to make everything easier for her—that's why I came to stay with them. And that's why I didn't bring up the past."

"Or tell her about Matthew's condition."

Anneke nodded. Hannah decided she was probably telling the truth. That sweet face would curdle with too many lies. She was willing to believe Anneke did care, in some way, about Rebecca. But her loyalties were with Stephen, the doctor-god.

"The family has been through so much," Anneke added.

Hannah had to agree with that. Family was all the Drummonds wanted. Now family was the source of all their problems. It made her think of something Anneke had said about malignant hyperthermia. "MH is inherited?"

Anneke nodded. "Laura had it, Dr. Drummond said."

Hannah felt the cold edge of another lie. She was almost certain there was nothing about a serious inherited condition in Laura's medical report. Just the opposite, in fact. "Anneke, when were you going to go back to the house?"

Anneke checked her watch. "We just got here."

"Stay for a little while longer, okay? I need to talk to the Drummonds."

She nodded, wiping the last traces of ice cream from her hands. "They don't talk to each other much lately."

For the slightest moment Rebecca hesitated before asking Hannah inside. "What's wrong?

"I need to look at Laura's medical report again."

Rebecca's face was grave. "Is it about Matthew?"

Hannah plunged into the lie, telling herself it was

necessary. "No. It's about Laura. The reporter that Susan enticed with this story told me Laura had been treated for an eating disorder. I'm pretty sure he's wrong." She really didn't like lying to Rebecca. Hannah vowed to tell her the truth, once she knew what it was.

Rebecca puzzled over the reporter's question and shrugged. "I don't remember anything like that." She paused now that they were at the door to Stephen's office. "We moved all the records inside, since . . ."

Hannah nodded. Since the shooting. Rebecca opened the file drawer of Stephen's desk and flicked her finger along the top of the folders. They heard Stephen's voice from upstairs.

"Rebecca!" He sounded whiny and aggrieved. "For Christ's sake, where are my jeans?

Rebecca signed. "They're blind as moles sometimes."

"Go on." Hannah wanted privacy anyway. "I'll refile this when I'm done."

When Rebecca was gone, she read the report slowly, skipping nothing. There was no mention of malignant hyperthermia. Hannah put the file back and sat quietly for a moment, trying to piece it together. If it was inherited, it didn't come from Laura. The father, then. And Stephen knew about it.

There was no other explanation. She searched her memory for something she saw or heard in Seattle to confirm it. And what she remembered was one of the registration cards at the Daybreak, the slummy motel next door to Laura's. It recorded a personalized license plate: IM MAD. She scribbled it on a piece of paper, and saw not an expression of emotion, but whose initials they really were. Not Maurice Anthony Dixon. Martin Drummond. And she suddenly knew the real middle name: Andrew, after his father. Was Martin Drummond at the Daybreak? She knew that he wasn't. But Martin's car was. It had been borrowed from him.

She riffled the files until she found the Drummonds' picture album, the record of Matthew's journey to them. She flipped to the page that held the Drummonds' newspaper ad.

Above it was a request for the services of a surrogate mother. Hannah punched in the phone number, and the extension. Almost two years later what were the chances it would be in service? But she had to try.

A clipped, professional voice answered: "Dr. Drummond's service."

"No message." Hannah's lips felt numb. She looked up to the picture on the wall in front of her. Jesus, she thought.

"Hannah?" Rebecca was on her way down the stairs.

Hannah scanned the picture, feeling her heart race. There was Stephen and his brother in the living room of an apartment. The clothes—pastel Izod shirts and acid-washed jeans—pegged the scene as the early eighties. Martin had told her that he and Stephen lived together, but never said where. She remembered the conversation: Martin worked at ACT, on Geary. Their apartment was south of Market. San Francisco.

Between the brothers stood another man. She knew him instantly, both his name and his history. This was the drug-using roommate, the would-be actor, whom Stephen had revived, whose life he saved. Hannah had met him when he masqueraded as Jerome Hoskins. And then she'd learned his real name: Tom Streeter, who still could play a role, when necessary.

Rebecca pushed the door open. "Everything okay?" She held a copy of Parents Magazine.

Hannah nodded, although nothing was okay. "I couldn't find anything about an eating disorder."

"This reporter still wants to talk to us?"

"I'm sure he does. That doesn't mean you have to go along."

"I'm so tired of all this," Rebecca said. And she did seem very tired. She seemed to be losing weight again. Her face no longer seemed sculpted, but hollowed out and scraped down to bone. Hannah didn't like to think about telling her the truth. It was premature now even to think about it.

"Lie down for a while," she said. "Sunday's a day of rest, right?"

"No rest for the wicked," she said. "Work is piling up. You know."

"I do. I've got some work to do myself."

At home, Hannah found Martin Drummond's number in Vancouver. His wife said he was out of town—a theater conference at SCR.

"South Coast Repertory?" It was in Costa Mesa. Not quite ten minutes away.

She found him smoking in the theater's front courtyard, and although there was no funeral that day, he still was dressed entirely in black. He waved when he saw her, thinking this was a happy, coincidental encounter. They were on a lunch break. He gestured to the table of sandwiches and soft drinks. Did she want something? Hannah shook her head. Martin saw her agitation.

"What is it?"

"I need to ask you about some things."

"What things?"

"About Matthew. And your brother."

He stared at her uneasily. She knew he couldn't imagine what she was talking about. "Okay, sure," he said finally.

"Did Stephen visit you the fall before Matthew was born? In October."

"Yeah. It was a week or so before Halloween. We were in rehearsal for a kids' show. *The Raven.* I remember that."

"And he borrowed your car?"

"Right. He wanted to see his ex-wife in Spokane. Sort of a peace mission, I guess."

"He didn't tell Rebecca, though?"

"No. She's not very understanding about friendly ex-spouses. It was a particularly sensitive time them. They'd only been back together a few months. What's this got to do with Matthew?"

"Let me ask a few more things: do you remember Tom Streeter?"

"Streeter? No."

Hannah's confidence faltered for a minute. "Your roommate in San Francisco? The drug-using one that Stephen saved?"

"Oh. You mean Tom Sweetzer. He must have changed his name. For Hollywood, probably."

Or to avoid arrest, Hannah thought. "Have you been in touch with him at all?"

"He called me a couple times, but I was busy and I thought he sounded flakier than ever. I mentioned him to Stephen. He asked me if I had Tom's number. I told Stephen I didn't think he'd be much interested in what Tom was up to."

"But you gave him Tom's number?"

He nodded, lit a cigarette, and said nothing for a moment, trying to put her questions into a framework that made sense to him. "So this has to do with Tom?"

"In a way," Hannah said. When Stephen called Tom Streeter, he might have reminded him that he'd saved his life. But in case that wasn't enough, Stephen probably paid him, too. Once Streeter targeted Hoskins as the man whose identity he would borrow, a few dollars spent with the right people would have produced an excellent fake driver's license. And then Streeter used his theatrical ability and knowledge he'd picked up in Hoskins's office to play the stockbroker. It was a critical role, from Stephen's perspective. And it would have worked, if Hannah hadn't called the real Hoskins one last time.

She paused before plunging in again. "What I need to ask you now is personal. But it's important."

"Is Stephen all right?"

Hannah wished she could say he was. "Just let me get through this, Martin. Is there a history of malignant hyperthermia in your family?"

Now he looked stricken. "It is Stephen. God, is he okay?"

"He's all right. Please tell me about the malignant hyperthermia."

"We had a cousin who went in for an appendectomy and didn't come out. The doctors told us we should be tested. There's only fifteen or so places that can do the test, a biopsy of skeletal muscle. I went to Toronto for it. Stephen planned on having it at UCLA this year, but with the baby and all . . ." His voice trailed off.

"Martin, there's one last thing. It's personal, too. You might not know the answer, but if you do, please tell me. Stephen had let people believe that he's infertile. But it's not Stephen, is it?"

Martin hesitated. "Hannah, I really can't . . ."

"Martin, listen to me. Matthew is your godson, right?"

"Yes," But spoke hesitantly. She was losing him. If Hannah couldn't convince him, he'd be on the phone to Stephen within minutes.

"I'm appealing to you as his protector. Some horrible things have happened, and they all lead back to Matthew's adoption. I'm afraid that more horrible things will happen to Matthew if I can't get to the truth. Just tell me this one last thing."

He looked at her, as though trying to weigh her sincerity, her trustworthiness. She had been hard on Stephen the first time they met. Martin might still regard her as his brother's enemy. But maybe he would tell her the truth for Matthew's sake.

Finally, he let out a sigh. "It's Rebecca who can't have kids. She was terrified her parents would find out."

"Terrified? Why?"

"When Rebecca when away to college—something they didn't want her to do—she rebelled. Ended up with this guy, a real jerk. He slept around, and she got sick."

"Venereal disease?"

He nodded. "Chlamydia. She didn't know what it had done to her until she and Stephen tried to have kids."

"It left her sterile?"

"She was devastated. She knew how it had happened, and there was no way she could tell her family that she couldn't have children, and why she couldn't. Especially that mother of hers, who thinks women were born to breed."

"So they made up this story about Stephen?"

"If Maura thought Rebecca had brought this on herself— and that's how she would have seen it—she would have made Rebecca's life miserable," he said. "She would have made Frank shun her. She would have bullied the other kids into doing the same thing. They would have cut her out of the construction business. Stephen just decided it was easier to pretend to be the sterile male. He wanted to spare her all that holier-than-thou bullshit."

Hannah nodded. "Thanks for being honest with me."

"Now I need to know something."

Hannah knew what was coming. Martin was perceptive, and the trail of her questions led him to the answer.

"Stephen really is Matthew's father, isn't he? Biologically?"

She feared confirming it. The brothers were close, and if Martin told Stephen what Hannah knew, there was no telling what he'd do. But something about the way he asked the question made her trust him. He understood his brother's failings. He loved his sister-in-law. Finally, he cared about Matthew.

"Yes," she said.

"I didn't want to believe it." Martin shook his head.

"You already guessed?"

"It was a feeling. Matthew doesn't look much like Stephen did at that age. But he looks a lot like me."

"Martin, please give me your word that you won't let Rebecca and Stephen know that we've talked."

He nodded. "I really wanted to believe Matthew was adopted. Because that would mean I was wrong about Jennifer."

The baby the Drummonds had tried to adopt. The little girl reclaimed by her mother. Hannah felt her heart sink. "What about Jennifer?"

"The mother didn't just wake up one day and decide she wanted her back. There was an incentive. From Stephen."

"Go on," Hannah said.

"I was at their house. Jennifer's mother called and she thought when I answered the phone that I was Stephen. She lit into me because the last payment was late."

"He paid her to take the baby back?" Hannah felt sick.

"He really tried to go along with what Rebecca wanted, since she wouldn't agree to surrogacy. But I could see it: that teenage girl, and her pimply boyfriend, and the trailer in Cudahy. He was bringing all that into his house with Jennifer. He couldn't handle it."

"Jennifer had bad genes? Was that it?" Hannah tried to keep the anger out of her voice.

"You didn't grow up like we did. Everything our mother told us, after our father died, was how fine he was, how smart, how determined. How the Drummonds were that way, since forever. How much we were like him, and how it was up to us to keep him and the Drummonds in this world. Always. That meant children."

"Blood children."

Martin sighed. "I don't remember our father very well. But Stephen does. He idolized him. He wanted to be him, and have a son. And that son would have a son. All of them would have a little trace of Stephen, and of our dad. That way, Andrew Drummond would never die."

"It was so important that he'd lie to Rebecca?"

"It was sparing Rebecca. It was saving their marriage, and having a child, which is all the Rebecca ever wanted. I know that's how it was. It's how Stephen thinks."

Hannah nodded. Stephen's thinking had cost two people their lives.

Martin was going home that night. He agreed to say nothing to his brother or Rebecca until he heard from Hannah. As she drove back to the office she imagined how Stephen's plan unfolded.

It probably seemed simple at first: hire a surrogate, set up the adoption cover story, and that would be that. But Laura had complicated it. She convinced Stephen—with wine, that slim body, the sad, sexy eyes—to bypass a fertility clinic in favor of a motel room. And when Laura met Rebecca, she preyed on her gratitude for receiving a child. Laura made the request for an open adoption something that Rebecca couldn't resist. Stephen must have been furious, but what could he do? Give up his own baby—and the money? He had to go along.

And then Kurt surfaced. Stephen could have just done

nothing, knowing that Kurt wasn't the father. But that gap—the father who never surfaced—might eventually have roused Rebecca's suspicions. So Stephen used Streeter, supplying his own blood for the DNA test, under the Hoskins name, signature, and thumbprint. But when? Then she remembered the Sunday that Rebecca got out of the hospital. Hannah hadn't been able to reach Stephen that morning—he said he'd been at the store. But Rebecca complained that they were out of everything—coffee, wine. It was a hunch, but Hannah thought it was a good one: Stephen flew to San Francisco that Sunday to supply his blood. Kurt was ruled out, and his own cover was preserved.

So Stephen had his son and his wife. He thought that was that. But something else had gone wrong. And whatever it was required Laura's death.

In the office case file, she found the notes she'd taken as Stephen and Rebecca recounted what they did on the day Laura died. Stephen hadn't been alone for more than a few minutes: a surgery in the morning, rounds, lunch at a restaurant with another doctor, office hours, a gym workout, another hospital visit, a medical-association meeting. She read through the notes again and stopped at the entry for three o'clock: *Workout w/ Ricky*. Hannah thought she knew why Ricky had never called her back.

Twenty minutes later she was at the gym. The neon bicep sign flickered and jumped, but the door was locked. She held her finger on the buzzer until a man came and glared at her. He was well over six feet, and his straight black hair was pulled back in a ponytail. Ricky Oso, she decided. He had brown eyes and thick brows, but not the expression of muscle-bound dullness she'd seen sometimes in bodybuilders. Actually, he wasn't quite the bear suggested by his last name. The lean musculature that showed under his sleeveless T-shirt and high-cut running shorts was feline. He shook Hannah's hand, but his smile disappeared as she told him why she was there.

"I left messages," she said. "You never called me."

He shrugged. "Sorry."

"Can we talk for a minute?"

He pursed his lips, and for a minute Hannah though he was going to find some excuse to refuse. But then he led her inside.

The gym was small: one treadmill, a stationary bike, a stairclimber, a circuit of exercise machines, and racks of free weights. A skylight, now covered with a paper shade, brought filtered sun into the room, making up for the lack of windows. Against the back brick wall, brightly colored clipboards hung on pegs under clients' names.

"I'm in the middle of a workout," Ricky said. "Gotta get in a few miles before my next client. You don't mind?"

"Go ahead."

He jumped onto a treadmill and punched in a brisk pace. "So you're Doc's lawyer, huh?" He'd decided this was about nothing important. She played along.

"Yup. How's he doing, workout-wise?"

"Pretty good. He should come more often, but you can't push people too much, you know?"

"Sure. If you do, they just don't come at all."

"Exactly." He pumped his arms. His feet landed lightly, with a catlike bounce, on the rubber belt.

"So you do individual workouts?"

"Best way. One-on-one. Costs the clients a little more, but they get all my attention."

Hannah nodded. One-on-one. Stephen's gym visit was the only time he was with just one other person on the day Laura died. "What do you do to make sure clients show up?"

Oso laughed. The extra expenditure of air didn't seem to bother him. "Charge them for the appointments they miss. It's the only thing that works with Doc Drummond, for instance. He bitches about it, but he understands. If it's worthwhile, you have to pay for it."

"Right." She didn't say anything for a moment, listening to the rhythm of Oso's feet, accompanied by the drone of the tread. He had barely broken a sweat.

"The police came and talked to you, about the day Laura Benson died? She was the birth mother of Dr. Drummond's little boy."

His loose stride tightened slightly. He seemed to be concentrating on his breathing now.

"Yeah."

"Did they look at those client charts?"

He nodded again, and with two punches on the console, he tweaked up his speed. The tread's pitch rose a tone higher. His feet fell more heavily now.

"So that day wasn't one of the ones Dr. Drummond missed?"

He hesitated for a split second before he shook his head. Beads of sweat clung to his forehead.

"Ricky, I know the truth." It was a bluff, but his pause had given him away.

He wouldn't look at her. "About what?"

"It was innocently done, I'm sure."

Ricky shook his head. "I don't know what you mean." He mopped the sweat with the hem of his shirt.

"Maybe you don't even realize what you did. But the effect was that you lied for him, and that's going to be a problem for you."

Oso frowned down at the console and punched the stop button. He let the belt pull him backward, then jumped off.

"You're Dr. Drummond's lawyer, right? This is going to help him?"

"Lies don't help anyone, Ricky."

"I'm going to have to call him."

"He'll lie, Ricky. It's gone too far for him to level with you, or anyone."

He sucked in a deep breath, as though it might be his last. "Come with me."

He took Drummond's clipboard off the wall, and flipped back through the pages to the date of Laura's death. "Doc was pretty steady for a year or more. Three times a week, no matter what. Once or twice he had to cancel—an emergency surgery or something. But most times he was here.

He'd take his clipboard, we'd do his workout, he'd check stuff off."

"But that changed?"

"In the last few months he's been really spotty. He'd call and cancel. Sometimes, just not show up. He apologized, and told me to bill him every time he missed. A fine, kinda. When that cop showed up, I couldn't really remember whether he was here that day or not. So I gave him this to look at."

Drummond had scribbled his name at the top of the page. It showed that he arrived at three, spent thirty minutes on the treadmill, fifteen minutes on the stairclimber, ran through a weight-training circuit, and left at four-thirty. An hour and a half, just as he told Hannah and Churnin.

"But he wasn't here," she said.

Ricky still was sweating. He brought two folders out of his desk drawer. "This was my old workout sheet—what exercises, how many reps, what cardiovascular we did. Fifteen categories. The client checks off what he does, see?"

Hannah nodded. "I'm with you."

He pulled a sheet from the second folder. "I bought a stairclimber, so I had to redo the sheets. Now it's sixteen categories." He put his finger on Drummond's workout sheet from the day of Laura's death. "What cardio did he do?"

"Treadmill and stairclimber," Hannah said.

"I didn't have the stairclimber then. It was delivered the next week. And that's when I made up the new sheets."

Oso wouldn't say it, but Hannah understood. Stephen had filled out the new sheet sometime after the real date, and added it to his clipboard.

"He came in the week after that girl died. He wanted to pay me for the month. I should have realized how weird that was—he could have mailed a check. He must have found the blanks and filled out a new sheet when I was busy with a client. I didn't realize the thing about the stairclimber until after I talked to the detective. I didn't know what to do. It would have seemed like I lied the first time."

"You didn't do anything wrong."

Oso sat down heavily on the desk and sighed. "Look. Dr. Drummond is more than just another client to me. A few weeks ago they found these polyps in my dad's stomach. He's not a young guy, not rich. I talked to Dr. Drummond about it. He took care of it—he did the surgery. Dad's fine. And he never got a bill."

That was how he'd secured Oso's loyalty—father love. Hannah tried again. "Ricky, was he here that day?"

Ricky dropped his head so he wouldn't have to look at her. "No."

Stephen had an hour and a half. More than enough time. Hannah pulled into her parking place and stared at the wall, collecting her thoughts. He drugged Laura and pulled the gas line from the stove. She knew the reason now, the only reason there could be: Laura had threatened to tell Rebecca that Stephen had fathered Matthew in a cheap Seattle motel room. That he'd submitted his own blood for the DNA analysis, under Jerome Hoskins's name. But what prompted Laura's threat? What did she want from the Drummonds that she didn't already have?

Hannah walked into the lobby. It was starting to be a hot summer, but the building's ancient air-conditioning system hadn't caught up with the season yet. She bought a diet Coke from Luisa, who ran the newspaper-and-sundries stand. Hannah only knew her name from her gold plastic name badge; she had been buying the *Register* and little packets of Oreos from Luisa for more than a year, and she had yet to say a word to Hannah. She didn't even look up from her copy of *Soap Opera Digest* as she made change.

Hannah took the stairs, hoping that the walk would help her focus. She remembered Laura's hungry gaze at Rebecca's clothes on the day the adoption was finalized. How Laura looked away when Rebecca and Stephen kissed. Her anxiousness, when she thought Stephen was angry at her. And the "suicide" note? There was no mention of letting

Stephen down. Because Stephen was staying in her life—she thought.

Vera acknowledged Hannah's arrival with a little wave. Hannah went to her office and shut the door.

The computer beeped with a message: *u ok?*

Hannah sent one back to Vera: *fine. drummond madness continues.*

It was a kind of madness for Laura to do what she'd done: try to take Rebecca's place in Drummond's life. It must have started in the motel—that was not the usual place for a surrogate pregnancy to begin. Hannah was sure that was Laura's idea—something about saving Drummond money, lies, paperwork. She might even have played up the idea of how natural and loving it would be—for the baby's sake.

But the deal must have had its more businesslike aspects—cash, of course. Drummond would have paid her to carry the baby and pretend to Rebecca that it wasn't his. She might even have been satisfied with mere money, for a while. But then she saw how the Drummonds lived. She had a life like that once, when she was a kid. She had left it behind, traded it for a sagging bed in a Seattle motel with Kurt, where she could watch the rain and think about the scattershot mess that cocaine and anger had made of her life. She might have talked herself into believing she was in love with Stephen Drummond. Maybe she actually was.

Hannah finished off the can of soda. She was beginning to feel a rush in her blood as certainty set it. This wasn't the work of Susan Beckett or her father. They had the guilty secret of their incest. They might have wanted to shut Laura up—and maybe the Fiat had done the trick. But they hadn't done this. Hannah knew who had, and why it happened:

Laura trapped Stephen. If he wouldn't leave Rebecca, Laura would just tell her the truth. Laura thought, as Matthew's birth mother, she'd be able to beat Rebecca in a custody fight. Hannah wasn't so sure, and she imagined Stephen's panic as he realized the bind he was in. Rebecca would make a custody fight sheer hell. Between lawyer fees and child support, Stephen would be left a cash-strapped half-time father. His consolation prize: Laura, full-time liar. That would have been fine with Laura. But not with Stephen.

He let Laura think she'd won him. He suggested that she write the note to Rebecca to soften the pain of the betrayal. He could have easily drugged Laura's drink. The Xanax might even have been Rebecca's—she had alluded to the pills she took after they lost Jennifer.

The pills and liquor were just to make Laura drowsy, Hannah imagined. Such mixtures weren't precise enough for someone like Stephen to count on. But he thought gas was. He hadn't expected that Laura would awake and call for help.

The phone rang. It was Anneke—Hannah could only make that part out. She was trying to talk, but kept choking on sobs.

"Take a deep breath," Hannah said. "It's okay."

"I told her."

Hannah closed her eyes. "Who? Rebecca?"

"I thought about it. Matthew is her son, and she had a right to know. I left the bracelet on him when we got home."

Hannah felt her heart sink. She should have warned Anneke. "She saw it?"

"Right away."

Hannah imagined the scene: Rebecca's hand on Matthew's plump, cool wrist. Turning the bracelet over to see the words *malignant hyperthermia*. Martin might have told her about the family's history, probably because Stephen hadn't. Protecting Rebecca, knowing what was best, stretching that condescension into lies—Stephen did such things almost reflexively.

"Tell me what happened then."

"She shook me like I was a little kid," Anneke said. "So I told her everything I told you."

"You told her Matthew inherited this illness from Laura?"

"Yes. Then she went into Dr. Drummond's office."

And like Hannah, Rebecca figured it out. She reviewed Laura's medical history, knowing she wouldn't find malignant hyperthermia. Maybe she even saw the surrogate ad, as Hannah had, and dialed the number that would link her to Stephen's exchange—a number she probably never dialed directly.

"Where's Rebecca now?"

Anneke's scant composure finally shattered. "She left. With Matthew."

"Where are you?"

"In the park. She told me to get out and never come back." She was crying hysterically. Hannah waited until she caught a breath.

"How long ago was this, Anneke?"

Anneke sniffled. "Oh, God. I don't know. I've been here about an hour, so maybe an hour and a half ago? Hannah, what did I do?"

You told the truth, Hannah thought. A dangerous thing.

Only Rebecca's car was in their driveway. Hannah rang the bell. No answer. She tried the door. Unlocked. And the alarm was off. She called their names. Her voice echoed, bouncing off the entryway's glass, metal, and slate. The windows concentrated the sun during this part of the day. The air-conditioning was off, and the house simmered, airless.

She called again. Silence answered her. At the top of the stairs, she paused, listening for what she expected: an argument behind closed doors. But she heard no voices. Strains of mechanical music came from a room at the end of the hall, from Matthew's room. "Pop Goes the Weasel." She clenched her hands. They were stiff with cold.

The door was three-quarters shut, muting the tune that now seemed to be slowing, the interval between notes longer than the notes themselves. She pushed the door open, trying not to think about what she could find. Rebecca loved her son. And he was her son, in the only way that really mattered. Hannah told herself that again.

The mobile above the crib barely turned now. It sputtered one final pinging note, the "pop," and fell silent. The crib was empty. Hannah slumped against it and then sat down in the rocker next to the window. The sloping garden was dappled green, yellow, and red, all the colors of summer. Under a stand of eucalyptus trees at the bottom of the yard, something stirred, stood, and fell. Rebecca.

36

She was trying to stand again when Hannah got to her. Exhausted and pale, Rebecca let Hannah ease her back to the ground. A bullet had grazed Rebecca's left shoulder, and blood was oozing from the wound there. Her linen shirt was sticky with it.

"Where's Stephen?" Hannah said. "And Matthew?"

"I don't know. Stephen took him. He tried to kill me."

"Is your office unlocked? I can call 911 from there."

Rebecca shook her head. "He ripped out the phone jack. You'll have to call from the house. You can leave me here. Please just help me get back my baby."

Hannah sprinted to the house and punched the emergency number, and then Churnin's. She tried to imagine where Stephen was with Matthew. They could have driven halfway to Mexico. They could be on a plane to anywhere.

By the time she returned, Rebecca had moved to the deck of the office. She sat in the bright sun, the blood drying on her skin.

"Let's get you inside." Hannah tried to help her stand.

"No." Rebecca pulled away. "I'm cold. I need to get warm."

"I'll get you a blanket. Come on."

Finally, she let Hannah help her to her feet. She stretched on the sofa in the office's reception room and ran her hand across her mouth. "Stephen is Matthew's father, isn't he? His real father."

There was nothing to do but tell her. Hannah nodded. "I'm sorry."

"I knew it, somehow." Rebecca was staring at the door to her office, the room where she'd shot Kurt to save her son from him. "Is the bracelet how you knew?"

"Yes. What happened with Stephen?"

"When Anneke told me about the bracelet, I understood what you were doing, looking at the files. When he came home, I confronted him. He had to have what he wanted. *His* baby. That was all that mattered. Another Stephen in the world. God, the selfishness."

Hannah couldn't disagree with any of that. "Go on."

"He betrayed me, with Laura, and then he killed her," Rebecca said. "I wasn't going to stand for it—any of it. Not the lies, and not covering up what he'd done. Not any of it."

"What did he say?"

"Tried to pretend, at first, that he didn't know what I was talking about. When that didn't work, he said everything would be all right, if we just stayed together, and hung tight. But I knew there was more to it than just that he was Matthew's father. I saw how Laura looked at him sometimes, and how he looked at her. They didn't do it in a fertility clinic, or even with a turkey baster, did they?"

Hannah thought about the Daybreak Motel. She imagined how a meeting between Laura and Drummond, which probably began over a nice dinner somewhere, took a steep slide, aided by wine and need and Laura's long-range schemes, into a double bed in Room 19.

"Rebecca, I don't think the details—"

"He wouldn't tell me either. He said he didn't mean to hurt me. Said it got out of hand. That she seduced him." She wiped her eyes and laughed weakly. "My God. He didn't need seducing."

"You mean he was looking for an affair?"

She shrugged. "Looking? I don't know. Sex was bad for months before we found Laura. Every time he wanted to, I thought: I can't get pregnant. What's the point of doing this?"

Love, Hannah wanted to say. But the act had come to mean despair, instead.

"Laura wasn't an innocent, but she wouldn't have had to do much seducing," Rebecca said. "He met her more than halfway, I'm sure of that."

"Did it go on, after she came down here?"

"He said it didn't. But sometimes I got a strange feeling about them. I told myself I was being jealous of a younger woman—one who could have children. But I was right. I should have trusted my instincts."

"So he confessed to you. And he asked you to forgive him. But you didn't."

"No. I told him it was over. I said I had no intention of lying, covering up and raising Matthew with a killer. I brought Matthew down here while I got my checkbook and some other papers. Stephen followed us."

Rebecca's face was turning a chalky white. Hannah checked her watch. Ten minutes since she'd called 911. Even though she'd reported a shooting.

"Let me get you some water," she said. There was a sink of some kind in Rebecca's inner office. Stephen had come from there, sipping water, on the night Kurt died.

Rebecca shook her head. "No. I'm okay. Stephen took out the gun and said if I told anyone, he'd kill me. He said he hadn't come this far to lose Matthew. And that's when he shot me. Then he took Matthew."

"Do you know where they went?"

"He has money. Their passports. They could go anywhere." Her eyes locked on Hannah's. "He killed Laura."

"He told you that?"

Rebecca hesitated. "Will I have to tell the police everything that happened?"

"I'll be there with you."

Rebecca put her hands over her eyes. "It's my fault."

"What do you mean?"

"What happened to Kurt. When you think about it, he cared about Matthew. Just like we did."

"Rebecca, Kurt broke in here with a gun. No one can blame you for defending yourself."

She shook her head. "You don't understand. It didn't happen that way. I think Stephen set him up. That first hang-up call was Kurt, I'm sure. But then Stephen did it. It would be easy. He could pick up a phone in the hospital. There's a pay phone around the corner from his office. He'd pretend the silence on the other end was Kurt. He did it to scare me, and to make everyone think Kurt was a threat to us."

"I thought Ed Westerland made those calls."

"I think some of them were from Ed. But Stephen wanted to terrify me so that he could justify what he was going to do. He got Kurt to come to the house."

"With money," Hannah said. She'd seen Stephen cramming cash into his humidor on the night of the shooting. Not a poker stake, but the bait he'd planned for Kurt.

"I think it was money. He made a withdrawal from one of our accounts the day before. He said it was to make an investment, but I never saw any statements for it."

Hannah nodded. "How was Stephen going to do it?"

She shook her head. "I don't know. But whatever the plan was, Kurt ruined it by coming early, before Stephen was home. Kurt saw the light down here. Do you know what he wanted?"

Something from the files, Hannah thought. He was playing both ends: getting money from Stephen, getting information on Matthew for Susan. She needed to know how much the Drummonds knew about Laura's birth family.

"I didn't know then that Stephen had lured him here, Hannah. That's the truth, I swear it."

"I believe you. Did Stephen talk about what he did to Laura?"

She nodded. "Xanax, mixed in carrot juice and gin first."

"And then the gas."

She shook her head. "He used something else, too. Another drug."

"The coroner's report doesn't mention about anything else."

"It wouldn't show up, he said."

"Go on." And as she talked Hannah could almost hear Stephen's voice.

"It was a muscle relaxant," Rebecca said. "Succinyl choline. It stops someone from breathing."

"That's what Laura meant when she said she couldn't breathe."

Rebecca nodded. "He said anesthesiologists use it in surgery, but they have it in the ER, too. Stephen had used it when he was a resident. When Laura was drowsy, he injected her. Stephen said they would never find the needle mark or the drug in an autopsy if they weren't looking for it. He was proud of himself." She shook her head in disgust.

"But something went wrong?"

"He didn't use enough of it. She stopped breathing, but only for a minute. Then she started again."

"And then what?"

"He pulled the gas line and left. She woke up again. And she called me." Rebecca winced as she tried to sit up. Her breaths were short, and her skin shiny with sweat. "Stephen killed her, and he almost killed Matthew and me."

"Why did Stephen do it, Rebecca?"

"Because of me, he said." She glanced up at Hannah. "He was right."

Hannah was pierced by the sadness of it. Rebecca had swallowed the guilt he fed her, as surely as Laura drank the cocktail of Xanax and juice and gin. "He wasn't right."

"But I am responsible," Rebecca said. "When Kurt first showed up and threatened to take Matthew, I got scared. Even if Kurt wasn't the father, there would always be a cloud over us. There was a father out there, somewhere, who might show up and try to claim Matthew. Or Laura might change her mind, just like Jennifer's mother did."

Rebecca still didn't know what had really happened with Jennifer. Hannah would tell her, but not now. "You were afraid Laura might never let go of Matthew."

"That's right." Rebecca seemed relieved that Hannah understood. "She would always be there, reminding him that she was his real mother."

"So you wanted Laura to move, to stop seeing Matthew?"

She nodded. "We would have to be careful not to upset her. But I thought we could slowly work her out of our lives."

"Didn't that mean breaking the promise you made to her?" Hannah said.

That made Rebecca angry. "How many lies had she told us, Hannah? How many trusts had she broken? I thought you understood."

"I'm trying," Hannah said.

"I just wanted my son's life to be secure. Stephen and I talked about it, and we agreed. Of course that's what he wanted, more than anything, because Matthew was his. He knew by then that Laura could undo everything. All she had to do was tell me who Matthew's father was."

"Did you talk to Laura about this? About spending less time with you and Matthew?"

"Stephen said he would. He wanted to spare me, he said. He didn't think I could stand up to Laura. I thought he was right. I thought he was less susceptible to her." She laughed harshly. "What an idiot I was. He said he called her, and tried to convince her to move back to Seattle. He said we'd help her."

"With money."

"If that's what it took. He said she agreed to think about it. She wanted us to leave her alone while she thought— that's what Stephen said. But now I know it didn't happen that way. He told me the truth today. She was going to tell me everything if he tried to make her go away. She knew what that would mean. I would divorce Stephen and sue for custody."

"So in Stephen's book, that made killing her your fault?"

She blinked at Hannah, amazed that she didn't understand. "If only I hadn't panicked about Laura, this wouldn't have happened. People betrayed and lied to Laura her whole life, and that's why she didn't trust anyone. Why she lied right back." Rebecca's eyes reddened. "The lies go back to before Laura was born, with Susan, when she was Ellen Burden at Paraclete School."

"I understand, but still, it's not your—" Hannah stopped.

She let herself hear again what Rebecca had said. Ellen Burden at Paraclete. And suddenly the room felt cold. Rebecca was staring at her, so she finished the thought. "It's not your fault."

Rebecca frowned. "What's wrong?"

"I'm getting you some water." She needed a minute to think.

"No, no," Rebecca said. "I can . . ."

Hannah opened the door. There, beside Rebecca's desk, lay Stephen.

He was on his back, a pool of blood beneath his head. A small bullet wound marked his forehead, like a smudge of bloody ash. One look around the room told Hannah that Matthew was not there. She knelt next to Stephen and touched his neck. He was warm, but Hannah couldn't get a pulse.

She looked up in time to see Rebecca stumbling up the path to the house. Hannah ran after her, grabbed her around the waist, wrestled her back to the office, and sat her on the sofa.

"No more lies, Rebecca. What happened? Where's Matthew?"

Before she could answer, they heard the sound of thudding footsteps. The paramedics had finally arrived.

37

They tried to check Rebecca, but she refused to be touched. So they started to work on Stephen. Hannah walked Rebecca up to the deck of the house. She was still trembling. Her skin was the color of chalk.

A paramedic stepped out of the office, called to Hannah, and shook his head. Hannah acknowledged Stephen's death with a nod.

"He's dead, Rebecca. Right now you tell me: what happened?"

"We were struggling for the gun. It went off, and I was hit. He was going to shoot again, so I grabbed for it. We were wrestling over it, and it went off again. And he was dead." She shuddered and dropped her head to her knees.

"You said Stephen had Matthew. Where is he?"

She glanced up at Hannah, measuring her to see if she could be trusted. "Safe. If you would just let me go to him."

Hannah understood the unspoken plea: I've been lied to, duped, mistreated by my husband. I'm a good woman, a good mother. I'll take my baby and disappear. Hannah almost wished she could do that, for Rebecca and Matthew's sake. But what Rebecca said about Paraclete and Ellen Burden stopped her.

"I'll be back here with Matthew in ten minutes," Rebecca said. She was giving Hannah an out—she could tell the police her rotten client had lied to her about coming back. There would be no repercussions.

Rebecca stood up. Took a step. Hannah considered it for

a split second. Then she shoved her—hard—on the wounded shoulder. Rebecca let out a shriek of pain and collapsed onto the bench.

"Listen to me," Hannah said. "You might be able to fool some people with the story of how awful Stephen was, what he did to you. I might even agree with some of it. But that doesn't mean I'm going to help you do this."

"Hannah, please."

Hannah felt the rage rising, thinking of what Rebecca had done, all in the name of keeping this perfect little life, this perfect little phony life. "I want to hear the truth from you. Just once. I can't tell anyone, because you're my client. But I want to hear it all."

"But I told you what happened."

"Those were lies."

Rebecca shook her head. "This is awful."

"The truth is worse, and you don't want to think about it. You were in Laura's apartment the day she died. You saw the report on Laura's birth parents—that's the only way you would know about Paraclete School and Ellen Burden. I didn't tell you that. Ivan Churnin certainly didn't."

Rebecca wouldn't look at her. She twisted the wedding ring on her finger.

"You didn't know that Stephen had been there already. You went, thinking you could reason with Laura, because of the bond you had with her. I imagine you took her some money. You didn't know that Stephen had already done that. When he tried to talk to her about cash, a payoff, it infuriated her. Cleve Gibbons heard Laura turn money down, Rebecca. Money wasn't what Laura wanted. She wanted to be you. She wanted to take your place in Stephen's bed. She was going to be Matthew's only mother."

Rebecca shook her head. "I don't know what you're talking about."

"You knocked at Laura's door. She didn't answer. Maybe you heard something. You let yourself in. You saw Laura had passed out, but she was still breathing. You found the investigator's report about her family. It was out in plain

ght, with the envelope. I imagine Stephen did that to point
e blame at Susan Beckett or Ed Westerland, just in case
e suicide scenario he'd come up with didn't convince the
olice."

"This is crazy," Rebecca whispered.

"You couldn't wake Laura up. The gas was doing its job,
nd you were going to let her die. After you read the report,
ou took it into the bathroom and burned it. You didn't want
nyone to know who Matthew's grandparents were. Things
ere messy enough without that."

Rebecca shook her head. "Why are you doing this to me?
hat isn't what happened."

She meant it as a blanket denial. But Hannah realized that
omething in the scenario was wrong. If gas was spewing
to the apartment, Rebecca would have smelled it once she
as inside. She would never have lit a match.

Hannah considered Rebecca for a moment. She seemed
o fragile, so in need of protection. That quality had made
annah see Laura's death differently, with Rebecca as a
assive participant, someone who could have saved Laura,
ut failed through weakness. But Hannah had misunder-
tood her, and forgotten what Rebecca had told her panicky
ssociate that night that she and Bobby came for dinner:
ometimes you have to think on your feet.

"You're right," Hannah said. "That's not what happened.
tephen wasn't the one who realized Laura had started
reathing again. If he had, he would have given her another
ose of the succinyl choline. She was breathing when you
ound her. You pulled the gas line, not Stephen."

Rebecca started to protest her innocence, but her eyes
ave her away. Hannah felt a column of something molten
nside, ready to explode. She calmed herself enough to
peak. "Tell me what happened. Or see Matthew wind up
ith Susan Beckett."

Rebecca's eyes went wide for an instant before she
ecovered. "You don't know where he is."

"We'll find him. And when we do, Susan Beckett will do
verything in her power to cut your parental ties to
atthew. You killed her daughter, Rebecca, and she won't

forgive that. She might win, too. Blood ties are in her favo
But if you tell me what happened, I'll fight her for you.
you don't, I won't. It's up to you. You read the report. Yo
know who fathered Laura. If you want Matthew raised i
that family, keep quiet."

Rebecca was ashen. When she spoke, her voice was tire
but steady. This time there were no pauses taken t
construct the next fact, to provide a heart-wrenching, lyin
detail.

"She was on the sofa. She had thrown up, and wa
half-unconscious. The phone was unplugged. I knelt next t
her, trying to wake her up, when I felt something under m
knee. It was a pill bottle. My prescription for Xanax. I'
taken it when we lost Jennifer. I guessed then that Stephe
had done this. I didn't know about the succinyl choline the
I just knew she wasn't dead, and he had dropped the Xana
bottle—with my name on it. That would have implicate
both of us."

"You had a bigger problem. Laura wasn't dead. So yo
pulled the gas line, just like that."

"No!" It was ridiculous, but she managed to look hurt. "
plugged in the phone and started dialing 911, but I stopped.

"Why?"

"If she lived, she'd go to the police and tell them wha
Stephen had done. She would tell them I was part of it. Sh
might even get a court to listen. If Laura woke up and g
to the phone, we would lose Matthew."

"So you unplugged the phone again, pulled the gas line i
the kitchen, and you left."

Rebecca's nod was almost imperceptible.

"But why did you go back after she called? Why not jus
erase the message?"

"I couldn't take the chance."

Hannah understood. If Laura could reconnect the phon
and call Rebecca, she could call her friend Gibbons. Or dia
911.

"So you stood there, knocking, waiting to see if she coul
answer. If there was no answer, you were going to leave.

She didn't respond for a moment. Then she whispered, "Then that Gibbons man showed up."

The words rang in Hannah's head, almost as loud as the explosion had been. What Rebecca had just said was the key to everything. Rebecca didn't realize it, wouldn't, as long as Hannah showed no reaction.

"You and Stephen never talked about what you'd both done?"

"He tried once. I just wanted to forget. Sometimes the painkillers I got after the explosion helped. And as time passed it seemed like it had never happened."

Now Rebecca's distance, silence, and preoccupation made sense to her. Pills, and guilt and the need to forget. Hannah could barely imagine the tension in the Drummond household. It was a bond predicated on what they would do to keep Matthew, but it must have felt like it was strangling them.

"Why did you kill Stephen?"

She blinked at Hannah. "I told you. It was an accident."

Hannah considered the minor wound to Rebecca's left shoulder. In a wild struggle, with Stephen determined to kill her, wouldn't the shot have done more damage? Rebecca was right-handed, and no longer afraid of guns. The pain must have startled her, though.

"I don't believe that, Rebecca. Where will Matthew go, once we find him? To Susan and her father?"

Rebecca's hands were clenched at her sides. The trembling, gone during her truth-telling, came back as rage. "Why? Simple. Stephen fucked that slut. And she had his baby."

Hannah heard car doors slamming in the driveway. A moment later the doorbell rang.

"Where is Matthew?" Hannah said to Rebecca.

"Do you know your Bible? Old Testament?"

Hannah felt a prickle of panic. If this was a clue to Matthew's whereabouts, she couldn't see where it led. The only Old Testament stories about children that she could remember were the awful ones—the death of the firstborn sons of Egypt. Abraham's readiness to sacrifice Isaac. The story of Solomon's wisdom, judging which of the two women who claimed to be the mother of a surviving child was telling the truth.

"Solomon?"

Rebecca nodded. "I thought about that story, there with Laura."

Hannah felt her heart sinking. "The real mother sacrifices. That's the point of the story. She gives up her baby rather than see him cut in half."

"No." She waved Hannah off, as if she hadn't properly studied her lessons. "I thought about what happened before that. The women were sleeping, and one rolled over on her baby. The baby suffocated. She took the other woman's child as her own."

Hannah heard the gate open and saw a uniformed cop, young and covering up his nervousness with a stern face, edging down the path to the deck.

"What does that have to do with Matthew?"

Rebecca watched him approach and then turned her attention back to Hannah. "She didn't think it through. It was shock, I guess. But Solomon wouldn't have the chance to decide who got that baby if the other mother never woke up. That's what I realized. That's what I had to do, Hannah."

As the cop came closer Rebecca dropped her face to her knees in a show of grief and pain. Hannah told the officer who she was and suggested a call to Ivan Churnin.

38

For an hour Churnin questioned Rebecca as Hannah sat at her side. Now the story had changed: Stephen was despondent when she threatened to leave him. He tried to kill himself. Rebecca was injured in the struggle for the gun, and once she was shot, Stephen finished himself off. Hannah bit down hard on the inside of her lip. Rebecca did indeed know how to think on her feet.

Churnin escorted Rebecca, hands once again encased in brown paper bags to preserve gunshot residue, to a patrol car in the driveway. Stephen's body would follow her downtown shortly.

"She won't say where Matthew is," Churnin said when he came back.

Hannah felt almost sick with fear for him. "She won't hurt him. I keep telling myself that."

"Even if he's Stephen and Laura's little boy? And she's the barren one? Something like that could drive a person crazy."

"I pray to God that's not it."

"Go back to your office. I'll call as soon as there's anything about Matthew. I've got cadets knocking on neighbors' doors, and we'll go wider when the next watch starts."

She was a few feet from the door of the office when she thought she heard a baby's whimper of displeasure. She stopped in the hall and listened again, but the sound didn't repeat. An auditory hallucination. Just something she wanted to hear.

Bobby was on the phone at Vera's desk. Vera, in an iridescent green-and-pink dress, hovered over him like some frantic hummingbird. She turned when Hannah opened the door, and let out a relieved sigh.

Bobby looked up and dropped the phone. "We've been trying to find you. Your damn cellular is dead."

"Sorry," Hannah said. "You know what's happened?"

Bobby nodded. "Churnin called a couple minutes ago. But there's no news."

"Christ, Bobby, what has she done with Matthew?"

Bobby shook his head. "I can't imagine."

Hannah dropped onto the sofa and tried to stop the frantic race of her thoughts. Where could Rebecca have hidden her baby? She got out the file and started the calls she was almost sure Churnin has already made: to Maura and Frank Malone, to Martin Drummond and his wife. She barely knew what to say to them—all the news was bad. A daughter had killed three times. A brother was dead. A baby was missing.

Vera brought her coffee and a bagel. But Hannah couldn't eat. All her thoughts had turned to Matthew. Her hand shook when she dialed the phone.

Nine o'clock. Bobby lay asleep on the reception room's sofa. Vera was at her desk. Hannah could hear her fingers on the keys, the tap dance of her Internet social life. Hannah had talked to the families. They were stunned, unbelieving, angry—she didn't blame them for any of that. But when she asked Maura Malone if she knew where Rebecca might have taken Matthew, the response was disquieting.

"I hope he is gone," she snapped. "It was wrong from the start, I knew it. Bad blood will out, and I always said it would."

Hannah scarcely knew what to say. Maura Malone made her grandson sound like a mutated cell, a disease of some kind. She hung up on the woman's rantings.

At ten-thirty, she called Churnin again. He had nothing to tell her. The neighborhood was canvassed. The media were waiting to do their eleven o'clock stand-ups. Missing children always led the news.

Hannah couldn't drink any more coffee. Her nerves were jangled, fried by exhaustion and suppressed panic. She remembered the coolness of Matthew's skin, the tiny fingers and solid arms, plump as overstuffed cushions. She put her head down on the desk. And on the edge of sleep, she heard the office door open. Vera let out a yelp, followed by a string of hiccuping sobs.

In the reception room, Vera had flung herself around the visitor. Bobby was on his feet, a stunned look on his face. Vera stepped back, and there was Connie Westerland—holding Matthew, who was disheveled, red-faced, grumpy, and furiously sucking on Connie's string of fetish-bear beads. Everything that happened that day caught Hannah then. She sat down on the edge of Vera's desk and let the feelings wash through her: grief, relief, and a flood of blinding love at the sight of Matthew. She cried.

After Connie gave Matthew a bottle, Vera volunteered to change his diapers. She took him to Hannah's office. Bobby went to call Churnin.

"I heard on the news," Connie said to Hannah. "Dr. Drummond is dead?"

Hannah nodded.

"But Rebecca's all right?" Connie looked strained to the breaking point. "I heard about Dr. Drummond, but is Rebecca okay?"

"No," Hannah said. "Not anything like okay."

"I knew it," Connie said. "As soon as I saw her, I knew."

Connie told the story quickly: Rebecca had come to Connie's motel, pleading for a favor. Stephen had an emergency surgery that interrupted their vacation plans. They were supposed to meet his brother at a house in Pismo Beach. There was no phone there, no way to let

Martin know about the delay. Rebecca and Stephen had the only key. Rebecca knew it was a long drive, and an imposition, but would Connie take the key and go ahead with Matthew, as planned? She and Stephen would join her later.

"She was all jumpy and nervous. I could see she really wanted me to do this. I wondered, was this some kind of test?" Connie said. "Did she want to know if I was a reliable person, someone she could trust? She gave me some money, for gas and such, and directions.

"It was all so fast, and I wanted to do it. Some time alone with Matthew. It's all I've wanted, really. So I said yes."

"But you knew something was wrong?" Hannah said.

She nodded. "It didn't half make sense. I thought Rebecca and Stephen might have been fighting, and maybe she needed time alone. So I went ahead. But up around Oxnard, I just turned around. I thought I'd better come here. I didn't want anyone to think I'd kidnapped him. There's been too much of that kind of craziness already."

With that, Hannah knew Connie had talked to Ed. She sounded disgusted with him, but at least they talked. That was a start.

"You did the right thing," Hannah said. Rebecca must have thought she'd have time to collect Matthew from Connie and run somewhere. She thought she'd have time to come up with a plausible story about Stephen's death. She was improvising, and Hannah didn't doubt that it might have worked. But Hannah's arrival had ruined her plan.

Vera brought Matthew back and put him in Connie's arms. She twisted a lock of Matthew's pale yellow hair in her fingers. Connie's eyes were dark-circled, and Hannah felt sure she wanted a smoke. Matthew had substituted his thumb for Connie's necklace. He was easing into sleep, occasionally letting out a wet blatting noise as he sucked away.

Hannah rummaged in her purse and handed over her house keys. "You could use some rest, and a little more space than you have at the motel. Take Matthew to my place, and I'll meet you there."

Connie's eyes widened. But she took the keys, and the sleeping baby.

39

Ken Bartel got his training at the William O. Douglas School of Law, just as Hannah had. He was with the public defender's office for a few years, and then went off into his own criminal-defense practice. Hannah had seen his name in the paper a few times. Domestic murder seemed to be his specialty, and by the look of his suits, car, and paralegals, he didn't come cheap.

Rebecca retained him the day after the shooting, after Hannah and Bobby declared themselves ill-equipped to handle a potential murder case. Now Bartel wanted Hannah to go over the facts of the adoption again. Rebecca apparently was sticking with the story she'd told Churnin: Stephen's lies about Matthew's parenthood came out, she threatened to leave him, he wounded her and then killed himself.

"The physical evidence is workable," Bartel said. Hannah took that to mean that he could concoct some story to convince a jury that the shot to Stephen's head was self-inflicted, and that Rebecca's wound wasn't.

"But Churnin seems to think Rebecca was involved in Laura's death," Bartel added. "But he's bluffing on that, right?" He looked up, waiting for Hannah's confirmation.

She didn't give it, not even with the merest swivel of her head. "I wish you luck with all this," Hannah said.

"There's something else," he said. "It's about Matthew."

"He'll be ready anytime Maura Malone wants to come get him," she said.

"No," Bartel said. "That's not going to happen."

Hannah thought she'd misheard him. "What?"

"Maura and her husband—Maura really, but she's the only one who counts—are stuck on the idea that Matthew is the reason for all Rebecca's trouble. And he's not even hers, really. They say."

Hannah felt like she'd been hit with a brick. Maura Malone had really meant all that crap on the phone. "He's just a baby. It's not his fault."

"Maura won't listen. Won't take Rebecca's calls, or mine."

"Well, Rebecca has scads of brothers and sisters, one of them . . ."

He shook his head.

"Why? Because Maura has forbidden it?"

"She's let them know her will can be changed. Bunch of wimps."

"So what does Rebecca want?"

"She wants you to take care of him. Until after the trial. She trusts you, she said."

It was cagey of Rebecca. With Matthew in her house, Hannah could never forget why Rebecca had killed three people. All for Matthew. She was preying on Hannah's sympathy, maybe laying groundwork for some further favor—a friendly bit of testimony, perhaps, since Hannah understood everything. Sisterhood was powerful, Hannah thought, but her sympathy lay with Matthew, and the truth. And nowhere else.

"Ken, I work sixty-hour weeks sometimes. I've only been able to handle Matthew so far because I have someone staying with me."

"That's Connie Westerland? Rebecca said she's wonderful."

Hannah thought about that. It would be a lot to ask of Connie. She loved Matthew, and that was good. But if she loved him too much, it would be a wrenching loss when he left. Going where, though? Her mouth felt dry.

"The only other alternative is foster care," Bartel said.

Hannah couldn't bear that. No matter how loving the

home, Matthew would feel lost without someone he knew. "But what about Martin, Stephen's brother? Doesn't he have some say in this?"

"Sure. I talked to him. He said he doesn't know anything about kids. He works crazy hours, and so does his wife. He said if the trial doesn't go Rebecca's way, he'll be there for Matthew. But he can't do it now. Now, of course, is the problem. In the long run, everything will be fine, because Rebecca's going to beat this."

Hannah was sure she wouldn't. But this was not the time to share that with Bartel.

"Martin said he'd like you to keep Matthew," Bartel said. "You have quite a fan club."

Hannah could think of one person who wasn't in her cheering section. It was probably time for Hannah to pay her a visit, and keep the promise she'd made to Rebecca.

Susan Beckett had heard the news, of course. The county's newspapers were splashed with the details of Stephen's death. Susan had made only one comment for the record: she was concerned for her grandson's future. Hannah knew exactly what that meant.

Susan was waiting for her in the living room of the glass-walled house. For the first time she and Hannah were alone, without a father, husband, daughter, or aide to act as shield or foil. Susan put down the newspaper she'd been reading. Hannah saw the headline: BECKETT RACE TIGHTENS. So the Republican lock on the district could be jimmied. Susan could lose.

"I heard you have my grandson," Susan said. "You can just let me have him now, or we can see each other in court."

Hannah watched her. The calculating eyes were bright with confidence. The predatory smile was freshly whitened for the fall campaign. Matthew would be a great prop for her, and a wonderful consolation prize if she lost the congressional race. Hannah gave her the envelope she'd brought. Susan opened it and pulled out the private investigator's report. Her eyes narrowed as she read, as if the words filled them with acrid smoke.

"What the hell does this mean?" She shook the pages at Hannah.

"This is what you thought the Drummonds had on you. That's why Kurt was rummaging in the files that night—helping you find out how much they knew. You were afraid they'd use it to shut you out."

"This is the craziest confabulation I've ever seen. You can't prove any of it."

"I don't need to," Hannah said. "I know you sent Kurt there, and he's dead now." He might have died anyway, but Hannah decided not to tell Susan Beckett that.

"And what are you planning on doing with this?"

"If you fight me on Matthew, the next person to see that document will be Judge Bitsy Baxter," Hannah said. "That's who would be hearing Matthew's custody case. You know her?"

Susan's lips tightened. Hannah knew she'd hit a mark. "So you know she has friends. Lots of them. Socialities, bankers, developers, businesswomen. Bitsy swims in contribution-rich waters. That report on Laura's parentage won't be in the newspapers, because this would be a guardianship case. But don't doubt for a minute that everyone who counts to you will find out what's in there. Do you really want to risk that? In a tight race? For what Amy will go through, once this slime oozes out?"

Susan sat silent for a minute, staring first at Hannah, and then at the newspaper.

"I know that you used some political clout to close the investigation into Kurt's shooting," Hannah said. "Don't try to have it reopened. One of the investigators is dying for a piece of you, and I'll help him get it."

Susan lifted her face, and Hannah saw, behind the political artifice, a glimpse of the girl at Paraclete. Young, violated, alone, bewildered, but with a core of something good.

It must have been like falling into quicksand, when Bill Beckett began coming to her at night. Susan had struggled—and won—by refusing the abortion. But after that? She was still a child, she still had to live in that house, in that sucking pit. She didn't go under as some victims did, choking on self-loathing and misplaced guilt. She'd stayed on the surface by not struggling, once she'd given Laura up. She stayed, treading a little, holding up her head. And finally, she was able to exact her punishment on her father. Daily—hourly if she wanted. But only by staying. So in the end he had won. She never left him. They were up to their necks in the muck together.

"I'm sorry for what he did to you," Hannah said. "You could still save yourself."

Susan blinked slowly at her. "Get out of my sight."

That was the last Hannah heard of Susan Beckett until November, when she beat a Latino accountant from Orange in the congressional race by a scant 817 votes. In the front-page picture, her father held up her hand in victory.

A few days after visiting Susan Beckett, Hannah dropped Connie and Matthew at the park, where one of Rebecca's sisters had arranged a clandestine visit with her nephew. Then she drove out of Las Almas and toward the coast, dropping down into Laguna Canyon. She had sent a get-well card, and in response, she'd been invited for a visit.

There was a strange line of businesses along the canyon road as it snaked toward the coast: a dog park, a gymnasium for women, a foundation that cared for homeless cats, a vintage-Jeep dealership, a frozen-food plant, a dulcimer studio, and a glassblower's workshop. She turned up a narrow street where shingled bungalows built in the thirties still stood, despite the floods and the fires and the escalating real-estate values.

She found the address: a house done up in red-and-brown paint. A wind chime made of spoons and forks dangled over the porch railing. Cleve Gibbons limped to the screen door, leaning on a stout shillelagh.

"Thanks for coming," he said.

"How long have you been back? I sent the card to Point Reyes Station."

"Long enough to know what's happened." His face clouded, and he motioned her inside. "I'll make some tea."

• • •

Gibbons poured out a brew that smelled of ginger and black pepper and eased himself onto the sofa. "I thought my memory was all screwed up."

He shook his head as if that would clear it and ran his fingers down his beard. The gray whiskers that had been confined to his mustache had spread. He looked older, exhausted, in spite of the wheat-grass juice and herbal decoctions.

"What made you think that?" Hannah asked.

"The night of the explosion, just after they put me in my room, Rebecca came in. She was apologizing over and over, telling me how sorry she was about turning on the light at Laura's apartment. I thought then that she had that wrong."

"Because she didn't turn on the light?"

He nodded. "From what I remember, she had the key in the lock. But then she just stood there, doing nothing. I was worried about Laura, so I pushed her back and opened the door. I was turning on the light when Rebecca screamed that I had to stop. Too late, though. We were blasted off the stairs. I thought we were going to die.

"So then she's at my bed in the hospital, apologizing, crying, telling me it was *her* fault, *she* had flipped the switch. She sounded so sure about it. I was so out of it. I kept hearing the noise, and feeling the heat, and knowing that Laura was in there."

"That's why you called me Rebecca at the hospital?"

"I was doped up. I thought you were her."

"Why did you tell the police that Rebecca turned on the light?"

He sighed. "I wasn't sure what happened. She was so certain, I thought she must be remembering it better than me. My head was all messed up. And then later, I guess I didn't want to think about it too much. Because if I turned on the light, that meant I killed Laura."

"No," Hannah said. "She was already dead. The gas killed her. Didn't you smell the gas?"

He smiled a little. "You don't remember? I had a cold. I couldn't smell anything. And Rebecca was outside, behind me, when she yelled to stop. Why? She was too far away to smell gas. But somehow she knew I shouldn't turn on the light."

He poured more tea and stirred his cup thoughtfully. "Do you think I should go to the police?"

"That's a decision you have to make for yourself."

Gibbons stared down at the vortex in the earthenware mug and nodded.

Epilogue

Hannah climbed into her car, wiped caked baby cereal from the elbow of her blouse and checked the time again. Eleven o'clock in the morning, and she already was ready for a nap. Motherhood was not a job for which she had been trained, but she was trying to rise to the challenge. These days she seemed to spend more time consulting Brazelton on babies that Prosser on torts. Matthew was settling into a routine during the day, but his nights were uneasy. He woke at three most mornings, first screaming, and then whimpering. Hannah and Connie took turns soothing him. He cried for mama, and Hannah felt it like a blow to the stomach.

The DA had hit Rebecca with his own one-two punch. On the day of her preliminary hearing in Stephen's death, he filed a murder charge in Laura's case. So Gibbons had made his decision.

Hannah tried to imagine Rebecca in the women's prison at Frontera. She probably would be a model inmate. Other prisoners might even like her for what she'd done: moms fighting for their kids were always popular. So were women who killed their lying, unfaithful husbands. But there were probably some women who'd either given up their babies voluntarily or had them taken away by the courts. They would certainly see themselves as Laura's sisters and avengers. Rebecca would have to watch her back.

Matthew's future still was murky. Two of Rebecca's sisters called occasionally and talked in whispers about taking him. But they were afraid of crossing Maura. Hannah thought that Matthew would be driving before any of them had the guts to defy her.

There was one other grandparent, whom Hannah had not been able to reach. When she finally got Gerald Lawrence on the phone, she wasn't surprised at his answer. Taking in his wild, resentful daughter's son would be too bitter a task. Besides, he wanted to keep Matthew out of Susan Beckett's orbit. Hannah appreciated that, and knew that Laura would have, too.

The only real hope came from Martin. He had visited twice since Stephen's death and seemed to enjoy Matthew's company. He liked Connie, too. Hannah was heartened by that. Connie was thinking of reconciling with Ed, who'd gone home to Seattle. The city was only a couple hours and a border crossing away from Vancouver, and Martin.

Whoever raised Matthew, Hannah wondered what they would tell him about the thicket of lies that surrounded the beginning of his life. Then she realized he might turn to her. She was the one who'd cut through the thorns, cleared a space for the truth. She understood the story best, even though she still was trying to fathom the jagged turns of heart that deprived Matthew of three parents.

She might be able to tell him, someday, how all three used him to fill up their own emptiness. All of them claimed to love him—they did love him. Hannah knew that. But their selfishness tainted the love, twisted it. She wondered how Matthew would live with that knowledge.

She was at the off-ramp for John Wayne Airport. She parked, tidied her clothes and spritzed on some cologne. These days her natural scent was Eau du Bébé.

She saw Guillermo coming down the Jetway, craning his neck to spot her. What if she and Guillermo married, decided to have a child, and Hannah couldn't conceive? Would they become the Drummonds? It would be totally different for us, she thought. We would never do what they did.

But then she thought of Matthew's face, and how he felt in her arms. His helplessness made her fierce, and a little crazy. She could be capable of what Laura and the Drummonds did. If Matthew was "hers"—whatever that meant—wouldn't she do anything to keep him? She didn't like the stirrings that came with thoughts like that. She made a promise to herself, and she would keep it: she was just a loving caretaker, not Matthew's mother.

Guillermo saw her and waved. Hannah could feel her heart racing. She had been with Matthew at the pediatrician when Guillermo called the house that morning. By the time she picked up his message, he was already on the plane. There was no way to tell him that she didn't live alone anymore. A man leaves, saying he wants a commitment. He comes back to an instant family, albeit an unorthodox and temporary one. How would he react to that? And what would he say when she told him about Feuer? She was determined to do that before the day was over.

Guillermo shouldered his way through the crowd, dumped his bags, and pulled Hannah close. His kiss lingered on her lips, warm enough to make her forget the cold peck she got when he left.

"God, it's been too long," he said. "I can't believe how many times we missed each other. So much for modern communication."

Hannah smiled and nodded. If she spoke, she'd cry. No tears here, she thought.

"You okay?" His brow lowered with worry. Jesus, she thought, he thinks I'm not happy to see him. Something crazy like that.

She nodded. "I'm fine." She picked up one of his suitcases. "You're coming home, right? To our house?"

He grinned at her. "Our house. That's great."

"Listen, you don't mind waking up in the middle of the night, do you?"

"If you're doing the waking." There was a lascivious gleam in his eye.

Hannah couldn't help herself. She started to laugh, and for a few moments she couldn't stop. She was bouncing from emotional pole to pole, feeling a little drunk at the sight of him, scared by what she had to tell him.

"It might not be me," she said. "I'm talking about babies

crying in the middle of the night. Sometimes they do, you know."

He smiled gamely, not sure where she was taking the conversation. "Well, sure. I guess I wouldn't mind that when the time comes."

She tapped her watch. "It's going to come about three tomorrow morning. I can almost guarantee it."

He looked utterly lost. Then he dropped his suitcase, and she could see what he'd deduced: she was pregnant, and was preparing him for the news of fatherhood in a weird time-leaping way. It made her laugh again, and it touched her, too. A baby—Matthew, or any baby—would be lucky to have Guillermo as a father. And any sane woman would realize how fortunate she was to have Guillermo in her life. Hannah wondered if she could be one of those sound minded women who lived and loved in the present, not worrying about the implications her past might have for her future. She would try to be one of those. She'd tame that gnawing, wary self. Or at least cage it.

"Let's go home," she said. "I'll explain everything on the way."

CARROLL LACHNIT

MURDER IN BRIEF   0-425-14790-8/$4.99

For rich, good-looking Bradley Cogburn, law school seemed to be a
lark. Everything came easy to him—including his sparkling aca-
demic record. Even an accusation of plagiarism didn't faze him: he
was sure he could prove his innocence.

But for ex-cop Hannah Barlow, law school was her last chance. As
Bradley's moot-court partner, she was tainted by the same accusation—and unlike him, she didn't have family money to fall back on.

Now Bradley Cogburn is dead, and Hannah has to act like a cop
again. This time, it's her own life that's at stake...

A BLESSED DEATH   0-425-1534-7/$5.99

Lawyer Hannah Barlow's connection to the Church is strictly legal.
But as she explores the strange disappearances—and confronts her
own spiritual longings—she finds that crime, too, works in mysteri-
ous ways...

AKIN TO DEATH   0-425-16409-8/$5.99

Hannah Barlow's first case is to finalize an adoption. It's a no-brainer
that is supposed to be a formality—until a man bursts into their
office, claiming to be the baby's biological father. So Hannah delves
into the mystery—and what she finds is an elaborate web of deceit...